In Want of a Wife

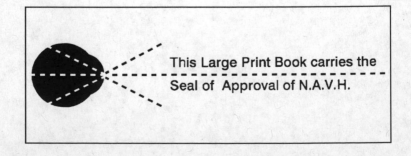

This Large Print Book carries the
Seal of Approval of N.A.V.H.

In Want of a Wife

Jo Goodman

THORNDIKE PRESS
A part of Gale, Cengage Learning

GALE
CENGAGE Learning·

Farmington Hills, Mich • San Francisco • New York • Waterville, Maine
Meriden, Conn • Mason, Ohio • Chicago

GALE
CENGAGE Learning®

LIBRARY OF CONGRESS CATALOGING-IN-PUBLICATION DATA

Goodman, Jo, 1953–
    In want of a wife / By Jo Goodman. — Large Print Edition.
        pages cm. — (Thorndike Press Large Print Romance)
    ISBN 978-1-4104-7159-8 (hardcover) — ISBN 1-4104-7159-4 (hardcover)
    1. Mail order brides—Fiction. 2. Ranchers—Fiction. 3. Large type books.
I. Title.
PS3557.O58374I5 2014
813'.54—dc23   2014015755

Published in 2014 by arrangement with The Berkley Publishing Group, a member of Penguin Group (USA) LLC, a Penguin Random House Company

Printed in Mexico
1 2 3 4 5 6 7 18 17 16 15 14

This one is for the ladies at the lake: Joann, Karen, Barb, Debbie, Sharon, and Jeannie. I wrote this book in spite of the distractions (temptations) of good company, good food, and the occasional dead squirrel.

PROLOGUE

September 1891
New York City

"My son says you are with child. His child. *My* grandchild."

Jane Middlebourne remained stoic in the face of Frances Ewing's censure. She said nothing. Every word bit at her flesh like a whiplash, and she did not flinch. Oddly, it was not as difficult as she had imagined it would be. Until this moment she had not understood how tolerant, even immune, she had become to the sharp, disapproving nature of her cousin's discourse. From Cousin Franny's lips, a passing pleasantry more closely resembled an accusation. When Frances Ewing said good morning, it was a clear indictment against the sun for rising on another day.

"I cannot say that I am surprised," Frances Ewing said. "Disappointed, certainly. But not surprised. You are your mother's daughter, after all, and blood will out. Cousin Eleanor was a source of tribulation to her family, and by extension, mine. And so it goes to the next generation. You are a failed experiment, Jane. You must see that it is so. I offered you every advantage when I took you in. All that was required was for you to demonstrate respect and a modicum of gratitude. I have evidence of neither."

Jane kept her hands at her sides. It required some effort. If she curled her fingers into fists, she would look like a combatant, and Cousin Franny would double her attempts to humiliate. If she folded her hands in front of her, she would present herself as a penitent, and Cousin Franny would seize the opportunity to drive her point home. It was better to do nothing, say nothing, *be* nothing.

Jane's gaze remained level, unblinking. She stared back at Frances Ewing with eyes that often had been likened to her mother's for their direct, sometimes defiant aspect, and hardly ever for their unusually deep emerald coloring. Jane took measured breaths, steeling herself without giving away the tension that kept her shoulders taut and her chest tight. Her hair, the exact shade of bittersweet chocolate, was scraped back from her forehead and secured in a coil at her nape. This style, approved by her mother's cousin as being modest and proper for a young woman with no particular standing in society, frequently provoked a headache. The dull throbbing behind Jane's left eye made her want to tear at the anchoring pins and combs and shake out the dark mane of hair that she was told required taming.

Jane did not flush in response to this last rebuke. In spite of her fair — and some would say wan — complexion, she rarely blushed. It wasn't that she did not feel the heat of shame or embarrassment; it was that she felt it in the pit of her stomach. Her belly was roiling now. Acid burned at the back of her throat. Pride, not defiance, kept her from being sick.

Frances Ewing leaned forward in the plump, velvet-covered armchair and lifted the teapot from the silver tray that had been placed on the table before her. She added cream and a carefully measured half teaspoon of sugar. She slowly stirred her tea, deliberation in the movement. Her eyes never left Jane's face.

Jane's summons to the parlor included carrying in the tea service. Although there were two china cups on the tray, Jane had no expectation that she would be invited to join her cousin, or even invited to sit down.

The cup was either meant for someone else who would be joining them, or it was another in a succession of pointed reminders of how she occupied no place as family or guest.

Jane Middlebourne was a sufferance.

"What do you propose to do?" asked Frances. She set down the teaspoon and raised the dainty hand-painted cup to her mouth. She did not sip. She pursed her lips in a manner that communicated her dissatisfaction with the temperature of the tea and blew. "The enormity of the disgrace your condition will visit upon this house is not to be borne. Consider that before you answer."

Jane did not respond. There was no correct answer here, no solution that she could provide that would be accepted. By offering any opinion on resolving this matter, Jane would actually be eliminating alternatives. Cousin Franny would dismiss her suggestions out of hand in spite of the fact that she had invited them. Whatever was to come of this — and there *was* a hoped-for answer — it had to be Frances Ewing's idea.

Over the rim of her teacup, Frances curled her lip. "You have nothing to say for yourself? Nothing at all?" She shook her head, sipped her tea, and lowered the cup until it hovered just above the shelf of her ample bosom. "I suppose I can credit you with enough good sense not to suggest that my son marry you. The idea is entirely without merit. I would never countenance it."

Jane remained quiet. She had expected this objection. It was actually welcome. She would not countenance that arrangement either.

"There are homes for young women such as yourself. I know because one of my charities is a house for girls in your indelicate condition. I have always considered it the duty of privilege to help those less fortunate. You see my dilemma, don't you? You must. *I* cannot count you as one of those with no advantages. *You* cannot count yourself among the less fortunate. Except for the early years you spent in the company of your mother and that fool of a dream-addled do-gooder who claimed you for his own, you have had an exemplary upbringing, a proper education, and the benefits of a society that would never embrace you if I had not embraced you first."

Jane narrowly avoided a visible reaction to her cousin's choice of words. Embraced? Jane could not recall a single instance in which she had ever been embraced, literally or figuratively. In those early days, months, perhaps for the duration of that long first year after her parents had died, Jane had wished she might be sheltered against the same plump breasts that pillowed Franny's daughter and each of her sons. She was never asked to come forward, never invited to be comforted. In time, Jane came to understand that she shouldn't expect it. There was good form for the public forum; in the privacy of the Ewing parlor there was . . . nothing.

Jane Middlebourne was a charity.

For the first time since Jane entered the room, Frances Ewing turned her gimlet eye on the plate of petit fours, iced cookies, and pastries and studied them at length before making her selection. She chose a rolled almond wafer and lightly tapped it against the rim of the plate until most of the loose dusting of powdered sugar fell away.

"I am not pleased with my younger son either," Frances said. "I am aware that your envious nature makes you sensitive to the relationship I enjoy with my children. You think I indulge them, hold them harmless. You wish that I would show you this same consideration, but I cannot since you quite mistake the matter, and what you imagine is special consideration does not exist except in your mind. I am familiar with Alex's predilections. I cannot explain or excuse these tendencies except to say it is in the nature of some men to behave incautiously."

Frances delicately bit off the end of the almond wafer and then sipped from her cup. "You know it, too. That is what I cannot forgive. You very nearly grew up in his pockets. You know him better than his brother and sister. It is with some pain that I admit that you may know Alexander better than I. Yet you behaved as naïvely as a dewy-eyed debutante. Do you tell yourself that he seduced you, made you lose all sense of what was right and proper?"

Jane knew Cousin Franny was posing what was essentially a rhetorical question. A reply would have been unwelcome.

"Alex wants to marry you. It is always what he wants to do when he learns that one of his dalliances has consequences. He tells himself that he is righting a wrong, but he knows he is safe to suggest it because I will always save him from himself. I will not permit it. Thus, we go on and inevitably arrive at this end."

Frances finished her rolled wafer and sipped more tea. After returning her cup to the tray, she folded her hands together and set that single fist on her lap. "I have no bastard grandchildren, Jane. You understand what I am saying, do you not?"

Jane's long stillness was what made her slight nod perceptible. She understood Cousin Franny clearly. There would be no marriage. There would be no home for fallen women. There would be no child. She would not give birth.

But there would be money.

"I will leave it to David to make the arrangements," Frances said.

It was then that Jane Middlebourne's heart fell into the acid bath that was her stomach.

Alexander Ewing surveyed Jane's sitting room before his gaze settled on the chair at her writing desk. He spun it away from the desk so that it faced the window bench and eased himself into it. He looked up when Jane paused in the doorway that led from the bedroom.

"Were you sick?" he asked.

She shook her head. "I thought I might be."

He waved her in. "Come. Over here." Knowing it was her favorite place to sit in reflection, Alex pointed to the window bench. "I should have brought you something warm to drink. I regret the lapse. I don't suppose Mother offered you any-thing."

Jane said, "She did not. It's just as well. I could not swallow my own spit."

Alex chuckled. "I doubt that. I am sure you did very well." He waited for Jane to sit. She curled into the corner of the pad-ded bench as he knew she would and drew her legs up and to the side, arranging and smoothing the skirt of her blue-and-white pinstriped gown until only the tips of her kid boots showed. "She suggested an abor-tion."

It was not a question. Alexander was ever confident. Jane told him, "That word never passed your mother's lips, but yes, that is her solution."

"As I said it would be. She would never countenance a marriage between us."

"Her phraseology precisely."

"I know my mother."

"Perhaps not as well as you think. She said that David would make the arrangements."

Alex regarded Jane for a long moment. "That explains why you are as pale as death." He shrugged carelessly. "You worry too much, Jane. Not everything is your cross to bear. I will take care of David. My brother will want to have nothing at all to do with this. He'll be happy to pass off the

15

duties. He will lecture me, of course. He takes pleasure in that. From his perspective it will be a fair punishment for me to handle this disagreeable situation on my own."

"Do you think he knows about the other times?"

"Perhaps. It doesn't matter. On his own he would arrive at the same solution as Mother. He is equally ruthless. A marriage between us would never be a consideration." He winked at her. "We're cousins."

"Cousins twice removed is the proper term, I think. We are hardly related."

"And you should rejoice in that." Alex observed that Jane's lips did not so much as twitch. "Jane. Cease your worry. I promise you it will all turn out exactly as I planned. David is a mere fly in the ointment. Mother will give him the money for the abortionist. He will give it to me. I will settle my debt with Eddie Hardaway and you will have enough to leave the city."

"I do not need the money to leave New York," said Jane. "Mr. Longstreet is paying for my ticket. It is included in our arrangement."

Alex quickly held up his hands, palms out. It was a gesture of apology, though not terribly sincere. "Yes, yes. Your arrangement. I understand. You need the money in the event Mr. Longstreet has a face more fit for the back end of a mule and the character to complement it. I know you, Jane. That little nest egg is your ticket out of Butter Springs."

"Bitter Springs," Jane said. "It's Bitter Springs."

Alexander Ewing leaned forward in his chair, his expression earnest. "Have a care that it isn't Bitter Pill, Jane. You don't have to go."

Jane held his gaze. The narrow smile that touched her lips was defined by sadness but not regret. "Yes," she said, "I do."

CHAPTER ONE

October 1891
Bitter Springs, Wyoming
"Hey, Mr. Longstreet."

Hearing his name, Morgan Longstreet broke stride. He avoided trampling eleven-year-old Finn Collins because the boy was as slippery as quicksilver and scuttled sideways at the last possible moment. Morgan looked down and gave him a brief nod. His acknowledgment was not meant to invite conversation, but Finn did not appear to understand that. The boy pivoted and loped beside Morgan, matching his pace across the platform to the station.

"Don't see you much at the station," said Finn. He glanced over his shoulder at the buckboard waiting at the end of the platform. "And you brought your wagon. I'm figurin' you're takin' delivery of somethin' pretty big. Am I right?"

Morgan ignored the overture and realized

after the fact that it was the wrong tack to take. Finn repeated himself, this time loudly enough to be heard by the couple standing ten yards down the platform. Their heads swiveled in his direction. It took Morgan a moment to place the pair. He was not used to seeing George and Abigail Johnson away from the mercantile they owned. He touched the brim of his hat and nodded once. Petite Abigail Johnson smiled fulsomely while George raised his hand in greeting. Morgan was satisfied, even grateful, that the exchange ended there.

Morgan gauged the distance to the rail station's entrance and lengthened his stride. He turned sharply when he reached the door. Out of the corner of his eye, he saw Finn make another artful dodge to keep himself from being bowled over. Morgan could feel the boy dogging his heels right up to the counter.

"Afternoon," Jefferson Collins said. The station agent raised himself a few inches above the stool he was sitting on, leaned over the counter, and extended an arm around Morgan Longstreet to grasp a handful of his grandson's shirt and pull him sideways. "You think I can't see you hiding behind Mr. Longstreet? What are you fussin' at the man for, Finn?"

"I wasn't fussin'."

Morgan looked down at Finn and saw the boy was regarding him hopefully, anticipating perhaps that there would be support for his denial. He promised himself he would make it up to Finn some other time. Today, Morgan said nothing.

Mr. Collins released Finn's shirt, smoothed the material over the boy's shoulder, and gave him a light swat. " 'Course you weren't. Go on outside. Find your brother and make yourself useful to Mr. and Mrs. Johnson. Their son will have bags, maybe a trunk. Mind you don't get underfoot."

"But I —"

The station agent stopped the protest with a stern look and pointed toward the door. Finn hung his head and heaved a sigh. Mr. Collins was unmoved. He kept his arm extended and his fingerpost firmly in place until Finn shuffled out. When the door closed, he sat back on his stool, adjusted his spectacles, and sighed almost as heavily as his grandson.

"He's a trial, Mr. Longstreet. Growing like a weed, but still a trial."

Morgan thought he heard more affection than complaint. He shrugged. "It's been remarked the same about me." It was his recollection that there had been more complaint and less affection.

Mr. Collins nodded. "I reckon it's a universal truth about boys. We are all of us trials." He set his folded hands on top of the counter. "What can I do for you, Mr. Longstreet? Don't often have the chance to inquire how I can help. You're still a stranger to town."

Morgan ignored this last observation and spoke only to the question. "Is the train running on time?"

"Since you're standing here now, I suppose you're asking about the two-forty train and not the one that passes through at eight."

"Yes. The two-forty."

The station agent checked his pocket watch. "You've got twenty minutes, Mr. Longstreet. Last communication was about an hour ago. No reason to expect No. 486 is going to be anything but on time." He pointed to the long bench in front of the window. "You're welcome to wait there. I offered the same to George and Abby, but they're too excited to sit. They've been waiting since one thirty just in case the train arrived early. Son's coming home from college. That's something, I can tell you. Buster coming home *and* being a college graduate.

Only one other person in Bitter Springs with that kind of education."

Morgan watched Mr. Collins's prominent Adam's apple bob as the agent took a deliberate pause and swallowed. Morgan supposed he was expected to ask after the identity of the only other person in Bitter Springs who could claim an alma mater, but he decided against posing the question. It would make him seem interested, and he wasn't. He also figured that Collins would tell him anyway, and he was right.

Bitter Springs was the kind of town where you learned things whether or not you wanted to know them, and guarding secrets required the kind of vigilance that wore at a man's soul. Morgan was better than content to live outside the town proper.

"That'd be the schoolteacher," Mr. Collins said, filling the silence. "Mrs. Bridger. The marshal's wife. But then, you probably guessed that."

Morgan thought he might actually prefer Finn's fussing to the station agent's familiarity. He made a quarter turn so he could see the platform. The Johnsons had not moved. Morgan did not like his choices. There was the rock, and then there was the hard place. Stepping outside almost guaranteed Buster's proud parents would lasso him, while staying at the counter meant he would remain Mr. Collins's captive. He did not want to sit, but the bare bench was looking more inviting.

"I think I'll wait over there," he said, lifting his chin toward the window.

"Suit yourself."

Morgan sat and struck a casual, even negligent pose. He leaned back against the window, stretched his legs, and tugged on the narrow brim of his pearl gray Stetson so that it shaded his eyes. If Mr. Collins read the signs meant to deter further conversation, he ignored them. Morgan sighed inaudibly when he heard the station agent draw a breath.

"You know my grandsons would have been happy to take your delivery out to the Burdick place. You could have saved yourself a trip to town."

"It's that kind of thinking that keeps me a stranger," Morgan said.

"How's that again?"

"It's not the Burdick place any longer."

Mr. Collins frowned. "Did I say that? Didn't mean to. Takes a while to get used to, the Burdicks bein' gone and all. Only been three years. And you're the second owner since the property was sold at auction. Reckon it'll be the Burdick place until folks know you're the sticking kind."

"I'm sticking."

"Saying so doesn't make it so."

Morgan recognized the hard truth in that. The Burdicks were early settlers to Bitter Springs, arriving as the railroad was being built. The rails moved on, so did most of the men, but those who stayed behind saw opportunities. Uriah Burdick had been a cattle rancher who benefited from the proximity of his spread to the new depot. The way Morgan understood it, Burdick had acquired land and power in equal measure until his ranch was the largest in the southeastern quarter of the Wyoming Territory. His influence extended beyond the bank, the land office, and the marshal's jurisdiction and marked a clear trail to Washington. For all intents and purposes, Uriah Burdick and his three sons had been the law in Bitter Springs for more than twenty years.

When the Burdicks were finally driven off like so much cattle, the spread was taken over by a consortium of eastern speculators. They lost interest when they were unable to acquire an important government contract for water rights and hydraulic construction. Morgan did not care about that. He was able to purchase the spread for well below the original asking price, below even what the speculators had paid for it.

Under the management of the speculators' foreman, the ranch acquired the legal name Long Bar B. It was a name of convenience since it meant adding only a single bar to the B brand that the Burdicks used. As far as Morgan could tell, no one ever called the ranch the Long Bar B. It wasn't clear that many people knew the Burdick place had a new name. What was clear was that it didn't matter. Morgan figured that at twenty-nine, he had maybe another twenty-five or thirty years to prove that he was the sticking kind. He would need every one of them. In all likelihood, his ranch would not be known as Morning Star until he was buried under it.

Mr. Collins tapped his thumbs together. "Must be a special mail order to bring you around."

"Must it?"

"I have a suspicion that you don't like coming to town."

Morgan shrugged. He didn't dislike it. Mostly he would rather be doing something else.

"So what are you waiting for?" Mr. Collins checked his pocket watch again. "In ten minutes."

"Just what you think. Mail order."

"From Chicago."

"From New York."

The station agent whistled softly. "We take a lot of orders shipped from Chicago, St. Louis, even Philadelphia. New York is just about as rare these days as Paris, France. 'Course, we do take delivery of books from Mr. Coltrane. He sends them regular. You heard of Nat Church? Whole series of dime novels about his adventures. Everyone in town reads them."

"Read them at the ranch, too."

"Is that right? Well, we get them from New York."

"Huh." Morgan shifted, crossed his ankles. He peered down at his boots. They were scuffed and dull with dust. He had not taken time to give them a shine. It wasn't that he didn't care; he hadn't wanted to be late. He considered giving them a spit and polish now but decided against it. He told himself that he would rather be judged for who he was than who he was pretending to be. It might even be the truth.

Morgan removed his hat, knocked it against his thigh a couple of times to dislodge dust, and raked his hair with his fingers before he returned the Stetson to his head.

"Funny thing how my mind plays tricks," said Mr. Collins. "I didn't recollect that you were a redhead. Folks ever call you Red?"

"Never twice."

There was a pause, then, "Oh."

Satisfied, one corner of Morgan's mouth lifted a fraction. The expression faded a moment later when the station agent had more to say on the subject.

"I'm thinking maybe I never saw you without your hat. There's more orange under that Stetson than red anyway. Seems like I would remember that properly."

"Seems like."

Jefferson Collins rubbed the back of his head where his own hair was thinning. He sighed and dropped his hand back to the countertop. "You staying in town long?"

"Haven't decided."

"I like to recommend the Pennyroyal if you care to take your dinner here. Ida Mae serves good fare."

"I'm familiar with Mrs. Sterling's cooking."

On the verge of another question, Mr. Collins's lips parted. They closed again, this time in a firm line when his grandsons raced past the window. He blinked once, and then they were pushing their way into the station office.

Morgan felt the telltale rumble under his boot heels before the boys pounded down the platform. He was on his feet by the time Rabbit and Finn worked out the contortions necessary for both boys to burst into the room simultaneously.

"Train's comin'!" Rabbit announced.

Finn echoed his older brother, but while Rabbit delivered the message to his grandfather, Finn had turned sharply at the point of entry and spoke to Morgan Longstreet.

It went through Morgan's mind that it was easier to hold ground in the face of stampeding cattle. The enthusiasm of two boys was a force to be reckoned with.

Morgan looked from Finn to Rabbit and back again. He imagined that at one time the boys were a closely matched pair of towheads, but the couple of years that Rabbit had on his brother had darkened his hair, broadened his shoulders, and added several inches to his height. Finn would grow, but he might never catch up.

Morgan hadn't.

Finn stopped toe-to-toe with Morgan Longstreet. "Train's comin'," he said again, this time an echo of himself. "You want some help? I saw right off that you didn't bring any hands with you."

"Just my own," said Morgan. He set those

hands on Finn's narrow shoulders.

Finn grinned. "You know what I mean, Mr. Longstreet. Your *ranch* hands."

"I know what you mean."

"Rabbit and me can carry just about anything."

"I'm sure, but then so can I." He slipped his hands over Finn's shoulders to his upper arms, squeezed just hard enough to get a firm grip, and lifted the boy off the floor. He set him aside as easily as a saltshaker. "Now, about that train . . ."

Morgan figured he'd be followed. Mr. Collins and the boys would take delivery of the mail and whatever parcels and crates the train was carrying to Bitter Springs. They probably would want to greet Buster Johnson, too. What he hoped was that those bits of business and the niceties of conversation would occupy them long enough to give him a measure of peace. Even a brief respite would be welcome.

When Morgan stepped onto the platform, the train was still half a mile away. He heard the whistle, the warning, and sensed the engine slowing as the brakes were applied. Beneath his feet, the platform shook. He felt the vibration roll up his spine. Something else accounted for the tension that pulled his shoulders taut.

Morgan moved away from the door to keep the path clear for Mr. Collins and the boys. They filed out just as the train was pulling in. Morgan noted that only Finn had a sideways glance for him. Mr. Collins and Rabbit were all about the business of the train.

Even after No. 486 came to a full stop, Morgan hung back. A minute passed before porters appeared and placed steps on the platform so passengers could disembark. He watched Abigail Johnson rise anxiously on her tiptoes to glimpse the travelers through the windows. Her husband's head moved back and forth between the coaches as he tried to anticipate the appearance of his son.

Morgan guessed the first flurry of passengers to leave the train were probably among the hungriest. Their visit to Bitter Springs would last approximately twenty minutes, about as long as it took to fill the tender with wood and the tanks with water. Sure enough, he watched them hurry toward the eatery adjacent to the rail station where something close to a hot meal awaited them if the biscuit shooters delivered it in a timely fashion. He surmised the experienced travelers were the ones carrying small baskets on their arms or large handkerchiefs in their pockets to take their food back to the coaches.

There was a lull after the first wave of passengers emerged. The mail car door slid open and Finn, Rabbit, and Mr. Collins veered toward it. Morgan's gaze followed them until he saw movement out of the corner of his eye. He turned. There was no wave of passengers this time. It was a trickle.

Morgan recognized Ted Rush as he emerged. Ted was the owner of the hardware store, and Morgan had had enough dealings with the man to know that he did not want to run into him now. Ted was a fair and honest tradesman, by all accounts a decent man, but he was an inveterate storyteller and every encounter began and ended with one. Morgan thought it was his good fortune that Ted spied George and Abigail first. Ted sidled up to them and began an animated conversation that only the arrival of Buster Johnson could have interrupted.

Morgan observed the tearful, happy reunion as Buster, lean and green as a string bean, was swallowed in his mother's arms and clapped soundly on the back by his father. Ted managed to find a hand to shake and pumped it gleefully. Buster disengaged himself long enough to be sick at the edge of the platform. Apparently the college graduate did not travel well.

Sympathetic and a little amused, Morgan set his shoulder against the station's wall and folded his arms across his chest. He shifted his attention to another of the passenger coaches. A man appeared carrying a large valise. He passed the bag to a porter. Once he stepped down, he took it up again. He was a stranger to Morgan, but then Morgan acknowledged that *he* was a stranger to most people in Bitter Springs. The man wore a black bowler, black wool trousers, and in deference to the chill permeating the dry air, a black scarf and heavy black coat. Morgan expected the man to move on, but after taking possession of his valise, he turned and held out his free hand toward the coach. Morgan watched as a woman emerged from the train and came to stand on the lip of the step. Bright red poppies trimmed her stylish black velvet hat. She wore a red scarf that matched the poppies exactly, arranged to wrap around her throat just once. The tails were so long the fringed ends brushed her fingertips.

Morgan thought he saw the briefest hesitation before she accepted the proffered hand, but he could only guess at the reason for it. She might be reluctant to accept help; she might be reluctant to leave the train. He would like to believe she paused because she had some slight aversion to the gentleman who offered his aid, but he doubted that was the case. This man was cut from the kind of cloth that women always admired, the kind that slipped like liquid over their skin and between their fingers and lay coolly against their cheeks.

"Hey, mister. Can I help you with that bag?"

Morgan's musings were interrupted by Finn's boisterous cry for attention. He watched the boy abandon his post at the mail car and hurry toward the gentleman in black, calling out a greeting to Buster as he sprinted past the Johnson family and Ted Rush. When Finn came to a stop, he held out both hands for the man's valise. "That's my wagon at the end of the platform. I can take you and your wife straightaway to the Pennyroyal." He bobbed his head in the direction of the woman, and asked, "That's where you'll be staying, isn't it? It's the best hotel in Bitter Springs."

Morgan noticed that Finn did not explain it was the only hotel. There was a boardinghouse run by the Sedgwicks, and the Taylors had rooms to let at their laundry and bathhouse, but the Pennyroyal Saloon and Hotel remained the place to stay if one cared about amenities, and Morgan had already formed the opinion that this man enjoyed his amenities. He hoped the same was not true of the woman.

Finn dropped his arms to his sides. "Maybe your missus has bags you want me to carry." He ducked past the porter and bent to hold the wooden steps steady. He looked up when he felt a hand on his shoulder.

"I have this, Finn," Morgan said. "She doesn't need these." He nudged the steps aside with the toe of his boot, released Finn, and inserted himself between the gentleman and the woman. He used his shoulder to disengage their handclasp. He did not reach for the woman immediately. Instead, he raised his face so she could see past the shadowing brim of his hat. "Do you know me?"

There was no hesitation. She nodded. "You are very like your photograph."

"You're not, but you can explain that later." He glanced pointedly at the red poppies adorning her hat. The flowers, not her features, were how he had identified her. In her last correspondence, she had described her new hat in great detail and wrote that she would be wearing it when she greeted him. It had been of a purpose, he supposed.

He would not have known her otherwise.

Without asking permission, Morgan placed his hands at her waist and tried not to think about how insubstantial, even fragile, she felt between his callused palms. Her smile was tentative, fleeting, but she placed her gloved hands on his shoulders as he lifted her. It seemed to him that she did not weigh much more than Finn. When he set her down, he noticed that after making allowance for the height of her hat, the crown of her head was level with his mouth. He was tall, but then so was she. He held on to that fact as perhaps the one thing she had not misrepresented about herself.

Finn straightened. Somehow he managed to convey surprise and skepticism, blue eyes wide as quarters beneath a deeply furrowed brow. "You know her?"

Morgan nodded, although it occurred to him that he knew her better before he met her. "I do."

"*She's* what you come to town for?" He did not wait for an answer. "Well, don't that beat all. Why didn't you say so?" Finn pointed to the gentleman still clutching his valise. "I thought she was with him."

"She is with me," said Morgan.

"I see that now. I surely do. But who *is* she?"

36

Morgan Longstreet had not planned on declaring himself on the platform of the Bitter Springs depot, and certainly not in front of Finn Collins, a gentleman whose name he did not know, and a porter employed by the Union Pacific. Still, the moment was upon him and . . .

The woman in his arms seized it. She removed her gloved hands from his shoulders and set them on his wrists. Using only modest pressure, she reminded him that he was still holding her by the waist. His fingers splayed, his hands fell away, and she took a step backward. It was not precisely a retreat, but it did reestablish a boundary.

"I am Miss Middlebourne," she said, holding out her hand to Finn. "And you are?"

"Carpenter Addison Collins," Finn said. He took her hand and pumped it once. "But everyone calls me Finn. I picked it for myself on account of I didn't cotton to the idea of being called Carp."

"A sensible notion."

"That's my brother over there. Rabbit. Cabot Theodore, but you see the problem, don't you?"

"I do."

"I've been speculatin' about what Mr. Longstreet come to town for, but I sure didn't speculate you."

"That's all right," she said. "I did not speculate your existence either."

Finn's eyebrows pulled together as he puzzled that out. "I reckon that squares it," he said finally. "Good to meet you, Miss Middlebourne." His eyes swiveled to the gentleman with the large valise. "I'd sure like to help you with that, mister."

Before the man could reply, Morgan Longstreet looked at him, one eyebrow raised. "I'd sure like it if he helped you, too." He kept his eyes on the stranger while he held out a coin to Finn. Morgan did not know if the man was influenced by the exchange of money or Morgan's own unwavering stare, but a decision was made in favor of moving on.

The stranger stepped around Morgan and handed his valise over to Finn. He tipped his bowler to Jane. "I hope there will be occasion to enjoy your company again, Miss Middlebourne." He glanced at Morgan, then back to Jane. He held her eyes for a long moment. "If you should have need of me, you will find me at the Pennyroyal. Good day." He might have said more, but Finn was already trotting away with his valise. He had to hurry to catch up.

Morgan waited until Jane stopped following the gentleman's progress and turned back to him. "What did he mean by that?"

"By what, Mr. Longstreet?"

"Why would he think you might need him?"

"Perhaps because you are glowering at me." She pointed to the porter still standing at his post. "He has not deserted me."

Morgan looked to the porter. The man was doing his best to seem uninterested, but there was no doubt he was hovering protectively. Morgan's cheeks puffed slightly as he blew out a breath. For a moment, his tautly defined features were softened. "Miss Middlebourne's bags, please."

Nodding, the porter stepped back into the car.

When Morgan was certain he was out of earshot, he said, "You are not what I expected."

"I understand. You are disappointed."

No, not disappointed. He felt betrayed. What he said was, "Angry."

Jane blinked. Her chin came up and she regarded him forthrightly. "Do you think I have deceived you?"

"Haven't you? Your photograph . . ."

"I explained it was taken two years ago. You wrote that it was acceptable to you."

He remembered writing exactly that. "It

was acceptable. It still is."

"But I am not."

"I don't know."

"Did I mistake your intention earlier?" she asked. "Were you not within moments of making a public proposal?"

"I was. I am a man of my word, Miss Middlebourne, but I should have thought better of the time and place . . . and the company. I am not accustomed to being rescued, but you saved me from making a fool of myself. That counts for something."

"You flatter yourself to think I did it for you, Mr. Longstreet. I did it for me. Perhaps I do not want to accept the proposal of a man who thinks I deceived him. Such a man will question all that follows." She paused. "Am I wrong?"

Morgan hooked his thumbs in the pockets of his long leather coat. "Perhaps we should find out, Miss Middlebourne. I am discovering courting by correspondence has its limitations."

"As am I. What are you suggesting?"

He shrugged. "That we sleep on it. See if twenty-four hours makes a difference in our thinking. The preacher will be there tomorrow, same as today. I don't suppose waiting a day will matter as much to him as it will to us."

Jane's reply was forestalled by the re-appearance of the porter carrying a valise under each arm. Another followed hoisting a small trunk on his shoulder. They looked to Jane for instruction. She looked to Morgan Longstreet.

Morgan pointed to his buckboard at the end of the platform and the porters set off. He noticed that the Johnsons and Ted Rush had already moved on. Finn and the stranger were pulling away. Rabbit was holding the station door open for his pap, who was carrying a leather mailbag and a wooden crate. The pair disappeared into the station, and then Morgan and Jane were alone on the platform.

Morgan held Jane's green eyes. Not merely green, he saw, but emerald, and startling for their radiance. Would she blame him when she regarded herself in the mirror one day and observed the brilliance had dulled? Hardship and isolation could do that. Could he bear to look at her, knowing he was at fault whether she said so or not? Morgan needed to consider that. He needed twenty-four hours.

"Well?" he asked.

"You will have to pay for my lodging, Mr. Longstreet."

"Of course."

"All right."

"You accept?"

"I do, yes."

He nodded. "This way, then."

The ride to the Pennyroyal Saloon and Hotel was filled with new experiences for Jane Middlebourne, chief among them being sitting on the thinly padded and springy buckboard seat. After being jostled sideways against the steely arm of her companion, she gripped the seat on either side of her and gamely held on. She expected that Morgan Longstreet would find some amusement in her efforts, but when she stole a sideways glance at his profile, she saw his mouth was set more grimly than it had been a moment before. She could not have imagined that was even possible.

The main thoroughfare of the town was wide and open. She had expected that from the reading she did prior to leaving New York. She had wondered how much she could trust the descriptions in periodicals and dime novels, but this detail was right. The town had erected itself around cattle drives and commerce, and shops of every sort lined the length of the street. She recognized a young man from the train ducking into Johnson's Mercantile with a couple she supposed were his parents. Another man, this one a gregarious older gentleman who had introduced himself to her on the train as the owner of Rush's Hardware, was engaged in animated conversation with someone sweeping the walk outside the drugstore.

Morgan Longstreet offered no narrative as the buckboard bumped along, and Jane did not ask any questions that might have invited one. She was curious about the fighting, or the lack of it. Her reading led her to believe she could expect to witness at least one brawl and perhaps a gunfight. The latter seemed especially unlikely since not one of the men she saw was wearing a gun belt. The only man she thought might be spoiling for a fight was the one beside her. Jane was unafraid that he would turn fists on her, but she felt some concern on behalf of the next man who crossed him.

She hoped it would not be Dr. Wanamaker. They had shared a bench seat on the train from Cheyenne to Bitter Springs, the last leg of her long journey. She had spoken very little during that time, as all of her thoughts had been turning inward. His comment that he had enjoyed her company was a mere pleasantry. Mostly her quiet had elicited his concern, which he continued to show when he reminded her that he would be staying at the Pennyroyal. Now so would she.

And so would Morgan Longstreet.

Perhaps she would be a witness to Western violence after all.

Jane pushed that thought to the back of her mind as the buckboard rattled past the marshal's office. The marshal was at that moment holding the door open for a woman who joined him on the sidewalk. He wore a star on his beaten brown leather duster; she wore a white ostrich plume in her blue velvet hat. They settled comfortably arm in arm as they began walking. They seemed to notice the passing wagon at the same time. Their heads came up. Jane thought the woman nudged the marshal with her elbow, but her coat was heavy and Jane couldn't be sure. She did not mistake that the marshal smiled in the way people do when they were sharing a secret.

Morgan, she saw, nodded coolly and then resumed staring straight ahead. "Who are they?"

"The marshal and his wife. Cobb and Tru Bridger."

"They know."

He looked sideways at her. "Know?"

Morgan Longstreet was not the only one

who did not like to appear foolish. "They know about us." When he said nothing, Jane shook her head. "I had an inkling."

"An inkling," he repeated. "Do you have one often?"

"Often enough to know that I should keep them to myself."

Morgan pointed up ahead and to the right. "That's the Pennyroyal."

"What if there are no rooms available?"

"There is at least one."

"How can you know that?"

"Because I reserved it earlier," he said. "For us. For tonight. For after we were married."

"Oh."

"I was thinking of your comfort."

She smiled a little at that. "That was kind of you."

"Morning Star is eight miles out of town."

"I remember." Jane looked over her shoulder at the trunk in the bed of the wagon. His letters were in there. She kept all of them, stored them in a black lacquered box with a brass hasp and lock. The lock was necessary to keep them away from Rebecca, who had been known to treat Jane's possessions as if they were her own. Until Jane left the Ewing household, she had worn the key on a necklace, keeping the slender gold chain out of sight with high, fitted collars. When that was not possible, she pinned it to her chemise. If Rebecca knew about the box and was frustrated by her inability to access the contents, she never indicated it. Jane was confident that Rebecca had never mentioned its existence to her mother. Cousin Frances would not have stood for Jane having secrets. Frances Ewing must know everything.

"I would not have minded if you wanted to return home tonight," she said. "I would have understood."

"Understood?"

"Yes, that you would like to be where *you* find comfort. Morning Star is that place, isn't it? You wrote as if it were." When he did not comment, Jane also fell silent. She stared in the direction of the Pennyroyal, feeling a mixture of excitement and dread as it filled her field of vision.

Morgan pulled up on the reins. The cinnamon-colored mare stopped in front of the hotel's porch entrance. "If Mrs. Sterling doesn't have a spare room, I'll find one at Taylor's Bathhouse. Maybe the Sedgwick place. Jail's probably empty. I can always bunk in a cell if it comes to that."

Jane did not have the impression that he was trying to inveigle an invitation to share her room. He said it without guile, without inflection. His manner was matter-of-fact. "I hope the jail will not be necessary," she said.

"So do I, Miss Middlebourne. So do I."

Jane thought this last was said with more feeling than she had heard from him before. She wondered at it but had no idea what she might ask to confirm it. The opportunity was taken from her when the doors to the hotel opened and a broad-shouldered man with hands as large as dinner plates loped across the porch and down the steps to greet them.

Jane felt the man's slow, wide smile as a physical force when it was turned on her. Disarmed, she could not help but return it.

Morgan said, "This is Walt Mangold. Walt, Miss Jane Middlebourne. She's going to take the room I reserved."

"Is that right? That's the sort of kindness that will come back your way tenfold. Believe it. Miss Middlebourne, is it? Well, I reckon you're plumb tuckered. Most folks that land at the Pennyroyal straight from the train are. Pleased to make your acquaintance."

"Likewise, Mr. Mangold." She put out her hand. It was swallowed whole in a grasp that was surprisingly gentle and gentlemanly.

"It's Walt." He released her. "Hardly recognize the other."

Morgan reached across Jane and handed the reins to Walt. "I've been thinking I'd stay in town tonight instead of heading back. Does Mrs. Sterling have another room for me?"

"We're full up. Just registered that Wanamaker fella."

Jane thought that Morgan handled the exchange smoothly. He had introduced her without offering an explanation for her presence, her connection to him, or why he was staying in town. The room he told her had been reserved for the two of them had been reserved in his name alone. He played his cards close, though whether it was because he thought she might not agree to stay or because he might not want her to, she did not know.

Jane wanted to press her palms against the knot tightening her belly. Instead she placed one hand in Morgan's as he offered to help her down from the buckboard and used the other to steady herself.

"Thank you," she said. She eased her hand out of his as he made another study of her face. "Is something wrong?"

"I was going to ask you. You're pale as a

salt lick."

Jane had no reply. She turned toward the steps and began to mount them. Behind her, she could hear Morgan giving Walt instructions about her belongings and the horse and wagon. It was only marginally reassuring that he thought of her first; his instructions regarding the horse were more detailed.

Jane was at the Pennyroyal's entrance when Morgan caught up to her. He reached for the doorknob before she could but did not immediately open the door. She stared straight ahead. "What is it, Mr. Longstreet?"

"Are you going to run off?"

The question surprised her. It was no good asking what she had gotten herself into. She was into it. "Not for at least twenty-four hours. Perhaps not even then." Jane felt him hesitate and wondered if he were trying to gauge the truth of her words. "I did not know you were a redhead," she said.

"How's that again?"

Jane's eyes swiveled in Morgan's direction. She regarded him from under slightly raised eyebrows. "I did not know you were a redhead. Your photograph failed to reveal that. I mention it because you are not the only one who must come to terms with expectations, whether they are reasonable or not. Perhaps if I had known you had hair the color of a lighted fuse, I would have made more inquiries about your temperament. We are both of us deceived, Mr. Longstreet, but I acquit you of intentionality. If you cannot acquit me of the same, no amount of time spent together will make a difference."

Jane set her jaw and faced forward again. "I am *not* going to run off."

Morgan lifted his hat, raked his hair once, and set the Stetson back on his head. "You really think it's the color of a lighted fuse?"

His hair was the color of the sun sitting low on the horizon. It was beautiful. Jane did not tell him that. "Please open the door."

Morgan did, and he held it open until Walt came through with Jane's bags and trunk. He joined Jane at the polished walnut desk while Walt set everything down at the foot of the stairs and called out for Mrs. Sterling.

Jane loosened her scarf as she looked around. It was a pleasant surprise to find the hotel's foyer so warmly inviting. The lemon yellow walls were a bright contrast to the walnut wainscoting. Sunlight dappled the damask cover on the narrow bench that ran parallel to the stair banister. There were two open archways, one that led to the dining room, and another that led to the saloon. From what Jane could see, the dining room appeared to be deserted, but the saloon had at least a few patrons. She glimpsed a young woman flitting between two tables holding an empty tray against her hip and a mug of beer in her hand.

Curious about the saloon, Jane would have liked to see more of it, but a door down the short hall swung open and the woman emerging captured all of Jane's attention.

Ida Mae Sterling was still drying her hands on her apron as she approached. The aroma of baking bread followed in her wake, a heady and seductive scent that had been known to stupefy a weary traveler.

Jane's nostrils flared as she breathed in the fragrance of rising dough and heat. The knot in her stomach vanished. In its absence, there was hunger.

Mrs. Sterling's smile was wide and welcoming as she greeted Morgan and stepped behind the desk. Her expression became more reserved when she regarded Jane over the top of her gold-rimmed spectacles and began to explain she had no rooms to let.

Morgan interrupted before Mrs. Sterling cited the options. "It's all right. Miss Middlebourne will have the room I reserved."

"She will? And what about you?"

"I can sleep anywhere."

She nodded. "I never knew a cowboy who couldn't." She pushed the registry toward Jane. "Guess you're a proper rancher these days, but I don't suppose that's softened you."

"I don't suppose it has," said Morgan.

Mrs. Sterling watched Jane fill out the registry. "New York City? Traveling by yourself? That's a far piece to go it alone."

Jane replaced the pen. "I do not think I was ever alone," she said. "And no one met as strangers. People were uncommonly friendly."

"You'll find the same in Bitter Springs, though some folks say it takes getting used to. How long will you be staying? Mr. Longstreet only has his room for the one night."

"I'm not certain. Will it be a problem if I require the room for several nights?"

"Not for me."

Jane observed Mrs. Sterling raise a questioning eyebrow in Morgan's direction. There was only one way Jane could interpret that look. Mrs. Sterling was inquiring if a prolonged stay at the Pennyroyal was a problem for Morgan Longstreet. Jane was uncomfortably reminded of Cousin Franny and the reach of her controlling hand. She meant to leave that behind in New York. It was not her intention to replace a mistress for a master.

Ida Mae gestured to Walt. "Take Miss Middlebourne's things to room four. You go on, Miss Middlebourne. We don't carry meals to the rooms, but if you'd like something before we open the dining room for dinner, we can surely set you up in the kitchen. It's no bother."

Jane realized her appetite was a mercurial thing. "Thank you, but I would simply like to rest." She unraveled her scarf, thanked Morgan for his kindness, and preceded Walt up the stairs.

Morgan watched Jane go. Her steps were unhurried. Her gloved hand rested lightly on the rail, gliding along the length as she rose. Her poise never wavered. She might have been going to her coronation. She might have been going to her death. She did not look back, did not see his eyes drink her in.

"How long have you known me, Morgan Longstreet?"

Turning slightly, Morgan leaned against the desk and rested an elbow on Mrs. Sterling's registry. "Long enough to know there's something on your mind and you're about to relieve yourself of it."

Ida Mae made a sound at the back of her throat that might have been disapproval or amusement. "That's right, which is why you should also know that bit of playacting didn't fool me one bit. Now, some people say Walt's a little slow-witted, but I can tell you I was watching him, and he wasn't fooled either." She pulled her registry free, causing Morgan's elbow to glance sharply off the desk. She was unapologetic when he made a face and nursed the pain. "Go on. I dare you to tell me it's different than I think."

"Mrs. Sterling, I have no idea what you think." But he did, and the moment he heard Finn's voice coming from the landing behind him, his suspicions were confirmed.

"Mr. Longstreet!" Finn called. "I just saw Miss Middlebourne in the hall. Fancy that."

"Fancy that," Morgan said, mostly under his breath.

"See?" Mrs. Sterling waved a finger at him. "You wanted to play at making me think you just met her at the station."

"I *did* just meet her at the station."

Mrs. Sterling continued to chide him, stopping short of clucking her tongue. "Pretending like you don't know her."

"I *don't* know her."

"Makin' it seem as if it were serendipitous."

Morgan said nothing. She had him there. His mouth curled to one side as Finn closed in.

"What'd I do?" asked Finn, sidling closer.

Mrs. Sterling reached across the desk and flicked Finn's stubborn cowlick. "Nothing but speak the truth, I expect."

Finn regarded Mrs. Sterling with suspicion. "That's something I'm thinkin' you should tell my gran. She harbors considerable doubts about my veracity. I heard her say so."

Morgan reached into his pocket for a coin. He held it out to Finn. "See if there's a room in town to be had for the night."

"You can have mine."

"That's generous."

"It will hardly cost you."

"And enterprising," Morgan said dryly. He dropped the coin in Finn's palm. "I'll take my chances that there's a bed somewhere else." Morgan tilted his head toward the door. "Out you go."

Grinning, Finn clutched the coin and hurried off.

"You spoil him," Mrs. Sterling said.

Morgan started to deny it, intercepted

Mrs. Sterling's faintly accusing stare, and merely shrugged instead.

Ida Mae Sterling shook her head. "You think you're such a stranger here that I don't see what's going on right beneath my nose? Could be that Finn reminds you of someone. I'm not saying who, because it's none of my never mind, but it comes to me every time I see you with him."

Morgan listened without comment.

"I guess I know you better than most folks. I've never forgotten that my Benton vouched for you all those years ago."

Morgan had not forgotten either. He did not say so aloud. He did not have to. Ida Mae knew the truth, his truth, and honored her husband's memory by keeping it to herself.

"So who is she, Morgan? The way Finn tells it you were waiting for her. Pushed Dr. Wanamaker aside and plucked Miss Middlebourne off the train like she was a Wyoming wildflower."

"He's a doctor?"

Mrs. Sterling cocked an eyebrow.

Morgan sighed. "It might have happened that way."

"There was something said about a photograph."

"Finn's gran is not the only one who

harbors doubts about his veracity."

"Are you saying that child is lying?" she asked. When Morgan looked away, she said, "You know what I figure? I figure you'll tell me what you're up to when you know it better yourself. That sound about right?"

"About right."

Mrs. Sterling reached across the desktop, laid her hand over Morgan's, and gave it an affectionate pat. "It's true I don't have any rooms to let, but there's the apartment on the third floor that the Coltranes use when they visit. I don't like to let it go, but for you, I could be persuaded, specially if it's just for the one night."

Morgan shook his head. "Thank you, but it's better if I bunk somewhere else."

"Better?" She removed her hand and cocked her head to one side as she studied him. "Yes," she said at last. "That's probably true. God knows you're a better man than you have any right to be."

CHAPTER TWO

Morgan waited for Jane in the Pennyroyal's dining room until half past six. He ate alone, politely but firmly refusing invitations to join Ted Rush, Harry Sample from the land office, or the other new arrival to Bitter Springs, Dr. Ellis Wanamaker. Morgan lingered over his meal and took a second helping of the apple brown Betty that he had not particularly wanted the first time it was put in front of him. When he got up from the table, he was not the last diner to leave, but only two latecomers remained. Everyone else had gone home, returned to a room, or wandered over to the saloon.

Morgan could not return home without speaking to Jane, and he was in no hurry to walk to the bathhouse, where Finn had secured him a room. That left the saloon. He wandered there.

Walt served him a beer at the bar, which he carried to an empty table in the corner.

He sat with his back to the wall, facing the open entrance to the hotel. If Jane appeared, he would see her. If she did not appear, it was a clear indication that she wanted nothing to do with him. Reflecting on his behavior, on the words they had exchanged, on the sense of betrayal he felt but had not explained, Morgan could hardly blame her for avoiding a second encounter.

Neither could he shrug it off. He had had an idea of how things would go when he met the train, and the only thing that squared with his imagination was the spray of red poppies on her black velvet hat.

The Jane Middlebourne he plucked off the train was no Wyoming wildflower. Finn Collins had that wrong. She was a hothouse orchid. Delicate. Rare. Cultivated for another clime. She was slender, not sturdy. Her skin was petal smooth, pale as milk. The length of her was a fragile stem. A flower like that required careful tending. Morgan Longstreet could not pretend, even to himself, even for a moment, that he knew anything about that.

Jane Middlebourne belonged on the arm of someone like Ellis Wanamaker. A doctor. A man born with a nature to heal, to help, to tend to those inclined to break. Morgan counted himself among those who were inclined to do the breaking. Jane probably sensed that right off. The doctor had extended his hand. Morgan had squeezed her between his.

Morgan realized he was white-knuckling his beer. He set down his glass and unfolded his fingers one by one. He stretched them, drew a long breath, and released it slowly. He reminded himself that Jane had come to Bitter Springs on the strength of his letters. She had come prepared to marry him, knowing only those things about him that he had chosen to write.

An echo of Jane's melodic voice drifted through his thoughts, reminding him he had not told her about his red hair. The right corner of Morgan's mouth lifted a fraction, more grimace than grin as he stared at his beer. That oversight was the least of his omissions, and probably one of the few he could honestly say was not deliberate. She had been wrong to acquit him of intentionality. There were things he had not merely failed to reveal but excluded on purpose. By leaving out details that would have surely meant an early end to their correspondence, Morgan acknowledged he had misrepresented his character and, oddly enough, revealed it at the same time.

He knew himself as a man who would do

what was needed to get what he wanted. Did he want Jane Middlebourne to know that man? The answer to that hinged on another question: Did he still want Jane Middlebourne?

"Another beer, Mr. Longstreet?"

Morgan looked up. He could not put a name to the pretty face that was regarding him expectantly. He had observed her circling the tables in the dining room earlier, usually with a coffeepot in hand and some chatter for everyone she served. She was uncharacteristically quiet around him, taking his order and bringing his food with a minimum of fuss. He had appreciated it then and hoped it would be the same now.

He pushed his glass toward her.

"That's what I thought," she said. "You've been nursing it so long I figured it's gone hot and flat."

"You figured right. Thank you."

"I'm Cecilia Ross. Cil. Renee's cousin."

"Renee."

"You know. Renee Harrison. Jem Davis's sweetheart."

Morgan finally put it together. He had hired Jem Davis and his two brothers away from the Bar G six months ago. He recollected now that he had heard Renee's name a few times from Jem but more often from his brothers, usually in the nature of some pointed ribbing.

"She's your cousin? I didn't know."

"You should come to town more, sit a spell like you're doing tonight. Of course, Renee would like it better if you brought Jem with you. I suppose he's holding down the fort, as they say."

"I think he's probably in the bunkhouse playing cards with Jessop and Jake."

"Cards? Without supervision? Sure to be a fight."

Morgan shrugged. "As long as they repair the furniture and tend to their shiners, they can be on their own."

Cil laughed. Dimples appeared at the corners of her mouth. "Oh, they know how to do that. Don't they just. I'll get you that beer now."

Morgan put out a hand to wave her back as she turned to go. "I wonder if you might do me a favor, Miss Ross."

"Cil."

"Cil," he repeated. "Would you look in on Miss Middlebourne for me? Room four."

Cil hesitated, frowning. "I don't know, Mr. Longstreet. I have it from Walt after he showed her to her room that she asked not to be disturbed."

"I see." He nodded. "That's all right. We'll

abide by her wishes."

"Probably better that way." Cil turned and wended her way back to the bar, where Walt poured another beer. She was within ten feet of reaching Morgan Longstreet's table when she realized he had left it.

Jane could not say what woke her, but she knew immediately that she was not alone. Opening her eyes a mere fraction, she lay very still while she searched the room from behind the fan of her lashes. She wished that she had asked Walt to lay a fire in the stove before he left. Whatever mean light it might have provided would have been a helpful addition to the flickering oil lamp at her bedside.

"You're awake."

Jane recognized the husky timbre of Morgan Longstreet's voice. Each time he spoke a slight rasp edged his words as though he were waking from a deep sleep or sharing his first thoughts after hours or days of silence. It was impossible to know how long he had been waiting for her.

Jane raised her head the few degrees necessary to find the deeper shadow that marked his location. She saw him standing with his back to the door. Remarkably, she was unafraid. She said the first thing that came to her mind. "I thought I locked that door after Walt left."

"It opened for me. I *did* knock first."

Jane nodded, supposed he could not see her, and said, "Yes. Of course."

"You never returned downstairs."

"No, I didn't, did I?" She turned on her back and levered herself up on her elbows. "Have I missed dinner?"

"Yes, but I brought you something."

"The Pennyroyal doesn't carry meals to the rooms."

"The Pennyroyal doesn't. I do. To this room."

Jane pushed herself upright and inched backward until her spine rested against the headboard. She wrestled the pillow free and laid it beside her. Her head ached abominably, a consequence, she supposed, of not eating since the night before. That meal had consisted of her last apple and a heel of brown bread. Money was not the problem. Her willingness to spend it was. "Is there a tray?"

"A plate."

When he did not move, she said, "May I have it?"

Morgan pushed away from the door. "Chicken and a biscuit. Both cold. No gravy." He held out the plate. When she took it, he gave her the napkin he had stuffed in a pocket. "You'll have to use your fingers."

Jane spread the napkin across her lap and placed the plate on top. As hungry as she was, and as much as the light made her head ache, Jane still wanted to see what she was eating. She leaned toward the lamp to adjust the wick.

"I'll get it," Morgan said.

Jane let him. When the golden glow from the lamp spilled over her shoulder and across her plate, she picked up a feathery piece of chicken stripped neatly from the bone and dangled it just above her lips. Her mouth parted and she dropped it in. It was a tender morsel, moist and tasty. Her enjoyment was so profound that she was unaware that Morgan was staring until after she had swallowed.

"You're not going to take it away, are you?" she asked.

He frowned. "Why would I do that?"

"Cousin Frances did. I was six. She said it wasn't done, not by a lady, not by girls in want of a good home, not by anyone, except perhaps by a fish. Did I want to be a fish? I said I did. She took my plate and frog-marched me to the kitchen, where she ordered the cook to fill a bucket of water. Whereupon she dragged the bucket and me

65

through the servants' entrance to the outside stairwell and emptied the bucket over my head. I was not allowed inside until my clothes dried. That would give me sufficient time, she explained, to reconsider my desire to be a fish."

"And did you?"

"Yes." Jane took another strip of chicken, this time eating it in a manner approved by Cousin Frances. It did not taste quite as fine as her first bite, but then how could it? "Reconsideration was only sensible. I am not stubborn to a fault. It was February."

"Your clothes never dried, did they?"

She shook her head. "Never. They froze." Jane felt his eyes still on her. She looked up from breaking her biscuit. He was indeed watching her, but she found his expression unreadable. She said, "I do not like the cold."

Morgan's nod was all but imperceptible. He glanced at the stove. "I can lay a fire."

Jane hesitated. She was uncertain if she wanted him to be useful to her, uncertain if she wanted him to stay, but then she noticed he had not taken a single step in the direction of the stove. He was waiting to hear her answer, and that decided Jane. "Yes, please. I'd like that."

Jane continued eating while Morgan

pulled kindling and coal from the scuttle and laid the frame for the fire. Her eyes strayed sideways as he hunkered in front of the stove. He patted down his pockets, came up with a matchstick, and struck it against the stove. The flame burst brightly, illuminating his face for a moment. Jane caught his profile as he briefly turned away from the light, and she had the wayward thought that he had features that were meant to be cast in bronze. The notion was disquieting.

Morgan shut the grate when the flames caught. He stood and approached the bed again. "I brought you an apple." He pulled it out from under the sleeve of his long leather coat and polished it against his shirt. "I can slice it for you."

Jane nodded. "I don't suppose you have something to drink up your other sleeve?"

"No. But there is a tap in your bathing room, and the water in Bitter Springs is better than the name implies."

Jane started to put her plate aside, but Morgan put out a hand to stop her.

"I'll get your water," he said. "You don't look like you're fit to stand." He opened the door to the adjoining bathing room and went inside. "When did you eat last?" he called out to her.

Jane was afraid he would know a lie, and what would it serve except to add to his mistrust? "Yesterday evening." She heard water running and then his voice above it.

"I sent money for your ticket *and* meals."

"I wasn't hungry. There's money left. Do you want it back?"

Morgan reappeared. He came abreast of the bed and held out a glass of water. "No. I don't want it back."

"Did I offend you?" asked Jane. "You sounded . . . I don't know . . . aggrieved, I suppose."

"I have thicker skin than that. It's not a generous gesture anyway. Depending on how long you stay, you might still need it." He looked around the room. The furnishings were spare, every piece practical. Besides the bed, there was a side table, a wardrobe, a straight-backed chair at the window, and a wing chair angled toward the stove. A chest for extra linens and blankets rested at the foot of the bed. His eyes moved from the valise sitting on the seat of the straight-backed chair to the valise sitting on top of the small brassbound trunk. "You haven't unpacked."

"I am not sure there is any purpose to it until I know where I'll be living."

Morgan released a long breath, nodded.

Jane drank half the water in her glass before she set it on the table beside her. "Will you sit down?" she asked. While he seemed to be debating the merits of accepting her invitation, Jane removed the empty plate from her lap and dabbed at her lips with the napkin. When she was done, she neatly folded the napkin and dropped it on the plate. Morgan Longstreet was still standing.

"Are you uncomfortable sitting?" she asked. "Because I am uncomfortable looking up at you. If we are at an impasse over this, I cannot imagine that we will settle well into marriage."

"Did you think we would?" he asked. "Settle well, that is."

"I did, yes. Didn't you? You must have, else why make the proposal?"

"I have my reasons."

A faint smile changed the shape of Jane's mouth. It touched her eyes. "Have a care, Mr. Longstreet, else I might believe you are a romantic."

"I suppose you *can* insult me. Practical, Miss Middlebourne, not romantic. Practicality is at the root of my proposal. Does that make you want to rethink your answer?"

"No."

"You sound certain."

"I am. Given the opportunity and the proper circumstances, someday I'll tell you why."

"Tell me now."

Jane shook her head. "You won't believe me."

Morgan waited, but when she remained silent, he shrugged. He removed the valise from the chair and dragged it closer to the bed. He sat down, tipped the chair on its rear legs, and set his feet on the bed rail. Holding up the apple, he asked, "Do you still want it?"

"Yes."

He removed a knife from the scabbard attached to his belt and scored the apple skin into eight parts before he cut it through. "Hold out your hand." Jane did, and he dropped the slender wedges into her palm one at a time until she said she had enough. He ate the last three slices, tossed the core on top of the plate, and used the napkin to clean his knife before he replaced it.

"Can I show you something?" he asked when his hands were empty.

"If you like." She finished her second apple slice, dropped the other three beside the discarded core, and brushed off her hands.

This time Morgan did not search a pocket.

What he wanted came from the inside leg of his left boot. He had to set the chair on all fours to get it, but when he was done, he tipped it again.

Jane could tell by the stock paper that it was a photograph. Not the one she had sent, she realized, because there was no writing on the back. He stared at it for what seemed a long time, so long that she thought he had decided against sharing it. That was not the case. He pinched one corner of the photograph between his second and third fingers and held it out to her.

Jane received it upside down. She turned it over, angled it toward the lamplight for a better view, and then she blinked. And blinked again. Her eyes swiveled from the picture to Morgan Longstreet.

"Where did you get this?"

"From you. You sent it to me."

"No." She shook her head vehemently and regretted it at once. The sharp movement magnified the ache behind her eyes and for a moment her vision blurred. She pressed the fingertips of one hand against her temple, closed her eyes, and took a shallow breath. Quietly she said, "No, I did not. I never sent this."

Jane heard, rather than saw, Morgan's chair being set back in place. It hit the floor hard enough to send a tremor under the bed. His boots dropped next, thumping in quick succession, and then the photograph was plucked from her nerveless fingers. Jane opened her eyes, shielding them against the glow of the lamplight with her hand. Morgan was already on his feet and bending over her. She was startled into rearing back. Her head knocked against the headboard. At any other time, the bump would have been insignificant. Now it triggered pain that made her cradle her head in both hands and squeeze her eyes shut. She sucked in another breath and held it.

She felt one of Morgan's hands come to rest at the back of her head, supporting her without adding pressure. The other hand worked carefully between her splayed fingers to remove pins from her hair. They made a faintly tinkling sound as he dropped them on the plate. When they were all removed, he carefully loosened the tightly wound coil just above her nape and let her hair spill down her back. Jane was not so numbed by pain that she was unaware of the intimacy of the gesture. A thread of tension pulled her shoulders taut as his fingers combed through the strands of her braid.

Morgan paused, his hand resting lightly against her back. "Would you rather I get

Dr. Wanamaker?"

Jane did not hesitate. "No."

"All right. Then let me help you."

Wasn't that what she was doing? She supposed he felt her apprehension. "There are headache powders in one of the valises. Small packets. I just need one."

"I'll get it. Lean back. Careful." He supported her so she did not bump her head again and then left her side.

Jane eased the fingertip pressure on her scalp but did not remove her hands. She kept her eyes closed. She heard the clasp on one of her bags being released. "I think the packets might be in the valise that was on the chair."

"Don't talk. I'll find them."

Jane wished she had asked him to bring the valise to her. It was not lost on her that perhaps the more intimate gesture was not allowing Morgan Longstreet to sift through her hair, but permitting him to sift through her belongings. She imagined the packets had slipped to the bottom of the valise by now; she had not needed them once during the journey. That meant he would have to look through everything.

"If you would just give me the —"

Morgan cut her off. "Found them."

Jane's stomach stopped clenching. She

heard him approach the bed and remove the half glass of water from the table. He walked away again before she could tell him that what remained in the glass was sufficient. She let him go, heard the tap running, and then his second approach. He did not have a heavy tread, but his rolling stride was distinctive in its rhythm.

She eased her eyes open when she heard him preparing the powder but continued to look straight ahead. She carefully lowered her hands from her head and held out one for the glass. When he placed it against her palm, her fingers closed over it and brushed his. Jane brought the glass to her lips, but before she drank, she asked, "Do you dance?"

He was standing too far to one side for her to see how he reacted to her question, or if he reacted at all. "Do I?" he asked. "Or can I?"

Jane thought she heard amusement edge his words, but that, she was coming to appreciate, was more difficult to identify than his walk. "Answer either," she said. "Answer both."

"Drink first."

Jane saw two fingertips appear at the bottom of her glass. There was a nudge, gentle but firm. Her lips parted and she drank, tipping her head back to get the last bitter dregs of the medicine. Wrinkling her nose and pressing her lips tightly together, she blindly held out the glass for Morgan to take.

He did, setting it aside before he sat on the edge of the bed. "Is it all right for me to sit here?" he asked.

"Yes."

"Then let me help you lie down."

"All right." Distress had made her unnaturally compliant. "This is not who I am," she said.

"The photograph can wait."

"No, I meant . . ." She did not finish. Morgan was tugging at the bedclothes, making a nest for her under the covers instead of on top of them. She pushed at the hem of her gown when it was trapped by the blankets and began to climb up her legs. He withdrew immediately, for which she was grateful, and let her finish arranging the covers herself. When she was done, he only held them up so she could ease under them. She patted the mattress, searching for the pillow she'd put aside earlier. Morgan reached it first. He plumped it once, slipped an arm under her shoulders, and lifted her just enough to put the pillow in place. When she lay back again, the world righted itself.

She smiled faintly as she closed her eyes. "Thank you."

Morgan reached for the lamp and turned back the wick until the light was no brighter than it had been when he entered the room.

"You did not answer my question," she said.

"You'll have to remind me."

"Do you dance?"

"No."

Jane waited for him to offer more, but he remained silent. She said, "It occurred to me that you might be a better than tolerable partner."

"You're still talking about dancing, aren't you?"

Jane's lips twitched. "Yes, Mr. Longstreet. I'm still talking about dancing."

"What put that notion in your head?"

"That you'd be better than tolerable? The way you walk, I suppose."

"The way I walk."

She opened her eyes a fraction and regarded him behind the shading of her lashes. "I thought I noticed a rhythm in your stride."

"More likely the pounding in your head."

"That might well be true." She laid the back of one hand across her forehead. "I apologize that I am unwell. I had hoped to sleep it away and join you at dinner. Instead I just slept. Did you think I was avoiding you?"

"It crossed my mind." He rose from the bed. "Are you sure you don't want me to go for Dr. Wanamaker? The town has a doctor also. Kent. I could ask him to come."

"No. I will be fine. Really." The light from the lamp was endurable. She opened her eyes the rest of the way. "Are you leaving?"

"Just moving to the chair," he said. "Unless you want me to go?" This last was said with enough inflection to make it a question.

Jane said, "No. Stay. By my reckoning, we have less than twenty hours remaining on your twenty-four-hour clock. Unless you have changed your mind about that, we should take advantage of the time we have."

Morgan sat. He did not tip the chair on its hindquarters but leaned forward instead and rested his forearms on his knees. He folded his hands and made a steeple with his thumbs. "Are you unwell often?" he asked.

The question was startling for its blunt delivery, but Jane understood the necessity of it. "Not often."

"You carry powders. I counted a dozen packets. To my way of thinking, that's about nine more than 'some.' "

"I did not know if I would be able to purchase them along the way or find them after I arrived. In my experience, it is better to have them and not need them than need them and not have them. The last time I used one of the packets was three months ago. To my way of thinking, Mr. Longstreet, that is the very definition of 'not often.' " She observed the narrow twisting of Morgan's mouth. He had a wry grin, accented by a faint, crescent-shaped scar at the right corner of his lips. The scar made a fleeting impression as a dimple but an enduring one as a wound. She wondered at it but did not ask.

"Your sass is back, Miss Middlebourne. I didn't imagine the powder could work so fast."

It was not working. Not yet. "You riled me," she said, and did not know what to make of it when he nodded as though her answer satisfied him.

Morgan tapped his thumbs together. "You wrote that you knew how to cook. Is that true?"

"Yes."

"I saw the cookbook."

"It's for reference. And for trying new things. There is a section of helpful hints for the young housekeeper. I thought I should learn as much as I could."

"You grew up in a home with servants."

"They preferred to be called the help. Cousin Franny called them servants."

"There is no house help at Morning Star."

"Your letters made that clear."

"I want to make it clearer. I have four men who work the ranch with me. The three Davis brothers and Max Salter. You'll be cooking for them sometimes."

"Who cooks for them now?"

"We take turns."

"But mostly I'll be cooking just for you."

"Yes."

"That doesn't seem fair. What do they think about that?"

"I don't know. They work for me. I didn't ask them."

"Securing a cook and housekeeper for Morning Star does not necessitate a proposal of marriage."

"I'm aware."

She wasn't sure how to respond to that. Her head was still foggy; she needed to think. His silence was welcome. Jane pinched the bridge of her nose and stared at the ceiling. "Whatever happens, Mr. Longstreet, I will not be returning to New York. What you decide does not determine my future. *I* do."

"I understand."

"Do you? I do not require coddling."

"All appearances to the contrary," he said dryly.

"Yes," she said. "All appearances to the contrary." Jane turned her head to look at him. "What did you do with the photograph? I think we should discuss it now. May I see it again?"

Morgan took a photograph from the table and handed it to her without glancing at it. "You were a very different person two years ago."

Jane ignored his sarcasm. Nodding, she turned the picture around so he could see it and pointed to the face. "I am still a very different person. This is my cousin Rebecca. I wrote about her. She is Cousin Franny's daughter."

"The one expected to marry well. The beauty, you said."

"Yes."

"Huh." He held out his hand. "May I?"

Jane gave him the photograph. "She sat for that picture six months ago in preparation for a charity gala that she was hosting with her mother. You can see that she's younger than I am."

"Yes, I can."

"You wanted a younger wife."

"I thought this photograph was two years old, remember? That's what you wrote. She's what? Twenty-one?"

"Twenty-two."

"So I thought you would be twenty-three or twenty-four."

A small vertical crease appeared between Jane's dark eyebrows. "Did I never reveal my age?"

"No. The photograph should have been sufficient."

Jane's cheeks puffed as she blew out a short breath. "How surprised you must have been to see me wearing the hat with red poppies."

"You were . . . unexpected."

"I was twenty-seven in June. Rebecca is five years my junior."

"And I am two years your senior. If I wanted a younger wife, you would still suit."

"I don't understand."

"How old you are doesn't much matter, Miss Middlebourne. I wanted a *stronger* wife."

Jane stared at him. "And you saw that in Rebecca?"

He looked at it again. "She has bold features and large bones. She is broad across the chest and shoulders. She's sitting down,

81

but you described yourself as tall — and you are — but now that I know you're you and she's someone else, I figure she's probably got a few inches on you. She's maybe as tall as I am. Am I right?"

She nodded. "Almost six feet." That elicited a soft whistle from Morgan. Jane bristled slightly. "Do you need your wife to pull a plow? Don't you have animals for that?"

Morgan ducked his head and stared at the floor for a moment. He cleared his throat before he answered. "No, Miss Middlebourne, I don't need my wife to pull a plow."

She sniffed. "You were laughing at me."

He shrugged and looked at her again. "A little."

"Rebecca is widely acknowledged to be a beauty."

"So you wrote."

"I wrote it so you would understand that I know I am not. I wrote it so your expectations would not be unreasonable. Rebecca closely resembles her mother, and Cousin Frances has always been accounted to be a handsome woman."

"She's very fair."

"Yes. She is. Waves of golden hair. Eyes the color of a cerulean sky. Alabaster skin. The photograph hardly does her justice."

"Your complexion is fair."

Jane shook her head. "An illusion. I have not been allowed to show my face to the sun in years. Not since Cousin Frances observed that I brown like a pie crust."

"I see. What did Cousin Frances have to say about your hair?"

"An unremarkable, unflattering shade of brown. She is straightforward in her assessments."

"Yes," he agreed. "She is. And your eyes?"

"You can see for yourself that they are green. Like yours."

"Not like mine," he said.

"No," she said. "Not like yours. You have flecks of blue and gray. Pine green. Spruce green. Evergreen, I would say."

"And yours are just green."

Jane did not flinch in the face of his plain speaking. "Yes."

Morgan finally leaned back in his chair. He did not tilt it backward, but he did slide down a few inches and stretch his long legs. His dusty boots disappeared under the bed. He removed his hat, tossed it over his shoulder. It landed squarely on the seat of the wing chair. He folded his arms across his chest.

"How do you suppose your cousin's photograph came to be in the letter you wrote?"

That was still a question in Jane's mind. What she said was, "I can only guess."

"Guess."

"I'm imagining that Rebecca put it there. She removed mine and inserted hers."

"Why? And I realize this will be another guess."

"Well," she said slowly, "I suppose because she wanted to make mischief."

One of Morgan's eyebrows lifted. "Mischief? That's your explanation?"

"That is my guess."

"She's twenty-two," he said flatly. "Finn Collins makes mischief. He's maybe half her age."

Jane said nothing for a time. Neither did Morgan. His silence felt like a tactic to prompt another response from her. Jane wanted to believe it only worked because the pressure of what she was trying to hold back was greater than the pressure of his silence. "Rebecca has always found a certain amount of perverse pleasure in creating situations that will end badly. More often than not, she creates them around me. I thought I was being clever and careful with our correspondence. I was so certain she did not suspect that it was my intention to leave New York. I told Alex, of course, but he would never have shared a confidence with his sister. David did not know."

Jane pressed her lips together briefly. Gathering her thoughts, she shook her head slightly. "It does not matter how she found out. The most obvious conclusion is that she did. She read the letter before I posted it and exchanged the photographs. She might have been trying to ensure that you would make a proposal and that I would leave, but it's also possible that she saw into the future to this very end and knew your disappointment would be profound and that I would be stranded."

Morgan unfolded his arms and examined the photograph again before his gaze returned to Jane. "Was that difficult to say?"

"Not as difficult as it should have been. Whatever little satisfaction comes from speaking ill of others is transitory at best. Making a habit of it poisons one's soul. If Rebecca were here, she would take issue with everything I told you, and you would believe her."

"Would I? How do you know?"

"Everyone believes Rebecca," she said simply. In Jane's mind it was as absolute a fact as the earth's revolution around the sun. "Regardless of what she's done, has thought about doing, or will do, it is unfair to lay all the blame at her feet."

"Cousin Frances," said Morgan. "I thought we would get around to her eventually."

Jane said nothing.

"That's what you meant, isn't it? She bears some of the responsibility."

"It's done," Jane said tiredly. "There is nothing to be gained from sifting through the confusion to the source of it. I am here. Your correspondence was with me. *I* wrote the letters you received."

"All of them? Are you sure?"

Jane suddenly felt cold to her marrow. A moment earlier there had been no doubt. Now it niggled at her, shaking her defenses. "I suppose it does not matter if I did or not," she said on a thread of sound. "You proposed to the woman in the photograph."

"It seems so." Morgan tossed Rebecca Ewing's picture sideways. It struck the beveled edge of the table and fell on the floor. He left it there. "How well do you think you know me, Miss Middlebourne?"

Jane turned on her side, slipping one arm under her pillow to elevate her head. She tugged on blankets until they covered her shoulder. "Much less than I thought I did."

"Not so different from me, then."

"I suppose not."

"Are there things you want to know?

Something more than, say, the color of my hair."

"Did you pen all of your own correspondence?"

The right corner of Morgan's mouth kicked up. Amusement gave way to a chuckle deep at the back of his throat. "Yes. I take it your question arises because I am more tolerable on the page than in person. Better written than spoken."

Jane smiled a little herself. He had spared her from making the blunt observation. "Have you ever been married?"

"Ah. So you do wonder what I left out. No, Miss Middlebourne, I have never been married."

"There must be single women in Bitter Springs."

"Yes. One of them trotted off to refill my beer in the saloon. That's when I left."

"You didn't want the beer?"

"I did, but I wanted to see you more."

Jane was skeptical and she let him see it in her narrowing eyes.

Morgan held up his hands, palms out. "I swear. I was concerned. I could see you weren't well when you stepped off the train."

Jane went from skeptical to frankly disbelieving. "I was fine and you know it, and I didn't step off. You carried me off."

"Not quite how I remember it, but it doesn't change the fact that you came a long way to be here. I thought I should look after you." He set his hands together again and rested them against his belt buckle. "You were right that I was set to propose back there at the platform."

"I know. In front of God and witnesses. You told me, remember? And then you thanked me for rescuing you from acting the fool."

"I should have made a better apology."

"You said what you meant."

"I would have written it better."

Jane's smile was a bit rueful, a bit wistful. "Yes," she said. "I'm sure you would have."

Morgan nodded shortly. "You want to know what I was thinking just before you interrupted my declaration?"

"I don't know. Do I?" When he said nothing, she finally nodded. "Yes, please. Tell me."

"I was thinking that I made a contract with you and that I needed to honor it."

"To be a man whose word means something."

"Yes," he said. "To be exactly that."

"That's important to you?"

"Yes."

"So it was no romantic impulse that I

forestalled."

"No. I told you I am not a romantic."

"I know what you told me." And perhaps he was right about it. "You reconsidered that contract quickly enough. What does that say about you and your word?"

"That I would make a fine lawyer if I did not have such a disgust of them."

Jane laughed quietly. Her eyes crinkled. When she sobered, she said, "Cousin Franny's husband was a lawyer. He was made a federal judge in the County of New York two years before he died."

"A judge," said Morgan. "Well, at least you were not related to him by blood."

"He was a good man, Mr. Longstreet, and I was heartbroken when he died."

Morgan sat up. "Then I'm sorry for that."

Jane accepted him at his word. Her eyes wandered to the door. "Where are you staying tonight?"

"The bathhouse."

"So no cell for you." She thought he might be moved to grin. He was not. "I still do not know why you did not look closer to home for a wife."

"Perhaps I did, and no one would have me."

"At the risk of flattering you, I think finding some young woman in Bitter Springs to have you would not have been a problem."

He shrugged. "I don't come into town often, and what I know about courting a woman is as much as I put in my letters. Sitting on a porch swing, holding hands, trying to be interesting, well, it seemed like more tiring work than mustering calves for branding and not nearly as satisfying."

Jane's eyebrows lifted. "Oh my. It seems you have given this some thought."

"I did. I heard about papers and periodicals that accepted inquiries. I wrote to several."

"I suppose there were dozens of replies."

"Not dozens," he said. "An even dozen."

So she was one out of twelve, Jane thought. Or rather Rebecca was.

"Your letter was the only one that I responded to with a request for more information."

Jane wished she were not heartened to hear that. There was no place for emotion, especially not the one that was seeking entry into her heart. Hope only crushed her.

"I answered the other letters," Morgan said, "but for the purpose of putting an end to them. I did that before I heard from you again."

"And if I had not written a second time?"

"Then I would have tried again. There are

churches that facilitate introductions, but it seemed wrong to apply through them the first time. I am not a godly man, and I did not want to be mistaken for one."

"Oddly scrupulous."

His quicksilver grin whitened the scar at the corner of his mouth. "Even a godless man can have scruples."

Jane's headache had subsided to a dull ache. If she slept through the night, it would be gone by morning. "I think you should go now, Mr. Longstreet. We still have the morning and part of the afternoon to come to terms. I would like to think about what I've learned. I imagine you will want to do the same."

Morgan said nothing immediately. He searched her face for a long moment before he slowly got to his feet. "Breakfast?"

"Yes. I'd like that."

"Very well. In the dining room. Does seven suit?"

"It does. I rise early."

He smiled a little then. "At Morning Star we call that sleeping in."

CHAPTER THREE

Morgan arrived at the Pennyroyal ten minutes before his meeting with Jane. She was already in the dining room, sitting at a table near the window that had the widest view of the main street. She raised her head as he walked into the room, and he knew she had seen his approach. Her smile wavered, veering toward uncertain, as if she wondered if it would be welcome or appropriate. He thought it was both.

He shrugged out of his coat as he walked toward the table and laid it over the back of an extra chair. He tossed his hat on the seat. "Good morning, Miss Middlebourne. You're early."

"So are you."

Morgan pulled out the chair at a right angle to hers and sat. "Have you ordered?"

"No. I was waiting for you."

She sat at the table very primly, he thought. The cotton napkin already covered her lap, and her hands were folded together on top of it. Her spine was straight, not quite touching the back of the chair. The smile she'd greeted him with had already faded. She held his gaze for a moment longer and then her eyes darted to the window and the street beyond.

"You look well rested," he said. She was wearing a crisp white shirt beneath a short-waist wool jacket the color of port wine. Her skirt was the same color as the jacket, and from what he could see, fit her closely at the waist and hips and then flared all the way to her ankles. He could not look at her shoes without an obvious examination but imagined they were as hopelessly unsuited to Morning Star as her fashionable New York clothes. "Your headache's gone?"

She nodded. "It was kind of you to help me." She smoothed the napkin over her lap and refolded her hands. "I thought about it again this morning, and I *do* remember locking my door."

"Is that right?" Morgan shrugged. "Passing strange that you should have that memory. It opened for me."

"So you said." Jane briefly directed her gaze toward the door that led to the kitchen. "That young woman you mentioned last night, the one who brought you your beer, she's working here this morning."

"How do you know that?"

"She was here when I came downstairs. She invited me to sit where I liked and told me that you had asked her to look in on me last evening. She said she declined because I had been particular to say I did not want to be disturbed, and she hoped she had done right by minding my wishes and not yours."

Morgan's mouth pulled to one side. He shook his head, torn between amusement and dismay. "Did she tell you that her cousin is the sweetheart of one of the men who works for me?"

Jane's brow furrowed. "No. She didn't."

"There's a wonder."

"She mentioned that you were sitting alone. She had some hesitation going to your table because you appeared to be deep in thought."

"See?" Morgan leaned toward her and set his forearms on the table. "There is nothing that happens in this town that is considered so dull that it doesn't bear repeating. I figure there are not more than four, maybe five, people who don't know by now that I was at the station to meet you yesterday. It doesn't matter that they don't know why. Speculation is a favorite way to pass the time in Bitter Springs, like playing dominoes or reading dime novels."

She lifted an eyebrow. Her smile was faintly mocking. "Do you imagine it is different elsewhere? I assure you, I am quite familiar with speculation passing for fact. In New York there are newspapers entirely dedicated to creating a story where none exists."

"There is no newspaper in Bitter Springs."

"That could very well be a point in its favor."

"I am forced to agree that you might be right."

Jane tilted her head toward the kitchen door as it opened. "She's coming now. Please don't scowl at her."

Undecided, Morgan grunted softly.

"Yes," said Jane when Cil Ross offered her coffee.

Morgan merely pushed his cup and saucer toward her. "Do you have cream and sugar for Miss Middlebourne?"

Jane raised her hand before Cil could reply. "Neither for me. I prefer my coffee black."

Morgan was skeptical, but he said nothing.

Cil said, "There's steak and eggs. Hotcakes so light you'll have to drown them

95

with molasses to keep them on your plate. Applesauce. Grits. Fried potatoes. Oatmeal. What's your pleasure?"

"Oatmeal," said Jane.

Morgan broke the silence that followed Jane's request. "She's waiting for you to say something else."

"Please?" said Jane.

Morgan grinned while Cil choked back a laugh. "Not that. She wants to know what else you want to eat."

"Oh." Jane looked up at Cil. "Nothing else, thank you."

"Oatmeal will sit in your belly," Cil said, "but it won't put meat on your bones. How about some bacon on the side?"

Morgan's look cautioned Jane about pitting her will against Cil Ross's. She said, "Bacon will be fine."

"Good. And you, Mr. Longstreet? Do the hotcakes tempt you?"

"They do, as long as you bring them with steak, two eggs, scrambled, potatoes, and that applesauce you mentioned." He intercepted Jane's wide-eyed astonishment. "I don't much like oatmeal," he said. "And I had grits at breakfast yesterday."

Cil winked at Jane. "Didn't I just say?" Chuckling under her breath, she pivoted smartly and headed back to the kitchen.

Morgan turned to Jane as soon as Cil was out of earshot. "What was that about? What *else* did she tell you before I arrived?"

Jane picked up her fork and fiddled with it, turning it over several times before she spoke. "I think she might have predicted what you would have for breakfast."

"Jesus," Morgan said feelingly. When he saw Jane's lips purse with disapproval, he reminded her that he was not a godly man. "Taking the Lord's name in vain is the least of the commandments I've broken."

"I'm not sure they were numbered for purposes of ranking. I believe they deserve equal weight."

"Maybe so, Miss Middlebourne, and maybe the next time I get the urge to invoke the Lord's name, I'll just kill Miss Ross instead."

Jane pressed her lips together, but it was an inadequate stopper for her amusement. Laughter bubbled anyway. "You have a wicked sense of humor, Mr. Longstreet."

"I was being serious, Miss Middlebourne." His tone was dry as the dust on his boots, but he saw Jane was unfazed by it. She did not believe him. He shrugged. "Suit yourself."

Jane set down her fork and returned that hand to join the one in her lap. "I will," she said. "I do."

Morgan picked up his coffee cup. It felt too small, too dainty, in his hand. Like Jane.

"You are scowling again. The coffee's not to your liking?"

"I haven't tried it yet."

"Then perhaps you should reserve judgment."

One of his ginger eyebrows kicked up. "You're still talking about the coffee, aren't you?"

Jane smiled. "You said something like that last night. Yes, Mr. Longstreet, I'm still talking about the coffee."

Morgan gave a short nod, took a swallow, and imagined he manfully concealed the fact that he burnt the inside of his mouth. Still, the swirl of cold air that entered the room was a welcome diversion. When Jane looked toward the dining room entrance in anticipation of more guests, Morgan sucked in a breath. By the time she turned back, he was returning his cup to the saucer.

"There's a pitcher of water on the sideboard over there," she said. "Shall I get it for you?"

Except to make her chuckle, his sour look had no impact on her. "Your concern is noted. I'll be fine."

"You ordered a big breakfast. It would be

unfortunate if you were unable to taste it." Her eyes swiveled to the pair entering the dining room. "Who are they?"

Morgan glanced behind him. "Howard Wheeler and Jack Clifton. They're here every time I am so I'm figuring them for regulars. They used to be with the railroad. Stayed behind when it moved on. That's about as much as I know, and I have that from Ida Mae."

"Mrs. Sterling."

"Yes. Her husband worked the rails with them and settled here same as they did. He was marshal after that. For years, in fact. Killed in an ambush on Morning Star land. It was the Burdick property back then. The story that went about at the time was that he was mistaken for a rustler. Everyone knows now that he was murdered, plain and simple."

"I never thought of murder as plain and simple."

"This one was."

"Was I wrong to have the impression that you are a relative newcomer to Bitter Springs? You seem to know a lot."

"I told you how it is here. Some stories you can't avoid. I didn't grow up in these parts, but I had a passing acquaintance with Benton Sterling years ago. His wife remembers it."

Jane nodded. "I thought she treated you familiarly."

"I don't know about that. She's good to everyone. 'Course, she makes everyone's business her own." He gave Jane a sharp, pointed look. "And if you tell her I said so, I'll —"

"Break one of God's commandments, Mr. Longstreet?"

Morgan's smile was wry. "Several."

Both of her dark eyebrows lifted. "Well, you can rest easy. I can keep a confidence."

If that were true, Morgan thought, she would be the first woman of his acquaintance who could.

Cil appeared with their food. Ribbons of steam rose from Jane's bowl of oatmeal and Morgan's plate of hotcakes. The distinctive aromas of bacon and steak hovered in the air. Cil set down a small pitcher of molasses syrup in front of Morgan. "Mind you eat them warm," she told him. "They'll be tastier."

When she was gone, Morgan looked over at Jane. "She winked at you again."

"Did she? Maybe she has something in her eye."

"Hmm. I'm sure that's it."

Jane picked up her spoon and slipped it

into her oatmeal. She tasted it, relishing the slightly nutty texture of the oats. "Aren't you going to eat?"

Morgan tore his eyes away from her mouth and drizzled syrup around the melting pat of butter dead center on his hotcakes. He cut a neat triangle from the three-stack and observed that Jane was watching him out of the corner of her eye. He wondered if her thoughts about his mouth were as darkly erotic as his had been about hers. Hunger put him on notice, but he wasn't certain that food could satisfy it. His lips parted and he closed them around a forkful of hotcakes.

He tasted the syrup first, but then . . . oh, but then the hotcakes all but dissolved on his tongue. Light, airy, with just a hint of crispness at the edge, these were splatter dabs worth coming to town for. He could imagine lingering at the breakfast table. Morgan cut another triangle and speared it and had it halfway to his mouth before he saw Jane was studying her oatmeal with an intensity that oatmeal never deserved.

His eyes crossed slightly as he stared at the bite on his fork before he took it in his mouth. He swallowed and then tapped the tines of his empty fork against the side of Jane's bowl. That garnered her attention.

"Yes?"

Now Morgan pointed to his plate of hotcakes. "You made these." It was more accusation than question. He already knew the truth.

"I made the batter," she said. "Mrs. Sterling made the cakes."

"That's why Miss Ross was winking at you. She knew."

"I still think she might have had something in her eye."

"All right. I'll let that go. Why?"

"Why?"

"Why did you do it?"

Jane set down her spoon. "It would have been insulting for you to test me, Mr. Longstreet, but I realized that if I showed you what I can do, I might persuade you I am not without some skills."

"Huh." He cut into the stack of cakes again, took another bite. "It was a risk. What if I didn't like them?"

"Then I would know one of two things to be true: Either the coffee scalded your taste buds or food is merely fuel to you and you take no particular enjoyment in a satisfying meal."

"You're surely confident about these cakes."

"With good reason, don't you think?"

"All right, yes. They're excellent."

"Did it pain you so terribly to say so?"

"Not nearly as much as letting them grow cold on the plate." He watched Jane's emerald eyes brighten with her expression of mischief and satisfaction. "Eat," he said. "Cold oatmeal's good for caulking pipes and mending fences but not for eating."

Jane picked up her fork and dug in.

After breakfast Jane asked Morgan if he would escort her along the main thoroughfare so that she might see the town. When he asked her why she wanted to do that, she told him, "So the four or five people who don't know that I'm with you are not kept in the dark any longer." He made a noise at the back of his throat that sounded suspiciously like a chuckle choked off. "If I am not to live at Morning Star," she explained, "then it is merely prudent for me to learn more about Bitter Springs. There might be opportunities for employment."

Jane had no difficultly reading his response this time. Both his expression and his grunt were disapproving. Still, he put his objections aside, reminded her she would need her coat and hat, and then waited for her at the front entrance of the Pennyroyal while she retrieved them.

The wind nearly lifted her hat from her head when she stepped onto the porch. Morgan stood by while she secured it but intervened when she looped the scarlet scarf only once around her neck. He picked up one of the tails and made a second loop, giving it a little tug at her chin so that it nearly covered her mouth. When they turned onto the sidewalk and were buffeted head-on by the wind, she was glad for his interference.

It was a good reminder of how much knowledge he had at his fingertips and how much she had to learn. She smiled gamely, and when he offered his arm, she did not hesitate to accept it.

Morgan did not have much to say along their walk. He dutifully read the signs on the storefronts. Barbershop. Johnson's General Mercantile. Bakery. Land Office. Leather Goods. Hardware. Feed Store. Taylor's Bathhouse and Laundry. Jane let him go on that way. It struck her that he was isolated at Morning Star and perhaps preferred it that way. If he knew details about the druggist or the milliner or the blacksmith, he kept them to himself. She realized that he had told her more about the former marshal of Bitter Springs than about anyone else, and Benton Sterling was dead.

They passed Ransom's Livery, the corrals where cattle were herded to wait transport on the trains, and stood near the platform at the station but never stepped onto it.

"What is the next stop west?" Jane asked.

"If you mean a town, that'd be Rawlins. The train has to stop for water and fuel before then, but it's mostly grass on top and coal below. It's rough country. There aren't many women."

Jane nodded, thanked him for the information. They were on the point of turning when a youthful and, in Jane's mind, a vaguely familiar cry stopped them in their tracks. Jane turned her head toward the station. Beside her, she thought she heard Morgan mutter something under this breath. Jane laughed under hers. The rascal she had met at the train yesterday was bearing down on them.

Finn skidded to a halt at the edge of the platform, waved an arm in a wide arc, and then dropped over the side. He no sooner alighted than he was spinning around and calling to his brother, who was at that moment emerging from the station.

"Hey, Rabbit! Come see who's here! It's Mr. Longstreet and his special delivery."

His head snapped around and he looked wide-eyed at Jane. "Sorry, ma'am, but I can't recollect what comes after 'Middle.' Burn? Bury? Borough?"

"Bourne," said Jane. "Middlebourne."

He snapped his fingers. "Got it." He hollered back to Rabbit, who was rapidly approaching. "It's Miss Middlebourne!"

"Finn," Morgan said, wincing slightly as he tugged on one ear. "You don't need to yell like he's standing at the other end of town. Besides, shouldn't you both be in school?"

"On my way. Got plenty of time. Mrs. Bridger is usually a little late these days on account of her condition is what you call delicate. I think there's a lot of puking so I'm not clear about what makes it delicate, but that's what Granny says it is."

Jane recalled seeing Mr. and Mrs. Bridger the previous afternoon on her way to the Pennyroyal. Perhaps the secretive nature of their smiles had something to do with Mrs. Bridger's condition and nothing at all to do with her being in the company of Mr. Longstreet. She liked to think that was it. It occurred to her that the marshal's wife could only be in the early stages of her pregnancy. There were no obvious signs.

Jane said, "How many children does Mrs.

Bridger have?"

Finn's eyebrows fused together as he counted on his fingers. His lips moved silently around the names of each child. "I make it to be thirteen," he said at last. "How many you got, Rabbit?"

Rabbit jumped down beside his brother. "Got what?"

"Mrs. Bridger's kids. How many?"

Rabbit used the same counting method as his brother. "Thirteen. Six that come and go, but mostly thirteen."

"Thirteen?" Jane blinked. "That can't be —"

Morgan interrupted. "They're telling you the number of children Mrs. Bridger has in her *classroom.*"

"Oh."

"She and the marshal have no children of their own."

"So this will be their first. She must be delighted."

Frowning deeply, Finn poked Rabbit hard in the side with his elbow. "What's she mean about Mrs. Bridger's first?"

Rabbit shrugged. "What did you mean?"

Jane looked from Finn to Rabbit and back to Finn, and when nothing came to mind that would extricate her from her dilemma, she turned to Morgan.

There was no sympathy from that quarter. He said, "From now on, you probably want to mind where you step around these two."

Jane sighed. It was sound advice even if it was offered after the fact. She regarded the boys again, who were regarding her expectantly in turn. "Perhaps you should ask your grandmother to explain 'delicate condition.' "

Beside her, Morgan whispered out of the side of his mouth, "You will not make a friend there."

Jane resisted the urge to follow Finn's suit and poke Morgan in the side with her elbow. She told the boys, "We are going back to the Pennyroyal. Would you care to walk with us as far as the schoolhouse? Mr. Longstreet has been telling me about your town." As an exaggeration, Jane rated it as somewhere between mild and moderate.

"Sure," said Finn. "Me and Rabbit know a lot about Bitter Springs."

"Rabbit and I," Jane said automatically.

Finn screwed his mouth to one side and shook his head. "I'm just not gettin' the hang of that one, Miss Middlebourne, and you ain't the first to point it out. Mrs. Bridger bemoans it real regular-like. So does the marshal, come to think on it." He shrugged. "C'mon. Which side of the street did you come down? We'll go up the other. That good with you, Mr. Longstreet?"

Morgan's ears were still ringing with Finn's enthusiastic narrative by the time he and Jane reached the Pennyroyal. Rabbit had only been marginally more restrained. "Well?" he asked Jane as he escorted her up the steps. "Was there a detail they omitted?"

"It beggars the imagination."

He opened the door for her, but his attention was diverted by the sudden appearance of Marshal Bridger at the foot of the steps.

"Marshal," Morgan said with a nod. As he held the door for Jane, he said to her, "Wait for me in the dining room. I need to speak to the marshal. I won't be long."

Jane glanced over her shoulder.

"Ma'am." Cobb Bridger lifted his hat.

Jane offered a faint and uncertain smile and then looked to Morgan.

"It's fine," he said, bending his head toward her. "He's not here because you told the boys his wife is pregnant." He thought Jane appeared relieved. For Morgan it was further proof that she was naïve. Perhaps hopelessly so.

Morgan closed the door behind Jane, then joined the marshal. "How long were you following us?"

"Not long. I watched you deliver Rabbit and Finn to the schoolhouse from my office. You afraid you're losing that sixth sense of yours?"

"Can't lose something I never claimed to have."

Cobb shrugged.

Morgan looked the marshal over. He and Cobb Bridger were of a similar build, tall, rangy, and with a tendency toward lean, although Morgan thought Cobb might be turning the corner on that, a consequence of his recent marriage and his wife's cooking. As far as Morgan could tell their similarities began and ended with their bones. Morgan held his ground as the marshal's cool, blue-eyed gaze bore into him.

"I thought the plan was for you to be back at Morning Star by now," said Cobb.

"It's still the plan. There was a . . . complication."

Cobb tilted his head toward the hotel. "She have a name?"

"Jane Middlebourne."

"She's not the woman in your photograph."

"No, she's not, but she *is* Jane Middlebourne."

Cobb rested his elbow against the railing.

"Look, Morgan, I don't have a problem with you. Never have. I have a problem with the people you might attract."

"No one's come, have they?"

"No," said Cobb. "No one's come."

"I brought you Jane's photograph as a courtesy, Marshal, not because I had to. I keep my distance because I like it that way, not because I'm trying to avoid a confrontation. And to that point, there might never be a confrontation. You said it yourself, no one's come."

"Yet."

Morgan nodded. There was no getting around the "yet." "Do you want Miss Middlebourne to stand in front of your Wanted Wall so you can tick her off your list?"

"That won't be necessary," Cobb said.

Morgan smiled narrowly, without humor. "You've already done it, haven't you? I bet you watched us across the way from your office. One eye on her. One eye on your wall."

"I made a study when I saw her in your buckboard yesterday. When you weren't gone this morning, I thought I better take a second look."

"And?"

"And she's not on my wall."

Morgan looked back at the dining room window. He couldn't see Jane standing there behind the glass, but that did not mean she wasn't. "What now?" he asked.

"Are you going to marry her?"

"Not that it's any of your business, but I'm inclined to honor my proposal."

"Really?"

Morgan just stared at Cobb.

The marshal shrugged. "You're right. It's your business. The photograph got me thinking, that's all."

"It got me thinking, too, but she's explained it, and I'm not exactly in a position to throw stones, now, am I? I had to think about that."

"Are you going to tell her?"

"I still like to entertain the notion it'll never come to that."

Cobb nodded, blew out a long breath. "Then I hope you're right, Morgan. Whatever you think, I'm not your adversary. I'm on your side."

"What I think, Marshal, is that it's better if we just bump along. Keeps things in balance. Standing on my side tends to tip the boat."

"If that's the way you want it."

Morgan nodded once. "I'll be packed up and out of here by three, four at the latest. I can't speak for Miss Middlebourne. She'll be making her own decision. She made that clear."

Cobb chuckled quietly. He pushed from the railing and touched the brim of his hat. "Nothing wrong with that. Could be the two of you will bump along just fine."

Jane looked up when Morgan stepped into the dining room. She set her cup of tea down and acknowledged his presence with a brief smile. Beside her, Ida Mae Sterling began to rise. Jane protested, but Ida Mae would hear none of it. She picked up her cup in one hand and patted Jane's forearm with the other.

"I have things to do if there's going to be ham and cabbage tonight. You and Morgan can sit here a spell, and if I have my way with the girls, you won't be disturbed." Instead of heading straight to the kitchen, she veered in Morgan's direction. "Here. Take this coffee. I just poured it." She thrust the cup at him, giving him no choice but to take it, and when his hands were occupied, she gave him an affectionate pinch on his upper arm. "I like her, Morgan. I like her just fine." Then she was gone.

Mortified, Jane stared at the tea leaves at the bottom of her cup.

Morgan set his coffee down, shrugged out of his coat, and dropped his hat on a nearby table. "You can't mind her," he said, sitting beside Jane. "She gets ideas in her head and just says what she thinks."

Jane lifted her head, glanced sideways. "I believe she holds you in some affection. I observed that yesterday when we arrived, and again just now. Who is she to you?"

"I told you. She's the widow of the former marshal."

Disappointed with his answer, Jane pressed. "I imagine she thinks of herself as someone separate from her husband."

Morgan shrugged. He kept his hands folded around his coffee cup. "Ida Mae's been free with her opinions since she realized she had a voice. That thought is not original to me. Benton Sterling said that, and I suppose he would have known." He sat a little lower in his chair, sliding his legs far under the table. His mouth curled to one side. "I guess you could say she's got me like a chick under her wing. Has for a long time. Even before I settled around here."

Jane tried to imagine Morgan Longstreet as a chick under anyone's wing. He stood head and shoulders above Mrs. Sterling, yet from what she had seen, it was probably an apt description of their relationship. Morgan might pretend to chafe at it, dismiss it as unimportant, but what he did not do was try to escape it.

"Does she have children?" asked Jane.

"Yes. And grandchildren. They're scattered, which makes the rest of us easy pickings."

Jane hid an amused smile behind her teacup. "Is her advice usually sound?"

"Why? What did she say?"

Jane blinked. His reaction was more reflexive than responsive. "She brought me tea, Mr. Longstreet, and kept me company while you were with the marshal. My question had nothing at all to do with our exchange." She accepted his suspicious regard without looking away. Mrs. Sterling had advised her to take Morgan Longstreet straight on. He would respect that, she'd said.

Looking away, Morgan raised his coffee cup and breathed deeply before he took a swallow. "I would have to say no one's gone too far astray listening to Mrs. Sterling."

"Thank you. That is all I wanted to know." Jane looked to the window as Walt crossed the porch in front of it carrying a broom. She watched him set it down and begin sweeping around the rocking chairs. "Is

Marshal Bridger a friend?"

"I don't know if he has friends. Friends don't necessarily settle well with the job."

It was not an answer to the question she asked, but Jane did not bring it to his attention. "I wondered why you did not introduce me."

"His business was with me."

There was nothing rude in Morgan's tone, but neither did it invite further comment. "You spoke for rather a long time."

"We have not seen each other in a while."

"It seems as if Bitter Springs is a quiet town. Is that his doing?" Jane saw Morgan press his lips together. He regarded her over the rim of his coffee cup.

"You have a lot questions, Miss Middlebourne. Is there something in particular you want to know?"

She shook her head. "Not one thing in particular," she said. "Everything." When he simply continued to stare at her, she added, "Why, for instance, does no one I've seen wear a gun? I read articles, pieces in the newspapers, which led me to believe everyone wears a gun. You don't. I'm not certain that even the marshal was wearing one."

"He was. But the rest have to abide the town ordinance. I checked mine at Bridger's office when I came in yesterday. I'll get it when I leave."

"Everyone does that?"

"I don't know. I do."

"It's unexpected."

"That I obey the law?"

Jane shook her head. "No, I meant it's unexpected that no one wears a gun." She caught a glimmer of a smile change the shape of his lips. "Oh, you knew that's what I meant. You were teasing me."

"A little."

"There was no opportunity to do that in our correspondence. I remember thinking I wanted to impress you with my serious nature. I was cautious. It seems it might have been the same for you."

"I would say I was restrained."

"Yes. Just so. Restrained."

He was still restrained, she thought. He contemplated his coffee as if it might hold answers to questions yet unformed.

"Why are you not already married?" he asked suddenly.

The question took her by surprise. "The simplest answer is that no man has ever asked me to be his wife. Until you, that is."

"What is the complicated answer?" he asked.

"That no man was ever allowed to ask."

"That *is* complicated. Something to do

with Cousin Frances?"

Staring into her own cup, Jane nodded. She said quietly, "I regret that you were able to draw that conclusion with so little difficulty. I disclosed more in my correspondence than was either prudent or proper."

"As I recall, you wrote very little. Last night's fish story was revealing."

Jane touched one hand to her temple, recalling her headache the evening before. *There* was the source of her wayward tongue. "There is no satisfaction in judging her harshly."

"If you say so. I could find some satisfaction in it."

His wry tone made Jane look askance at him. She returned her hand to her lap and surprised herself by confessing, "Sometimes I hate her."

After a moment, Morgan said, "That's not always a bad thing."

"Do you think so?"

"I do, but I told you I'm not a godly man. I reckon you have to make peace with the hate and every other way you feel about her." He shrugged. "About anyone." He took another swallow of coffee. "I guess I always knew you were running more than coming."

"Pardon?"

"Coming here because you're running from there. I accepted that when I posted my advertisement. A woman with opportunities where she is doesn't look for opportunities where she isn't."

"I am disturbed that I understood that, Mr. Longstreet." She watched his mouth take on that vaguely sardonic twist she found a trifle alarming for its effect on her heartbeat. "I wish I could deny it, but you are right, of course."

"Did you discourage suitors, Miss Middlebourne?"

"Discourage them? Whyever would you think that?"

"Because if you gave a man the slightest hint that his attentions would be welcome, there is no fence that Cousin Frances could have put up that would have stopped him."

Jane stared at him blankly. His words were slow to register. When she understood what he was saying, laughter rolled lightly at the back of her throat. "It is your humor again, isn't it? You are teasing me."

"You embrace some peculiar notions about yourself."

She sobered. "What do you mean?"

Morgan shook his head slightly and released a short sigh. "Maybe it doesn't matter. Maybe it's for the best."

Before Jane could ask him to explain further, he rose and headed for the kitchen. This was done without so much as a by-your-leave. Watching him go, Jane realized he was not in the habit of excusing or explaining himself. It was not that he had no acquaintance with manners. He walked on the street side of the boardwalk when he escorted her, tipped his hat to acknowledge passersby, did not slurp or spit or slouch. She caught herself and amended this last point. Morgan Longstreet did slouch. In fact, he had not been introduced to a chair that could keep him upright or all four of its legs on the ground. Jane accepted this as pardonable since there was no evidence of poor posture when he stood, and his rolling, rhythmic stride kept him straight and tall.

It was probably good that she had defined some standards, she thought, no matter how arbitrary they were. Otherwise, she risked seeing him not as he was but as she wanted him to be. He had already done that where she was concerned; it was the only thing that accounted for his observation about men who would not be discouraged by fences. If he truly had not said it to tease her, then the comment meant he was deceiving himself into believing that she was more like Rebecca Ewing of the photograph than she was like Jane Middlebourne of the letters. He could say that he wanted the virtues of strength, but what he wanted was to walk with beauty.

Jane recalled what he'd said before he left the table. Perhaps it applied here: *Maybe it doesn't matter. Maybe it's for the best.*

Her thoughts were interrupted by Morgan's reappearance. He was not alone. He had Mrs. Sterling with him.

Without preamble, Mrs. Sterling said, "Morgan wants me to tell you straight up that if you think he has a sense of humor, you are the only one."

Jane blinked and needed a moment to orient herself. She supposed Mrs. Sterling's statement was in response to her own comment about Morgan teasing her. "Is it true?" she asked. "I understand he wants you to say it, but is it true?"

Mrs. Sterling pushed her spectacles up until they rested above her salt-and-pepper widow's peak. She regarded Jane with slightly narrowed eyes. "You think he could convince me to lie for him?"

"I do, yes."

Ida Mae's head snapped sideways, and she looked sharply in Morgan's direction. "Did I not say she is no one's fool, least of all yours? Now, I did what you asked, and you can see for yourself what's come of it."

Morgan's lip curled, but the tips of his ears reddened. "It was not one of your finer efforts." He dodged Mrs. Sterling's attempt to give his earlobe a tug and put up a hand to forestall her second attempt.

"He *should* have the grace to blush," she said, turning back to Jane.

"Then he *does* have a sense of humor?" Jane asked.

"Oh my, yes. Not so you can tell right off, but it's there. Wicked, too. I don't suppose many folks know that about him, so he really should have asked someone else for an opinion." Mrs. Sterling wiped her hands on her apron, reset her spectacles on the bridge of her nose, and looked askance at Morgan. "Anything else?"

"No, you have been extraordinarily helpful. It's hard to know what else I could possibly ask."

Ida Mae Sterling winked at Jane. "See? That's his wit. Dry as four-day-old cake." She turned smartly and headed back to the kitchen.

Shaking his head, Morgan sat. "Lesson learned."

"Then something has been accomplished. Why did you do it?"

He shrugged lightly. "An attempt to remove the scales from your eyes, I suppose. I was probably right that it doesn't matter."

Since Jane had been thinking along similar lines, she thought she understood. "It is in our nature to see what we want to see first and come to the truth later." She hesitated, thoughtful. "Or never come to it at all."

Morgan did not argue her point. He checked his pocket watch. "We have almost five hours. What do you propose we do?"

"Will you take me to Morning Star?"

Jane was not surprised when he did not answer immediately.

"I suppose I could take you to see the house," he said finally. "You're probably most interested in that anyway."

"I would be pleased if you would show me the house."

"All right. I have to get the buckboard at the livery first. And my gun. You stay here, and I'll come back for you."

Jane agreed and stayed seated until he was gone. Then she went into the kitchen to speak to Ida Mae Sterling.

They were five miles beyond the Bitter Springs town limits when Morgan announced they were on Morning Star land. Beside him, Jane leaned slightly forward as though this posture might improve her distance vision. "You won't see the house from here," he told her. "We have three miles to go." He was aware that Jane was still straining to see something.

"How do you recognize the edge of your property?" she asked.

"How do you recognize the back of your hand?"

Her smile was a quiet one. "Of course," she said.

Morgan pointed off to his left. "See that rise in the grassland? And the slip of cotton-woods just beyond it? That's the marker most folks use to distinguish my property from what can still be homesteaded. If it stops being respected, I'll have to stake it or put up a fence. There's enough fence al-ready, in my opinion, so I don't like the idea of it. I keep what the Burdicks put up in good repair and try not to unroll more barb-wire."

"I thought fence was good."

"Something else you read?"

"Yes."

He did not miss the slight defensiveness in her tone and realized he had not sup-pressed the sarcasm in his. "I'm sorry. It's good you wanted to learn things before you came, but most of what I read in New York papers that make it this far west is wrong-headed. Some of it is just wrong. Like everything else, there're two sides to putting up fence."

"Explain it to me."

He wondered if she was interested or merely being mannerly, and then wondered why he thought she couldn't be both. "Well, the fence keeps the cattle in. That's the obvious advantage. Limits the open range. Makes pulling the herd together or sectioning it off easier. That's helpful when your cattle number in the tens of thousands."

"You have so many?"

"Not now. Market for beef is down some after the boom. I'm building the herd back, testing what the market will bear. I understand the Burdicks had near that many head at one time, but lost about twenty-five percent in the blizzard in '86 and fifteen percent of what was left during the drought that followed. When the ranch was sold at auction, they barely had two thousand head. You see, when a big snowstorm is gathering, the cattle will move out ahead of it. It's in their nature. I don't know how they know what they know, but you can depend on it. When the weather calms, there they are where the grass is, or at least where they can get to it. With the wire up, they move until they're stopped by it, and then they pile up against the fence and die. It's not in their nature to push through."

Jane whispered, "How awful. Those poor creatures."

"Cattle would have died during the blizzard regardless of the wire, but there's a case to be made that wire made it worse. Weather here is unpredictable. It can happen again, did actually the following year, but by all accounts that winter was not as hard as what came before it. 'Eighty-six is the marker folks around here use for comparison."

Morgan noticed that Jane was no longer holding the seat under her as tightly as she had when they started out. He guessed she had learned to relax and roll with the juddering instead of trying to fight it.

"Fence has critics in Washington, too," he said. "Ranchers settled the territory, claimed the land that their cattle roamed as their own. Hundreds of square miles. Entire valleys. They could do that because no one was there to dispute it. The railroad and the federal government had already beaten back the Indians. Fence went up to mark ranch land. The problem came when Congress granted homesteads to encourage more settlement. The homesteaders were given plots and proper deeds and told to go west. They ran right into the fences, and unlike cattle, they pushed through."

"The range wars," said Jane.

Morgan nodded. "Ranchers accused the homesteaders of something worse than taking their land; they accused them of taking their cattle. There's swift and widely accepted justice for cattle thieving, and the ranchers enforced it. Land disputes were usually settled with a gun or a rope before they ever had a chance to be settled in court. Around here, the Burdicks had influence with the land office, so homesteaders were usually bought off. Scared off, if it came to that. Their deeds were turned over to the Burdicks."

"Is all of Morning Star deeded now?"

"Yes."

"So you benefited from the tactics the Burdicks used."

"Not just from them. The eastern speculators that came after had a hand in securing what the Burdicks hadn't. They wanted government contracts for dams and hydraulic works. If they had gotten them, they would have parceled out the land and sold off the pieces they didn't need. Homesteaders would have populated this entire area. One more way the government works against its own interests. Now I'm here, alone, on almost seven hundred square miles, and I'm not inclined to put any of it up for sale."

"Do you have problems with rustlers?"

"When I first took over, I did. It's been a couple years now. There was some testing of the waters, I suppose you'd call it. Cattle thieves looking to see if I was an easy mark."

"Were you?"

Morgan glanced sideways. "What do you think?"

"I think you applied swift justice."

He did not deny it. He gave the reins a little snap instead and lifted his chin toward the horizon. "Look there. You can just make out the house sitting low on the curve of the earth." He risked a second glance at Jane's profile and saw nothing in her finely etched features that hinted at her thoughts.

CHAPTER FOUR

Jane's eyes never strayed from the house as they approached. She wanted to take in everything about it. Morgan wrote about the house at Morning Star in his first response to her inquiry, but it was clear to her that he viewed it as a shelter from the storm, not a home. In Jane's mind, it should be both.

The long log house was larger than she had permitted herself to believe it could be. She said nothing to Morgan about the photographs of rough-hewn cabins that she had seen and upon which she had based her expectations. This house looked solidly built, the mortar lines straight and parallel to one another, the corners squared off at what appeared to be true right angles. It sat low to the ground and was so wide that it looked as if it squatted on the land. The house was sturdy, in service of its purpose, and had none of the architectural embellishments that distinguished Manhattan mansions along the avenue.

From what she could tell at a distance, and then again as they drew closer, the house was in good repair. The porch did not run the length of the front of the house, but it was long and wide enough to hold a swing. That swing, she noted, looked as if it had recently been given a fresh coat of white paint, and the thought that this might have been done in anticipation of her coming to Morning Star both warmed Jane and made her anxious.

The windows were glass, another feature she had not been certain she could expect, and where the sun did not reflect too brightly, she could see lace curtains framing them on the inside. The empty flower boxes beneath the windows were also freshly painted, and Jane permitted herself the indulgence of imagining what she might plant there.

As Morgan guided the buckboard abreast of the house, Jane's eyes were drawn to the large door front and center. In contrast to the dark, weathered frame of the house, the door was varnished and polished so that it fairly gleamed from under the protective roof of the porch.

Jane stayed in her seat as directed until

Morgan secured the horse and wagon. She took his hand when he offered it and let him assist her descent. It fell to her to release his hand when she was steady, but Jane held it longer than that because there was comfort and calm in his support.

"What are those buildings?" she asked, pointing off to her right.

"Woodshed. Smokehouse. That's the barn next to the corral. The bunkhouse is on the other side of the barn. Hard to see from this angle, but the men have a good view of the road leading up here from where they are."

As Jane's eyes were drawn to search for the outbuilding, a figure appeared on the far side of the corral. "Someone is coming."

"I see him. That's Jem Davis. I think I mentioned him. He's the one set on marrying Renee Harrison."

"Cecilia Ross's cousin."

"Yes. That's the one. Did you see Renee at the Pennyroyal this morning?" When Jane nodded, Morgan added, "Good. Because Jem will want every detail. It's better if you don't have to make them up."

Jane clutched the sleeve of Morgan's duster as he turned back to the house. "Who am I?" she asked. "I mean, who are you going to say I am?"

"If I know Jem, I won't have to say anything. He'll figure it out for himself." He gestured to the front door. "This way. He'll come in the back."

In the entryway, Jane allowed Morgan to help her remove her coat and scarf. She gave him her gloves but kept her hat. He hung her things on a hook beside the door before he shrugged out of his coat and took off his hat and gloves. He put his outerwear next to hers.

It was the first time Jane had seen his gun belt and holster. She stared at the weapon at his side.

Morgan unfastened the belt and held it out to her. "Would you like to see it?"

Jane leaned in for a closer examination but kept her arms at her sides. "Is it safe for me to touch?"

"If you don't squeeze anything. Here." Morgan unstrapped the holster and removed the revolver by its pearl handle. He tossed the belt over his shoulder, freeing his hand. He opened the Colt's cylinder, took out the bullets, and pocketed them before he reversed his grip and held the gun out to Jane by the barrel. "It's empty. Now I'm certain it's safe for you to touch."

Still, she took it gingerly. The pearl grip was cool and smooth in her palm. "Is this what is called a six-shooter?"

"Some call it that. Folks also call it a Peacemaker, though I've always thought that name mocks it some. It's a .45-caliber centerfire, made by Colt and mostly favored by lawmen and shopkeepers. I like it because it's lighter than other models, accurate, and the short four-inch barrel means it clears the holster easily."

"The fast draw," she said. When he did not comment, Jane looked up at him. She sighed. "It's another fiction, isn't it?"

"Afraid so. Leastways, I never saw it practiced or done. No shootouts at high noon either, none that are actually scheduled anyway. I guess it made for some exciting reading for you."

She had to admit that it had. "I'm not disappointed by the facts," she said. "Only surprised by them."

Morgan took back the revolver, holstered it, and then set the belt on the entry table. "For a rifle, I favor a Winchester. There are three resting in a rack by the back door. More in the bunkhouse. No one rides the property without a rifle in his saddle scabbard. That's something you'd have to get used to. I don't suppose you had guns in your home."

"Not a one."

"Do you object to learning how to shoot?"

"Object? No. I should like that." Given the way Morgan was studying her, Jane was not certain that he believed her. "I have always admired Annie Oakley." She paused, frowned, and regarded him with consternation. "She's real, isn't she? Annie Oakley is real."

Morgan nodded solemnly. "Yes, Miss Middlebourne. Annie Oakley is real."

"Well, I am heartily relieved to hear it."

He pointed to the left. "Come, I'll show you the rooms."

Jane stayed at Morgan's side as he escorted her through the house. A stone fireplace dominated the front room. The sofa had wide arms, a curved back, and was covered in navy blue velvet that was shiny in places from wear. There were two armchairs similarly covered. One showed evidence of more use than the sofa while the other showed less. The upright chairs had seat covers that revealed skilled embroidery work. The French knots numbered in the thousands. There were two tables with lamps, and candles on the mantelpiece. Other than an empty vase, the room was devoid of items that might grace other front rooms. There were no photographs, no figurines, no little boxes that could hold small treasures or even a deck of playing cards. The piano was unexpected, but Morgan told her that it came with the house, a gift from Uriah Burdick to his wife. It neither kept the wife faithful nor kept her on the ranch. She ran off with a railroad surveyor, and as far as Morgan knew, the piano had not been used since.

He did not ask Jane if she played, and she did not volunteer the information. Instead, she lightly dragged her fingertips across the keyboard's lid as she passed.

In addition to the front room, there was a dining room, a study that Jane judged to be seldom used, two bedrooms, one half the size of the other, and a loft space that Morgan told her had two more beds. The ladder to reach the loft was put away since he had no use for the space now. Someday, he had said, rather more offhandedly than not, and Jane kept her eyes averted, afraid he would know all her secrets at this casual reference to a future that figured children into it.

They ended in the kitchen. Jem Davis was waiting for them, one hip cocked against the sink while he drank his fill of water from a jar. Jane observed a broad face, square jaw, shoulders that extended like planks from an iron ship, and without conscious thought, she edged closer to Morgan. If

Morgan was aware that she had inched toward him, he gave no indication. He made the introductions and told Jem to wash his hands before he offered one to Jane.

Far from taking offense at the directive, Jem grinned so widely Jane thought she could count his entire mouthful of teeth.

"Sure, and I was going to do just that," said Jem. He set the jar down, turned to the sink, and scrubbed up while he hummed "Sweet Betsy from Pike." He shook off his hands, looked around for a towel, and when none magically appeared, wiped his hands on the front of his green flannel shirt. He stepped around the table, nodded, and waited for Jane to extend her hand first.

She did. His hold was gentle and put her immediately in mind of Walt back at the Pennyroyal. Something of her surprise must have shown on her face because Jem gave a lopsided, oddly endearing smile.

"Renee says I have hands like hams and fingers as thick as sausages, but it's all tender cuts." He added, "Renee's my fiancée, except she doesn't always own that she is."

"I see," said Jane. "It is a pleasure to meet you."

"Well, that's what I would call a mutual feelin' except I *know* there's more pleasure on my side." He looked at Morgan. "So you finally gone and done it. Hired yourself a cook and housekeeper. And none too soon. We were just jawin' about having to cook for ourselves this winter, and there wasn't one of us looking forward to it. Me and my brothers probably could survive, but that runt Max Salter hasn't got but a minute's worth of meat on his bones and no stores of fat. He wasn't going to make it, Morgan."

"Uh-huh."

"I'm serious. It was going to be a problem."

Jane found herself once again the target of Jem's hopeful expression. "Do you make fritters, ma'am? Corn. Apple. Cauliflower. Celery. Calf's brains. Tomato. It don't matter much what you put inside it. I'm partial to corn, but I like them all."

Before Jane could respond, Morgan put up a hand. "Jem, settle yourself and give her a chance to breathe. I noticed you are less concerned about her housekeeping talents."

"Sorry, ma'am. My mouth runs and the rest of me is hard-pressed to keep up." His eyes shifted to Morgan again. "I figure the housekeeping doesn't include the bunkhouse. Hard for me to get excited about that. Unless she's going to do our laundry?"

"No."

Jem shrugged. "Well, maybe we can pay her under the table."

"I'll beat you *with* the table."

Jane heard no rancor in Morgan's tone and saw no fear in Jem's expression. She reflected on what Morgan had said about telling Jem who she was. *I won't have to. If I know Jem, he'll figure it out.* What Morgan hadn't revealed was that he'd known all along that Jem would figure it wrong. She was aware that Morgan had subtly influenced Jem's assumption by introducing her as Jane Middlebourne, not *Miss* Middlebourne. It would be in keeping with Jem's assuming nature that he thought there was a man somewhere. Then again, Jem was single-minded about the fritters. Perhaps it was no matter to him if she was single, married, widowed, divorced, or had two heads. Propriety was about the only thing she could not batter dip, fry, and serve to Jem Davis.

Morgan could not interpret Jane's silence on the ride back to Bitter Springs. She responded when he spoke, but in the absence of her questions, it was too difficult to know what to say. He did not have a good sense of what she thought of the house. Her expression, except for the brief exchange with Jem, was largely neutral. There had been her interest in the gun, but for all he knew that interest was a prelude to shooting him.

Before they left, he took her out back to see the garden, the pigs, and the henhouse. The chickens scratched the ground when he scattered corn for them and ignored Jane, but the rooster marched right up and tried to peck at her shoes. He was encouraged when Jane bent, firmly picked up the bird in both hands, and tossed it away. The bird left her alone after that. She looked over the smokehouse, saw the woodhouse was full, and stood beside him at the corral until one of the mares came over to see if Morgan had anything for her. He noticed that Jane was initially shy around the animal until Morgan told her the mare's name was Periwinkle, but answered better to Winkle. For whatever reason, that seemed to make a difference. She stroked the white star on Winkle's nose with increasing confidence. It was only when Winkle tried to nuzzle her that Jane backed away.

Morgan decided to bypass the barn after that and escorted her to the bunkhouse. Jem had already gone back there and turned out the troops. Wiry Max Salter was wedged between Jessop and Jake Davis, but he managed to get a hand out and gave a good account of himself. Jane was polite, reserved, and deeply thoughtful by then, and she sat beside Morgan in that same vein now.

"That's the town's cemetery on your right," said Morgan.

"Yes, I know. I saw it on the way out."

Morgan grimaced slightly. Of course she had. He might have even pointed it out to her; he couldn't remember. "We'll be at the Pennyroyal soon." Out of the corner of his eye, he saw Jane nod. "By the time we return, it will be almost exactly twenty-four hours since your arrival."

"Yes. I'm aware."

"I know what I want to do. Do you?" Jane caught him off guard by grabbing his wrist. There was considerable strength in her grip. She made him pull up on the reins.

"Stop," she said. "Stop the wagon."

Morgan slowed and then halted. She was still clutching his wrist in her gloved hand. He looked from it to her ashen face. "What is it?"

"Those bedrooms in the loft, and the small one beside your room, you said there might be use for them someday."

Morgan frowned. "Yes. I said that."

"You were speaking of children, weren't you?"

"I suppose so. They're a vague notion right now." His ginger eyebrows drew closer together as he studied her features. "You're going to have to tell me. Frankly, I don't know if it's what precedes the getting of them that has you twisted three ways from Sunday, or the having of them. It's probably something we should discuss."

"That's what I'm trying to do, Mr. Longstreet. Do you expect me to give you children?"

Morgan blew out a protracted breath that was part whistle, part sigh. "I don't know that I *expect* it exactly. I figured it would happen in the course of things. Naturally, you know." He had a sudden thought. "That's been explained to you, hasn't it? Someone's talked to you about what's natural between a man and a woman."

"I am not completely ignorant."

"Oh, I know you've done your reading. I'm just not sure I trust your sources."

"Mr. Longstreet, it is my intention to have a serious conversation."

Morgan thought she could not possibly be prissier, but then her mouth flattened in a prim, disapproving line, and he concluded he had been wrong. "Pardon me, Miss

Middlebourne, but my intention is the same as yours. I meant what I said. I am not sure I trust your sources."

"Please put that from your mind," she said. "I am trying to understand what you want from me in regard to children. What if I am unable to give you any?"

"You're not past your childbearing years."

"I know. You are not being helpful. If I said to you now, I cannot have children, what will it mean to your proposal? Or if we marry, and time passes, and I never conceive, what will it mean to your vows?"

"Is this about that photograph? Do you think I looked at the picture of your cousin and thought about her childbearing parts?"

"Why not? You gave a good deal of thought to her *bones.*"

Morgan looked Jane over. Her face was no longer pale. There were rosy coins of color in her cheeks, but what put them there was frustration, and perhaps, he thought, fear. "You're pretty riled about this."

"Because you refuse to answer my question."

"Well, I reckon that's because I don't know. You put it to me kind of sudden."

Jane said, "I did."

Morgan saw Jane shiver. A few more minutes in the wind, and her teeth would start to rattle like dice in a cup. "Can we go somewhere warm to discuss this?"

"We have no private place, and please don't suggest my room. Not in the middle of the afternoon."

"All right. If you're going to pin me to the wall, then I guess the answer is I want children. I would be lying if I said my mind never came around to it. Probably Finn and Rabbit got me thinking."

"Because of what they said about Mrs. Bridger being pregnant?"

"That's part of it, but mostly it's the boys being who they are. I like them. I like them just fine, and I wouldn't mind a couple of rascals underfoot. That said, the particulars of begetting some rascals require two parties, and who's to say that if there weren't any children the problem would be yours? I don't have any children, least none that have ever been presented to me. You understand what I'm saying?"

"I understand that you've had opportunity to beget."

"That's one way of saying it, I suppose."

"It never occurred to me that you would be inexperienced."

Morgan's eyebrows lifted slightly. "Do you mean to insult or flatter me?"

"Neither, but you can take it as you like."

Morgan faced forward. "You know, Miss Middlebourne, this is a peculiar conversation. Perhaps the most peculiar conversation I've ever entertained, especially when I account for the location and present company. You think you have another one like this in you before we reach the Pennyroyal?"

"I have no idea."

He sighed. "Let's finish this one, then." He gave her a sideways glance. "What about you?"

"Me, Mr. Longstreet?"

"Children," he said. "We are speaking of children. I've heard some women fear childbirth. Do you?"

Jane did not answer immediately. "No," she said at last. "At least I don't think I will."

"And you'll welcome children?"

"Of course."

"Of course," he repeated softly. "It's been my experience that not all women do."

"I am aware. It is difficult to imagine that I would ever count myself as one of those women."

Morgan fell silent. He had one question left, the one he had never considered until Jane got him to wondering with her talk. He could let it sit, never say a word and hope for the best, but if the best turned out to be something literally ill conceived, he would have to live with knowing he could have asked her straight and trusted her answer.

He said, "I don't know any way to put this to you except direct, and since that's mostly how I am, it seems that's how I should be."

"What is it?"

"Are you already carrying some man's child?"

Jane sucked in a breath.

Morgan waited, didn't look away. He did not trust himself to read what he glimpsed in her eyes. She might have been stricken, embarrassed, shamed, or even hurt. What he needed was her word.

"No," she said quietly, letting the breath ease out of her. "Let me say it plainly, Mr. Longstreet. I am not going to present you with anyone's bastard."

"You got me speculating with your talk," he said. "I had to ask."

Jane pressed her lips together, nodded faintly.

Morgan picked up the reins. "I think we're done. You?"

She was long in answering, but finally she said, "Yes, I think we are done."

"Very well, Miss Middlebourne, then I suggest we go back to the Pennyroyal by way of Grace Church. Pastor Robbins will make time for us, and I suppose we can scare up a couple of witnesses." Morgan shifted so he had a clear view of Jane's face, and then he regarded it for a long moment. Her emerald eyes were luminous, her smile just a cautious slip of a thing. "What do you say to that?"

"Yes," she said on a thread of sound. "I say yes."

By Jane's reckoning, the ceremony took only fifteen minutes. It was formally witnessed by the pastor's wife, and at Jane's suggestion, Ida Mae Sterling, but this being Bitter Springs, there were also bystanders to the exchange of vows. Walt Mangold came courtesy of Mrs. Sterling's invitation, and then Walt hailed the marshal on his way to the church and said sure, they could walk over together. Ted Rush had business with the marshal so when he stepped out of his hardware store and spied Cobb and Walt loping toward the church, he followed, partly for business reasons, but mostly out of curiosity. Buster Johnson, the sole customer in the hardware store when Ted stepped outside, finally made his selection among the hammers and went looking for Ted. Catching sight of Ted on the church steps, Buster took off after him, swinging the hammer as he went. Abigail Johnson left the mercantile in search of her son, who had been sent to the hardware store for half a pound of nails. It was simply in her mother's nature to hurry after Buster before he hurt someone — or more likely himself — with a hammer he had no business carrying. She would later confide to Jane that her boy had a college degree and the sense of a squirrel.

Jane was entirely pleased with the ceremony. In Pastor Robbins's capable hands, the reading was done with particular care for the serious nature of marriage and amusing acknowledgment of the adventure. Morgan demonstrated no hesitation in repeating the words that would bind him to Jane, and although he made every declaration quietly, it seemed to Jane that he was not reciting, but speaking from his heart. She wanted to hold that thought close, embrace it, no matter that it was the feeling of a moment, a wildly improbable notion that might annoy him if she shared it. Jane doubted that she ever would. The ceremony they had concluded had infinitely more in common with a business arrangement than a love match, and she cautioned herself that she would be wise to remember that. A business arrangement might end amicably. A love match never could.

Morgan escorted Jane back to the Penny-royal with the intention of collecting her belongings. This did not come to pass as quickly as she thought he might have liked, as they were trailed to the hotel by Pastor Robbins, the two witnesses, and all five of the bystanders. There were congratulations and best wishes all around, and the celebratory air evolved into a reception with food and drink and laughter. Customers from the saloon came to the dining room to observe the fuss and stayed to enjoy it. Diners crossed to the saloon to take more drink. After an hour, Jane believed she had been introduced to all of Bitter Springs, certainly to everyone who was able to squeeze into the Pennyroyal.

For herself, Jane did not mind, but she thought Morgan suffered the attention. On the few occasions when they were separated by well-wishers, she noticed him sidling toward the edge of the room only to be drawn back by someone calling him over to their circle.

A young woman whose name she could not recall was pressed to play the piano. Terry McCormick, the town's mayor, held up a fiddle and joined her. The music moved people to push aside the saloon tables and make room to jump and stomp and carry on. The raucous energy on display was wholly unknown to Jane. The walls of the Pennyroyal shook. The floor trembled under her feet. The mirror behind the long mahogany bar reflected golden, rippling light as the lamps and lanterns wobbled in place.

Jane stood with Morgan on the perimeter of the dancing, fascinated by the frenzy but not inclined to join in. She did not know when she slipped her arm in his, and once she was aware of it, she did not try to disengage. For the longest time, neither did he, but when Buster Johnson swung Cil Ross too close to where Jane was standing, it was Morgan who pulled her out of harm's way and kept her there, one hand at the small of her back.

Jane did not expect that Morgan would invite her to dance, but there were those present who had expectations contrary to her own and were not shy about voicing them. She hoped that Morgan would hold firm, as much for her sake as his, but when the crowd began to clap and chant, only a pillar of stone would not be moved. She held her breath when Morgan turned to her.

"Shall we?" he asked.

She looked at the perfect arch of one of

his eyebrows and wondered if it hinted at wry humor or resignation. "I don't know the steps," she said.

"No one does."

Thinking she could save him from himself, she tried again. "You told me you don't dance."

Morgan angled his head toward Buster Johnson gamely trying to corral Cil Ross in his arms after another spin that went wild and wide. "That's not dancing," he said. "I can do that."

Jane's eyes widened. "I don't think I want you to." If he heard her, he didn't acknowledge it. She was lifted off the ground as easily as he had lifted her from the train. His hands at her waist were at once familiar and foreign. She did not try to resist.

Morgan set her down in the midst of the dancers, faced her, and took one of her hands in each of his. "Ready?"

She was not. It didn't matter. The clapping quickened and then he was leading her sideways, always with the shoulder first, dipping into the rhythm. Three steps right, three steps left. Backward. Forward. Around and around. He made her dizzy. He made her light. She caught sight of herself in the mirror once, head thrown back, beads of perspiration glistening on her brow, pink blossoms on her cheeks, and only knew her reflection because she recognized the man she was with. He seemed unchanged to her, his features set with a Spartan's grit even while he guided and spun her across the floor. The music moved his feet, but it did not move him. His narrow smile never touched his eyes, and when he watched her — and it struck her that he had never stopped watching her — she could not see her way through to his thoughts. His impenetrable green gaze made her shiver suddenly. In spite of the heat, she felt a frisson of excitement, and yes, of fear.

As the improvised reception went on until well after dark, Mrs. Sterling invited Morgan and Jane to spend another evening in Bitter Springs, this time as special guests of the Pennyroyal at no charge. Morgan politely declined the offer. Mrs. Sterling gave him a pointed look for making this decision without consulting his bride. For his part, Morgan pretended to be oblivious, which provoked Ida Mae's heaviest sigh.

They left as soon as Walt loaded Jane's trunk and bags on the bed of the buckboard. People spilled out of the Pennyroyal to send them off. Morgan singled out Cobb Bridger at the forefront of the crowd and tipped his hat to the marshal and Mrs. Bridger before taking up the reins.

The night was clear. The Milky Way laid out a trail of stars across the black sky. There was no visible moon to diminish the majesty of the heavens. Morgan saw Jane glance behind her and imagined she was seeking a last glimpse of town before the lights disappeared. He felt no such urge. It was not long after that he heard the last of the music and laughter.

"Did you want to stay?" he asked.

"No."

"Good."

Jane sifted through the fringed ends of her scarf, straightening and smoothing them over her knee. "I would have liked to have been asked."

"So Mrs. Sterling was right."

"Yes. I did not think you noticed her disapproval."

"I've never learned to dodge her darts. Ignoring their sting is how I get by." Morgan looked sideways at Jane. "I'm used to making decisions on my own. Taking your opinion into account will require some getting used to."

"So you *do* intend to take it into account."

"When it suits," he said.

"Of course."

Morgan thought he might have seen Jane's lips twitch, but it could have just as easily been a grimace. "You were satisfied with the ceremony?"

"Yes. You?"

"Seemed a little crowded." He could not mistake her soft laughter for anything but what it was. "I suppose back in New York there would have been a hundred people at your wedding."

"Back in New York," she said, "there would have been no wedding. Regardless, it seemed to me that there were at least that many at the Pennyroyal. That was unanticipated."

"That was free liquor and curiosity."

"Powerful motivators," said Jane. "Still, it was kind of everyone to wish us well."

"I didn't know the half of them."

"I never noticed that it mattered. They greeted you as a friend."

Morgan grunted softly. He did not want to be their friend.

Jane said, "Why did you ask me to dance?"

"Should I have asked someone else?" His flippant response was met with silence. "It was only a matter of time before we were pushed onto the floor. It seemed wiser to take it on my own terms."

"I thought it might be something like that.

153

I wanted to believe that you enjoyed it, but I do not think you did."

"Did I make a fool of myself?"

"No."

"Did I make you feel foolish?"

"No!"

Morgan shrugged. "Then that'd be as much as I hoped for."

There was only silence after that.

Jane stood beside the bed that she was meant to share with Morgan while he carried in her bags and trunk. She had offered to take one of the bags, but he would not allow it. He told her that tomorrow morning was soon enough for her to start toting, lugging, and hauling, and that when she looked back on it, she would be grateful he had spared her the chore tonight.

Jane was not sure that was true. She needed something to do. She had already placed her gloves, scarf, and coat at the front door, and now she stood with her hands at her sides, fidgeting with the folds in her flared skirt.

Morgan dropped both bags on the chest at the foot of the bed. "Do you sleep in that hat?"

Jane's hands flew to her head.

Morgan cocked an eyebrow. "I guess not."

He turned and headed out. "Getting your trunk now."

Jane removed her hat and looked around for somewhere to put it. She was reluctant to shift any of Morgan's personal items on top of the dresser to make room for hers. There was no vanity, and the table on the far side of the bed already held a lamp and two books. An empty water glass and carafe sat on the table closest to her. There was a rocking chair beside the window, but she could foresee either herself or Morgan crushing the hat if she left it on the seat. The hook on the inside of the door that led to the small, utilitarian washroom was most likely meant to hold a towel or robe, although she saw evidence of neither. Still, living with the Ewings had taught her the importance of territory, both having it and respecting it. She was determined not to encroach.

Jane eyed the wardrobe again and settled on placing the hat on top of it. She also decided that she would buy a hatbox on her very next trip to town. It pained her some that she had left a very nice one behind.

She was standing on tiptoe, pushing the black velvet hat in place, when Morgan reentered the room.

He set the trunk down, came up behind

her, and gave the hat a nudge. It slid several inches beyond Jane's reach. "I suppose you're going to need a footstool."

"If you continue to help in this manner, I will." She lowered herself from her tiptoes but could not step back. He was there, right behind her, and when his outstretched arm came down, his palm brushed the curve of her shoulder. Jane went very still. For a moment, she could not breathe. It could not have been long at all before his hand fell away, but it seemed to Jane as if time slowed, stopped, and only resumed its march when he retreated one step, then another, until he finally put enough space between them that she could no longer feel the heat of him at her back.

Jane expected to see Morgan standing near the bed when she turned. He wasn't. He was facing the dresser, his Stetson overturned in one hand, and he was filling the crown with the very items that she had been too respectful to move aside. She watched, her dark eyebrows rising in conjunction with her astonishment, as he picked up his hairbrush and comb and dropped them into the hat. In short order, these items were joined by the bottle of Dr. Horace Johnstone's Peppermint Tonic, a baking soda tin, toothbrush, box of matches, hand mirror, and shaving cup, soap, and razor. There was a leather strop hanging on one of the spindles that supported the dresser's large mirror. He removed it, wound it neatly around his hand, and then slipped the coil off and added it to the contents in his hat.

"You can put your things here. Mrs. Sterling said that your kind of female would have little pots of creams and lotions and such. Perfume. Hair combs. Maybe a box for jewelry."

Jane stared at him. *Her kind of female? What did that mean?*

"Do you?" he asked.

She nodded slowly.

"Well, you can put them here." He waved one hand over the dresser's cleared surface. "Will it be enough room?"

Jane found her voice. "Mr. Longstreet, I assure you I can —"

Morgan's mouth twisted wryly. "About that. I figure since we're married, you should call me Morgan."

"All right. Morgan. As I was saying, I believe you and I —"

"And I should call you Jane."

"Yes," she said. "Yes, of course. I think we can —"

"It's a good name. Jane."

"I suppose. Now, if I could . . ."

Morgan studied her, head tilted slightly to one side, eyes narrowed a fraction.

Finding herself the object of his intense interest once again, Jane sighed and asked somewhat impatiently, "What *is* it?"

Morgan would not be hurried. He continued to regard her thoughtfully. "I'm trying to decide if it suits you."

"Does it really matter? It is my name. It is the one you will have to use if you hope to attract my attention. As you said, it is a good name."

"Plain," he said.

"Yes. Which is precisely why it suits. Now, if you would allow —"

"You believe that, don't you? Plain Jane."

Jane said nothing.

Morgan's eyebrows lifted, and he made a sound at the back of his throat that could be interpreted as skepticism or satisfaction. "What was it you wanted to tell me?"

Jane's lips parted before she realized her mind had gone perfectly blank. She blinked, and then recovered enough to give Morgan an accusing look. "I have quite forgotten."

He shrugged. "That happens."

"Not to me," she said. "Not until now."

"Could be a consequence of you being so tired. I noticed your eyelids were drooping back at the saloon." He held his hat in front of him like an offering plate. "That's why I collected my things. I'm taking them to the bedroom next door. I'll sleep there. I expect the bed is comfortable enough. That will give you some time to accustom yourself to whatever it is a bride accustoms herself to. It's new days, Jane."

Jane remained perfectly still in spite of the fact that she thought her knees might buckle. All the anxiety she had harbored about sharing his bed had been for naught. He did not want her. She was going to sleep alone on her wedding night. Jane was sure she did not know how she was supposed to feel about that. Relieved? Worried? Frustrated? Offended? It seemed that she experienced all of those things but none so profoundly as unsettled.

Morgan had explained his thinking in a manner that made it seem he was acting out of consideration for her, but it was Jane's experience that such consideration could mask contempt. She was afraid to trust it. Plain Jane. He had said the words aloud, the ones that had struck at her heart since childhood, the ones that she thought she had accepted, even embraced with the fierceness of ownership.

Cousin Alex liked to tease her that she

imagined herself as that other Jane, the Gothic novel heroine who found love with the equally unappealing, but infinitely more tortured, Mr. Rochester. Jane found it best not to respond to Alex's sardonic remarks, especially when it was liquor that pickled his wit, but there were times she had wondered if there might not be some element of truth in his observations. It was not necessarily uncomfortable to be Plain Jane. Acceptance merely hinged on reduced expectations; not for herself, but for how others regarded her.

Now that he had met her, married her, Morgan Longstreet had reduced expectations. She suspected he was trying to come to terms with them. Jane could appreciate that. She did not make the mistake of supposing he was Mr. Rochester. No doubt he required time alone to master his disappointment.

To stop fiddling with the fabric of her skirt, Jane folded her hands in front of her. "It is new days," she said quietly. "I am not averse to sharing the top of the dresser with you. I think we might manage to find room for your things and mine. I think you will agree it is a beginning. Sharing. One of the things I expect a bride — and her husband — must accustom themselves to. The bed can wait, if you think that best, but perhaps we should learn to dance in each other's space."

"You want me to keep my things in here?"

"I want you to do as you wish. I am merely saying I do not mind if you keep your things here."

Morgan cradled the crown of his hat in one hand while he raked his hair with the other. He scratched behind his ear. "I'm feeling my way here."

"So am I."

"I didn't expect you to be so accommodating."

"Compromising."

"If there's a difference there, I'm not grasping it." He held up a hand when Jane would have explained. "It's all right. I don't need to learn about it now." He carefully turned over the Stetson so the objects he collected began to spill out. He arranged them on the left side of the dresser top. "Will that do for you?"

"It will do fine."

He nodded. "Do you want to use the washroom first? That's what you meant by learning to dance in each other's space, isn't it?"

"Yes. That's what I meant. But you use it first. I have to unpack some things."

"All right." Morgan picked up the toothbrush and baking soda tin. On the point of entering the washroom, he paused. "Towels, soap, sponges. They're all in here."

"I saw."

"A washup will have to do tonight," he said. "Tomorrow, I'll help you draw and heat enough water for a bath."

"I would like that."

"Maybe not, once you take notice of the work involved."

"I'm not afraid of work, Mr. Longstreet."

"Morgan."

"Morgan," she repeated. "Another thing to which this bride shall have to become accustomed." Before he disappeared into the washroom, Jane thought she glimpsed his wry grin and a faint headshake. Both responses puzzled her, but by the time a question occurred to her, he was closing the door and shutting her out.

Jane worked quickly, emptying the valises first. Each of them was packed tightly with cotton, wool, and flannel undergarments that included petticoats, corsets, camisoles, and drawers. Tucked between those items were stockings, suspenders, gloves, and the various pots of cream and lotions that Morgan had suspected comprised the whole of their contents. At the bottom of one bag was the cookbook she had purchased expressly for her new position as wife of a rancher. At the bottom of the other, she discovered an item that she had not packed, another book, placed there by Alex, she suspected. When she lifted it and saw it was *Jane Eyre,* her suspicions were confirmed. She imagined he thought it was a very good joke. If he were within sight, Jane would have thrown the damn thing at his head.

The man she had bound herself to was *not* Mr. Rochester. The most obvious distinction was a physical one. Morgan Longstreet had a pleasing, symmetrical countenance that was only saved from true beauty by the scar at the right corner of his mouth. Although it pained her to admit it, she was selfishly glad of that flaw. For his features to be so otherwise cast in a fashion that evoked thoughts of marble gods was a burden to her, and she had dwelled on it nightly while examining his photograph in the privacy of her bedroom. She also took some comfort that his coloring was different than she had been able to imagine. As it happened, he was no blond Adonis in the drawing room style of Alexander Ewing. Jane counted that as a mark in Morgan Longstreet's favor. It was yet another way she had risked so much by accepting his invitation. No amount of study could have prepared her for the thatch of orange that he kept mostly hidden under his hat. And his fair complexion was lightly freckled where it was unprotected from the sun. Alex would have hated that. Jane was relieved by it.

Morgan Longstreet had a narrow chin, defined cheekbones, a sharply drawn jaw that made his facial muscles jump when he set it tightly, and blue-and-gray-flecked green eyes that could be implacable, impenetrable, or inviting. Jane had observed all of that. In turn she had felt small, slighted, or swallowed whole, and having felt those things, had vowed not to allow him such influence. It was a familiar promise, one she knew to be easier made than carried out. Guarding one's thoughts always presented fewer challenges than guarding one's emotions.

The door to the washroom opened. In the process of folding a pair of stockings at the bedside, Jane intended to merely glance over her shoulder to acknowledge Morgan's presence. What she did was stop folding and stare.

Morgan stood in the open doorway wearing a pair of flannel drawers and nothing else. The damp towel slung around his neck did not qualify as any sort of substantial

164

garment. Droplets of water clung to the shaggy tips of his hair, darkening it. He had not carried a comb with him. The runnels made by passing his fingers through his hair were visible. He leaned one naked shoulder against the door frame and held each end of the towel in his fists.

He gestured toward the bed with his chin. "Is that all of it?"

Jane tore her eyes away from the marble statue come to life and looked back at the bed. Most of the contents of her bags were strewn across the coverlet. What wasn't there was occupying the space on the dresser that he had ceded to her. "I have not opened the trunk."

Morgan's eyebrows lifted. He looked at the wardrobe already in the room, and then he looked around the room. "Another cupboard would fit over there next to the window."

"Do you think so?"

"There's one in the loft. I'll measure first. If it will fit, I'll get Jake to help me bring it down tomorrow. There's one in the room next door, but it's too small for what I'm imagining you're going to lift out of that trunk." His eyes swept the bed again. "You have a magician's flair. How many scarves do you reckon you still have up your sleeve?"

"Don't concern yourself with the scarves." She pointed to the top of the wardrobe where her hat rested. "But have a care for the rabbit."

The right corner of his mouth creased. The crescent-shaped scar whitened. "There's some sass in you, Jane."

"Pardon?"

"Sass," he repeated. "Maybe they don't call it sass where you're from."

"I know the word. I didn't know if I heard you correctly."

"I see."

Jane finished rolling the stockings in her hand, set them down, and picked up another pair. "Cousin Frances said I was impudent."

" 'Sassy' sounds better."

Jane smiled. "I believe you are right."

Morgan pushed away from the door frame. "Mostly I am."

Jane looked up to see if his wry grin was in place. It wasn't. She could not make out if he was stating a fact or poking fun at her. She hoped it was the latter; she could not abide arrogance.

"I'll get my things out of the washroom," he said. "And clear out that top drawer. Unless you think you can squeeze most of what you have there into it."

She shook her head. "No, there are immutable laws of physical science that apply here."

"You're talking about the conservation of matter."

Jane nodded slowly. "I am."

"You can't fit a pig through a straw without turning her into sausage first."

"Yes, I suppose." There was no mistaking his grin now.

"How about I just 'move my things, like I said."

"That would be fine. Thank you."

Morgan opened the drawer, scooped out the contents, and held them against his chest with one arm. He returned to the washroom, collected his clothes with his free hand, and then padded out barefoot.

Jane could hear him moving around in the bedroom next door. They were engaged in similar activities, folding, smoothing, hanging, sorting. She suspected she completed her tasks with more care, but when she finished before he did, she wondered if she had been mistaken.

When she entered the washroom, Jane discovered that Morgan had set out a towel, washcloth, and sponge. The basin was empty, and she realized he must have tossed the water he used out the small window. She poured fresh cold water into the bowl before she stripped down to her shift. It felt as if she washed away a week's worth of grit, when in reality she had bathed only that morning in a tub at the Pennyroyal with hot and cold running water. Less than twenty-four hours had passed, and she was already reflecting fondly on that memory. She thought she probably should not mention it, even in passing. It was quite possibly the sort of thing that would have Morgan questioning his decision to marry her.

She thought he probably already was, perhaps from the exact moment they had finished exchanging vows. He had not kissed her. He had avoided it, in fact. When Pastor Robbins had given him leave to do so, Morgan had done nothing. She had covered the awkward moment by leaning into him and pressing her cheek against his, and for then it was enough.

It was not enough now, but when she stepped back into the bedroom and saw that Morgan had not returned to say good night, she counted it as a blessing that she was familiar making peace with disappointment.

CHAPTER FIVE

Morgan lay on his back in bed, head cradled in his hands. His stare alternated between the ceiling and the starlight beyond the window. Light from the bedside lamp flickered. He wondered if Jane had fallen asleep yet. She should have. It had been over an hour since he'd left, and in his estimation she had been ready to fold then. He wished he could say the same for himself.

What the hell had he been thinking? He did not know a damn thing about women, so why in God's name had he concluded it was a good idea to marry one? He should have stood behind a mule and taken a kick to the head. He would either be dead or so dumb that the idea of marriage would have been knocked clean out of his mind. Now he was just out of his mind, and he had a woman lying in a bed in the room right next to his to prove it.

Mrs. Sterling had pulled him aside at the

hotel and suggested that he just leave Jane be tonight, that she would be one taut nerve, fatigued, and fearful, and it would be a kindness to let her breathe some before he exercised his conjugal rights. Thinking back on it, Morgan wished he had pressed Ida Mae to be clearer. For instance, should he have included Jane in the decision to sleep apart? Given her an opportunity to tell him that she would have welcomed, or at least tolerated, him in bed? When he had cleared the dresser top, she had suggested they share that space. Maybe if he had asked her, she would have been similarly inclined about the bed. ✦

And if she had been, would he have taken her up on it? It was true he had some experience with women, but that did not mean he knew them. He recalled Jane's words. *I understand that you've had opportunity to beget.* He wondered what Jane would have thought if he told her his opportunities had been limited to a few whores, two of whom he paid for a poke, and one who took him upstairs because she felt sorry for him. There was another woman: the one who claimed him first, taught him about a woman's body and fed his soul. She was seductress, siren, a young boy's savior. Or so he had thought for a time. And how could he have known differently when she laid waste to his mind and made herself everything to him in and out of bed? Even now, after so many years had passed, it was easier to think of her as a witch than a whore, but he no longer harbored any doubt that she was the latter.

Morgan had an urge to go to Jane and no idea what he would say to her. If nothing occurred to him when he got to her room, he would have to invent some reason for being there. Just thinking about it seemed like too much trouble.

It bothered him that he had not kissed her. He should have done that. At the wedding ceremony, the witnesses accounted for his reluctance. Maybe if it had been only the minister, Mrs. Robbins, and Ida Mae, Morgan thought he would have taken the opportunity presented to him, but with Walt, Ted, Cobb, Buster, and Buster's mother all looking on, he felt as if he and Jane had become an attraction in a sideshow. The problem was, that excuse did not hold up very well when he considered that he had not even tried to kiss her once they were alone.

The night had been ripe for it. There was a moment riding back to Morning Star that he thought she might not bolt if he angled his mouth to hers, but the moment came and went as he was plotting it. He had been accused before of thinking too hard and too long, but mostly that had kept him out of trouble. Mostly. He wasn't sure if this was one of those times.

He thought about those few moments when he had helped Jane put her hat up. He had stood right behind her, laid his palm on her shoulder. His thumb could have made a pass against her neck. He could have turned her, kept her there against the wardrobe, his arms on either side of her. Maybe she would not have felt trapped. Maybe she would have felt embraced. It was hard to know when he had thought all of it and done none of it.

Morgan threw off the covers and sat up in bed. He rubbed his eyes with the heels of his hands and then swung his legs over the side. He needed to get out of this room, this house. He needed open sky and space that stretched beyond his fingertips. He reached for his pants and began to dress. He was going for a walk, maybe a ride, but he was going.

Mrs. Sterling might just as well have been talking about him tonight. He was a single stretched nerve, exhausted to the point of restlessness, and about as scared of his wife as any husband had the right to be.

God. What a mess.

Jane was up before it was light. Her sense from things Morgan had told her was that if she waited for the rooster to announce morning, she had already slept too long. She washed, plaited her hair, put on a robe over her shift, and went to find the privy. It was so dark she walked into the smokehouse first. When she found the outhouse, she knew it.

Returning to the house, she lit a lamp and set it on the kitchen table. Her first order of business was to become familiar with this area, in particular the cast-iron cookstove. In her experience, a cookstove either possessed a personality or was simply possessed. She had worked with both types and found the former infinitely preferable to the latter.

Hands on her hips, Jane faced the cookstove and stared it down. "You will not get the best of me," she whispered. "You will not belch smoke, throw ash, heat unevenly, or burn my biscuits. Know that and we will get along just fine."

Jane picked up a blue-and-white checked towel lying beside the sink and wrapped it around her waist before she opened the firebox. It was empty. No kindling had been set for the next fire. Before she did anything else, Jane put covers on the stovetop, closed the front and back dampers, and opened the oven damper. She turned the movable iron grate in the firebox so the ashes fell into the receiver below it. After giving it a shake for good measure, she flipped it over, and then removed the covers from the top. Everything she needed to start the fire was there in a large tin box beside the china cupboard. She imagined that in the future it would be her responsibility to make certain that the box was filled.

Jane covered the grate with pieces of paper that she tore and twisted in the center and left fanned at the ends. She then covered these with small sticks, mostly pine, and made certain the wood reached the ends of the firebox. She took care with this, arranging it so air would be admitted. Over the kindling, she placed pieces of harder wood and added two small shovelfuls of coal from the scuttle. She replaced the covers, opened the closed dampers, and chose a match from the box on the table. She blinked as the phosphorus and sulfur flared. Her nose twitched at the unpleasant odor, but she bent and set the lighted match under the grate. She wondered if men at the dawn of time had had any more sense of accomplishment than she did creating this fire.

Now her job was to master it. Jane scoured the kitchen to find the stove black. She located the tin of polish in a drawer with string, tweezers, penny nails, scissors, an eggbeater, brushes, two wooden spoons, an empty flask, cotton balls, and a paring knife. Another challenge, she told herself, but first the cookstove.

Beginning at the front of the stove, she applied the polish evenly, rubbing it in a circular pattern and working her way to the back while the surface gradually heated. She could not guess when the stove had last received the equal of her attention, perhaps never, but when she was done, she was hopeful that it looked as good as it had upon delivery. She recognized the model. It was not very old, certainly not a relic from the days when Uriah Burdick built the house, but that did not mean that Morgan had purchased it either. Her only hint that he might have came from the fact that it was similar to the cooking stove at the Pennyroyal. It was conceivable that Mrs. Sterling had advised him.

Jane returned the polish to the drawer, tossed the cleaning rag on the tin box, and checked to see if the wood was thoroughly kindled. When she saw that it was, she added more coal and waited for the blue flame around the coals to change to a white one. It was then that she closed the oven damper. In a few moments, she was able to mostly close the front damper, leaving enough space for oxygen to flow and nourish the fire. Finally, when she was certain there was a good draft and the coals were sufficiently caught, she half closed the chimney damper.

She could finally appreciate the warmth coming from the stove. What she had felt before was the effect of her own exertions.

Jane explored the pantry. It was well stocked. She had supposed yesterday that it must be the case because Morgan had had two opportunities to purchase staples in Bitter Springs and had brought nothing back. He impressed her as someone who would not have returned with a bride alone if he was also in want of molasses.

For some reason, that made Jane smile.

She measured flour, salt, baking powder, and sugar and then mixed and sifted them over a green glass bowl. From the cold store she took an egg and some fresh, cool milk. She beat the egg in a separate bowl and added the milk. There was no point in mixing them together until someone joined her.

She'd have to add more baking powder, spoiling the proportions, and the hotcakes would not taste the way they should. Someone drowning them in butter and syrup might not be able to tell the difference, but she would.

Jane decided to make coffee. She suspected that would rouse Morgan, and perhaps he would invite his hands to come and sit at his table. She made enough for them. It did not seem right to her to do otherwise.

Jane found finely ground coffee in an airtight glass jar in the pantry. She measured out a cup for the strainer, returned the strainer to the pot, and put it on the table. She pumped enough water at the sink to fill the kettle and set it on the stove to boil. That left her with time to dress. A shift and robe was not suitable for greeting anyone, even if her husband was the only one who came to the table.

Jane thought she heard the back door open and close while she was dressing, but she did not give it any thought except to suppose that Morgan was finally up and making his morning visit to the necessary. When she returned to the kitchen and saw him standing at the stove pouring boiling water from the kettle into the coffeepot, she realized that she had been wrong. The door had certainly opened and closed, but he had been coming in, not going out.

"I will do that," she said, skirting the table. "I just went to the bedroom to dress."

Morgan did not relinquish the kettle, but he did look at her sideways. "I see that. Are all of your dresses like that one?"

Jane glanced down at herself. "I don't know what you mean."

"Fancy is what I mean. Sunday fancy. Going-to-a-social fancy."

"This?" The dress was apple green calico with white polka dots on the skirt and the hint of a white ruffle around the scooped neckline. The sleeves were plain and fitted, with none of the puffery that was becoming the fashion in the East. Jane wore a corset but deliberately had set aside her bustle. It seemed to her that the appendage had no place here. The hem of her skirt hovered just above her ankles, a good length for walking and working. She thought she had chosen practically. He thought she had chosen fancy.

She understood then that she had nothing that he would pronounce suitable.

"What's wrong with what I have on?" she asked.

"It's pretty. That's an observation, not a

compliment."

"I was not in danger of mistaking one for the other." She left Morgan at the stove and applied herself to making the hotcake batter.

Morgan looked over at Jane and watched her tie a towel around her waist. "I have no objection to pretty," he told her. "But it goes against my grain to see it come to a bad end. Someday you'll look at it and not recollect that it was ever once the color of summer apples or that it had that little ruffle at the neck."

"It's for wearing," she said, stirring the batter. "It goes against my grain to tuck it in a wardrobe and only visit it from time to time."

"Is that right?"

She looked at him sharply to gauge whether he was mocking her. Unfortunately, he had turned away so that only his profile was visible. "I shall miss the sewing machine I had in New York, but I do well enough with a needle and thread. There is no reason I cannot make one or two aprons, or even a dress. It will merely take longer."

"Is that a compromise or an accommodation?"

"The latter, I think."

Morgan nodded. "Coffee's ready," he said,

179

removing the pot from the stove. He held it over the table where he had placed two cups. "Can I assume you want some?"

"Yes, please."

He poured coffee into both cups and set the pot on the table. Jane traded places with him at the stove.

"Did you invite your men to breakfast?"

"No."

"There will be plenty."

"I wasn't sure you would be able to fire up the dragon."

"The dragon? Oh, you mean the cookstove. I was able."

"I see."

Jane paused before she began to pour batter onto the greased griddle. "So? Are you going to invite them? I know from experience that the batter's best when it's freshly made."

"That might be true, but they won't know and won't care. It seems to me that you and I should have our breakfast first. Together. Alone."

Jane's nerves jangled unexpectedly. It was his tone that did it. When he spoke in certain ways, low and husky with that slight rasp that put her in mind of callused fingers sifting silk, it was as if those same fingers were walking up her spine.

"All right," she said, keeping her back to him. "These won't take long." And they didn't. She made a stack of six, put four on a plate for him and gave two to herself. He had syrup, butter, and utensils on the table when she handed him his plate, but he waited for her to sit down before he tucked into his meal. Jane owned there was a certain amount of pleasure watching him eat because his pleasure was that obvious. She liked that he had unguarded moments. Genuine moments. She drew her coffee cup closer and took it in both hands. She lifted it, sipped, and smiled over the rim of the cup. "This would not be a satisfying beverage if it were not for the aroma."

"Can't you say the same about all foods?"

"Probably, but I think it is most true of coffee." She set the cup down and picked up her fork. "I heard you coming in this morning, but I never heard you leave. I thought you were sleeping when I got up."

"You were sleeping when I left."

"I was?"

"I left last night. If you didn't hear me go, I think we can assume you were asleep."

"Yes. Yes, of course, but why did you leave? Where did you go?"

"I left because I couldn't sleep. And where I went was out."

The area between Jane's dark eyebrows puckered as she frowned, but she did not ask another question. She cut out a bite of the hotcakes, stabbed it, and put it in her mouth.

"How did you sleep?" he asked.

"Well enough."

Morgan took another bite. His gaze slid to the cookstove. "How did you conquer the dragon?"

Jane shrugged.

"Jake says she breathes fire."

"She probably does when her dampers aren't regulated."

"All right," he said. "I am going to ask. How do you know how to do it?"

"What do you mean? Why wouldn't I know how to do it?"

"You lived on Fifth Avenue. Even strangers to Manhattan know that address. Home to brownstone mansions and gilded parlors. Some things you wrote led me to believe that you come from money."

"I lived with it," she said. "I did not come from it."

"So you lived with it. The Ewings had help. You told me that. There were things I expected I would have to teach you, so now I'm wondering how you learned to slay the dragon in a home where servants would have done it for you."

Jane cocked her head to one side and regarded Morgan with a faintly mocking smile. "You have misapprehended an important point," she said. "And it would be a disappointment for both of us, I think, if you married me for love of money. I have no claim to the Ewing fortune. None. In every way that was important, Morgan, I was a servant to Cousin Frances. There were appearances to be kept, and this was done. I accompanied the family to any event that Cousin Frances deemed appropriate and always had a place at the table. I had a foot in both worlds, but I was only truly welcome in one. So, yes, I can slay the dragon. Yours is smaller, newer, and less bad-tempered than the one I am used to. Mrs. Shreve, the cook, was easy with a compliment, and she told me that I had the right touch, the right temperament, and knew all the right words when the situation called for them."

"The right words?"

"Curse words."

One of his eyebrows lifted. "Oh?"

She thought he seemed a little too interested and perhaps too impressed. "You probably know more. I do not take the name of the Lord in vain, even when provoked by the beast."

"The dragon."

"In Mrs. Shreve's kitchen, we called her the beast." Jane warmed her coffee by adding some from the pot. "I find that I am still curious about your offer of marriage. You seemed to have imagined that I came from privilege. I don't know why that would influence you to propose. If it were true, I would be hopelessly ill prepared for Morning Star."

"You still are."

"I won't argue that point. It supports mine. I don't understand why you did not continue corresponding with women whom you must have thought were better suited to this life."

"You mean someone who did not hail from Fifth Avenue, New York City."

"Yes. I understand it was not Rebecca's photograph that persuaded you because we had not yet exchanged pictures, but you told me that you wrote back to the other respondents with the express purpose of ending the exchange. It seems to me that you cut them off rather precipitously."

Morgan set his forearms on the table on either side of his plate. He leaned forward a fraction, never once taking his eyes from Jane. "That's why," he said.

She frowned. "I don't understand."

"You write like you talk, or maybe it's that you talk like you write. I figured you for an educated female, and I liked the idea of it right off. What I know I mostly learned on my own, and I have no objection to learning more. It's possible that someday you'll hear me say 'precipitously' like it belongs in my mouth same as it belongs in yours."

Jane opened her mouth to speak and all her fine words failed her. When that happened, she simply shook her head.

Morgan finished off another bite and drank more coffee. "Do you ride?"

Jane watched him set down his fork. He rubbed the ginger stubble on his jaw with his knuckles. She guessed that it had been almost forty-eight hours since he shaved. He was looking faintly disreputable, a little dangerous, and he was sitting at the table with a napkin on his lap and politely inquiring if she rode.

"A bicycle," she said. "But I don't think that's what you meant."

"No, but tell me about it. I've only ever seen bicycles in pictures. Are they hard to learn to ride?"

"Balance is really the only thing to master. Steering, pedaling, braking. All of that is not so difficult if one remains upright."

"Huh."

"It is a pleasant pursuit for women," said Jane. "The park was a favorite place to go."

"But you didn't learn to ride a horse?"

"No. Rebecca is the accomplished rider. Our educations diverged in a number of ways, and that was one of them. The difference in our ages accounts for some of it. Cousin Franny's expectations account for the rest." Jane put her fork down and scooted back from the table. "Will you teach me to ride?"

"Have to. It's not a choice here. Same as seeing that you're comfortable with a gun."

"When will we begin?"

"Not this morning. We'll see about this afternoon."

Nodding, Jane stood. She picked up her empty cup, plate, and utensils, and carried them to the sink. She would have returned for Morgan's dish, but when she stepped back, he was there just as he had been the night before. She did not dare turn around. Her chest would have been flush to his.

"How do you do that?" she asked.

"Do what?" Reaching around Jane, Morgan dropped his things in the sink on top of hers.

"Move around without making a sound."

"Why does it have to be something I do?

186

Maybe you have old women's ears."

"There is nothing at all wrong with my hearing." He was so close that Jane could feel his shrug. "I hear perfectly well."

"If you say so." •

Jane was aware when Morgan straightened, but what he did next she did not anticipate. He nudged aside the dark braid at her back with a fingertip and laid his mouth against the curve of her neck. In contrast to the warmth of her skin, his lips felt cool. The kiss, if it could be correctly called that, lasted only a moment, just long enough for her to know that something was different, that something had changed.

"Thank you," he said, stepping away. "I'll let the others know you have breakfast for them before I wash up and head out."

Jane stayed where she was, hands curled around the rim of the sink as much for balance as support. Out of the corner of her eye, she saw Morgan open the door and step onto the porch. She saw him again, this time through the window as he took down the brass bell hanging on one of the posts and gave it a good swing. And that, she supposed, was letting the others know that breakfast was ready. By the time Morgan reentered the house, Jane was greasing the griddle for the next round of hotcakes. She waved him on without looking up, but in her mind's eye she imagined his wily smile was firmly in place.

Jane had no difficulty filling her time between breakfast and the preparations for dinner in the afternoon. She had it from Jem Davis first and then from Max Salter that they would be riding out with Morgan and checking on the cattle in the Blue Valley, but there was no reason they shouldn't be back in time for dinner. This last was said with considerable hopefulness, and Jem also managed to mention fritters.

Jane suspected that on any other morning they might all have ridden out, but on this particular morning Jessop and Jake were being left behind to do chores that would keep them close to the house. Over breakfast, Jane had listened to them fuss as brothers were apt to do about how they would split the work, and while she had the sense that their tasks were genuine, she occasionally intercepted darting looks in her direction that made her think she was also one of their responsibilities.

She doubted Morgan thought she intended to run off when his back was turned, especially since she couldn't ride and did not know the first thing about harnessing an animal to the buckboard, so she supposed he was thinking of her safety or perhaps that she might not want to be alone. He never said as much to her, and she did not ask, preferring to believe he meant well and leave it at that.

While Jessop and Jake attended to their outside chores, Jane took a second tour of the house and began a list of things in need of doing, some of them sooner than others. The hardwood floors and furniture deserved more care than they had been given. She noted to check for linseed oil and turpentine so she could make her own furniture polish. The floors would benefit from a paste of beeswax and turpentine. She lifted the lid on the piano and ran her fingertips over the keys. In addition to needing tuning, the keys were in want of a good cleaning with alcohol. She regarded the smoked ceilings with some consternation until she remembered that a small piece of washing soda dissolved in water would remove the stains. The curtains at the windows required washing, and they did not slide easily on the rods. Hard soap applied to the rods would take care of that. It was also the remedy she would use on her creaking bedroom door and two of the drawers in the dish cupboard. The carpets needed a thorough sweeping, but the brooms she found were not in a condition that she deemed good enough for the task. The linens were clean, neatly folded, and stored properly, and the hucka-back towels were perfectly serviceable if in need of bleaching.

Jane hesitated when she came to the wardrobe where Morgan still had most of his clothes. Would he see her examination as an intrusion or understand it as merely one of her duties? Last night, when she was adding her clothes to this wardrobe, she had given his belongings only a cursory glance, primarily to judge what she could move out of the way.

Putting aside her misgivings, Jane opened the doors wide. She removed Morgan's shirts one at a time and looked them over for stains, tears, and general wear. She found two that needed mending, one at the elbow, and the other on the tail. A third shirt had a loose button. There was a blue cham-bray shirt that was so thin at the elbows that it would require patching if it were one of Morgan's favorites. If he could bear to part with it, she was going to shred it for clean-ing cloths. Grass stains in his trousers could be removed with alcohol; grease would require Ivory soap and cold water. She made another note to herself to look for the soap.

As Jane went through the house, she looked for the ladder that would allow her to reach the loft. She never found it, but she did find Jessop Davis hammering on the henhouse roof and asked him about it. He was happy to stop what he was doing and fetch it from the barn for her. When he reappeared, so did his brother. They carried the ladder into the house together and set it up so she could access the loft. Neither of them was comfortable letting her make the climb alone, so Jake went up first to lend her a hand when she reached the top. Jessop remained vigilant below, anticipating a fall.

The loft was more spacious than she anticipated when she had regarded it from below. It covered the same area as both of the bedrooms beneath it. There were two iron rail beds, a pair of matching dressers, and the clothes cupboard that Morgan had mentioned to her. She looked it over inside and out and agreed with his assessment that it would fit beside the window in their bedroom. How to lower it over the side of the loft was the problem.

Jake and Jessop shared none of her trepidation. Jake removed the two drawers at the bottom of the cupboard and carried them down while Jessop went back to the barn for block and tackle. One brother made a show of lassoing the cupboard while the other tied it off. Jane estimated it took them all of ten minutes to complete the task. They transported the cupboard to her bedroom, put it precisely where she wanted, and managed to do this without scratching the wood. Jane thought they had accomplished a marvel of engineering and told them so. She also promised them fritters. Her praise elicited identically lopsided, if slightly embarrassed, grins, and they kept their heads down as they shuffled out to get back to their chores. Jane believed they could not have cleared the porch before she heard one of them whoop and the other one laugh.

Smiling, shaking her head, Jane applied herself to moving Morgan's clothes to the cupboard.

Morgan dismounted when he reached the summit of Mechling Hill. Jem and Max followed suit. They all stood beside their horses for a time, looking out over Blue Valley. One by one, they took up their canteens and drank.

"Looks like the grazing will be good this winter," said Jem. "You were right about grubbing the land. Grass is more plentiful here than before. Came back thicker." He sloshed water side-to-side in his mouth, and then he spit before he took another drink. "Never could tolerate the taste of the first swig from a canteen."

"That's because you've never been thirsty," said Morgan.

Jem looked over at him. "Sure felt like that's what I was."

Morgan did not reply. He fixed his gaze on the fast-running stream that cut through the valley. On a clear summer day when the sun was starting to lower, the water reflected all of the sky. It put him in mind of a curling blue ribbon, the kind that a pretty woman might use to tie back her dark, bittersweet chocolate hair. This morning the stream had a silver cast. The white water sparkled as it rushed over stones.

The white-faced Herefords ignored the stream; most of them favored the pool of water in the basin. Here the water was more or less like the cattle it served — tranquil, wide, and shallow. Come winter, it would freeze. When that happened it would be up to him and his men to chop holes in the ice. If it froze solid, then they would drive the herd to water somewhere else.

Max Salter put his canteen away first.

"I'm going to ride over to the next ridge and look around. I figure there're about six, maybe seven strays. I'll bring 'em back."

Morgan nodded. "You've got a good eye, Max."

Max swung his wiry frame into the saddle and pulled his horse around. He clicked his tongue, and then he was moving on.

Jem watched him go. "Probably started to feel crowded what with the two of us standing beside him. He's not one for company."

"Ever think it was the company?"

"Me? It's not me."

Morgan shot him a pointed look.

"All right," Jem said. "I suppose it could be me."

"Damn straight. You haven't shut up since we left the barn. Maybe you should say what's on your mind instead of talking all around it. Or just talking."

Jem shrugged.

Morgan blew out a long breath. "No parlor games, Jem. I'm not one for animal, vegetable, mineral. Out with it."

"It's animal," said Jem. Before Morgan clubbed him with his canteen, he added quickly, "It's about Jane."

"You mean Mrs. Longstreet."

"She give us leave at breakfast to call her Jane." In response to Morgan's arched eyebrow, he said, "But Mrs. Longstreet suits just fine."

"Good. What about my wife?"

"Well, I guess I've been wondering what it's like being married."

"You guess? Have you been wondering or not?"

"Okay. I've been wondering. I reckon you know I've been fixin' to marry Renee. I've had the thought rattlin' around in my head for about ten years now, since I was fourteen and she was twelve, but early on mostly what I thought about was just kissin' her. Haven't changed my mind about that, and since she lets me have the chance now and again, I think we suit. For sure, we fit."

Morgan used his index finger to tip back the brim of his hat and regard Jem dead on. "Wind it down, Jem."

Jem shifted his weight. "It's like this. I've known Renee pretty much all my life, been in love with her near to half of it, but sometimes when I actually think about being *married* to her, I just sorta freeze up inside. Maybe she knows it. Maybe that's why she ain't marched down the aisle to meet me yet. How'd you know you'd be a good enough husband?"

"Jesus, Jem. What the hell kind of question is that?"

"You think I should ask Jane? I mean Mrs. Longstreet?"

"You think I should stake you out here for the wolves to find?"

"No."

"Right. There's your answer."

Jem shook his head. "C'mon, Morgan. You must have a notion or two about marriage since you went and did it. I don't pretend to know you like I know my own brothers — none of us do — but I'm not wrong about you bein' real thoughtful about the way you do things. Real particular, too. You put me a little in mind of the marshal that way."

"I'm not flattered," Morgan said dryly.

"All right. Maybe you don't like him much, so forget I said that. Just tell me about bein' married. What made you sure that it was so right that you could convince a lady like Miss Middlebourne to take you up on it?"

"A lady like Miss Middlebourne wouldn't have me any other way."

"Is that it?" asked Jem.

"Part of it."

Jem's mobile mouth worked side to side as he chewed on that. "What's the rest?" he asked finally.

Morgan shrugged. "Maybe the person you

should be asking is Cobb Bridger. He's been married a spell, and he's real free with advice."

Jem looked to his left, his right, off in the distance, and then back at Morgan. "D'you see him around? You're the only married man in spittin' distance."

"Well, then, ask him next time you can spit on him. Hell, Jem, I wasn't married when I saw you yesterday afternoon. I'm not exactly flush with experience."

Jem packed up his canteen. "You played your cards close there, letting me think she was hiring on. Seems like you could have said something about why she was really at Morning Star."

"Seems like some things are still my business."

"Sure, I get that. It's just strange, is all. You knowin' her about a minute compared to all the time I've known Renee. And here you are married, and I'm still wonderin' what it's like."

"Have you thought about where you'll live, Jem?"

"I'm savin' money. She won't live outside of town."

"What about your brothers? You three are about as tight as a square knot and you come as a set. God knows, it took me better than a day to know who was who, and a week to tell you apart at a distance. If Renee is sensing your doubts, could be it has something to do with your brothers. You probably want to make some decisions about family."

Jem nodded slowly. "Maybe you're right. Guess that wasn't a consideration for you."

"No," Morgan said quietly. "It wasn't a consideration."

Jane was the last one to sit down for dinner. When Morgan started to get up to hold a chair for her, she almost waved him back before she caught herself. Here, she thought, it felt right to observe convention. She had already changed the routine by deciding this meal would be served in the dining room. Crowding around the smaller kitchen table was fine for breakfast, especially if they continued to eat in shifts, but for the most substantial meal of the day, Jane wanted to enjoy it separate from where she had prepared it. She explained that to Morgan when he asked her about it, owning that it was a selfish indulgence on her part. Oddly enough, it was this last part that seemed to make him reconsider the objection she saw hovering on his lips. Instead, what he said was, "As long as it suits you."

How could it not? she wondered. This was an appreciative audience. They were sufficiently well mannered so as not to fall on the food, but the speed with which the platters and bowls made the first pass around the table was nothing short of remarkable. They layered their plates with slices of baked ham, boiled potatoes with butter and parsley, creamed peas, and apple fritters.

Jem had his fork poised to stab a fritter when he suddenly came to attention and jabbed the tines in his brother Jake's direction instead. "Did you do that?"

Jake frowned at him across the table. "Do what?"

"You know."

"I asked, didn't I? That means I don't know. And stop pointing your fork at me."

Jem looked sideways at his other brother Jessop. "You?"

Jessop held up his hands, palms out. "I didn't do anything."

"Then who kicked me?"

Across the table, on Jake's right, Max Salter said, "I did." If he was concerned that he took up half the shoulder space of any of the Davis brothers, it did not show. "Didn't expect you to fuss about it. Polite thing to do before you poke at your food is to say a prayer over it, or at least wait until the boss's wife finishes hers."

Jem sat back. "Oh." His gaze swiveled to Jane. "Sorry, ma'am." He put down his fork, folded his hands, and bent his head.

Until Max spoke up, Jane was unaware that she had called attention to herself. She looked to the other end of the table where Morgan sat. He still had his hand around his fork and was closer to spearing a fritter than Jem had been. She waited to see what he would do. There was all his talk about not being a godly man.

Morgan grunted softly, darted a narrow look at Max, and set his fork down slowly and deliberately. He did not follow Jem's example and bow his head. He stared straight ahead at Jane as she bowed hers.

Jane did not hurry through her thanksgiving, but in deference to her company's hunger, she kept it short. When she closed with "Amen," it was as if a pistol had been discharged on opening day at the races. From Jane's vantage point, it was difficult to tell who dug in first. It might have been Max who led the charge.

"Good fritters," said Jem. "Damn if they aren't the best I ever had. Ow!" This time he jabbed his fork in Max's direction first. "What'd you kick me for now?"

"Didn't."

Jake held up a finger. "Me. Mind your language."

Jem frowned as he reviewed what he'd said. "Oh. Sorry, Mrs. Longstreet. Just sorta slipped out."

Jane smiled. "I heard the compliment, not the curse, but for the sake of your shins it might behoove you to temper your enthusiasm."

"Consider me behooved." Grinning, he returned his attention to his plate.

When Jane glanced at Morgan to gauge his reaction, he was simply shaking his head, but what remained of his faint smile struck her as indulgent. It came to her then that he genuinely liked the men working the ranch with him, enjoyed their company, and probably only intervened when they failed to police themselves. She had seen evidence of the men's respect for Morgan, and here was evidence that it was returned.

Jessop smashed his potatoes with the back of his fork and pushed creamed peas onto the pile. "How'd you find things up at Blue? Herefords okay?"

Morgan said, "Mostly."

"Wolves," said Max. "A pack of seven or eight from what I could tell."

Jem said, "Max set off to round up some

strays and ended up following the pack's trail."

"I brought back five strays. Wolves cut out a calf."

"Seems early," Jake said. "Winter's not set in."

Max lifted the platter of ham and slid a second thick slice onto his plate. "The herd's easy pickings in the basin."

Jessop asked, "You find the den?"

Max shook his head. "Tomorrow. I'm going out again tomorrow."

Morgan said to Jessop, "You're going with him."

"Sure thing."

Jane set her fork down and smoothed the napkin in her lap. "Is it safe?" She blinked as the men and Morgan turned on her as one. She did not know how to interpret their regard, although she certainly felt foolish.

Morgan said, "Safe enough. They know what they're doing."

Jessop carefully balanced a forkful of ham, potatoes, and peas all the way to his mouth. Before he swallowed the bite, he said, "What it is, ma'am, is necessary."

"Will the wolves attack you?"

"Not likely. And Max here is a sharpshooter. We'll set up a blind and pick them off if we can. Might have to sacrifice a steer. It's something we've done before, so you shouldn't worry about us." He paused. "Though I have to say, there's something real nice about you bein' concerned."

Morgan's expression was wry as he looked at Jane. "Perhaps the answer is just to pretend to worry."

Jane sighed. "It appears to be the only sensible solution."

Jem scratched his head. "So from now on when you say you're worried, it'll be for show."

"See?" Morgan said. "The seed's been planted."

She nodded and looked at Jem. "If I'm very good, you'll never know."

"Huh." Jem went back to his meal, ignoring the smiles all around.

Morgan caught Jake's attention. "I noticed the henhouse coming in. Looks like you finished the roof."

"Sure did. Got most of the things done on the list. Jess and me also brought down that clothes cupboard from the loft like your wife wanted."

Morgan looked at Jane. "You asked them to do that?"

"Yes," she said. "Yes, I did. Was that wrong?"

"I told you I would do it."

"You said you would get one of them to help you do it. It's almost the same thing."

"Except it isn't."

Jane opened her mouth and closed it again when she observed Max and the Davis brothers fiercely concentrating on their plates. Her point could wait. She could only hope that Morgan appreciated her discretion.

Morgan said, "Seems as if you found everything you needed. I guess we didn't know half of what we had in the pantry."

Jane accepted the change of subject. "It's an impressive inventory but in need of organizing. I intend to do that tomorrow."

"If you make a list of what you think is missing, Jem will pick it up in town tomorrow afternoon."

Jem's head snapped up. "I'm going to town?"

"It's your turn, isn't it?"

"It was my turn two turns ago."

"Well, that makes it your turn now." He arched an eyebrow at Jem. "Do you really want to argue?"

In the event that Jem did not know how to answer the question, both of his brothers kicked him under the table. "No," he said, jerking his chair back until his shins were out of danger. "You'll get no argument from me."

Morgan eyed Jem's distance from the table and crooked a finger to encourage him to return. "You heard me say tomorrow, didn't you?"

Jem grunted, glanced under the table, and glared at his brothers. "I heard." He carefully scooted his chair back into position and took up his fork.

Jane pressed her lips together and kept her eyes on her plate until the urge to laugh passed. Mercifully, at least in her opinion, the remainder of the meal passed without further assault on Jem.

Jane learned that if she positioned herself a little to the right of the sink, she could see most of the corral from the kitchen window. That was where her attention was fixed while she dried the dishes. At Morgan's direction, Max had helped her clear the table after dinner and stayed to wash. Jessop and Jake were sent off to the barn to finish chores. It was Morgan and Jem who were working with one of the mares in the corral.

Jane only knew the horse was a mare because Max told her it was. Occasionally he would look up from his washing duties and explain what was going on. Jane learned that the recalcitrant mustang was a recent acquisition, not purchased, but captured. It was Jessop who first spied the wild herd that had moved onto Morning Star land, but it was Morgan who was successful in cutting the mare out. The rest of the wild horses were driven off so they would not compete with the livestock for grazing land, but according to Max, they had not strayed far, and he and Jessop still had a notion of getting a mustang for themselves.

Jane watched Morgan simply stand beside the horse for the longest time. He appeared to be talking to her. Sometimes he would stroke her neck. If she shied sideways, he would wait until she calmed and approach her again. He held a halter in his left hand. He showed it to the horse, let her smell it, rub her nose against it, and when he held it up in front of her in both hands, he let her toss her head and nudge at it so in effect she helped him get it over her head. Morgan quickly attached a lead line. There was some push and pull after that, but Morgan gave up some of the length to let her have distance and then gradually guided her back.

"He's gotten this far before," said Max when Morgan started leading the mustang around the corral. "It's the bridle that makes her bolt. She wants no part of the bit. That's why Jem's holding it out. See how the boss is nosin' her closer to where Jem's sittin' on the rail every time he makes a pass? He's trying to accustom her to the sight of it, although how she knows it's different than what she's wearin', I ain't figured out yet."

Jane had been wondering the same thing. "What's her name?"

"Doesn't have one. Boss said he wanted to think about it. He's like that. A thinker, I mean, but I expect you know that about him."

Jane merely smiled. She picked up a wet plate, wiped it down with a towel, and set it behind her on the table. She did this without ever looking away from the window. She felt a twinge of sympathy for the mustang. Harnessing that beautiful animal struck her as vaguely cruel, although she certainly understood the necessity of it. The mare's coloring and glossy coat made her think of cinnamon sugar glaze.

"She looks to be a very fine animal," said Jane. "Is she?"

"Well, she's no dink, I can tell you that. The boss wouldn't cut a dink out of the herd."

"Dink?"

Max shrugged his thin, ropy shoulders. "Nothing special, I suppose you'd say. Ordinary. Mustangs are just mixed-breed horses. You can't be sure what you've got. There's some spirit in that one, maybe a little thoroughbred in her lines. She's strong and quick. Pretty, too. Definitely not a dink."

"Oh," Jane said softly. She felt unaccountably sad. It was that sudden rush of feeling that made her finally look away from the window.

That was how she missed Morgan being thrown against the fence and Jem falling backward over the rail. That beautiful and spirited animal had decided she was done being led around by the nose.

CHAPTER SIX

"I can walk, damn it," Morgan said. His snarling declaration had the effect of forcing him to prove it. Max and Jessop simultaneously ducked out from under the arms they were supporting and stood by to see what would happen. Morgan's next step would have put him on his knees if they hadn't caught him.

"Sure you can, boss," said Max.

Kneeling beside Jem on the outside of the corral, Jane found it painful to look at Morgan's white-lipped grimace. She put a hand on Jem's shoulder and helped Jake get him into a sitting position. Jem had had the wind knocked out of him when he fell flat on his back, but he had demonstrated to Jane's satisfaction that nothing was broken, except perhaps his pride. When he shook himself off and got to his feet on his own steam, Jane accepted the hand he held out to help her rise.

"Not lookin' too good there," Jem said, following Morgan's halting progress to the gate. This earned him a sour look that had absolutely no effect. "What do you suppose made her so skittish?"

"Maybe you juggling that bridle like a bear with a ball."

"I wasn't juggling. Just changin' hands. I had a splinter in my —" Jem stopped, glanced at Jane, and in deference to her presence said, "Backside." He pointed to the offending part. "Still do."

Jake took a step back from his brother. "You're on your own there. I'm not taking it out."

Jessop and Max voiced similar sentiments as they helped Morgan move to the outside of the corral. Jake went to close the gate behind them.

Jane brushed dirt off her gown. "Is someone going to go for the doctor?" This brought every head turning in her direction at once. She was on the receiving end of looks that were mostly amused. The expression that didn't live in the same state as amused belonged to her husband. He looked aggrieved.

Jem said, "Splinter's just a bitty thing. Don't need a doctor for that."

Jake and Jessop snorted with laughter.

Max and Morgan just shook their heads. The empathy Jane felt for Jem did not keep her from smiling.

"She's talking about fetchin' Doc Kent for the boss," said Max. "You sure you didn't rattle something loose in your head?"

"Oh." The tips of Jem's ears reddened as he addressed Jane. "Heck sakes, ma'am. The boss probably only has a couple of cracked or busted ribs and a twisted ankle. No cause to send for the cavalry."

This elicited some snickering from his brothers and Max, but Morgan said, "Jem's right. I don't need a doctor."

"The same way you don't need help," said Jane. "Yes, I see that. I'll get the door." She turned toward the house but not so quickly that she missed Morgan's arched eyebrow and the rather astonished looks of all of his men.

At Jane's direction, Jessop and Max supported Morgan all the way to the bedroom. They left him wobbling on one foot beside the bed and hurried out when Jane indicated they had done enough. She shut the door behind them.

"There's no audience," she said. "Sit. Down."

Morgan sat.

Relieved, Jane's cheeks puffed a little as

she exhaled. "Good." She approached the bed and held out her hand for his hat. When he gave it to her, she turned it over in her hands, examining it. "How is it that this did not get knocked off your head? Jem did not lose his either."

"Cowboy secret."

It was his flat, expressionless delivery that assured Jane his humor was still as twisted as his ankle. She dropped it on a post at the foot of the bed. "Are you going to wrestle that boot off yourself or allow me to do it?"

"If it comes off, my ankle's going to swell."

"That is why if nothing is broken, I am going to get a pan of cold water, have you soak your foot in it, and then bind that foot tight for you. But the boot has to come off sometime. It might as well be now." She thought Morgan was going to offer another objection, but then he took a deep breath and was obviously and painfully reminded that his foot was not his only injury. Grimacing, he set one forearm tight against his rib cage. "I will get the pan, water, and bandages," she said. "We will see how far you get with that boot while I am gone."

"She-devil," he muttered.

On the point of leaving, Jane turned and gave him her most indulgent smile. "If we are already come to a point in our marriage where endearments are an appropriate form of address, you should know that I prefer 'devil's handmaiden.' " She felt very good about leaving him speechless.

Only Jake was still present in the kitchen when Jane got there. He had drawn the short straw that meant he had to stay behind to help while the others returned to work. He assured Jane that she was not what made this duty a short straw; it was the boss. Jane appreciated the distinction.

He fetched a galvanized steel tub from the barn, cleaned it out, and filled it with water to which Jane added a portion of Epsom salts. It was too heavy for Jane to carry to the bedroom so Jake was engaged for that onerous task as well. He set the tub at Morgan's feet and left without a word.

"What did you do to him?" Morgan asked when Jake was gone.

"Do to him?" Jane dropped the bandages on the bed. "Nothing. Shall I hold up a mirror so you can see the scowl you are casting?"

If anything, Morgan's scowl deepened. "I got the boot off."

"I see. And the sock, too." She knelt beside the tub and held out her cupped hands. "May I?"

His heavy sigh was both sufferance and

surrender. He slid sideways to avoid hitting the tub and gingerly lifted his injured foot. He placed the heel in her hands.

Jane carefully pressed her thumbs against his flesh, feeling her way over and around the bones of his ankle and foot, hoping she would know that something was out of place by touch alone. She made an effort to portray more confidence than she actually felt.

When she looked up, she saw Morgan's teeth were clenched. A muscle jumped in his jaw. The scar at the corner of his mouth was a very white crescent. "I'm sorry." She guided his foot to the salt bath and gently lowered it. She heard him suck in his breath as cold water washed over his skin. "It seems as if nothing is broken."

"I know it's not. You had to be convinced. I didn't."

"You are right," she said. "I did." She nudged the tub closer to the bed so he could rest his foot at a more comfortable angle. "What about your ribs?"

"What about them?"

"Alex broke some ribs falling down the stairs, and —"

"Clumsy?"

"Drunk," said Jane. "Dr. Stiles swaddled his chest in bandages."

"No swaddling."

"But —"

"No swaddling. You can wrap up the ankle. Nothing else."

"All right."

"I've had cracked ribs before. I'll be fine."

"Yes."

He was quiet a moment, studying her upturned face. "I don't trust you when you're too agreeable."

"That places me in a rather awkward position, then. I am not disagreeable by nature, although there are some who would say differently."

"Cousin Franny."

"She would be one, yes."

It was insult, not injury, which made Morgan grimace. "I don't think I like being painted with the same brush."

Jane gave him a helpless shrug and nothing else as she stood. She went into the adjoining room and washed her hands. When she returned, she was carrying a basin of water, a washcloth, and soap. A towel was slung over her shoulder. She set the basin on the bedside table and handed Morgan the cloth and soap.

"You might as well clean up," she said. "Do you want your nightshirt?" Jane gave him no quarter, even when he stared at her as though she had suddenly sprouted the three heads of Cerberus.

Morgan jerked his thumb in the direction of the window behind him. "There are still a couple of hours of daylight left."

"I am aware."

"I am *not* an invalid."

"No, that would be overstating it, but you *are* injured, and that is sufficient cause for you to remain in bed. You employ four capable men." She held up a hand when she saw he was about to interrupt. "Very well. Three capable men and Jem." It probably wasn't what Morgan intended to say, she thought, but it did raise his reluctant smile. "They are all going about your business and theirs now, and none of them will think less of you for staying here."

"They might not think less of me, but I sure as hell will never hear the end of it."

"That cannot be true. To a man, they would be happy of my attentions."

"They would wallow in your coddling like pigs in mud, but that's because you're not married to any one of them."

"My, but marriage changes so many things. I had no idea."

Morgan's green eyes glinted as he eyed Jane more sharply.

Her artless expression did not waver.

They were at an impasse.

Jane said, "I'll come back in half an hour and examine your foot again. If the swelling has lessened, I'll bandage the ankle." Her eyes moved past Morgan to the books on the stand at the opposite side of the bed. Without asking if he wanted a particular one, she retrieved both. "I'll leave these here in your reach. The time will pass more quickly if boredom does not set in, and reading will distract you from the pain."

Morgan grunted softly. "I doubt it. Slamming a shovel against the back of my head might do the trick."

"Is that what happened to Jem?"

In spite of the pain, Morgan's lips twitched. "No, that's what being in love with Renee Harrison's done to him."

"That's good to know."

"About Miss Harrison?"

"About love."

Jake was sitting at the kitchen table when Jane reappeared. He started to rise, but she waved him back. "How is he?"

"Annoyed, frustrated, and on his way to mad."

"Then he's doing pretty well."

"That is what I was thinking, but you are more familiar with his moods." She put a kettle of water on the stove. "He says that if he stays in bed you won't let him forget it."

"He's probably right, but that's because we have so few opportunities to take a poke at him."

"Oh. I had not thought of that."

"Is there somethin' else I can do for you?"

Jane shook her head. "Supper will be ham sandwiches and apple bake. Will that be enough? I think I underfed you at breakfast. You all work so hard."

"You fed us fine. And supper's hours away. Don't forget, ma'am, we've been doin' all right on our own for a time now. If you don't want us muckin' up your kitchen, that's one thing, but if you need us to do for ourselves and don't ask, that's another."

"Thank you, Jake."

He stood, tipped his hat. "If there's nothing else . . ."

His pause was longer than her hesitation. Jane said, "I have noticed that all of you are calling me ma'am. I thought we settled that at breakfast."

"True, *we* did. The boss doesn't like it. That's what Jem told us when he got back from Blue Valley. Guess it must have come up."

"Well, that explains it. Thank you again."

"Sure thing."

When he was gone, Jane put away the dishes from dinner. She realized belatedly that Jake had finished washing everything that Max had left in the sink. Even the cookstove and griddle had been wiped down. That made her smile. He had done that for her. •

She made half a pot of coffee after the water boiled, and then gave herself permission to sit at the table and drink it. Perhaps she had been wrong to invite Morgan's men to call her Jane. It was not what she would have done back in New York, but the mood at the breakfast table had been friendly, informal, and then there was that niggling sense that she was a fraud every time one of them addressed her as Mrs. Longstreet. It was not merely that her husband had not slept in her bed, or at least she hoped that was not the sum total of her discomfort. Becoming Mrs. Longstreet must mean more than sharing a bed.

Jane wanted to believe that it meant sharing a life.

Taking on her husband's surname was like wearing a new corset on the outside of her dress. It so obviously did not belong that it was easy to imagine that everyone was staring.

Not liking the direction of her thoughts,

Jane held her cup in both hands and watched the ripples in her coffee as she tightened her fingertips. She was a dedicated worrier. She knew that about herself, and it gave her no satisfaction to own something she had been unable to change. She supposed it was only a matter of time before Morgan realized it as well. Uncovering those things about her character that she wished might remain hidden was the unfortunate consequence of sharing a life.

Jane finished her coffee, set the cup in the sink, and then headed back to the bedroom. She suspected he heard her coming because when she opened the door, his posture was a shade too upright and the books on the table were stacked differently than she had left them. She pretended to notice neither of these things. If he wanted her to believe he had not taken her advice, she could allow him that much latitude.

"You're late," he said. "You said thirty minutes."

"If you mean to quote me, I said 'half an hour.' If you mean to hold me to my word, then your point is well taken. I am indeed late. Bearding the lion does give one pause."

"I don't believe it. You are fearless."

Jane was careful not to show her surprise. Fearless? "All right," she said. "I was drinking a cup of coffee. Time got away from me."

He made a sound between a grunt and snort that sounded like *"umeh."*

"I have no idea what that rumbling at the back of your throat means. I understand Morse code better and my knowledge of that is merely rudimentary."

"That so?"

"Is what so?"

"No, I was trying to explain what I meant." He repeated the sound. "It means: Is that so?"

"Umeh," Jane said.

Morgan blinked. She had perfectly captured his nuance if not his pitch. "I'm not sure it means the same thing when you say it."

"Umeh," she said again. She let him mull that over while she knelt beside the tub and examined his foot. "I think this is the best we can hope for now." She slipped one hand under his heel and lifted it. "Give me the towel, please."

"I can dry it myself."

Jane set her mouth stubbornly and extended her free hand. Morgan passed her the towel.

"Thank you," she said. She patted his foot dry and then encouraged him to ease himself onto the bed until he could stretch comfortably. She removed two blankets from the chest at the foot of the bed, folded them, and then slipped the pair under his foot to keep it elevated. "Where are the bandages?" she asked.

"I think they might be under me." He lifted a hip and reached under it, pulling out half of what she had carried in. He found the remainder under the other thigh and handed over the lot of it. "Do you even know what you're doing?"

"No, but it is fortunate for you that I am willing to be instructed. I imagine you *do* know." She held up the bandages and smiled. "Where do I begin?"

"So many answers occur," Morgan said dryly, looking pointedly at her mouth.

Jane did not take offense. In his place she would want to stuff the bandages in her mouth as well. Her smile actually deepened. "Your restraint is admirable."

Laughing hurt, so Morgan did the only thing he could in the circumstances. He co-operated.

Jane looked admiringly at her work when she finished tying off the bandage. "I do not think a doctor could have done better."

"I don't know that a doctor would have bothered."

"Well, that is too bad. It feels better now,

doesn't it?"

Morgan looked down at his foot, rotated it slowly one way and then the other. "Yes," he said. "It does."

"Good. I should have offered one of my headache powder packets earlier. Would you like one?"

"I don't have a headache."

"That doesn't —"

He pointed to the washroom, stopping her. "There's a bottle of laudanum in the cabinet."

"I'll put it in some tea."

"Bring the bottle here."

She rose from the bed, taking the leftover bandages with her. "I'll put it in some tea."

"Am I ever going to have the last word?" he called after her as she stepped out of the bedroom.

Jane did not respond, which was answer enough to his question. Smiling rather smugly to herself, she wondered if he found it as satisfying as she did.

Morgan groaned softly when he gauged Jane to be out of earshot. He did not know what hurt more, his ribs, his foot, or his pride. The pain seemed to be evenly distributed at the moment. He suppressed an urge to beat his head against the pillow under it. That was about as stupid a thing to do as allowing himself to be blindsided by the mare. The men knew it was a freakish thing, but Jane didn't, and while he had not been aware of any desire to impress his bride when he approached the mustang, he certainly had not wanted her to see him handle the horse so ineptly.

He knew what could be seen from the kitchen window, and he knew from the speed with which Max and Jane arrived at the corral that they had witnessed what happened. Max vaulted the fence to get to him while Jane remained motionless on the other side. She probably did not know that her face drained of color when she saw him, but for Morgan, the picture of her chalk white features was still fixed in his mind. It had occurred to him then that she might faint. He still did not know if it was concern for Jem's condition or gravity and weak knees that put her on the ground at Jem's side.

Morgan had to allow that whatever Jane's immediate thoughts were, she showed that she was adept at reining them in. By the time Max and Jessop had him on his feet, Jane was in full command of herself and, it seemed, everyone else. She had them all dancing to her tune, while it came as a surprise to Morgan that she played an instrument.

When she reappeared in the bedroom a few minutes later carrying a cup of tea, she was actually humming. Morgan thought that could not possibly bode well for him.

Jane put the teacup on the nightstand before she retrieved the laudanum. "How many drops?" she asked.

"Three."

She added them to the cup and stirred. "Do you need help getting up?"

"No." Morgan eased into a sitting position. He leaned against the headboard and stuffed the pillow behind the small of his back. His foot no longer rested comfortably on the folded blankets, but Jane began repositioning them before he could point to the problem. He accepted the cup when she handed it to him, folding his hands around it. He did not realize until then how cool his palms felt or that a chill was creeping under his skin.

"Are you cold?" asked Jane.

Morgan had no idea what she had observed to prompt her question. His teeth hadn't chattered. His skin was not prickled. He had not pulled the coverlet over him. "Are you a witch?"

Jane responded by placing the back of her

hand against his forehead and resting it there for several seconds. "Just as I thought," she said, drawing back. "You're clammy." Without giving any indication of her intentions, she left.

Morgan's eyes followed her until she disappeared. She looked as fine going out as she did coming in, so he did not waste a breath asking her what she was doing. The thing to do, he decided, was enjoy the view. All would be explained when she returned. In the meantime, he drank his tea and waited for the laudanum to take effect.

Jane came back with a kettle of hot water, which she added to the basin on the nightstand. After testing the temperature, she soaked the washcloth in it, wrung it out, and then sat beside Morgan on the edge of the bed.

He finished off his tea and gave her the cup. She put it aside but did not surrender the washcloth. Morgan shook his head. "You are not mopping my face with that."

"What should I use?"

"That's not what I —" He stopped when he glimpsed one corner of her mouth curl ever so slightly. "Give it to me," he said. "I'll do it myself."

"All right."

Morgan took the washcloth and wiped his

face and neck with it. He rolled up his sleeves while Jane soaked it again, and then he ran it along his arms from wrists to elbows. At her insistence, and because there was no point arguing, he unfastened three buttons on his shirt and union suit and used the warm cloth on his chest.

When he was done, he dropped the washcloth into her overturned hand. "Satisfied?"

"I am, yes. Would you like to lie back or remain sitting?"

Morgan ignored the question. "You can stop trying to impress me."

Jane's delicately feathered eyebrows pulled together. "Is that what you think? That I've been trying to impress you?"

"Haven't you? Hotcakes all around for breakfast. Sunday dinner on a Thursday. Moving the clothes cupboard on your own. Telling me you've got plans to organize the pantry and beat a year's worth of dirt out of the rugs. Firing up the dragon without instruction. Pretty much putting me to bed and attending to me like you're Clara Barton in a field hospital. Yeah, I'd say you've been trying to impress me with your competence and concern."

Jane looked away. She said nothing. Her face was a mask, unreadable.

Morgan sighed. "That probably sounded

as if I were ungrateful. I'm not. I appreciate all of it." He paused, rethinking this last. "Well, most of it. I guess I'm saying it still feels a little awkward what with you doing so much right out of the gate, like you think I might put you on the next train out of Bitter Springs. That's not going to happen, not unless you decide to go. That would be your choice."

Jane kept her face averted.

"Look at me." When she didn't, he said, "Say something, then."

"I am not fearless."

"What?"

She turned her head to look at him then. "You said I was fearless. I am not. Perhaps you are right. Perhaps I *am* trying to convince you I can be a good wife. Certainly I have been trying to convince myself."

Frowning, Morgan said slowly, "That's not exactly what I said."

She did not argue the point. "It's what I heard." Her faint smile faltered. She brushed away a tendril of hair that had fallen across her cheek. "I want to stay here, but not so much that I would take a role for which I have no talent or regard. I do not mind terribly that you see me as trying to impress with my competence, but it is disturbing that you think it is the same for my concern. I *am* concerned. You might have been killed."

Morgan started to object, but he allowed her to cut him off with a shake of her head.

"No, you will never convince me differently, and you should not try to. You know very well there are dangers you face every day. They are part of your life and that makes them part of mine. So, yes, I am concerned that you are properly rested and healed before you lead that animal around the corral again. Because I know you will."

"You know that, do you?"

"Yes."

Morgan plowed his fingers through his hair and regarded her thoughtfully. "That sounds like something a good wife would say. She might add a couple or three words about not making her a widow before she's lost her virginal blush, but everything else about that speech seemed right."

"I am not opposed to poking you in the ribs or twisting your foot, so you might want to temper your observations."

It was difficult for Morgan to take the threat too seriously when Jane's virginal blush was already coloring her cheeks. He was tempted to kiss her splendid and saucy mouth and was prevented from doing so by the stitch in his side every time he took a breath, but when Jane began to rise, he risked sharpening his pain by reaching for her arm and managing to capture her wrist.

"Yes?" she asked, looking from him to his clasp.

"You're going?"

She hesitated. "Not if you don't wish it."

"I thought you could sit here for a while longer."

"You're tired."

He did not deny it. "Maybe you could read to me for a spell."

Jane glanced at the books at his bedside. "From one of those?" When he nodded and released her wrist, she picked up the books and held them up. "*Treasure Island* or *Daisy Miller*?"

"Do you have a preference?"

"Whichever will put you to sleep more quickly."

"That's easy. *Daisy Miller*."

Jane set *Treasure Island* down, walked around the bed to the rocking chair, and sat where the late afternoon sunlight could spill over her shoulder. "I confess to being surprised you are in possession of *Daisy*."

"Mrs. Bridger lent it to me on one of my previous trips to town."

"The marshal's wife?"

"The schoolteacher," he said firmly. "She

believes everyone should read. She's going to build a library."

"Really? Here?"

"Well, in Bitter Springs."

"That's what I meant. It is quite a wonderful contribution to the town." Jane opened the book to where Morgan had inserted a ribbon marker. "You do not seem to have read very far."

"Second time through."

"Oh."

"I didn't much care for Daisy the first go-round. It occurred to me that I should give her another chance before I returned the book."

"I wish the author had liked her half as well as I did. He might have decided to end her story differently. He wrote her as a woman who did not behave in conventional ways and then punished her for it. It seemed so unfair."

"I thought she behaved naïvely. I would have liked her better if she acted out of some conviction, but it seemed to me that she was insensible of her society or the stir she created."

Jane blinked. "You really *did* read it."

"You thought I lied?"

"I — no, not — well, perhaps that —" Jane shut her mouth.

"Maybe you should start reading," Morgan said. "Let Henry James speak for you."

Jane lifted the book and did as he suggested.

Morgan slept through supper, which Jane believed was exactly as it should be. By his own admission, he had gotten very little sleep the previous night. Jane prepared sandwiches and baked apples for the men, which they carried outside and ate on the back porch. She considered joining them but decided against it. Morgan's view of the flirtatious Daisy Miller might have factored into her reluctance, but Jane was also aware that the men were not as comfortable around her alone as they were when Morgan was in their midst.

It was after seven when she finally stepped outside to take their plates and cups and bid them good night. After she washed dishes, sorted through the ash receiver for cinders and clinkers, and swept the kitchen floor, she checked on Morgan. He had changed positions since the last time she had looked in on him, but he was still sleeping. Since she had never managed to get him under the covers, she drew half the coverlet over him and added a quilt from the chest.

Jane checked his brow. She took some comfort from the fact that he was no longer clammy. She removed the basin, cloths, and soap to the washroom, tidied the bedroom, and pushed the steel tub that Morgan had used as a footbath under the bed. She would ask Jake to carry it out tomorrow.

When she returned to the washroom to ready herself for bed, Jane indulged in a moment of yearning for the copper hip bath to be filled with hot water and sprinkled with lavender salts. It was surprisingly easy to imagine and a good reminder that wishing did not make it so.

Jane removed her dress and examined it for stains. She had been careful, but she could see where she had knelt in the dirt beside Jem and where the tea she had made for Morgan had splashed her wrist. Remembering what Morgan had said about her fancy clothes, she thought it would have been better to burn her skin than ruin her gown.

She washed up at the basin, brushed her hair, neatly plaited it again, and put on her robe over her nightgown. She wore kid slippers but acknowledged that a pair of woolen socks would have been a better choice. She thought about the money she had secreted away under the lining of her trunk and wondered if she dared use some of it for practical necessities. Her funds were not nearly what she had hoped they would be. Alex had been mistaken about how much she could depend on. Jane shivered, not from cold, but from memory. Alex had been mistaken about many things.

Jane returned to the bedroom and put up her gown in the wardrobe. She closed the door quietly, darted a look toward the bed, and moved to leave the room in what she considered a stealthy fashion.

"Sneaking out?"

Jane stopped short of reaching the door. Perhaps stealthy and silent were not quite synonymous. "I did not want to wake you."

"Why not? We haven't finished *Daisy Miller.*"

"No, and we are not going to." Lamplight bathed Morgan's face, but his expression was shuttered and Jane could not tell if he was disappointed or relieved. "I put your supper on a tray in the dining room. Would you like it?"

"I'll get it on the way back."

"On the way back? What do you mean?" But she understood precisely what he intended when he struggled into a sitting position and slid his legs over the side of the bed. Jane threw up a hand. "Stop right there. I'll get the pot for you."

"The hell you will." Morgan mostly swallowed a groan as he got to his feet. In deference to his injury, his weight was not distributed evenly. "If you want to be helpful, you'll lend me your shoulder; otherwise, you'll get out of my way."

"You need your boots."

"I can only wear one."

One was better than none, Jane decided. She retrieved it, helped him pull it on, and then found a sock to put over the bandages on his injured foot. Jane put his arm around her shoulder when he hesitated. "You really do need my help," she said. "You said it yourself." He grumbled something under his breath that she did not ask him to clarify. Jane accepted his weight, although she realized he did not bear down on her heavily.

In this manner they hobbled through the house to the back door, across the porch, and then across the yard to the privy. The return trip was equally halting. He sent her back to the dining room to get his supper while he washed up. When she returned, he was back in bed.

She set the tray on his lap. "You are a stubborn man, Morgan Longstreet. I did not suspect how deeply that streak ran when I read your letters."

Morgan picked up one half of his sandwich and bit into it. "But you had a suspicion it was there."

"I supposed a man who lived the way you described must be stubborn." She paused and looked at him askance. "Or crazy."

"Or both," he said.

"Perhaps." Jane went to the rocking chair and sat. "Tell me about the mustang. Max says she's no dink."

"Max is right. I knew I wanted her the moment I spotted her in the herd. She wasn't easy to cut out; the stallion wanted to keep her. He interfered as much as he could, but he had a harem to protect. That's how he lost her. I wanted her more."

Jane met Morgan's eyes. She had the sensation of his fingers wrapped around her wrist, the pad of his thumb brushing the delicate blue webbing on the underside. She remembered his mouth on the curve of her neck, how light, how gentle his touch had been.

I wanted her more.

Jane tucked those words away where they could do no harm. It served no purpose to dwell on them. "She should have a name," Jane said. "I do not think you can know her properly if you do not give her a name."

"You might be right." Morgan tossed Jane

the extra blanket she had pulled out for him. "Take it before your teeth crack."

Jane did not argue. She drew up her legs, folded them so her knees almost reached her chin, and tucked the quilt around her.

When she was settled, Morgan asked, "What name would you give her?"

"Sophie."

"Sophie," he repeated, one of his eyebrows kicking up. "Why Sophie?"

"I am fairly certain that is her name."

"And you know this because . . . ?"

Jane shrugged. "It is of no account. In fact, it is a ridiculous notion."

"I'm not laughing."

He wasn't, Jane realized. There was some skepticism, but there was also curiosity. "Well, when I ran outside after you were injured, she was already turning away and going to the far side of the corral, but when I got there, she turned back. It seemed as if she was looking directly at me. Scared, you know. But sorrowful, too. And in my mind, I thought, 'Oh, Sophie, how could you?' It just came to me to call her Sophie, and that was when she shook her head. I don't mean that she tossed it as if she did not care. She shook it as if she *did* but couldn't explain it to her own satisfaction."

"Huh." Morgan said nothing while he

searched her face. Finally, "You know she really doesn't think like that, don't you?"

Jane nodded. "I know. It just seemed as if she did. I told you it was a ridiculous notion."

"What it is, is a nice story, but probably better if it just stays between us."

"I am sure you are right."

"So when Jem or his brothers or Max ask why we're calling her Sophie, we're going to say it was your great-grandmother's name."

"Sophie? She's really going to be Sophie?"

Her pleasure was arresting, and Morgan felt his breath seize when she smiled without inhibition. "Yes," he said after a moment. "As a remembrance of your great-grandmother."

"No, she was Frances," said Jane. "Like my mother's cousin."

"All right, then we'll say she was *my* great-grandmother."

"Yes, let us do that."

"Oh, good," Morgan said with a touch of sarcasm. "That's settled."

Jane nodded agreeably, her smile only slightly less fulsome than it had been seconds earlier. "What *was* your great-grandmother's name? On your mother's side first."

"I have no idea. Before you ask, it's the

same on my father's side."

"I suppose not knowing makes it easier to repeat the story, doesn't it? The devil is in the details. Or so I've been told."

"Umeh."

"Yes, that's so." Jane smoothed the quilt over her knees. "What about your grand-mothers' names?"

Morgan shrugged. "I didn't know them. Is it important?"

"No, not important. I was merely wonder-ing. Your letters contained nothing about family. I think I might have written too much about mine."

"Broad strokes," he said. "For instance, I know your parents died when you were young. Of cholera, I believe, but you never explained how you came to live with the Ewings."

"Did I write that my parents were mis-sionaries?"

"No. You did *not* write that. I would re-member."

"Yes, I imagine you would. I also imagine I would not be here if I'd told you, although that had nothing to do with my omission. I did not know you were a godless man then." Jane was not certain that he was now, but she kept that thought close. "I did not write about their missionary work because as a

239

child I did not fully understand it, and it was a bone of contention growing up in Cousin Franny's house. My mother was 'in a bad way' when she married my father. That is how my mother's 'delicate condition' was explained to me until Alex explained it better when we were twelve. There is also some disagreement in the family as to whether or not Robert Middlebourne is my father."

Jane tilted her head to one side, raised her hands in a helpless, but uncomplaining, gesture. "I think you can appreciate why I did not put this tawdry tale to paper. My father accepted a mission in India sometime before my second birthday. I traveled with my parents, but I have no memory of the voyage, and few memories of India except for the heat and the animals. What I recall is the return to New York, alone this time. My parents sent me away when they heard the sickness was coming. I do not know what they understood about cholera, but they meant to protect me. I lived with my mother's mother for a short time, not out of graciousness on her part, but out of duty. When word came that my parents were dead, she would not have me any longer. My father's parents did not claim me as one of their own so there was no room for me there. I am not certain how it happened, but I eventually came to the attention of Samuel Ewing, Esquire."

Morgan removed the supper plate from his lap and placed it on the nightstand. Only crumbs remained. "Samuel Ewing," he said. "That would be Cousin Frances's husband. He took you in?"

"He did more than that. He welcomed me."

"But not your cousin."

"No, but she tolerated me, and she did not send me away when her husband died. She showed considerable forbearance. I will always believe it was the best she could do."

Morgan's soft grunt was noncommittal. "Did you make a list?"

His question made no sense to Jane. She stared at him, puzzled. "Pardon?"

"A list. Jem's going to town tomorrow. I suggested you make a list of things you need. Did you?"

So he was changing the subject. And rather firmly, too. "No, I did not. Truthfully, I had forgotten. Thank you. I will do it first thing in the morning. Is there any particular thing you want?"

"Maple syrup."

"Really?"

He nodded. "If you're going to feed us

hotcakes, I prefer mine with maple syrup, not molasses."

"All right." Jane unfolded her legs, stretched, and started to rise.

"What are you doing?"

She thought the answer to that was so obvious that his question must have a deeper meaning. She pointed to the door. "I am going to bed."

"This is your bed."

Jane froze. "I don't think that —"

Morgan did not allow her to finish. "My bed is on the other side of that wall."

It required a little effort, but Jane managed to unlock her knees and straighten. "I am not helping you walk next door."

He shrugged.

"Good night, Morgan." She snapped the quilt and let it flutter across his legs. "Shall I turn back the lamp?"

"I'll do it."

Jane nodded. "Sleep well."

Morgan watched her go. He picked up *Daisy Miller* and opened it in his lap. He had been thinking about naming the mustang Daisy, but that was before he knew her name was Sophie. The memory of Jane's explanation surprised a chuckle out of him. Sophie. Morgan could only shake his head. He wondered if Jane knew that it meant "wisdom." From the beginning, the mare struck him as more wily than wise, but then Jane was disposed to see the better side of all God's creatures. If she could do it for Frances Ewing, she certainly could do it for a feral horse.

Whether or not she could do it for him remained to be seen.

CHAPTER SEVEN

The first thing Jane noticed about occupying the bed where Morgan previously slept was that the scent of him lingered. It was faint but clearly identifiable, and not at all unpleasant. She felt a little foolish that she had mistaken Morgan's meaning when he referred to the bed he was in as her bed. She thought he meant to invite her to join him. For an instant in time, hope had warred with alarm. Of course, neither was warranted. He had only been pointing out that they should return to the accommodations of the previous night.

Her disappointment, and surely that was what she had momentarily felt, disturbed her. She knew herself well enough to know that she did not love Morgan Longstreet, not today, probably not tomorrow, but the idea that it might be hers to grasp at some future time was both tantalizing and terrifying. What if it was in her reach and she hadn't the courage to embrace it?

Fearless. No, she wasn't that.

What she was, Jane reminded herself, was practical. So, apparently, was Morgan. It made no sense for her to share his bed when she might cause him further distress by crashing into his cracked ribs or kicking his sprained foot. He had arrived at the same conclusion and because he was gallant in his own fashion, he was willing to surrender some of his comfort to assure hers.

Except Jane was not entirely comfortable, not with the scent of him on her pillow and between the sheets. Closing her eyes only created disturbing images in her mind of the two of them lying together. Was it truly possible to become so entangled? She could not quite define where she ended and he began; he was that close.

She did feel his heat. She felt his fingertips grazing her throat and following the line of her collarbone. She felt his mouth in the sensitive hollow below her ear. He laid his palm on her shoulder, let it slide down her arm. His thumb made a pass across the delicate underside of her elbow. He cupped her breast. There it was again, the warmth of his hand, the comfort. He was easy with her, easy because it was his way to go slowly and tread lightly.

She thought she might have moaned, but it might have been the sough of the wind passing through the eaves or the sound of the mattress shifting under their weight.

Jane felt her cotton shift sliding against her skin. Her hem was at her calf, her knee; it rose as high as the curve of her hip. Fingers curled around her thigh. They were still at first, but inevitably they began to move. They were gentle in their seeking but always deliberate, insistent. No quarter was given. Jane asked for none.

Those fingers nested between her thighs. They fluttered there like small fledglings. Hungry and hungrier. Their tiny heads bumped as they scrabbled in their seeking. They found nectar and drank deeply. It brought her satisfaction to feed them.

It brought her pleasure. Sharp, intense pleasure. Pleasure that could not be contained by biting her lower lip or digging her heels into the mattress. It rippled through her, a tremor that seemed to begin in the fingers of one hand and ended in the fingertips of the other.

Jane woke with the shudder. At first she thought the movement came from outside herself, the bed, the floor, the walls, but it was only a fleeting notion, one she would have liked to retain but could not because she could not ignore the truth. *She* was the source of the tremor. She understood that even before she removed her hand from between her thighs.

Jane pushed herself into a sitting position and huddled against the headboard. She pulled the covers up to her hunched shoulders and lowered her chin. The last inklings of pleasure made her shiver. She was afraid to close her eyes, afraid of what might happen if she fell asleep and the unsettling feelings collided.

Jane required an ordered mind, and like the pantry, that required an inventory. She searched for shame and could not find it. Was she truly shameless, then, or was it that she had committed no transgression? Cousin Frances would say it was the former, but knowing that made Jane lean in the other direction.

There was no guilt. It would have been there beside shame the way pepper paired with salt. No shame. No guilt.

Jane was able to locate little more than a modest amount of embarrassment. It was not even enough to make her blush when she reflected on what had happened. If anything, reflection made her breasts ache and her womb contract. She warned herself that she would have to be careful about reflection.

She felt a certain sense of satisfaction. Discovery was like that, and this particular discovery was a revelation.

It was also disturbing. She had been sleeping, and by her reckoning, not for very long. This thing that she had done to herself had happened outside her consciousness. She had been thinking of him, she remembered that, but then she had surrendered to sleep and dreaming, and the dreams made it seem as if he were with her. It had been real, but not real at all, not in the way she wanted it to be.

Finally, Jane found disappointment. It was there, deep and abiding, squeezing her heart more than just a little. Discovery, she knew, was better when it was shared.

Morgan bumped around in the kitchen until he found where Jane had moved the lamp. The matches at least were in the same drawer he always kept them. He struck one, lit the lamp, and put the glass globe back in place.

Once he could see well enough to keep from banging his foot against a chair or a table leg, Morgan hobbled over to the sink and pumped water into the kettle. Jane had not set a fire in the cookstove to keep the kitchen warm overnight so Morgan had to build one. He started out trying to be quiet, but it did not take long for the dragon to frustrate him, and then he was slamming the dampers and the covers and the firebox door. He swore some, too.

"It would have been better if you had called for me," said Jane.

Morgan pivoted on his good foot. She was standing in the doorway, sleepy-eyed and tousled, belting her robe in what he could only think of as a Gordian knot. He thought absurdly that it was a shame broadswords had gone out of fashion. A carving knife wouldn't get through that.

"Did I wake you?" he asked.

She looked around the kitchen and then returned to him. "Unless there is someone else in here making a fuss, I would have to say yes, you woke me. What are you doing?"

"Slaying the dragon."

Jane sighed. "Sit down, St. George." She gestured to the kettle. "You want hot water?"

"To start. I want tea to finish." He reached in the pocket of his pants and showed her the bottle of laudanum. "And some of this. I think you're right. It works better with tea." He thought she might want to seize this opportunity to underscore that she was always right, but she didn't. She merely pointed to a chair, and this time he sat.

He could appreciate Jane's efficiency as she brought the stove to life. He did not think she wasted a motion, and she knew the precise order of opening and closing the dampers so the fire could breathe. When Jane turned away from the sink after washing her hands, she caught him staring at her. He did not look away, and she did not shy away. Morgan liked that about her.

Jane said, "I would ask you if I had smut on my nose, but you were not staring at my face."

That made Morgan blink, which he supposed meant that she had just stared him down. "You say unexpected things."

"Do I?"

"I don't mind."

Jane's eyebrows lifted as she dried her hands. "Good. I doubt I would be able to change if you did." She looked around. "Where is the tea?"

"Pantry. I hadn't gotten that far."

"What possessed you to get this far?" Shaking her head, Jane went to the pantry and brought back the canister. "Did you say something? Because I did not hear you."

"I thought maybe it was one of those rhetorical questions."

"If you truly thought that, you would not sound hopeful."

Resigned, Morgan blew out a breath. She had him there. "I couldn't sleep, and I couldn't see the point of waking you because of it. I know how to fend for myself."

"Yes, I am sure. All evidence to the contrary, I do not doubt it."

Morgan's mouth took on a sardonic twist. "You enjoyed saying that, didn't you?"

"Perhaps a little." Jane finished preparing the tea ball and set it in the pot. "I am sorry that you were injured, and I know that if I were not here you would manage on your own, but since I am here, I wish you would allow me to be useful to you."

"You are asleep on your feet, Jane."

"On *two* feet." Her gaze moved to his leg that was stretched out and away from the table. "You should put that up."

Morgan yanked one of the empty chairs closer and set his bandaged foot on the seat. "Satisfied?"

"I have annoyed you. I'm sorry. I will go."

It was impossible for Morgan to reach Jane as she turned to leave, but he put out an arm anyway. "No," he said. "Don't." When she paused but did not look at him, he added, "Please."

She nodded faintly and sat.

"The truth is," Morgan said, "I tend to forget about the pain when I'm around you."

"If there is a compliment there, I am not finding it. If you are less attentive to your pain when I am around, it is because I annoy you."

"You make it difficult for me to figure out if the right thing to do here is argue with you or let it be." He observed the corners of her mouth edging upward, although she seemed to be trying hard to have it otherwise.

Jane said, "That certainly is a conundrum."

A chuckle vibrated in Morgan's throat. He knuckled the underside of his chin as he studied her from across the table. She was so tired that her eyelids were barely raised to half-mast, and the thick fan of her dark lashes almost obscured the color of her eyes. Her mouth was narrowly parted. The separation between her lips was like an invitation. Once again, the vision of him hobbling awkwardly and painfully toward her forced him to reject it.

"It's rude to stare," she said. "And you've done it twice."

Morgan could have told her that he had done it a lot more than twice, but he supposed she was only referring to this brief encounter in the kitchen. "I'll beg your pardon if you like, but it will probably happen again. I don't mean anything by it."

Jane averted her eyes. "No," she said softly. "Of course you don't."

Morgan could not see her hands. He wondered if she was twisting them in her lap under the table. He did not understand the shift in her mood, the sudden avoidance. She usually met him head-on. It seemed out of character for her to turn away.

It was a relief to Morgan when the kettle started to jump. He did not have to say anything, and it gave Jane something to do. He made sure she did not surprise him in the act of watching her while the tea steeped and she set out cups. She poured and added a dollop of honey to her cup. He added three drops of laudanum to his.

Jane sat. "It occurs to me that I have crossed a line. Several times, in fact."

"How's that?"

"Being your wife and acting as if I'm your mother."

"I wouldn't know. I've never had a wife."

"But you've had a mother."

Morgan did not correct her assumption. It was true to a point. He blew on his tea before he drank.

Jane went on. "You railed some this afternoon about not needing to be coddled. I think I understand it better now."

"What does that mean? You'll nag me instead of nipping at my heels? And don't ask me which is being my wife and which is acting like the mother. I sure as hell don't know."

Jane stirred her tea. Her mien was thoughtful.

Morgan said, "You could probably ask Mrs. Sterling. She would know which side of the fence is which. She's been both."

"Maybe I'll do that." The smile she turned on him was a shade regretful. "And maybe the problem will take care of itself if I stop nagging and nipping altogether."

"Seems a mite excessive." He thought Jane might be hiding a smile behind her teacup. What he could see of her brightening eyes led him to believe that could be the case. "I don't think you should change your ways on my account. Besides, you don't exactly flinch when I rail at you anyway. More or less, it rolls off your back like water off a duck. I wasn't convinced you were paying attention."

"I pay attention."

"I know that now. And you're a worrier,

too, thinking over things the way you do long after they should be tucked away. I didn't realize that."

"Now you do. It is remarkable that laudanum and lack of sleep have not deprived you of your faculties. Would you like a pencil? Some paper? Perhaps you will find it helpful to make a list of my shortcomings while I am here to assist you."

Morgan grinned so widely that he would not have blamed Jane if she had thrown her teacup at his head. She looked as if she were tempted. He put up his hands and prepared to duck in the event she gave in to the urge. It fascinated him how curiosity got the better of her temper. In moments she had completely reined it in and was regarding him with a puzzled expression, not an angry one.

"What is it you found amusing in that?" she asked. "I was serious."

"That was entirely evident."

"Well?"

"It's your tone. It's real tidy. Your mouth is so full of sauce it should choke you, but it doesn't on account of you're so tidy."

"I see," she said slowly.

He nodded. "I guess if I were making a list of the things that aren't among your shortcomings, I'd put 'real tidy with her words' on that one."

Jane pressed her lips together.

Morgan asked, "Are you doing that with your mouth because you don't want to laugh or because you don't know what to say?" He shook his head. "No, don't answer that. I'll come to it eventually."

"I'm sure you will," she said on the back of a sigh. She finished her tea, rose, and moved her cup and saucer to the sink. "I am going back to bed. I know you do not *need* help, but do you want it?"

"You go on. I'm going to sleep in one of the chairs in the front room. I'll keep my foot up." He thought she seemed on the verge of objecting but caught herself. She nodded once and turned to leave.

"Jane?"

She paused, looked at him over her shoulder. "Yes?"

"Pain wasn't the only reason I couldn't sleep."

"There's something else?"

"The pillow. The sheets. They smell like you now."

Morgan figured those words would be enough to keep her away from him for the rest of the night no matter what she heard. What surprised him was how deeply they made her flush.

Max and Jessop rode out early the next morning. Jem left for town with Jane's list soon after that. Jake had chores to do in the barn. He came out once to present Morgan with a crutch he had fashioned from some scrap wood. It was sturdy and functional and about as comfortable under Morgan's arm as the splinter in Jem's ass, but Morgan thanked Jake and fashioned a pad for it out of a worn huckaback towel that Jane gave him. After that, he got around well enough to harness Sophie and lead her into the corral. He thought the crutch might bother her, but it was more like she thought they were on equal footing.

Jane avoided looking out any window that presented a view of the corral. She had her hands full keeping the water warm in the copper boiler so she could wash sheets. She stripped the beds as much for her peace of mind as for Morgan's. *They smell like you now.* He would not be able to say that tonight, and she would not be able to think it.

Jane did not spend much time preparing the afternoon meal with only three of them present to enjoy it, but in anticipation that the others would be back by supper, she braised beef and served it with carrots and mushroom gravy. The biscuits were what drew everyone's attention when she set the basket on the table. They were so warm, puffs of steam rose from the flaky centers each time one was split.

Jem smeared his biscuit half with butter, looked as if he meant to shove the entire piece in his mouth, but in the end took a surprisingly dainty bite. "What?" he asked when everyone stared at him. "A man can savor a thing, can't he?"

"Sure," said Jake, shrugging. "Nothin' wrong with that."

"That's what I thought." Jem set his biscuit on the edge of his plate and patted down his pockets. "Here you go, boss. I brought this back special for you." He reached across Jessop to hand Morgan a cobalt blue bottle.

"What is it?" Morgan said. He wiped his hands on his napkin and took it.

"Go on," said Jem. "Read the label. It's good for about every kind of thing."

Morgan read, first to himself and then aloud, "Dr. Ellis Wanamaker's Miracle Liniment and Medicinal Rub. With the healing extracts of aloe and willow bark." He stopped reading and cocked an eyebrow at

Jem. "Looks like it has about every kind of thing in it. Oil of petroleum. Alcohol. Sodium chloride. Tar ex—"

Max said, "That sodium chloride. That's salt, isn't it?"

"Fancy salt," Jem said. "That's why they call it that."

No one corrected him.

Morgan went on. "Tar extract. Camphor. Black cohosh. Poke root. And here, look at this. Lemon zest. He has brass, I'll give him that, to list the ingredients. There aren't many who will do that. It makes me wonder what he *isn't* revealing." He started to pull on the cork stopper.

"Please don't open it at the table," Jane said quickly. "It cannot possibly smell good."

"Oh, it doesn't," said Jem. "That's the first sure sign that there are a couple or three things in there that will work. There's no such thing as medicine that's good for you that doesn't smell like it's gonna kill before it cures." He looked at his brothers for confirmation. "Remember that plaster Ma used to slap on our chests?"

That memory set them back a dozen years. They had to agree he was right. "It's probably safe enough to use on the outside," said Jake.

"That's why it's called a liniment," Jem said. "You don't drink it."

Morgan set the bottle to one side and picked up his fork. "Did you buy this directly from Wanamaker or was Mr. Burnside selling it in his drugstore?"

"From the doctor himself."

"I see." Morgan looked at Jane. "Did he tell you he was a snake oil salesman when you met him on the train?"

She shook her head. "No. He introduced himself as a doctor. I took him at his word. I thought he had equipment in his valise, not samples. It is possible that he is a doctor, you know."

"Uh-huh."

Jane laughed. "All right. I do not believe it either. Not now. Thank goodness you did not insist on asking him for help when I did not feel well. There is no telling what he might have done."

"She's right, boss," said Jem. "Wanamaker's smooth with the ladies. I watched it myself. Renee only gave him the time when he asked for it, if you know what I mean, but Cil Ross kept circling. So did Marianna Garvin. That's the milliner's daughter. The one who's not married to the undertaker. She kept comin' around like —"

Morgan pointed his butter knife at Jem.

"Swear to God, Jem, you'll take your supper on the porch if you keep going on."

Jane leaned toward the much-chastened ranch hand and patted him on the forearm. "It's all right," she said softly. "You can tell me everything while you are helping me with the dishes."

"I sure will," Jem said, beaming. "I sure will."

Across the table, Morgan gave Jane a grateful look before he addressed Max. "What about the wolves? How far did you ride?"

"Ten miles or so past Whiskey Knob. Followed the pack's trail for a while, then Jessop here saw something else worth following so we took it on ourselves to take a different course."

Morgan switched his attention to Jessop. "When were you going to tell me about that?"

Jessop's eyes swiveled the smallest degree in Jane's direction. "I figured it could wait until after supper."

Morgan caught Jessop's guarded expression. He nodded. "I'm sure it can."

Jane said, "Am I to be excluded, then?" She looked around the table until her gaze landed on Morgan. "That's what you mean to do, don't you? Discuss whatever it is outside of my hearing?"

"Yes," said Morgan. "That's exactly what we mean to do."

"That is very disappointing."

"How you feel about it is up to you. You could choose to believe we're doing you a favor and be grateful."

Jane started to say something, but Morgan gestured to the other men at the table, who were currently staring at their plates and at least trying to give the impression they were uninterested. She put a forkful of braised beef in her mouth instead.

Over the course of the next three weeks, while Jane was establishing a routine for herself, she observed that her husband and his ranch hands seemed to be more comfortable working outside of one. Or at least they were trying hard to be unpredictable. She stopped asking who would be present for dinner or supper because the only thing she could depend upon was that one or two or even three of them would be missing. They ate breakfast in shifts. Some nights the men stayed on the range instead of returning to the bunkhouse. They did not talk about where they were or what they did in her presence.

Morgan did not ride out, although Jane

could tell that he wanted to. She was not certain if she were the reason he stayed behind or if his injuries kept him back. He was improving daily. His limp had disappeared so completely that sometimes Jane could not recall which foot he had injured. His ribs, though, still bothered him. Sometimes when he took a deep breath Jane could hear crackling in the area under his bruise. He allowed her to apply cream to it, but it came from Burnside's Drugstore. Dr. Wanamaker's Miracle Liniment and Medicinal Rub was good only for the bottle it came in. Jane had cleaned it out and placed it on the windowsill in the kitchen. It looked pretty to her when it was filled with sunlight.

Morgan walked Sophie every day but not at regular times. He finally got the bridle on her. He could not put himself on her back until he could tolerate the pain if she threw him off. Jane could tell that it frustrated him, but he never talked about it.

One afternoon she walked out to the corral while he was taking a turn with Sophie. He sent her back inside within minutes and refused to explain his reasoning. His refusal to explain himself was something Jane was coming to expect, but it was in no way something that she could tolerate in the long term. She settled on biding her time, watching, and when the right moment presented itself, she would tell him that keeping so many things to himself was unacceptable.

He took out his Winchester and sometimes his Colt and shot at mud bricks or stones that he set on fence posts away from the house but always within earshot of the dinner bell. Jane knew better than to suppose that the bell was only used to announce that meals were on the table. Jem, then Jake and Jessop, Max, and finally Morgan had all come to her at one time or another and found a way to mention the *other* use of the bell. Yes, she understood she should use it if she needed to bring them to the house; yes, she understood it was not to be moved from the porch because everyone expected it to be there. She believed the intention of this instruction was to make her feel easy that someone would come if she needed help. In fact, their instruction only eased their minds. Jane was much more than merely alerted; she was alarmed.

She asked Morgan several times about teaching her to shoot, but he always put her off. It further supported her impression that he did not want her outside. It did not help her understand why.

Jane overheard Morgan telling Jake that

his aim was off with the rifle but true with the Colt. Jake put it down to recoil and Morgan's ribs, and Morgan seemed to accept that, but Jane noticed that he took particular care that evening with cleaning and examining the weapon. The next day, he spent half again as much time practicing. In the house, Jane found herself snapping to attention every time she heard a shot.

They slept apart just as they had done every night since their marriage. It was not something they planned or even spoke about. It was just the way things were.

In Jane's mind their separate sleeping arrangement was not unlike Morgan's trouble with the Winchester. It had something to do with recoil and his ribs. She tried not to think about the day his ribs would finally be healed. Then there would only be his recoil to explain why he was not in her bed.

She was sleeping in the larger room again. Morgan had insisted that she have it, and Jane did not argue. He never moved his belongings from the room. They shared the dresser, the washroom, the clothes cupboard, and the wardrobe, but what they did not share, as she had intended, was the space. They did not dance around each other in preparation of either their day or their night. They acted more familiarly in the kitchen than in the bedroom, but Jane believed that Morgan's behavior there was predicated on whether or not they had an audience.

The presence of one or more of the ranch hands made for odd moments of intimacy, and Jane could not permit herself to attach too much importance to them. To pretend they meant anything except keeping up appearances was to recklessly endanger her heart. There was no bell she could ring to summon help for that, so she did what she watched the men around her do. She raised her guard and kept her silence.

Morgan threw his cards on the table. "Fold," he said, getting to his feet.

"Where are you going?" Jessop asked without looking up from his hand. "You can't leave. We haven't even started this round, and you owe me money."

"You lost money. There's a difference. And I'm going to do something about the fire in this stove. Why don't you ever complain about how cold it is in this bunkhouse?"

"Figured you knew," said Jake. "Give me a card, Max. I've got my eye on adding a pretty lady to the pair I already have."

"Here's your card," Max said. "But you're a liar."

Morgan opened the door to the stove and poked at the fire. He tossed in a piece of wood and a shovelful of coals and then poked at it some more. "Jane makes a better fire than you do."

"Jane's got the dragon," said Jessop. "What we have isn't big enough to be the dragon's smallest egg."

Morgan pushed the door closed with the tip of the poker, leaned the poker against a post, and warmed his hands in front of the stove.

"Blocking the heat," Max told him.

"Don't care." Still, he moved out of the way and back to the table. He spun his chair around and straddled it, resting his forearms along the back rail. "How much longer do you think Jem will be?"

"Is that the burr under your saddle tonight?" asked Jake. "I stopped keeping count of how many times you've been in and out of that chair."

Jessop looked up at the door as if he expected his brother to walk through it. "He'll be along directly, I expect. It'll be something about Renee that's kept him."

Max tossed two cards at Jessop when he asked for them. "I gotta say what we're all thinkin', boss. Seems like these rustlers have you spooked." He held up his hands when Morgan pinned back his ears with a look. "I said 'seems like.' Maybe it's because you haven't been able to ride out yourself, and I figure that's because of Mrs. Longstreet, not because you got hurt."

"You can't be in two places at once," said Jake. "You gotta trust us to do right by you here or there."

Morgan said nothing.

"Well, I said it," Max said, more to himself than anyone at the table. He threw a chip into the pot. "And whaddya know? I still got my head attached to my neck."

"Jesus," Morgan said.

Max simply shrugged, but Jessop said, "You've been kinda touchy lately."

"Jesus," Morgan said again, this time mostly under his breath. He looked at the men. "How long has this been rattling around in your heads exactly?"

"Exactly?" asked Jake. "Couldn't say. Upwards of ten days, though, would be a good guess. About the time you came to me complaining about your shot being off. Couldn't have been off more than a couple of inches, and at the distance you were firing that Winchester, seemed a little odd to me that you'd be fussing about it. Got me thinking."

"Bit longer than that for me," said Jessop. "I understood that you didn't want to talk about it right off in front of the missus. We didn't know much at first, but when you told us not to say anything ever, well, that sort of spooked *me.* Like maybe you knew something we didn't."

Max folded his cards and tapped a tattoo against the table with one corner of the stack. "About the same for me. None of us talked about it until yesterday. Guess since Jem isn't here, we can blame him. He brought it up."

"Jem," Morgan said flatly. "Jem brought it up."

"More or less. He said something about Mrs. Longstreet bein' just about the quietest woman he knew. I guess that's when we realized she hadn't always been that way. Only natural that words would come to be exchanged about you."

"Only natural."

"Well, it does seem as if she should know," Jessop said. "If you think we have notions rattlin' around in our heads, what kind of things do you suppose she has rattlin' around in hers? They're rustlers, boss. Cut the fence, take a few head of cattle, hightail it off your land, and come around again when they think it's safe to take a couple more."

"And what if they're not rustlers?" Morgan asked quietly. No one said a word. An ember popped in the stove and Max jerked, but other than that they were still. "What if they're not *only* rustlers?"

Jake asked, "What do you mean?"

"How often do rustlers make off with just a few head of cattle? And how often do they come back in so short a time?"

Max said, "We'd have caught up with them already if they'd run off with more cattle."

"Maybe. I hope so. But again, if not getting caught is that important, why return?"

"Hunger," said Jessop. "Could be they're rustling for food, not profit. Feeding a group, say. Squatters."

Jake shook his head. "No squatters on this land."

"Of course they ain't squatting here," Jessop said. "But there's plenty of unclaimed land north of here and only four of us that can ride out."

"Not homesteaders," Max said thoughtfully. "The whole point of homesteading is to put down roots. Same with squatters. These thieves are movin' around. Hiding out, I reckon you could say."

"Outlaws?" Jake sat up straight. "Is that what you're gettin' at?"

"Rustlers *are* outlaws," said Jessop.

"I know that. Max knows what I mean, and I was talkin' to him anyway."

"You should be talkin' to the boss," said Max. "I reckon it's his thinkin' that matters."

Jake looked at Morgan. "You think it's outlaws?"

Morgan knuckled the stubble on his jaw. "It's better to entertain the possibility than pretend it can't exist."

"You mighta entertained it with us. I can see why you don't want Mrs. Longstreet fretting about a thing like that, but the rest of us should be prepared."

"And what would you be doing that you aren't already? You ride out every day armed and alert. You know what I know. More, probably, since you've been out there. I just have another thought about it, is all, and it's the kind of thought that I want to keep from my wife. So now you know."

Jessop laid his cards down and pushed them toward the pot. "You have some suspicion about who the gang might be? Cassidy, maybe?"

"He and Sundance are up at Hole-in-the-Wall," said Jake. "Everyone knows that."

"Well, *everyone* ain't found them yet, have they?"

Jake flicked a card at his brother. It struck Jessop in the chest. Jessop started to come out of his chair, but Morgan threw out a restraining arm before there were blows and blood.

Morgan waited for the air to become less agitated. For a moment there Jake and Jessop were putting out more heat than the stove. "Done?" he asked them, looking at each of them in turn. "So help me God, if I see one or both of you sporting shiners in the morning, I'll keep Jem on and exchange the pair of you for Rabbit and Finn Collins."

Neither brother had anything to say to that, although they did exchange squinty looks.

Morgan said, "I don't have any suspicions about a particular gang, so let's just leave it."

"What about saying something to the marshal?" asked Max. "I've seen his Wanted Wall. I reckon he has a notice of just about every miscreant in three states tacked up there. Maybe we should let him know what's been happening out here."

"Bridger's jurisdiction is Bitter Springs, not the county. The last marshal that came out here on town business got himself killed for his trouble. I'm not going to risk that happening again."

Max leaned back in his chair and poked the brim of his hat with a fingertip, causing it to lift a fraction so that it no longer shaded his eyes. "There's still the sheriff."

"I don't want the law. We'll handle it ourselves. We are the law at Morning Star."

Max nodded. "That's what I thought you'd say, but I thought I should hear you say it."

Morgan stood, spun his chair around so that it once more faced the table. "Good night. If Jem isn't back in an hour, someone come up to the house to let me know." He picked up his winnings, which elicited a collective groan. "What? You thought I would leave this behind? I have a wife, gentlemen, and she has set her sights on bankrupting me."

In truth, Jane had not asked him for a thing. Morgan was not even sure why he said what he did. The men chuckled in that way men did when they believed they'd happened upon a universal truth about women. The real universal truth was that men didn't know a damn thing about them. Morgan knew himself to be part of that great collective.

He found Jane in the front room sitting in

one of the large armchairs beside the fireplace. She was wearing her nightdress and robe and had her dark hair neatly plaited in a braid that fell over her right shoulder. He could not tell if she was wearing slippers. Her slim legs were curled to one side and her feet were hidden under the hem of her robe. She had one of his shirts in her lap and a small red enameled sewing box on top of that. The lid was open, and she was staring into the case, poking at its contents with the thimble that was on her middle finger. There was a small vertical crease between her eyebrows, and her concentration was so focused that Morgan did not believe she knew he was in the room.

He stood there, watching her, wondering how to make his presence known without scaring her, but then her head lifted and she stared directly into his eyes.

"Did you win?" she asked.

Morgan regarded Jane without hearing her.

Jane's smile faltered. "Did you win?" she asked again. "You were playing cards in the bunkhouse, weren't you?"

"Why have you never asked me for anything?"

Every trace of Jane's smile vanished. "Pardon?"

Morgan repeated his question. He pointed to the enameled case in her lap. "Where did you get that?"

Jane glanced at the sewing box and then looked back at Morgan. "This? Max purchased it from the milliner for me. At least I think it was Max. It was whomever you sent to town after Jem went."

"Max," he said flatly. "Max bought that."

"Yes. I asked him to. I packed an etui, but it holds only the most basic needs. Scissors. Needles. Tweezers. Very small items. To hem my gowns, I needed matching threads." She pointed to the blue chambray shirt. "And I could find nothing here to properly mend this."

"I don't recall seeing a receipt for that box."

"I did not give it to you."

"Max paid for it?"

"I did."

"With what?"

"With money, of course. My own."

Morgan took off his hat and slapped it against this thigh. He saw Jane start at the violence in the gesture, but she did not cower. She sat perfectly still, her eyes as sharply cut as the emeralds they resembled. He sighed heavily, tossed his hat on the empty chair, and sat down at the end of the sofa that was closest to her.

He said, "Why would you buy threads or a box to keep them in or any other damn thing you need with your own money?"

"Do not swear at me," Jane said with quiet dignity.

"I wasn't swearing at you. I was swearing at any other damn thing."

When she spoke again, she was even quieter than before. "Are you done? Because it felt as if you were swearing at me."

Morgan collapsed against the back of the sofa, pushed his legs out in front of him, and plowed one hand through his hair. He stared up at the ceiling and was confronted with the absence of smoke stains. That was Jane's doing.

"Sorry," he said.

Jane made no reply.

He turned his head and looked at her. "I am sorry."

She nodded. "I believe you."

Morgan looked at her for a long time before he slowly released the breath he had been holding. There was resignation in the long exhalation. "Tell me about the box," he said. "Please."

"I didn't ask you for it because the case is a luxury. Any little box would have done to hold threads. When we walked through town that first morning, I saw this one in the milliner's window, and I remembered it later when I realized I needed something like it. Or something exactly like it."

"You could have asked me."

"And feel small and foolish for wanting something pretty when I could have something practical?"

Morgan turned his head and looked up. This time he did not stare at the ceiling. This time he closed his eyes. "What a goddamn mess." He heard himself. "Sorry, damn it. I mean, oh hell, you know what I mean."

"I do," said Jane. "It's the damnedest thing, but I do."

Morgan's lips twitched, but he was quiet.

"Would you like a drink? I can pour you a whiskey."

"Yes, I'd like one. Don't move. I'll get it myself." He stayed precisely where he was, head back, eyes closed, slouched against the sofa. "In a minute."

Jane let him be. She found the spool she wanted and threaded her needle. It was difficult. Her hands had a slight tremor that only the precise coordination required for threading a needle could reveal. She began mending the rent in Morgan's shirt with an occasional glance in his direction.

"What are we going to do, Jane?"

Jane almost pricked herself with the needle. "I thought you had fallen asleep."

"No. Sometimes I just think real quiet."

"Yes, I've noticed that."

"I want you to ask me for things," he said. "Fancy things, if you are of a mind to have them. I noticed you kept that Wanamaker liniment bottle. It looks real nice sitting on the sill. Come spring, maybe you'll want to put flowers in it."

"I was thinking I would."

Morgan laid a forearm across his eyes. "I could show you some patches around here where they grow wild. Pinks and blues and yellows. Lavender."

"I'd like to see that." Jane's vision blurred. She dashed away a tear. Another followed, and this one landed on Morgan's shirt cuff. Instead of trying to rub it out, Jane used the cuff to quickly dry her eyes before Morgan lifted his forearm and looked in her direction.

"So you'll be here in the spring."

Jane heard the smallest inflection at the end of his sentence that made it seem more question than statement, but if he expected a response he didn't prompt again for it. Jane was glad for that. Tears were still clogging her throat.

"I noticed you finished your courses," Morgan said.

That non sequitur dried her eyes, dissolved the lump in her throat, and drove an invisible fist into her diaphragm. Jane hiccupped.

Morgan's arm fell away as he sat up. "Maybe we could both use a whiskey?"

This time it was clear he was asking a question. Jane nodded. Her breath hitched again and she hiccupped. Her eyes were wide above the hand she clapped over her mouth.

"Yes," he said. "Definitely whiskey."

Morgan got up and went to the drinks cabinet, retrieved two cut glass tumblers and a bottle that was three-fourths full. He poured two fingers for himself, then looked over his shoulder at Jane for direction. She held up one finger. He gave her that and a splash.

Jane slipped her needle into the shirt cuff where she could find it easily and accepted the tumbler that Morgan handed her. Her thimble clinked against the glass. Smiling a bit self-consciously, she removed it and dropped it in her sewing box. She moved the box to the table beside her.

"Drink up."

Jane looked up at him. He was still standing in front of her. When she hesitated, he tapped the bottom of her glass with his forefinger, giving it just a nudge to move it toward her mouth.

"There you go."

She thought he sounded, if not quite pleased, then at least satisfied. As soon as she took her first sip, he moved back to the sofa. This time he sat in the far corner so that one of his legs could rest on the cushions while the other angled out to the floor.

"Is it going to distress you to talk about your courses?"

Jane hiccupped. Her fingertips tightened on the tumbler until the tips were white.

"I reckon so." He lifted his glass and knocked back half of his drink. "I only ever had a conversation like this with a woman once before, and she was the one who began it."

"Was she a . . ." Jane took a sip, hiccupped, and tried again. "Was she a whore?"

"A whore? No, not so anyone ever had to pay her, but that's probably a fine distinction. I came around to thinking she was."

"Oh." Jane understood enough to know she did not want to hear more.

"Whether she was or wasn't doesn't really matter. The important thing is that she told me that the goings-on in a woman's body shouldn't be a mystery, and to make sure it isn't a mystery, it needs to be talked about now and again."

"The *goings-on*?" asked Jane.

"Too plain? How about the mechanics?"

"Why don't we simply say the biology?"

"All right. So I've been noticing your biology."

Jane wished she had asked for more whiskey. Would hiding her face in Morgan's shirt make her distress more or less obvious? "What about it?" she asked, carefully enunciating the *t* at the end of every word.

"I already said I'm aware that you're done bleeding."

"Oh, God," Jane said. "You did *not* say that." She knocked back what remained of her drink, threw off the shirt, and stood. Morgan held out his nearly empty tumbler as she passed, and Jane smoothly took it on her way to the liquor cabinet. She gave him another generous finger and, after eyeing it, poured herself the same. When she went to hand the glass back to him, he caught her wrist and gave it a tug.

"Sit," he said. "Here." He patted the space beside him.

Jane looked at her captured wrist, then at Morgan. She realized suddenly that her hiccups were gone. That decided her. She supposed that she had made choices in her life that were influenced by flimsier logic, but she could not recall one of them now.

Her hiccups had disappeared. She sat.

CHAPTER EIGHT

With one hand, Morgan carefully pried his drink from Jane's cold fingers while holding on to her wrist with the other. He was relieved when she did not attempt to pull away. Her wrist was so delicate under his palm, so fragile, that he was afraid that any attempt to hold her would crush her bones.

He waited until he felt her settle onto the cushion before he let her go. Even then, he released her slowly, unfolding his fingers in succession, not all at once. Her hand hovered in the air for a moment, almost as if it were no part of her. He nudged it. It fell into her lap like a stone.

Morgan did not ask Jane to look at him. He was comfortable looking at her profile, and she was obviously comfortable staring straight ahead. "In five days it'll be a month that we've been married." If he had not been watching her closely, he thought he would have missed her nod. It was that faint. "I don't guess it ever crossed my mind that you and I would mostly be sharing a bedroom and never a bed. Did it ever cross yours?"

Jane's lips parted around her answer, but no sound accompanied the word.

"How's that again?" asked Morgan.

"No." She used both hands to raise her glass. She sipped quickly. "No, I never thought about it."

Morgan frowned. "I'm not sure what you mean. You never thought about sleeping with me, or you never thought about *not* sleeping with me? You can see they're horses of a different color." When she did not reply, he said, "All right. I'll just keep going." He thought he might have heard her moan softly, but he couldn't be sure.

"You asked me once if Ida Mae Sterling gave good advice," he said. "I figure that's because she gave you an earful about me, and you were wondering if you could trust her. Is that about right?"

Jane nodded.

"Well, she was pretty free with her advice to me about you." Even in profile he could make out the lift of Jane's eyebrows. "I know. It probably seems strange since she's known me a spell and you for about a minute, but she's like that. Maybe I should have taken that more into account, but some of the things she said, I was already thinking. It made them seem truer. More like we had facts instead of just two wrong-headed opinions."

Morgan paused, waiting to see if Jane would look at him. She did not. He judged her interest by the angle of her chin. At the moment, she was about as alert as anyone could be and still be sitting. If that chin came up another notch, it would yank her right off the sofa.

"When I lifted you off the train, my hands just about circled your waist. Holding you was like holding a flower stem. You had all those red poppies on your hat, so it wasn't exactly a stretch for me to think like that. You're so slight. Tiny bones, narrow hands. You can see how I thought I might snap you in two."

"You were expecting Rebecca."

"I suppose I knew that would come up. I can't very well deny it, can I?"

"No. Her photograph is the reason you wanted another day to decide whether or not you'd have me for a wife."

What had made sense to him at the time, sounded on the other side of appalling when he heard it coming out of Jane's mouth. "Mostly because I thought I'd been lied to.

It struck at my pride. No man likes to think he's been made a fool."

"No woman either."

"No," he said quietly. "No woman either."

Jane said, "I am stronger than I look." For the first time since Morgan drew her onto the sofa, she stole a sideways glance at him. "You are the one with broken ribs."

"I surrender to your superior argument."

Jane went on anyway. "Rebecca would not have been able to lay a fire in the dragon."

Morgan nodded. "I got there on my own."

"She does not know how to make hot-cakes or goulash or honeyed ham."

"Or fritters, I'll wager."

"Or fritters," said Jane. "She has a fine hand for embroidery, but she has never mended anything in her life."

"Probably has a personal maid to thread her needles."

"She does not wash, hang, or fold clothes."

"I already figured she doesn't dress her-self."

"She could ride your horses, play your piano, even read to you if —"

"If the words weren't too big?" he asked.

Jane clamped her mouth closed.

"Jane?"

She shook her head.

"It's all right. Were you listening to me at

all? It was early days yet when I came around to thinking all of those things you just said. You didn't tell me anything I didn't already know." He paused a beat. "Except maybe about the piano." He glimpsed Jane's small smile as humor asserted itself. "I'll bet she's ham-handed."

Jane's smile deepened. "No. She plays beautifully."

"Oh. That's a shame."

"I have always thought so."

Morgan appreciated her wry tone. "Give me your hand, Jane." She swiveled a little toward him then, searched his face, and after a moment in which he could not begin to guess her thoughts, she gave him her hand. "Look at it," he said. "Can you appreciate how impossibly delicate you seem to me?" His thumb made a light pass across her knuckles. "I can be afraid for you with a man like me."

"I think you are confusing delicate with weak. I will not break if you touch me. You have only to look to your own hand to know that truth. A man like you? You have nothing to fear on my account. See how you hold me. That is the man you are."

Morgan wished to the God he didn't believe in that that was true. He stared at their hands and said nothing. When Jane withdrew, he let her go.

Jane rolled the tumbler between her palms. "What advice did Mrs. Sterling share with you?"

The question brought Morgan back to the present. "She told me that a woman like you would need time to adjust to the idea of marriage and —"

"A woman like me?"

"I took it to mean she meant refined. Delicate in your sensibilities."

"There it is again," said Jane. " 'Delicate.' I believe I am beginning to dislike that word."

"Maybe I should have said she thought you might be easily offended."

"I am not sure she thought that at all, but you certainly did. And what is it that you thought would offend me?"

"Me, I suppose." Morgan wondered how Jane had come to occupy the high ground because he certainly felt as if he were no longer explaining things, but defending himself instead. "You are rather particular about your manners, and there's not an edge on me where you can't find a rough spot."

"That is not true."

Morgan saw Jane's eyes drop to his mouth. She tore them away, but not soon enough.

He touched the crescent-shaped scar at the corner of his lips. "It *is* true. Even here." He raised his tumbler and drank. "There I was, already thinking that I could snap you in half if I wasn't careful, and then I've got Ida Mae in my ear telling me I should be real easy with you when I took you home, and to have a care how I introduced you to the marriage bed."

Jane dropped her head and stared at the glass in her hands. "She did not say that."

Even though she wasn't looking, Morgan crossed his chest. "Swear."

"I am not sure that even a mother would take the liberty of saying that to her son."

Morgan shrugged. "It's no good trying to reason out what Ida Mae does or says or thinks. She's a force of nature. You duck or run or get swept up. I guess you realize now that I got swept up."

Jane lifted her head again. "Tell me true," she said, her voice not much above a whisper. "That very first night, did you want to . . . to . . . that is, did you want —"

"Yes." He smiled a little crookedly as Jane polished off her drink and handed him her glass. He set it on the table beside him and then added his unfinished drink as well. "That first night and every night since. You can't know how sorely I regret heeding Ida

Mae's advice."

"No," she said. "I only know how sorely I regret it."

She said this so feelingly that it surprised a laugh from Morgan. He took her hand again and squeezed it this time. Jane was right. She did not break. "I left the house that night," he said, "to keep from going to your bed."

"Did you suspect you were capable of such noble sacrifice?"

He liked the way her eyes sparkled when she tried and failed to temper her wry humor. She could never quite contain her amusement. "Humor will out," he said under his breath.

"Pardon?"

"Nothing." He shook his head. "Just something I'm realizing."

"You're staring again."

"So I am." He did not look away. "I've been thinking we should start over, Jane."

"Start over?"

"No, that's not what I mean exactly. I think we should just start."

"You are not going to talk about my . . . my . . ." She winced slightly. "That is, you're not going to —"

"Talk about your *biology*? No. I'm not going to talk about that." Jane's relief was so palpable that Morgan did not point out that he had not promised to never talk about it. He did not believe he had offended her with his plain speaking, but it was clear that he had embarrassed her. He regretted that. He remembered the first time Zetta Lee Welling had explained the goings-on to him. He'd been embarrassed then, too, and Zetta Lee had seen it. She called him an ignorant no-account orphan son of a whore and slapped him so hard that all these years later he could still feel the heat of her palm. The only word that had stung was "ignorant." He reckoned he couldn't do anything about the others.

"Morgan?"

He came out of his reverie to find Jane searching his face.

"Are you blushing?"

He wasn't, but he understood why she thought that. It was the scalding imprint of Zetta Lee's heavy hand against his cheek that she was seeing. "I guess I am," he said. "A man can be embarrassed by his rough edges." She did a surprising thing then, and Morgan was so unprepared for it that he almost reared back. He did not, though. He held himself very still while she laid her cool palm against his cheek and kept it there.

At first he suffered her touch. It was painful before it was healing, like alcohol in an open wound. He withstood it and it passed. She held his eyes. He never thought for a moment that it was the other way around. Curling his fingers around her wrist, he drew her hand to his mouth. He kissed the heart of her palm. He heard her take a sweet sip of air.

She asked, "Shall we go to bed, Mr. Longstreet?"

Morgan folded her hand in both of his and lowered it to his lap. "I think we should, Mrs. Longstreet. I really think we should."

Jane's eyes widened ever so slightly. "That's your biology," she said.

He grinned, released her hand, and stood. "It certainly is." Giving her no chance to rise herself, Morgan cupped her elbows, drew her to her feet, and swung her into his arms.

She threw her arms around his neck. "What are you doing?"

"Testing the ribs." He gave her a little bounce to prove he was better. Her squeak of surprise covered up his deeper groan. With her face buried against his shoulder, she also missed his grimace. He thought he might have pulled something, but he would be damned before he let her know. Better, he was realizing, was not the same as good as new. "See?"

Jane lifted her head. "Put me down."

"I never carried you over the threshold. I should have done that."

"We're not going outside, are we?"

"No. The threshold to our bedroom will do."

"Oh, thank goodness." She made herself as small in his arms as possible so he could get her through the doorway without banging either one of them against the frame. "I am not so insubstantial as you thought," she said as he carried her into the room. "Admit it."

"I admit nothing."

"That so?" She gave a little yelp as he pitched her on the bed. It was not a graceful landing. Jane scrambled to untwist her robe and push the hem of her nightgown over her bare knees.

"Take your time, Jane. I'm going to turn back the lamp in the front room, make sure there's enough coal in the firebox to keep the chill out tonight, and wash up in the kitchen. That'll give you enough time to work up a worry or two."

"Perhaps I will just read," she said primly.

"You could do that." He started to leave, stopped, and turned to face her again. He cocked an eyebrow at her, gave her a considering look. "Or you could think about where I'm going to kiss you first. And here's a hint: It's not going to be on your mouth." He grinned and ducked out of the room. He had already turned the corner when one of the bed pillows sailed through the doorway.

Once he was out of Jane's sight, Morgan pressed his right forearm against his ribs and breathed in slowly. His bones crackled. He swore under his breath and then waited, half expecting Jane to have heard him. When no scold came, Morgan proceeded with the tasks he had named in the order that he had named them. He was washing at the kitchen sink, shirt open, suspenders hanging at his sides, thinking about where he was going to kiss Jane first, when the back door swung open.

Morgan's fingers squeezed the bar of soap so tightly that it jumped out of his hand and into the sink. "No," he said. Just that. No.

Jessop pulled the door closed and turned down the collar on his wool coat. "Warm in here. Feels good."

Morgan's eyes narrowed a fraction, and he wondered if Jessop could feel *that* heat.

"Jem's not back," said Jessop. "You said to give him an hour and let you know if he wasn't back. It's been an hour and he isn't."

Morgan wrung out the washcloth and laid it over the lip of the sink. He pulled up his suspenders. "Who wants to go with me?"

"With you? Jake and me figured we would go together."

"No. I'm going. I'll take one of you with me. Do whatever the two of you do to decide these things. Someone stays here with Max." So there would be no mistaking what he meant, Morgan pointed to the floor. "Here. In the house. With Jane."

"Jem's probably playin' cards. I bet Renee's working in the saloon tonight. He likes to keep an eye on her when he can."

Morgan hoped Jessop was right. "If that's what he's doing, then I'm not passing on a chance to drag him out by his ear."

Jessop nodded. "Then I hope I win the coin toss. I sure would like to see that."

Watching Jessop go, Morgan could only shake his head. Coin toss? He had been so sure they arm-wrestled. ✦

Jane could see that something had changed the moment Morgan reappeared in the bedroom. She was sitting up, her back against the headboard, her hair unwound and finger-combed so that it lay across her shoulders. She was under the covers. Her robe was lying at the foot of the bed.

Everything about the way she had intended to greet him was wrong now.

Jane hastily pulled her hair back with one hand and threw off the covers with the other. Leaning forward, she grabbed her robe. Morgan was at her side before she could put it on.

"Stop, Jane." He sat on the edge of the bed and took the robe from her. Instead of helping her put it on, he covered her with it in place of the blankets she had pushed away. "There," he said, resting his hands on her shoulders. "I have to go."

"I knew it," she said on a thread of sound. "I knew something was wrong. What's happened? Was that Jem I heard in the kitchen?"

"Not Jem. Jessop. Jem is the reason I'm going out. He's not returned from town. He's probably playing cards at the Pennyroyal, but it's better to know. His horse might have come up lame, or it could be that he's sleeping off too much whiskey on the lee side of that rocky knoll. If that's the case, we all want a piece of him, but only one of his brothers is going with me."

"They could go. Just them."

"They could, but Jem's as much my responsibility as theirs. Maybe more. I owe something to the men who work for me." Morgan's hands fell away. "Look at me,

Jane. I forgot I even asked one of them to come and get me if Jem didn't show up. I took one look at you curled up in a chair with a thimble on your finger and a needle between your teeth and that pretty much pushed every other thought clean out of my mind."

"I didn't have a needle in my teeth."

He chuckled low at the back of his throat. "All right. It must have been the sharp edge of your tongue that I saw."

Jane tried to smile. It faltered and then faded. "You're not well. You haven't ridden for weeks."

"I'll manage. I carried you in here, didn't I?"

Jane made herself accept what he was telling her because he needed her to. "How long will you be?"

"A few hours, I imagine. It's not a long trip to town on horseback. It will be shorter if we meet Jem on the way." He looked her over. "Good?"

She nodded, closing her eyes as Morgan bent his head toward her. She felt his mouth hovering just above her lips, but he was a man of his word, and he did not kiss her there. Instead, he slipped his hand behind her neck and lifted her dark cascade of hair. He looped it around his fist and tugged, lifting her chin and exposing her throat.

That was where he kissed her. He left his mark on the soft hollow of her throat where her pulse fluttered like a hummingbird.

Jessop won the toss, so he rode out with Morgan. Between them they had blankets, a flask of whiskey, bandages, and a lantern. They saddled up with the thought that Jem might be in trouble. They each carried a rifle in their scabbard and a gun holstered at their hip in the event they stumbled into trouble when they found Jem.

It was a cold night, not unbearable, just bone-deep cold when the wind gusted. They rode with their collars turned up and their hats angled low and considered themselves lucky that the wind was not steady. Snow on the ground would have been a help to them, provided tracks they could have followed if Jem — or anyone — had wandered away from the road. There was a fingernail moon suspended in the sky, but its meager light came and went as the cloud cover thickened.

Twice, Jessop saw something that was worth investigating, but nothing came of it either time. After the second incident, Jessop admitted to being a little jumpy since his conversation with Morgan back in the kitchen. Morgan said he hadn't noticed.

Sometimes it took a lie to calm a man.

"What are we gonna do about our guns?" Jessop asked when they reached town. "Marshal won't like it if we're strapped when we walk into the Pennyroyal."

"The only person in danger of being shot is your brother. That's why you're going to hold my gun while I go in the saloon and get him."

"You figure you'll kick his ass?"

"Depends on how drunk he is. Why?"

"Jake and me talked about it, and we reckon that to do right by our little brother, we should be the ones to kick his ass."

Morgan looked over at Jessop as they drew abreast of the hotel. Light from the windows bathed the younger man's broad, square-jawed face. "All this time you've worked for me, and I had no idea Jem was the little brother."

"Oh, yeah." Jessop tipped the brim of his hat upward. "You understand I'm talkin' about his age, not his size."

Dismounting, Morgan nodded. "Sure. I understand." He removed his Colt from his holster and handed it to Jessop. "I've got no problem leaving Jem to you and Jake's tender mercies."

Jessop grinned. "Tender mercies. Yeah.

Sounds just like us."

The Pennyroyal was not crowded. Morgan looked around as he approached the bar. He knew before he reached it that Jem was not in the saloon.

Walt Mangold stopped rubbing down the top of the bar. "What can I get for you, Mr. Longstreet?"

"Information."

At first Walt stared at him blankly, then his smile emerged slowly, splitting his face and showing teeth almost as big as his fingernails. "That's a good one. People don't much come to me lookin' to learn things."

Morgan had heard Jake Davis remark once that Walt was slow off the mark. Jessop had jumped in with an opinion in the same vein. It was Jem who had come to Walt's defense, pointing out that Walt just considered his words more carefully than most folks, and anyway, people were suspicious of someone who didn't talk much, especially when the talk was about other people. That exchange had taken place over cards in the bunkhouse, and Morgan remembered it because it was the only time he'd seen Jem shut his brothers up. He felt a little sorry they were going to kick his ass.

"Has Jem been in here tonight, Walt?"

"Sure. Miss Renee's workin' tonight. That's her over there talkin' to Ted."

Morgan did not turn to look. He did not want to attract Ted Rush's attention. "Do you know where he is now?"

"Yep."

Morgan waited, but when Walt did not expound on his answer, Morgan realized he had to ask another question. "Where is he?"

"That'd be the jail."

"The jail."

"Yep. You know where that is?"

"I do."

"You look like you could use a drink, Mr. Longstreet. You sure I can't pour you a whiskey? On the house. I can do that for certain people. Mrs. Sterling won't mind. She likes you."

"Thanks, but I'll pass. Jessop's waiting for me outside." He straightened, and a thought occurred to him. He'd made an assumption. Talk about jail could put a hitch in his thinking. "When you said Jem's at the jail, did you maybe mean that he was dropping by the marshal's office to say 'hey' to Bridger? Maybe pick up his guns if he left them there?"

"No. Didn't mean that at all. Jem said 'hey' to Marshal Bridger when the marshal arrested him."

Morgan placed a quarter on the bar and slid it toward Walt. "Not what I wanted to hear, but I don't kill the messenger."

Grinning, Walt pocketed the quarter. "Much obliged, Mr. Longstreet. Much obliged." He went back to polishing the bar as Morgan walked away.

Jessop was flapping his arms and pacing up and down the walk when Morgan came out. "Tryin' to keep warm," he said as Morgan made him the subject of his withering stare. "So where is he?".

"Jail." Morgan loosened the hitch on the reins and mounted. He was too irritated to take notice of the pain. "*In* jail."

Jessop stopped flapping and hurried to follow Morgan's lead. It was a short ride to the jail, and he did not ask any questions along the way, but he did tell Morgan that if he changed his mind about kickin' Jem's ass, he and Jake would understand.

Cobb Bridger was sitting back from his desk, chair tilted, legs stretched, boot heels resting on the desktop. He had a book open in his lap, but he closed it and tossed it on the desk as the door opened.

Morgan glanced at the book when it stopped just short of falling over the edge. *Triumphant Democracy*? He asked, "One of your wife's recommendations?"

Cobb shook his head. "Jim Phillips thinks everyone should read it. You can take it if you like."

"Some other time." Morgan felt Jessop at his back. He used his thumb to point over his shoulder. "Jessop would like to see his brother, and I want to talk to you."

"Sure." Cobb moved his feet off the desk and dropped his chair to all four legs.

Jessop stepped out from behind Morgan. "We're carrying," Morgan said, spreading his long coat to reveal his gun. "Rifles, too. On the horses."

"I figured as much." Cobb showed no concern. "Jem mentioned you've been having some trouble out at your place. Go on back, Jessop. You know the way. Take the keys if you like. You can sit with him a spell while Morgan and I talk."

Jessop removed the key ring from the peg by the door that led to the cells. "What'd he do?"

"Ask him." Cobb started to wave him off, then paused. "Maybe you'd better leave your gun on this side of the door. So far, no one's been shot tonight. I'd like to keep it that way."

Jessop grinned. "Sure. I guess you know us pretty well." He unstrapped his belt and used the buckle to hang it on the peg.

Jingling the key ring, he stepped into the jail and closed the door behind him.

"You want a cup of coffee?" asked Cobb. "Tru made it before she left. You just missed her, so coffee's fresh." He pointed to the basket on the desk close to where his feet had been. "Apple tarts from Jenny's bake shop. Tru brought them when she heard Jem was a guest." In response to Morgan's doubtful look, he shrugged. "Apparently they're a favorite. I don't inquire anymore how she knows these things. So, coffee?"

Morgan nodded.

"You might as well take a chair. Jem's going to rattle on awhile." He went over to the small stove that was the single source of heat for the office and jail and used a towel wrapped around his hand to pick up the coffeepot. He poured a cup for Morgan, passed it off, and then added coffee to the cup on his desk. He returned the pot to the stove, and when he came back, Morgan was sitting in his chair. Cobb did not object. He sat in one of the chairs facing his desk that visitors typically took when they were invited to sit.

"Did you know the Davis boys were deputies for me once?"

"I heard that."

"They did a good job. I'd take them back,

but the town can't afford three deputies and there's not enough to keep them busy anyway. I considered hiring one but couldn't decide between them. They don't come apart easy."

"That's what I'm finding." Morgan stripped off his gloves, stuffed them in a pocket, and opened his coat. He wrapped his hands around his cup and drank. He kept his eyes on the marshal and avoided the Wanted Wall on his right. "They're a set."

"Not like you and your brothers."

"I don't have any brothers."

"Right. Like I was saying. You have nothing in common with the Davis boys."

Morgan felt acid rising in his throat. He washed it down with more coffee. "So what did Jem do?"

"Near as I can tell, started a fight or ended one. Depends on whom you ask. The thing everyone agrees on is that he was in the thick of it."

"You arrested him for fighting?"

"I arrested him so I could keep an eye on him. I figured someone would come to fetch him sooner or later. Before you ask, I escorted the other combatants to the station and put them on the first train out. They're on their way to Cheyenne."

"If they're out, why is he still in?"

"Because he was talking like he was going to go after them, and I thought he might just be crazy enough to do it."

"Did this have something to do with Miss Harrison?"

Cobb gave Morgan an arch look. "What do you think?"

"All right, but maybe you should arrest her."

"Believe me, I've thought about it. She keeps Jem on a short leash while she entertains all comers."

"How many comers were there tonight?"

Cobb held up three fingers. "Just in town this afternoon. They stopped by here looking to find out who might be hiring. I told them I didn't know if anyone was with winter coming on."

"They were looking for ranch work?"

"That's what they said."

"And you put them on a train? What about their horses?"

Cobb sipped his coffee, nodded. "Struck me as strange, too. Three men showing up, looking to hire on somewhere without gear or guns or mounts? They didn't look like shopkeepers, but they sure didn't come prepared to take a job on the range. They didn't give me a reason to run them out, so

I pointed them in the direction of Whistler's Saloon and figured there'd be a to-do once they had a few shots in them."

"But they went to the Pennyroyal instead."

"Sure did. Passed up Whistler's and went straight to the Pennyroyal."

"Jem was already there?"

"He says he was. I only saw him earlier when he was going into the mercantile."

"So you weren't all that disturbed that Jem got himself in a tangle with them. Looks like he gave you the excuse you were looking for when you sent them to Whistler's."

"He did. That's why I'm going to let him go with you and forget that he clobbered me with a broken chair leg." He pointed to his left shoulder. "I couldn't get out of his way fast enough."

"I thought you got there after the fight was over."

"Uh-huh. Jem took it in his head to start it up again while I was herding the other fellows to the door." He looked Morgan over. "So what's this about rustlers out your way?"

"Nothing to say except that we're handling it."

"You certain? Those men came in on the train that went through here at two forty. I checked with Jeff Collins. He watched them get off. We get people coming and going all the time, Longstreet, but I'm pretty good at spotting the ones that just don't fit." He looked purposely at the Wanted Wall. "They're not up there. I checked. Of course, neither are your brothers. I don't have a notice for them anywhere. Deputy Sugar got rid of a lot of old posters after Marshal Sterling was killed. I've asked around the county, even sent a letter to Leavenworth, but no one's got a picture for me. Except maybe you. Do you have a photograph?"

"I don't have any brothers."

Cobb leaned forward in his chair. "Look, I appreciate that you came to talk to me when you took over the old Burdick place. I know you didn't have to, so I've always thought you were on the right side of this thing, trying to keep people safe by letting me know who you are. We can split hairs about whether or not Gideon and Jackson Welling are your brothers by circumstance or biology, but the fact is, you were raised with them. Raised hell with them, too. Now they're out, served their time same as you. There's plenty of people that think it wasn't enough time — me included — but then, it was only the one robbery they got sentenced for, and no one died in the commission of it."

"You sound like a lawyer."

"Do I? Well, I've been studying."

"And I thought I couldn't dislike you more."

Cobb just smiled. "So do you think one or two of these men might have been Gideon or Jack?"

"Didn't you ask them?" The thinly veiled sarcasm in Morgan's voice earned him the steely edge of the marshal's icy blue eyes. Morgan did not flinch. He'd done it to see whether or not Bridger could be riled. It was good to know the man had blood, not ice water, in his veins.

Cobb held up his fingers again and ticked off the names. "Joe Pepper. Edward Ravenwood. Jud Wilcox. Any of those sound familiar?"

"No."

"They didn't to me either. Not at the time, but I was telling my wife about them, explaining how Jem got to be here, and she recognized their names."

Morgan tasted acid again. He let it sit at the back of his throat rather than swallow.

"Characters in a Nat Church novel. One of the recent ones, that's why she remembered. *Nat Church and the Runaway Bride.*

She says Jud Wilcox is actually Judge Wilcox, but you get the idea."

Morgan did. "Could be a coincidence."

Cobb appeared to think about that for a moment. He said, "Yep. That's about the stupidest thing I've ever heard come out of your mouth."

"You haven't known me long."

"Right. So what about it? You think it could be the Welling gang?"

"What makes you so sure there's still a gang? Maybe they were reformed by their prison experience. I was."

"No. Mrs. Sterling says differently. She says your ways were different before you ever saw prison. That's what her husband knew about you and why he vouched for you going in."

"Benton Sterling was a good man, but that doesn't mean he was always right."

Cobb finished his coffee, set his cup down on the desk. His lips vibrated as he blew out a breath. "Have it your way, but we both know they'll be coming for you. It might be better if you have someone watching your back. It can't be the Davis boys or Max Salter. I know from what Jem's said that he doesn't have a good sense about what might be going on at your place. I'd guess that's true for all of them. You think about that,

Longstreet, on your ride home, and keep looking over your shoulder. It won't surprise me at all to learn those men jumped the train somewhere between here and Cheyenne since that's the direction they came from. It'll have been somewhere close to where they left their horses and guns and gear."

Morgan's features remained impassive as Cobb paused to let his words settle. He said nothing.

"I'll ask some questions, find out what happened to them after they boarded, and I'll let you know because that's my job, not because I think I owe you for coming to me in the first place."

Morgan put down his cup and reached for his gloves. He stood slowly. "Don't ride out alone with your information, Bridger. In fact, it'd be better if you don't ride out at all. If it's the Wellings, now that they know what you look like, they won't pass on an opportunity to kill you. The best thing you can do until this sorts itself out is to look over your own shoulder."

Jane sat with Max and Jake at the kitchen table. She had made a pot of coffee for them. She was drinking tea. At her elbow was a battered green tin half-full of gingersnaps. More gingersnaps were in a pile equidistant from the three of them. In addition to the pile in the middle, they were each guarding short stacks of gingersnaps with their forearms.

Jane was learning to play poker. Max and Jake were trying to eat each other's chips.

"Now," said Jane, "if I have five cards almost in sequence and not in the same suit, is that worth anything?"

"It's worth folding," Jake said. He tried to lean in toward Jane to get a glimpse of her cards, but she pulled them close to her chest. He feigned a wounded, innocent look. "I was trying to see if I could advise you."

"Uh-huh." Jane stole a glance at her cards again. She waved Jake's hand away as his fingers walked slowly toward her winnings and addressed Max. "I will have one card, please." She placed her discard on the table.

"Are you sure, ma'am? Just one?"

"Yes."

Max peeled a card off the top of the deck and slid it toward her. "I don't think you're gettin' the hang of this, if you don't mind me sayin'."

"If that's true, then why do I have more cookies in front of me than either of you?"

"Well, we're eatin' each other's, for one

thing, and you're sneakin' them out of the tin when you think we're not lookin'."

Laughter tickled Jane's lips as she tried to hold it back. She picked up the card Max gave her, looked at it long and carefully, and then closed her hand. She picked up a stack of four cookies and added them to the middle. "I call."

"Three snaps is a call," said Jake. "Four is a call and raise."

"All right. That is what I will do."

Max folded, but Jake stayed in. "Let's see what you have, ma'am."

Jane was halfway to revealing her hand when her head snapped up. She tossed her cards on the table and jumped to her feet. "I hear something. They're back."

She had not taken a full step from the table when Max put out a restraining arm.

"Let me look first." He cocked his head as he stepped in front of her. "I think you're right, but this is one of those times no one should be wrong."

Behind Jane, Jake Davis was also on his feet. He edged toward the window and tried to see out. Until the lantern light appeared, all he saw was his own reflection in the glass. "It's them," he said as Max began to open the door. "That's Jem holding up the lantern. He's got the whitest damned teeth.

Sorry, ma'am, but it's God's honest truth about his teeth."

Jane was hardly listening. Once she knew it was Morgan returned to her, she squeezed past Max and ran out the door.

Jake jutted his chin toward the yard. "Bet she's gonna kick my little brother's ass."

Chuckling, Max held the door open for Jake and they followed Jane as she sprinted toward the barn.

Morgan was dismounting when Jane caught up with him. She appeared so suddenly that he had no opportunity to hide his grimace or pretend his groan was anything but what it was. She had a sharp look for him, but a sharper one for Jem. It faded quickly enough, replaced by genuine concern as she took in the extent of Jem's injuries.

With the skill of an old cowhand, she cut the two of them away from the others and herded them up to the house. Jake, Jessop, and Max were left to take care of the horses.

Jem was obliged to sit at the kitchen table and suffer Jane's ministrations. He protested a few times, but every one of those was for form's sake. He was quick to turn the other cheek, even when she was applying astringent. Every once in a while, she would put some pressure on a particularly tender spot, and Jem would wince mightily. That's when she would give him a gingersnap.

When Jane was done, she sat back and examined Jem's face with the critical and objective eye of an artist. She studied *her* work, not the battered and bruised features of her subject, and concluded she had done her best by him. She gave him another cookie and sent him on his way.

Morgan, who had been standing with his back to the warm stove, took a seat at the table when Jem was gone. "You are diabolical."

Jane continued to gather up the detritus of her medical attention. She did not look at him. "How is that?" She returned the soap to the sink, emptied the basin of water, and washed and dried her hands.

Morgan waited until she was done and held up a gingersnap. "These. The last man tortured by so much kindness was me. I know your methods." He broke the cookie in half, grinning when it snapped rather loudly. "I was watching him. It hurt him like hell to chew on one of these, and you gave him three. Four, if you count the one he left with. He's probably sucking on that one like a lozenge since he's got nothing to prove to an audience."

"I'm not saying I did it on purpose, you

understand, but if I had, it would serve him right."

"Uh-huh." Morgan put both halves of the cookie in his mouth and savored the flavor before he chewed. He waved a hand over the table as Jane began to return ginger-snaps to the tin. "What's all this anyway?"

"Chips. Max and Jessop were teaching me to play poker to pass the time."

Morgan picked up the five cards scattered in front of him and looked them over. "Who was sitting here?"

"I was."

"Did you know you had straight flush?"

She nodded. "I discarded an eight of clubs and Max gave me a six of diamonds. I told them I had five cards almost in sequence but not in the same suit. They advised me to fold."

Morgan chuckled. "Diabolical *and* lucky. They didn't realize you were holding four diamonds and one club. Even so, it wasn't the wrong thing to tell you. The chances of drawing to a straight flush are awfully small."◄

Jane reached across the table and plucked the cards from his hand. She laid them on top of the ones in front of her, squared off the deck, and pushed it aside. She gave Morgan her full attention and frank regard.

316

"Are you going to tell me what happened tonight?"

"You heard Jem."

"I did. Now I want to hear what Jem did not, could not, or would not say. I am imagining you used the ride home to be very clear with him about that, but because you are a cautious man, and Jem is . . . well, *Jem* . . . you stood over my shoulder so you could cue him in the event he forgot his lines."

"There's nothing to tell —" He stopped because Jane was already getting to her feet. "Where are you going?"

"To bed. I don't want to hear that 'there's nothing.' It is the beginning of an evasion. You do not seem to understand that you make me vulnerable when you try to protect me from the truth." Jane stepped behind her chair and pushed it under the table. She set her hands firmly on the top rail. "The only time you offend me, Morgan, is when you doubt my strength."

Morgan's eyes followed her, but he did not. He sat where he was, listening to her words as they echoed in his mind. Was she right? Clearly it was her opinion, but was she right?

Still stiff from his ride after so long an absence from the saddle, and feeling every thread of tension between his shoulder blades, Morgan stood slowly. He rubbed the back of his neck, rolled his shoulders, and then went to the sink to begin washing up all over again. This time there was no interruption, and when he was done, he picked up the lamp and headed to his room.

On the point of entering, he hesitated. He held up the lamp. The bed was still neatly made. He always threw the covers over it, and sometime during the day, Jane would go into his room and smooth and tuck and plump. At first it amused him that she would give so much attention to a bed that was going to be slept in again that night, but later he came to appreciate it, even found it oddly comforting.

But not tonight. Tonight there was nothing about the sight of that perfectly made bed that Morgan found either comforting or inviting. Just the opposite. Morgan did not want to disturb it. He wanted to move on. Lamplight flickered as he inhaled deeply. By the time he slowly released that breath, his decision was made.

Jane had not closed her door. Morgan wondered if it was an oversight or a hopeful sign. Lamp in hand, he stepped into the room. Jane did not look so very different from the last time he had seen her in bed.

She was sitting up with the headboard behind her to support her back. The bed-covers were pulled across her lap. Her robe lay at the foot of the bed, folded as neatly as before, but the room was colder than it had been earlier, and now Jane had drawn a quilt around her shoulders and tucked it under her arms. She did not glance up from the book that was open in her lap, although Morgan believed she was aware of his presence. If nothing else, the addition of more lamplight gave him away.

"I've been thinking about something," he said.

Jane's eyes remained on her book. "Oh?"

"I remember what you said about taking your opinion into account."

Jane closed the book, but she marked her place with her finger. She looked up. "I am listening."

"I want to sleep here. With you. Tonight."

"I see. And what about what I said in the kitchen? Have you taken any of that into account?"

"Still trying," he said. "I'm not sure I'll ever come around to your way of thinking, Jane. It could be that the best we're going to make of it is to agree to disagree."

"There is a part of me that wishes you would tell me what I want to hear, but I appreciate that you are being honest about the struggle. It will do," she said. "For now." Her eyes fell to the lamp in his hand. "Put that down before you drop it."

"Yes, ma'am." Morgan saw that amusement made her lips quiver. He used his heel to kick the door closed before he crossed the room and set the lamp on the dresser. He turned back the wick to extinguish the flame. That left Jane bathed in the golden glow from the lamp on her bedside table. When he looked at it, he noticed the book she had been reading was now beside it.

"Which side?" asked Jane.

Morgan barely heard her. He was staring at her mouth, the way her lips remained parted after she spoke. She had a lovely mouth, wide and sensual, plump and provocative. As he watched, Jane raised one hand. She did not try to cover her mouth. Instead, her fingers went to her throat, to the last place his mouth had been.

He saw the mark he had left on her pale skin. His brand. His mouth went dry; his eyelids drooped. Beneath his lashes, his eyes were darkening.

"Move over," he said. There was a rasp in his throat that he did not try to clear. "You're on my side."

CHAPTER NINE

Jane lifted the covers and inched sideways.
The quilt around her shoulders bunched
uncomfortably. Morgan was suddenly there
to take it away. He tossed it toward the foot
of the bed. Jane let him because she realized
she was no longer cold. Every inch of her
skin was flushed with that peculiar sort of
heat that had its source inside her. Her toes
curled. She slid down until she was lying on
her back. She barely noticed that in this new
spot the sheet under her was cool. She set
her arms on either side of her but outside
the blankets. She wriggled once to get
comfortable and then she was still. Actually
she was stiff.

She stared at the ceiling, waiting for Morgan to do something. When he didn't, she
looked at him askance. He was sitting hip-
shot on the edge of the bed, turned slightly
in her direction. His fingers hovered over
the fourth button on his shirt. The three

above it were already unfastened. Watching her appeared to have arrested his movements. She had no idea why.

He said, "You have to breathe, Jane."

Her chest fell as she released the one she had been holding. "I hadn't realized," she said. "I expect it won't be the last time you will have to remind me."

"You're anxious."

It wasn't a question, but she confirmed it nonetheless. "Yes. I cannot precisely pretend I have experience when I so clearly do not. Quieting my nerves is out of the question."

"Then stop trying. Your heart will not explode no matter that it feels as if it might. Breathe."

She sunk her teeth into her bottom lip, nodded. This time her nostrils pinched slightly as she took a deep breath through her nose.

One corner of Morgan's mouth curled upward. "Perhaps a drink." He started to rise, but Jane struck out with an arm and stopped him.

"No. It is always possible that I will regret it, but I prefer to be clearheaded."

"Are you going to take notes?"

"You are not amusing." But her primly set mouth and the fact that she was breathing easier hinted that she thought differently.

Jane turned on her side and folded the pillow so her head was angled upward. She watched him finish unbuttoning his shirt. "When did you sit for the photograph you sent me?"

"About three months before my personal notice was published. Why? Do you think I've changed since then?"

"No. Your appearance is the same. Very fine, I would say."

Morgan turned his head as he shrugged out of his shirt.

"Did I embarrass you? I did, didn't I? It is no good denying it. Your coloring gives you away. Did you curse your red hair growing up? I'll wager you did, but it's quite beautiful, you know. It is —"

Morgan tossed his shirt over Jane's head and leaned forward to yank off his boots. Behind him, he heard her sputtering as if he had pitched a bucket of water at her. He also could hear her laughter bubbling under it. That decided him. He dropped his boots so they landed one at a time with a recognizable thud. All the sputtering and bubbling stopped. He stood, dropped his trousers, and slipped between the covers beside Jane before she was properly out from under his shirt. He lifted it away with a magician's flourish, but he did not dwell on his accomplishment.

What he did was take advantage of her perfect astonishment and cover her open mouth with his own. And that was when he lost his mind. Gone was his intention to tease a response from her. He forgot about coaxing her lips to move under his and quieting her fears. He forgot his intention was to care for her anticipation, not crush it.

Instead, he went to a darker place. He had thoughts of devouring her, of not merely stealing her breath, but suffocating her, of making his claim so complete that her eyes would betray her desire every time she looked at him. And then, just when he thought he could not come back from that black hole, he remembered what it was like to be on the surrendering, helpless end of selfish passion, and he jerked his head away.

Jane whimpered. The sound lodged at the back of her throat. Her eyes were closed. She was senseless to everything but his mouth on hers. He held her head in his hands, held her still. His mouth plundered hers. Heat flared. At first she thought the damp edge of his tongue was meant to cool it, but he licked her lips with the ferocity of a flame. He sucked her lower lip into his mouth and bit down. She had sunk her teeth into her bottom lip earlier, but this was nothing like that. When he sawed and tugged, he set some thread of tension in motion that vibrated all the way to her womb. A ribbon of heat curled and twisted, rose and fell and crackled. He had built a fire in the pit of her belly.

When he tore his mouth away, it was not lost that she felt, but a loss. She could have found her way back from one, but she grieved the other. Startled into awareness, her eyes opened, and she reached for him.

He had not gone away after all. He was there, looking down at her, searching her face in the lamplight, just as she was searching his in the shadow. Her hands rested on his shoulders; her fingers fluttered once and then were still.

"God." She heard him say it softly, and even though he professed not to be a godly man, it seemed very much like the beginning of a prayer to her, perhaps thanks, perhaps relief.

Morgan bent his head again, this time with gentle intent. His mouth brushed hers. He nudged her lips carefully, laying down the kiss like a balm. He had inflicted a wound that needed tending.

Jane moved her hands from his shoulders to his elbows. She felt the strength in his arms, the cut and definition of muscles that bunched under her touch. He still held her head in his palms and there was still pressure in his fingertips. His kiss was soft; the way he cradled her head was not.

She wrapped her hands around his wrists and made a pass across the undersides with her thumbs. She stroked lightly. Once. Twice. She felt his fingers open, the pressure ease. It made her smile, and her smile changed the shape of her mouth and the tenor of their kiss.

Morgan teased her now, tasting her mouth in a way he had not done before. He nibbled her lips. Nudged them open. He also nudged her knees apart, found a space between them with one of his. She stretched, arching just a little, and her restlessness allowed him to settle solidly against the curve of her hip. He slipped his tongue between her lips and ran it along the ridge of her teeth. She reciprocated, touching her tongue to his, experimentally at first, and then with more confidence when he hummed his pleasure against her mouth.

He drew away gradually, first kissing the corner of her mouth, then her chin, then trailing kisses along her jaw until he reached her ear. His teeth found her again. He worried her earlobe. His breath was warm against her cheek. When he released her ear, he dragged his mouth along the sensitive cord in her neck to her throat.

Jane swallowed. She lifted her chin, exposing the underside of her jaw. She felt his lips against the hollow in her throat, and he took his time there. He buried his face in her neck and his fingers in her hair, and he breathed in like a man who had been denied air until this very moment.

He used his teeth again, this time to fold back the neckline of her gown and reveal her collarbone. He lifted his head to study it, nodded to himself, and then put his mouth against it in what was the beginning of a journey along its length. Jane felt her breasts swell. They grew heavy. She recalled her dream, the one in which she had awakened with one hand on her breast and the other between her thighs. She wanted his hands in there. In time, perhaps. She would be patient. And then his mouth was covering hers again, and she wondered if she could.

Morgan moved his head, changed the slant of his mouth. She tasted faintly of gingersnaps and tea and innocence, and it was a powerful reminder that he was also inexperienced. There had been no other woman like her in his bed . . . in his life. Jane was not the only one who was anxious. Morgan had to remind himself to breathe.

Their mouths muffled his rough gasp, but Jane understood enough to know pain had prompted that sound, not pleasure. She moved her head sideways. His lips grazed her cheek. She ducked a little, took his face in her hands, and made him lift his head.

"Tell me," she whispered. "I will know if you lie to me."

"There's a stitch in my side." He dropped a kiss on her mouth. "It's tolerable." He brushed his lips against hers again. "And it is not deserving of your attention." He caught her mouth just as it was parting. It could have been a breath or a word that gave him this small opening, but he wanted to believe it was her anticipating him.

The promise he made to himself that he would go carefully was broken and remade and broken again. That he had not been with any woman for a long time accounted for some of it, and this particular woman accounted for the rest.

He wanted her. He wanted her under him. He wanted her hands on his back, her fingertips white against his flesh, the tips of her nails impressing his skin with pale crescents. He wanted to lie between her thighs, her knees raised on either side of him, and move inside her. He wanted to move her.

So he kissed her again, softly, carefully, and began a second trail of kisses that took him to her breasts. Her fingers wound through his hair and twisted the strands at his nape. They splayed and stiffened over his scalp when he took her nipple into his mouth and sucked. He laved the areola. Her nipple was a little pink bud that he could worry between his lips and flick with the tip of his tongue. He could tease it and hear her breath catch. She made it tempting to linger, but there was her other breast that was equally worthy of notice, and a lovely little valley to explore before he got to it.

Jane wondered if Morgan could feel the steady thrum of her heart. Every beat drove blood to her head. There was a distant roar in her ears that made it hard to hear any sound but her own breathing, and it seemed so loud and discordant that she put the back of one hand over her mouth so Morgan would not hear it, too.

What her movement did, though, was bring his head up. He looked at the hand covering her mouth and then at her eyes, wide and a little wild, above it. His smile was slow in coming. First there was concern and uncertainty and the question of whether it was too much and should he go on, but then she shifted, stretched, and the manner in which she did it told him what he needed to know. That was when he smiled. That was the moment he was sure that it would be all right.

He moved her hand out of the way so he could kiss her on the mouth, but first he whispered, "You shout if you want." He did not know she couldn't hear him.

Jane nodded because she read his lips. He made her feel as if nothing she did was wrong. He made her want to do more. So when he kissed her this time, she held nothing back. There was no lead for him to take. She met him as a partner, a friend, a lover.

She slid her hands between their bodies and found the buttons on his union suit. She unfastened three, parted the flannel, and slipped her palms inside. She had touched his chest before, but determining the extent of his injuries and seeing to his comfort were not uppermost in her mind now. She did not proceed cautiously. His skin was warmer than her palms and she wanted that heat under her skin. She opened the last two buttons and tugged on the sleeves to lay his shoulders bare. He did the rest, yanking and twisting until the top of the suit rode low on his hips.

It was not for very much longer that his drawers were any kind of impediment. When the suit was bunched at his feet, he kicked it out of bed, and then he was lying back, not naked precisely, because what he was wearing was Jane.

She moved over him. Wherever her cotton shift covered her, it covered him. It felt as thin as a membrane, as insubstantial as gossamer. It existed to frustrate. It existed to excite. Neither of them tried to strip it away.

Jane remembered all the things he had done to her. She cradled his head in her hands, communicated her intent with a smile that came and went so quickly it left only an impression of wickedness. She nudged open his lips, tasted them with the tip of a darting, flicking tongue. She kissed the corner of his mouth, his chin. The ginger stubble on his jaw tickled her lips. She nibbled on his earlobe and blew ever so lightly in his ear. She buried her face in his neck and nipped his skin with her teeth. She laughed when he growled. The sound of it rumbling in his throat vibrated against her mouth. She knew where she found the courage to sip his skin and leave her own mark. He gave it to her.

She felt his hands moving up and down her back, drifting lower with each pass, sliding over her hips once, then again, and finally palming her bottom and urging her to ride up just a little. He was hot and hard against her belly, and when her thighs parted, she felt the wetness between them.

Between the kisses, the long ones that made her heart pound, and the short ones that made it stutter, she finally understood the purpose of her body's response. She was being made ready for him.

Good. She wanted to be ready.

Jane knew the time had come when Morgan caught her by the elbows and turned her on her back. He followed, his mouth not much more than a hairsbreadth from hers, and when he raised his head, his eyes had lost their vaguely slumberous look. They were watchful, alert.

"Raise your knees," he said.

She did. She would have done it regardless of his direction. Some instinct made her want to cradle him. Jane pressed her heels into the mattress, and she was already lifting her buttocks when he rose to his knees and his hands slid under her bottom. She looked down at herself and then at him. It was too late to ask him to extinguish her reading lamp, and she wasn't sure that's what she wanted anyway.

He was startlingly beautiful to her. She

could see the runnels her fingers had made in his thick hair. The color of it was strangely darker in the lamplight, no longer orange, but coppery instead. His eyes, though, seemed greener. They did not stray. His features were somehow more defined, and she had the sense that he was exercising restraint. She did not know why; she only knew that it was unnecessary.

"Please," she said. And it was enough.

Morgan angled his hips and pushed into her. She was slick and tight and warm, a dewy sleeve around his cock. He watched her press her lips tightly together, but there was no help for that except for him to wait it out with her. He knew how to do that. He had been taught how to do that.

He felt her begin to accommodate his entry. It occurred in slow degrees. Her fingers uncurled where she gripped his shoulders, then she sucked in a little breath and let it sigh out of her. Her knees relaxed. The cradle she made for him was softer. And where she held him most intimately, the contraction eased.

There was still tension, but it was meant to be exploited, to be endured. Morgan knew how to do that. He had been taught how to do that.

He withdrew. Thrust again. He moved

slowly, deliberately, watching her. Always watching her.

Jane closed her eyes. She could not look at him any longer. What he was doing to her, what he was making her feel, made her only want to look inside herself. In her mind's eye she thought she could see the inception of pleasure, and although it was white-hot, she could not look away.

Her hips moved. They rose and fell. She responded to a rhythm that she only heard distantly but was deeply felt. It was something that he did to her and she accepted it, not out of any sense of duty, but because it was what she wanted.

She felt as if she were being lifted, as if she were coming out of herself, out of her skin, when in reality, she was only coming. She was a single nerve, taut and twisted and trembling. Her eyes flew open and she saw Morgan's face above her. She threw her head back. She dug in her heels. Between those two points, the entire length of her body bowed like an electrical arc.

Jane gasped. She might have said something in that moment, but if she did, it was unintelligible and unimportant. She shuddered, shuddered hard, and then she was still. The lightness that had lifted her vanished but not the awareness that Morgan was still moving inside her. It was only a short time before he was not.

He did not gasp. He groaned. Jane heard the sound as something that was in response to both relief and suffering. She did not mind his weight on her. They were joined in their lethargy. She put her arms around him and stroked his back. She combed her fingers through the hair at the nape of his neck. She rubbed his calf with the sole of her foot.

When he hoisted himself up, Jane did not try to stop him. He rolled away and collapsed onto his back. She turned just enough to see him put his forearm over his eyes. She was becoming familiar with that posture. He did it when he was looking into himself, evaluating, reflecting. He did it when he found that even the flickering light of a lamp was too distracting.

Jane quieted her breathing, said nothing, and waited.

"Do you regret becoming my wife?"

When he finally spoke, Jane only wondered why she was not more surprised by his question. "I was your wife before tonight," she said. "At least it seemed so to me."

"And tonight?"

Jane refused to answer. Instead, she said,

"Tell me what there is to regret."

"The absence of love, perhaps."

That pricked her heart, but she knew it was true. Under the covers, she found his hand and took it. He did not try to pull away as she thought he might, even when she squeezed it. "You will never convince me that of the pair of us, you are not the more romantic." He snorted, which made her chuckle. "I saved all your letters. Sometimes I reread them."

"Do you? Why?"

"Because sometimes, like now, you can't help but hold on to a dark thing so tightly it swallows your joy, and those letters remind me that there is light in you. You would not have named this place Morning Star if that were not true."

He did not lift his forearm. Under his breath, he said, "Jesus."

Jane let it be. She moved his hand to his chest and inched closer before she released it. "Is it proper to tell you that you made me happy tonight?"

"I don't know. Does it seem proper?"

"Yes. Yes, it does."

"Then it probably is." He finally removed his arm and looked at her sideways. "I trust your sense of what's fitting. You have my men saying grace before meals."

336

"This is a little different from that."

"Hmm." He crooked his finger at her and pointed to his shoulder. She put her cheek against the spot he intended for her. "I don't want to sleep in the other room tonight. Or any night from now on."

"I am not asking you to." When he was quiet, she lifted her head and looked at him. "Did you think I was going to argue?"

"Maybe. I don't know. I'm still working out how marriage changes things. No woman's ever let me stay in her bed."

Jane blinked. She was quite certain it had required considerable effort for him to squeeze out these last words. "You mean I will be the first woman you've slept with?"

"Once we actually go to sleep, yes."

Jane's head dropped back to his shoulder. "I feel as if the appropriate response here is 'I'll be damned,' but I defer to you on matters of blasphemous phraseology."

Morgan gave a shout of laughter, turned, and pressed Jane's shoulders into the mattress. "That mouth of yours," he said, and then he brought his down on it and kissed her long and hard and deeply.

When he eventually let her go, Jane lay there, stunned into silence. After a moment, she carefully touched her lips with the back of her fingertips. It had been a very thorough kiss, and her mouth felt a bit tender and her lips still tingled. She wanted to hold on to the sensation awhile longer. Morgan, she noticed, was looking rather pleased with himself, and she bathed in the light that finally shone through his eyes.

"My parents slept together," she said. "I remember that. In India, the accommodations were often cramped, and sometimes I shared a room with them. Sometimes a bed. What about your parents?"

"I don't know."

Jane let that pass. "Mr. Ewing and Cousin Frances had separate bedrooms. They did not even adjoin, but I have no idea who insisted on that arrangement. I suppose that means people can do as they like. You might discover you are not comfortable sleeping with me. I could jab you in the ribs or kick you. Steal the blankets. Rub my cold feet against your legs. I might talk in my sleep."

"It would still be a respite from how much you talk when you're awake."

Jane poked him in the ribs with an elbow. "I might snore."

"Do you?"

"I don't know."

Morgan yawned in dramatic fashion. "I am not opposed to finding out."

Jane turned so she was held in the crook

of his arm again. "I like you, Morgan. I do."

Morgan reached for the lamp and extinguished the light. He set his mouth at the crown of her head and whispered against her hair, "I'll be damned."

Jane heard Morgan get up in the middle of the night, but she let him go. The back door opened and closed. She did not remember him coming back to bed, but he was there when she woke. She carefully removed his arm from around her waist and slipped out of bed without disturbing him. In fact, she managed all of her morning rituals while he slept.

It was the aroma of coffee that brought him out to the kitchen. He stood directly behind Jane at the stove, peering over her shoulder as she poured. His hands rested at her waist. To keep her steady, he said, and she did not disagree. She needed a little steadiness this morning, especially when he put his lips to her ear.

Jem and Max came in the back door, each of them carrying a tin cup of coffee from the bunkhouse. They stopped so abruptly that coffee splashed the backs of their hands.

"This, uh, this a bad time?" Jem looked at Max, eyebrows raised nearly to his hairline. He mouthed the words "say something."

When Max just jerked his head toward the door, Jem cleared his throat. "We will, uh, that is, we'll just show ourselves out, if it's all the same to you."

"Stay," Jane said.

"Go," Morgan said.

Max started to back up, but Jem pulled out a chair and sat down.

Morgan changed his mind about what he was going to whisper in Jane's ear, and said, "We'll talk about what you've done to Jem later." He backed away, cup of hot, black coffee in hand, and took a chair himself. He waved Max over. "Jessop and Jake out already?"

Max nodded and sat. "They figured they'd go out to Hickory Lake first, seein' as how the rail line cuts that way going to Cheyenne. We all thought about what you said last night." He darted a look in Jane's direction. She was humming to herself while she cracked eggs over the skillet. He still dropped his voice to a near whisper. "Seemed the most likely place to look around for jumpers."

Looking at Jane's back, Jem said more loudly, "Never know what one of those Herefords is gonna do."

Max rolled his eyes. Morgan sighed and shook his head. Jane dropped both halves of an eggshell into a bowl and turned around. "Cows *jump* fences?"

Jem said, "Sure. One jumped over the moon, didn't she?"

Jane gave him an arch look. "Clever, Jem. Very clever." She turned back to her skillet and eggs.

When breakfast was over, Jem and Max headed to the barn. Morgan lingered at the table for coffee and conversation.

"Jem's face looks worse today than it did last night," Jane said. "But I suppose that's to be expected." She began gathering plates and utensils, pulling them toward her to stack.

"Leave them," said Morgan. "Drink your coffee. I'm not sure that you've ever finished a cup that was still warm."

"Morgan. I have things to do."

He pushed the plates out of her reach. "So do I, and all of it will be there in ten minutes when I get up from this table."

"All right."

"Cows don't jump," he said. "A steer will buck and charge and carry on like he has no sense, but he won't jump barbwire."

"I knew that. I remember what you said about the cows stopping at the fences in a snowstorm."

"I figured you did, especially after Jem

used a nursery rhyme for supporting evidence. The jumpers that Max was talking about are the men that beat up Jem. Marshal Bridger put them on a train going east. We're only supposing they might jump the train and circle back this way. That's why Jessop and Jake went out to Hickory."

"What in the world has Jem done to these men that they might come after him?"

Morgan shook his head. "If they do come back — and, again, there's no certainty that they will — it's the cattle that they're after, not Jem."

"Rustlers."

"We think so."

Jane did not reply. She slowly turned her cup in its saucer.

Her prolonged silence finally prompted Morgan to speak. "What is it?"

She shrugged, sighed. "I appreciate that you want to offer me the explanation I've been asking for, but I had hoped for something that might at least rub shoulders with the truth. Frankly, Jem's cow over the moon reasoning was easier to swallow."

Now it was Morgan who fell silent.

Jane said, "I'm sorry. It is just hard to believe."

"I don't know why."

"The risk, for one thing."

"Thieves aren't necessarily smart, just determined. What's the other?"

"The coincidence. As far as I can tell, you have no reason to suppose the men that fought with Jem are cattle thieves unless you know of some connection between them and the rustling happening here at Morning Star. If there is a connection, you should tell me that, because it seems incredible that they would stop bedeviling you and your men and your cattle to go into Bitter Springs and pick a fight with Jem."

Morgan sat back in his chair. "How long have you known there's been rustling here?"

"About as long as you have been trying to keep it a secret."

"Huh."

"One of the things I have not understood, other than why you thought I should not know, is why you have been so insistent that I remain indoors. That insistence has taken away my opportunity to learn to ride, to shoot, even to gather eggs and work in the garden. When it comes time to hang the laundry, there's always someone else around to do it. I went to the corral one day, just to watch you and Sophie, and you shooed me away like one of the hens. What danger do you suppose rustlers present to me that someone's always close by? They are interested in cattle. Why would they come here?"

Morgan's mouth twisted wryly. "This is just a guess, you understand, but I'm thinking what you know about rustlers you got from a book. *Nat Church and the Hanging at Harrisonville* comes to mind immediately, but I will allow that some badly researched story in one of those important New York newspapers could also account for it."

Jane pressed her lips together.

"I thought so," he said. "They're cattle thieves, Jane. Horses are cattle, too. Taking stock from the barn and corral is easier than rounding up mustangs on the range. Not only easier, but the stock is better. Our saddle horses are good animals. Put aside all your thoughts about what you think they'll take, and consider nothing else but the fact that they're thieves. They have no honor, no scruples, and no respect for what rightfully belongs to someone else."

Morgan leaned forward, set his arms on the table, and regarded Jane frankly. "For all kinds of reasons I'd rather not say out loud, I don't want them anywhere near you. Maybe trying to keep what's been going on from you was a mistake — you've proven to me that we've been pretty clumsy at it — but I did it because I thought it was the right thing to do."

Jane laid one hand over his. "I know that. I've always known that."

"Doesn't mean I won't do it again, Jane. That part about it maybe being a mistake, well, that's when I look at it sitting where you are. From where I'm sitting it still doesn't strike me that I did something wrong."

"I suppose it's a disagreement that we'll have from time to time." She squeezed his hand before she released it. "Now tell me why you think there is any possibility that Jem's fight was with the same men you've been hunting."

"Marshal Bridger said they came to town together by train with a story about looking for range work. They didn't have gear, which bothered him some. He directed them to Whistler's place, but they went to the Pennyroyal instead. That bothered him more. He didn't know about the trouble we've been having until Jem told him about it after the fight. By then, he had already sent the men on their way. Too late to do anything except maybe speculate. What the marshal got from the witnesses, and what I got from Jem, is that Jem had a bull's-eye on his back from the moment those men walked into the saloon. Miss Harrison might have encouraged it some because she can't always help herself, but those men were spoiling for a fight, and not with anyone. They wanted it with Jem."

Jane nodded slowly. "So the speculation is that they recognized him because they've seen him on Morning Star land. Is that right?"

"Yes."

"But it *is* speculation."

"If that's a question, the answer is yes. That's all it is."

Jane considered that. "Thank you." Her chair scraped the floor as she pushed back from the table. Standing, she reached for the dishes. "Now I have work to do, including laundry. With everyone else away this morning, it will be your turn to hang the wash on the line for me."

Morgan finished his coffee, watching her as she turned her back on him and faced the sink. Damn, but she had enjoyed saying that. He grinned a little then because he couldn't really blame her.

As it happened, Morgan got out of laundry line duty because of the timely arrival of Rabbit and Finn Collins. Morgan saw them when they were still a far piece from the house. It was not their first visit to Morning Star, and he recognized them by the meandering route they were taking, as if staying on what passed for the road was just not interesting enough. They were driving the old buckboard they used to deliver visitors and luggage from the station to the hotel, and it was fairly certain in his mind that they were fussing over who should be holding the reins.

Morgan made a point of intercepting them before they reached the house. He had a pretty good idea what had brought them out his way, and when they announced importantly that they were on official deputy business, he knew he was right.

"You better show me that business before we reach the house," he told them, walking alongside the wagon. "Are you carrying something for me?"

Finn pointed to his temple. "Carrying it right here, Mr. Longstreet. Marshal Bridger didn't give us anything to pass along. Put it in our heads and made us memorize it. We're pretty good at that. Rabbit here knows all the presidents up through Mr. Benjamin Harrison, and I know just about everything there is to know about General George Washington on account of Mrs. Bridger thinkin' there might be a lesson in it for me about tellin' the truth and all."

Morgan did not know why he thought

Finn could be hurried. "You're referring to the cherry tree."

"Ain't I just? It's a sorrowful tale. I figure he got a butt whuppin' for what he did, but no one wrote that part down."

"I'm sure Mrs. Bridger will want to hear your opinion on that, but I don't. Not right now." Morgan reached across Finn's lap and took the reins from Rabbit. He pulled up on them and brought the mare to a halt. "Boys? What do you have to tell me? Rabbit, you go first."

Rabbit lowered his scarf and tucked it under his chin. "Marshal says Pepper, Wilcox, and Ravenwood never did go as far as Cheyenne. He says it could have been around Westerville, but he doesn't know for certain, and he says you might want to have a look around Hickory Lake."

"Is that all?"

Finn said, "Except for the part about dropping by his office first chance you get to look at some sketches he made. I told him we'd bring them out, but he said he'd rather have you look at them there."

Morgan could think of two reasons Bridger wanted it that way. The first was to keep them out of the boys' hands; the second was so the marshal could have a look at his face while he studied the drawings. It was a good strategy, except that it wasn't going to happen.

Still holding the reins, Morgan glanced in the back of the buckboard. There were two parcels of equal size in the bed of the wagon, both wrapped in brown paper and tied with string. The similarities ended there. One of them had obviously been opened, though a serious, if clumsy, attempt had been made to rewrap it. "What else are you boys bringing out here on official deputy business?"

Rabbit said, "Marshal Bridger said we should have something to show for our trip, so he bought an apple pie out of his own pocket from Mrs. Phillips."

Morgan did not inquire about the contents of the other parcel. From the way the boys were nervously licking their lips, it was probably safe to assume that they had already helped themselves to the contents. Cookies, Morgan guessed, but he was hoping for tarts.

He handed the reins back to Rabbit. "How about coming up to the house for something to eat? Mrs. Longstreet will enjoy your company."

"That's what Marshal Bridger said, but he was kinda chucklin' out of the side of his mouth when he said it. You know what I mean?"

"I know exactly what you mean. C'mon. Let's get you up to the barn, take care of your horse, and then maybe you'll want to meet Sophie. She's the mustang I captured a while back."

There followed a rather philosophical discussion as to whether "Sophie" was the proper name for a horse, especially one that had been running the range all her life, but once the boys were properly introduced, they agreed that Mrs. Longstreet had got it right.

"We have guests," Morgan told Jane as he came through the kitchen door. "They'll be in directly. They're putting up that basket of wash you set out for me."

Wiping her hands on her apron, Jane sidled from the cookstove to the sink and looked out the window. She got there in time to see Rabbit jump up and toss one of Morgan's shirts over the clothesline. Finn was standing on the other side to catch it in case Rabbit overthrew his mark. They did not have a good strategy if the throw was short. "You are shameless," she told Morgan.

"So are they. The marshal sent them out with two parcels of baked goods. You'll be able to see right off which one they were sampling."

That made Jane laugh. "Will they stay for lunch?"

"I don't think we can get rid of them without feeding them first." He lifted his hat, ran his fingers through his hair, and reset it on his head. "Will you be all right with them for a while? I have chores in the barn to finish up."

"Of course." She put out a hand when he started to go. "Just a minute. Tell me why the marshal sent us baked goods."

Morgan shrugged. "My guess? To get Rabbit and Finn out of his hair on a Saturday morning."

"He's very clever, isn't he?"

"That's one word for it," he said, stepping outside. " 'Devious' would be another."

Jane had some time to appreciate that as the boys shared the piano bench in the front room and fingered the piano keys in every combination they could think of. First all the white keys, then all the black, then alternating, then every other. In thirty minutes, they had not happened upon a tune, and she was starting to twitch.

From the kitchen, she called to them, "Why don't you come in here, boys, and keep me company? I'm making potato cakes." She winced as the bench crashed to the floor. "Are you all right?"

"Sure thing, Mrs. Longstreet," Rabbit called back. "That was Finn."

"Was not," said Finn.

"Was."

"It doesn't matter," Jane said, raising her voice above theirs. "Pick it up and come in here." She directed them to opposite sides of the table when they slunk in.

"It's real nice of you askin' us to sit with you," said Rabbit.

"Yeah," Finn agreed. "Mostly our gran wants us out of the kitchen. Same with Mrs. Sterling when we're up at the Pennyroyal, but at least she gives us somethin' to eat when she sends us off. Granny shows us her broom." He craned his skinny neck to see what Jane was doing at the stove. "We havin' anything besides potato cakes?"

Jane turned a little sideways as she worked so she could keep an eye on the boys. "I have what's left of yesterday's roast warming in the oven. I thought you would have smelled that."

Finn sniffed the air. "I think I have apple pie in my nose."

Rabbit snickered. "That's what you're callin' your boogers now?"

Before Finn came out of his chair, Jane

put her hand down hard on the table. Except for coming to sharp, military-like attention, neither boy moved. "Good," said Jane. "I have a broom, too. I also have cookies. Think about that."

They fell quiet as Jane began shaping cold mashed potatoes into small cakes and rolled them in flour. "Do you boys generally visit the marshal on Saturday mornings?"

"Sure," said Rabbit. "After we get our chores done. Sometimes we drop by on our way home from school."

"We're pretty much deputies now," Finn said.

Jane saw his small chest puff. Only the fact that he was seated kept him from strutting. "So Marshal Bridger probably looks to you for help from time to time."

Rabbit nodded. "Sure he does. He came for us this morning. Ain't that right, Finn? He had to wait around while we finished up, but I don't think he minded much. Granny had coffee and crumb cake for him."

"I see. So Marshal Bridger must have had an important assignment for you today."

Finn sat up on his knees and leaned forward, supporting himself by the elbows. "Did he ever. Swore us in special."

"Goodness. I have to believe you brought

us the best apple pie in Wyoming. The best cookies, too."

"That's a fact," said Rabbit.

Finn nodded. " 'Course, the pie and cookies are what you call a red hair. Ain't that right, Rabbit?"

Rabbit shrugged. "Something like that. That's when Marshal Bridger was talking to Gran. I wasn't really paying no mind."

Jane asked, "Did he say red *herring,* perhaps?"

"Might'uv." Finn sniffed the air. "Butter's melted in your pan, Mrs. Longstreet. Just about ready to burn. That would be a shame."

Jane saw he was right. She quickly began adding the potato cakes. They sizzled immediately and started to brown on the edges. Picking up the turner, Jane gave her attention to her cooking.

Red herring, indeed. She had a good mind to serve Morgan from *that* kettle of fish.

Morgan knelt beside the copper tub where Jane was sitting with her knees almost tucked under her chin. The water was not quite deep enough to cover her breasts. "Bend your head," he said. When she complied, he raised a kettle of warm water and poured it over her hair while she sifted through wet strands to squeeze out the last of the soap.

"That's enough." Jane pulled her hair to one side and began wringing out the water. "May I have a towel?"

Morgan set the kettle on the floor and handed her one. He watched her deftly wrap it around her hair and make a tuck that kept it securely on her head. He picked up a second towel and held it up for her to take.

Jane shook her head. "I am not getting out of this tub while you are in here."

Tossing the towel over his shoulder, Morgan sat back on his heels. "Why not?"

"Because I am not wearing anything." She pointed to the washroom door. "Out." When he did not move, she said, "Please."

Morgan rose slowly. "I don't understand. I'm your husband."

"Please?"

"All right." He dropped the towel on a chair and backed out of the room, closing the door behind him. "I wouldn't ask you to leave." When Jane did not reply, Morgan shrugged, but he was grinning.

He got ready for bed while Jane was in the washroom and was turning back the covers when she reappeared. She had the kettle in one hand. He took it from her and pointed to the bed. Morgan recognized it as one of the few times since Finn and Rabbit left that she did not fuss at him. By the time he returned from the kitchen, Jane was in bed. She had a book open in her lap and did not look up as he crawled into bed. He lay on his back and did not try to engage her in conversation. Neither did he try to figure out what he had done wrong or what she thought he had done wrong. He could not imagine a more futile exercise in cogitation. When Jane was ready, she would tell him.

What he did instead was plan his apology. Fairly certain that one was going to be required, Morgan went through several drafts while Jane read. He also did not pretend to be sleeping when she finally closed her book and put it aside. She glanced at him before she extinguished the lamp. Morgan met her with a raised eyebrow and a question in his eyes.

Jane slid down in bed and pulled up the covers. She did not turn on her side as he did. "I would like to go to church tomorrow," she said. "I hope that will not be a problem."

Her request surprised Morgan into a longer silence.

Jane said, "I understand that you might have objections. If you do not want to accompany me, then perhaps you'll ask one of your men to do it."

"How long have you had this raspberry seed stuck in your teeth?"

"I've been thinking about it most of the day, if that's what you're asking."

"Most of the day," he repeated. "How about since Rabbit and Finn were here? Something's been different since then."

"Are you saying that because I asked you to leave before I got out of the tub? One has nothing to do with the other. I am simply —"

"Jane. No. You're modest, and mostly we're still strangers. You let me help you rinse your hair. It's a place to start, like you said from the first about sharing space. I'm talking about how prickly you've been since the boys left. Little things. Now I'm wondering if you've spent all the time that they've been gone working yourself up to telling me that you want to go to church. I thought you had more on your mind than something like that."

"I have many things on my mind. That's the one I want to talk about now. May I go to church tomorrow?"

"You can't wait until the rustlers are caught?"

"I can wait, if you insist, but it's been

nearly a month of cat and mouse, and all there is to show for it are a few missing cows and poor Jem's battered face. If I have been prickly since the boys left, it is because their visit made me long for different company than the company I usually keep. I was not expecting that. If you had asked me yesterday, I would have told you I was content. Today . . . I am not certain I can explain how I feel today."

Morgan wished he had not turned back the lamp. He wanted to see more than Jane's shadowed profile. "Last night . . ." His voice trailed off because he didn't know what he wanted to say.

"Yes," Jane said quietly. "Last night."

"You still have no regrets?"

"None." Jane turned her head toward him. "I feel more alone, Morgan. I can hardly ask you to understand something I don't understand myself. I thought if I went to church, if I talked to someone . . ." She reached for his hand. "I am where I want to be."

"Are you?"

"Yes. I mean that." She slipped her fingers through his and squeezed. "Morgan?"

"So you're not leaving me."

Jane sat up so suddenly the bed frame banged against the wall. She tore her hand out of his. "Why would you say that?" she said. "Why would you *think* it?"

He did not answer. Couldn't. He started to sit up, but Jane stopped him. She laid a hand on his shoulder and he did not resist. He figured he owed her that.

"Don't go," she whispered. "I am not letting you leave *me.*" She slid down and lay on her side against him. Drawing up a leg, she placed it over his, and then she put an arm across his chest. "Where else do you have to be but here?"

His voice, when he could push it past the constriction in his throat, was a little rough. "Nowhere, I guess."

"No guessing. Be certain." Jane raised her face and bent toward him. She kissed his cheek, the corner of his mouth. "Where else do you have to be but here?"

"Nowhere."

"That's right." She kissed him again, this time on the mouth. "Now show me why I should believe you."

CHAPTER TEN

Several times during the service, Jane caught her thoughts drifting away in a direction that hardly seemed appropriate in a house of worship. She tried to stay grounded by sitting with her spine pressed rigidly against the pew, but sometimes she could still feel Morgan's fingers walking up her back and her best efforts at attention came to nothing.

Last night, he had loved her. She had no other word for it, but the thought that it was her vocabulary that was impoverished worried her. Perhaps he would have described it differently, but then what word would he have used?

Jane spared a glance up and down the pew where she had been invited to sit. No one else seemed to be having difficulty attending to the sermon, but she could not recall any of the last three points Pastor Robbins had made. She could, however, distinctly recall every word Morgan had whispered to her in the dark, in the quiet.

"Tell me what you want, Jane." Even now she could feel his warm breath at her ear and hear the nuanced tone in his husky voice that made what he said as much a plea as a command. He made her think she could tell him anything, so she had. *You,* she had said. *I want you.*

Her confession emboldened him. His mouth dipped to the curve of her neck then. The touch of him against her skin was hot and humid. She had turned her head as he swept away her hair and surrendered herself to the maddeningly slow exploration of his lips and tongue.

He suckled at her breast and made her breath come lightly. And when his lips returned to hers, there was nothing quick about his kisses. No teasing. No nibbling. His mouth mattered. The response he drew out of her was a revelation to Jane. He taught her the fine distinction between pleasure and passion.

"Tell me what you want, Jane." And this time she answered differently. *I want to be bold,* she had said.

So he had let her. She did not have his patience, but he did not seem to mind. She wanted to know all of him at once, and so

361

her hands were as busy as her mouth, learning the planes and angles of his body with her fingers and lips, seeking those places that made his breath hitch and his heart stutter. ◆

She hesitated only once. It happened when her palm rested against the curve of his inner thigh and for several moments neither of them moved. She waited, but then so did he. It was the low, rumbling, and vaguely challenging chuckle at the back of Morgan's throat that ended her indecision. She took his cock in her hand and knew a certain satisfaction that she had also ended his laughter.

He was hot and heavy in her hand, and she could feel the pulsing of his blood against her palm. She held him too gently until he showed her how it could be different. He guided her to stroke him more deliberately, to hold him in her fist with pressure in her fingertips. He swelled, grew harder, and she wanted nothing so much as to take him inside her.

"Tell me what you want, Jane." So she did. She laid her mouth against his ear and told him in words so plain and simple she could not be misunderstood.

He rolled her onto her back and followed her with his body. He drugged her with a kiss that made her senseless to everything but his mouth on hers and the weight of him between her thighs. She knew what to do now, and it was her hand that guided him. She knew what to expect, and still she marveled in their joining. She knew how it would end, and she savored the journey.

Jane stood with the rest of the congregation for the final hymn, although she did not join the singing until halfway through the second verse. The bent of her thoughts had made her mouth curiously dry, and she had moments of apprehension that her knees might not adequately support her. Afraid that some trace of her wandering thoughts might be stamped on her face, she did not dare look around. Cobb Bridger was on her immediate left, sharing a hymnal with his wife. On her right was Mrs. Burnside, the druggist's wife, and between her and her husband were their children, all of them singing so enthusiastically that Jane was certain that her voice was not missed.

The congregation began to file out after the benediction. Jane stayed where she was. The Burnsides sidled out to the right of the long pew, but Cobb and Tru Bridger did not move. Neither did Jim and Jenny Phillips on the other side of them. Jane sensed that she was about to be engaged in conversation. She had left it to too late to follow the Burnsides.

Jane decided to take the initiative and make the first overture her own. Smiling, she addressed Marshal Bridger. "Thank you for the pie and cookies."

"So you *did* get the cookies. With Rabbit and Finn, one never knows."

"Yes. And your message also." For a moment Jane wondered if she had it all wrong, but then, because she was looking for it, she glimpsed the surprise that came and went so quickly in the marshal's eyes. Encouraged, she said, "My husband was appreciative, even grateful, but I imagine the boys told you that."

"Not in those words."

Jane realized she had spoken for Morgan in a manner he would not have spoken for himself, and Rabbit and Finn would surely have complicated anything Morgan might have said. Cobb Bridger was suspicious. She said, "No, probably not, but the fault would lie with Mr. Longstreet. He expects people to do what they're supposed to do, doesn't he?"

"Maybe," said Cobb.

His cryptic reply left Jane without a response. That was when he took over the reins of the conversation that she had been trying to hold on to. Jane felt her polite smile waver.

"Where is he?"

"At the Pennyroyal." She thought Cobb looked relieved, but she couldn't be certain or understand why he would be. She added, "He's visiting Mrs. Sterling."

Tru Bridger leaned around her husband so she could address Jane. "That means he's sampling one of everything she's preparing for Sunday dinner. He will not be hungry for your cooking."

"I hope not. It is my intention to dine at the Pennyroyal also."

"Very wise." Tru tucked a tendril of spun gold hair behind an ear and indicated the couple beside her. "You remember Jim and Jenny Phillips, don't you?"

"Yes. Yes, I do. From the reception." She held Jenny's frankly inquisitive gaze. "I understand it was your pie and cookies that I had the pleasure of receiving yesterday."

"It sounds as if you did." She had a disapproving look for Cobb. "You might have told me you intended to send them out to Morning Star, especially that you were sending them out with those rascals. I would have tied them up real pretty."

"The baked goods?" Cobb asked dryly. "Or the boys?"

Jenny snorted while her husband and Tru laughed. Even Jane found herself smiling right up until the moment she looked around and saw that the church had all but emptied.

"Excuse me," she said. It was difficult to keep the sense of urgency she felt out of her voice, but she believed she was successful. "Was Dr. Kent here this morning? I wanted most particularly to meet him."

"Not this morning," said Jenny. "He was at the Johnsons' house until the wee hours. I saw him walking home as I was getting up." She launched into an explanation of how Buster Johnson had a congestion in his lungs that was worrying his mother something terrible. Believing in the miracle of Dr. Wanamaker's liniment and rub, Abigail used two bottles of it on Buster's chest before she sent for Dr. Kent. Jenny shook her head in the sorrowful manner of one who is contemplating the foolishness of another.

Jane was grateful for Jenny's diversion. "I'd like to speak to Dr. Kent about Jem Davis's injuries before I meet Morgan. Would someone point out his home to me?" They did better than that, of course. They escorted her to the doctor's door and made certain he received her before they left.

■ ■ ■ ■

Morgan stood as soon as Jane entered the dining room. He waited while Walt helped her with her coat, scarf, and gloves, and held out a chair for her when she approached. She returned his welcoming smile, but he could tell it was forced. He remembered what she'd said last night and tried not to be overtaken by anxiety.

"I didn't eat," he said. "I was waiting for you."

Jane nodded. "Mrs. Bridger said you would sample one of everything in Mrs. Sterling's kitchen."

"Not quite."

"How is she?"

"Feisty." He showed her the knuckles of his right hand. "Quick as ever with a spoon." When Jane's smile was a mere shadow of the one he expected, Morgan abandoned any hope of gently drawing her out. "What's wrong?"

"Not now," she said quietly. "It can wait until we're home. It *should* wait."

Morgan thought he should be grateful that she had not lied to him, but her answer was not enough. "People began arriving here from church a while ago. Ted Rush said he saw you talking to the marshal after services were over."

"Yes. I was also speaking to his wife and Mr. and Mrs. Phillips. I took the opportunity to thank Marshal Bridger for his gift and compliment Mrs. Phillips's baking."

"All this time?"

"No. Afterward, I went to visit Dr. Kent. I am surprised no one told you that." Her tone sharpened infinitesimally. "Now, can you let it rest?"

Morgan thought it was just as well that Renee Harrison came rushing out of the kitchen then. She made straight for their table, thanked him for getting Jem out of jail after he was set upon by the no-account strangers, and poured coffee for him and tea for Jane. She did not linger but returned to the kitchen to get their food.

"She did not ask how he was doing," Jane said when Renee was gone.

"I suspect she already knows. I told Mrs. Sterling. Word like that gets around."

"Buster Johnson has chest congestion. And this will surprise you: Dr. Wanamaker's Miracle Liniment and Medicinal Rub was inefficacious."

For Morgan it was his first moment of real enjoyment since leaving Jane at the church. "I'll be darned," he said, and the fact that he tempered his language made her smile genuine at last.

Neither of them did justice to their meal, but Morgan made a larger dent in his chicken and dumplings than Jane, who, by some sleight of hand, was able to give the illusion of eating while leaving her food almost untouched. When he suggested that they leave, her agreement was immediate.

They spoke very little on the drive back to Morning Star. Morgan did not trust himself not to begin an interrogation, so it was easier not to initiate conversation. It seemed to him that Jane felt similarly. Restraint had made her tense. She touched her temple frequently with her fingertips and massaged the area. Sometimes she closed her eyes. Morgan wondered if she had gone to see Dr. Kent about her headaches. It had not occurred to him until now that she might have been hiding them from him. He wondered what stupid thing he had said that might make her think he wouldn't want to know.

When they arrived at the ranch, Morgan told Jessop to take care of the buckboard and followed Jane into the house. She went right past Jem at the kitchen table without speaking. So did Morgan, but he added a gesture that communicated to Jem that he should leave and not return until he was invited.

Jane was already in the washroom preparing one of her powders when Morgan got there. He hovered in the doorway just long enough to see that she took all of it, and then he stepped aside and waited for her to return to the bedroom.

He thought she might lie down, but she went to the rocking chair instead. She substituted her coat, gloves, and scarf for the quilt at the foot of the bed. The last thing she did before she sat was to remove her hat and place it on top of her scarf. Bundled in the quilt, Jane drew her legs under her.

"I want to show you something," she said. "Will you bring my trunk here? It is in the loft, remember?"

Morgan did. Without asking for an explanation, Morgan brought it down and carried it into the bedroom. He started to bring it to her, but she stopped him.

"Put it on the bed," she said. "I want you to open it. I already know what's in there."

He knew from hefting it that it was no heavier than it had been when he put it in the loft. It did not seem that Jane had added any material weight to it. He had assumed it was empty when she asked him to put it up. It didn't matter whether it was or not; he would not have looked inside without her permission. Now she was giving that to him, and he was not sure he wanted to take her up on it.

Morgan lifted the latch and raised the lid. The aromatic fragrance of cedar was strong at first, making him rear back. After a moment, he peered inside. "There's nothing in here." Indeed, he could see the bottom of the trunk. It was lined with cedar blocks that were connected in such a way as to resemble the wood pattern of a parquet floor. Morgan looked over at Jane and asked, "You must have left what you want me to see somewhere else."

"No," she said. "I didn't. Press down on the right side of the block in the bottom left corner. That will lift the left side and you will be able to remove it."

Curious, Morgan followed her instructions. The block came out with relative ease. As soon as Jane told him to press down first, not lift, he knew the blocks were a cover for some space beneath them. "How many do I need to take out?"

"Only a third of them can be removed. I think you will see what I put there after you take out —" She stopped because Morgan had gone into the trunk with both hands and was already bringing out the envelope she had secreted away before she left New York. "Go on. Open it."

Morgan slid his index finger under the flap and lifted it. He knew before he looked what he would find. "There's money here."

She nodded. "One hundred twenty-seven dollars. I came with one hundred thirty-one."

"You told me you had money. I had no idea it was this much."

"It should have been more. I had thought I would leave New York with two hundred fifty dollars. I had some money saved from things I made and sold, or things I just sold. Most of it is accounted for there."

"What happened to the rest?"

"It was used to pay the abortionist."

Morgan said nothing. He closed the lid on the trunk and set it on the floor. He was still holding the envelope in one hand when he sat on the edge of the bed and angled himself so he could see Jane. Beyond the window at her back, the sky was turning gray. Morgan had seen signs that morning that made him think snow was coming soon. If it did, it would be the first since Jane's arrival, and he found that he was not minding the prospect of it all that much. Now, watching the cold gray light leach the color from Jane's face, he was not as certain.

He slid his thumb and index finger across the edge of the envelope and raised his eyebrows a fraction. "There's probably something you want to explain about that."

Jane put three fingers to her temple again and closed her eyes while she nodded slowly. Returning her hand to her lap, she opened her eyes and settled her gaze on Morgan. "You were kind to take me to town this morning, and I want you to know that I appreciate it. I realize you had reason to be reluctant to make the trip, but you did it anyway. For me."

Morgan merely returned Jane's regard. His features were grave while hers were almost without expression.

"It was not a fabrication that I wanted to go to church," she said. "But it was an excuse. I needed to go to Bitter Springs in order to speak to Dr. Kent. I wanted him to —" She stopped, considered her words. "I wanted him to examine me."

Morgan was tapping one corner of the envelope against his knee. When Jane's gaze flitted there, he realized what he was doing and stopped. He offered no comment about this last admission. He said, "Go on."

"I want you to understand that no one except Dr. Kent knows the reason for my visit. I asked for directions after church, and the Bridgers and Mr. and Mrs. Phillips escorted me there." She paused when Morgan swore softly. "I told them I wanted to talk to the doctor about Jem. They thought nothing of it, and it was true as far as it went."

"I don't know, Jane," said Morgan. "I'm beginning to think that with you the truth sprints about as far as the barn and the lie walks on forever."

"That is unfair," she said quietly. "And hypocritical."

The scar at the corner of Morgan's mouth whitened as he set his lips together. His narrow smile was sardonic, and his eyes gave no quarter. He was admitting nothing.

Jane went on. "I've told you things here and there about my cousin Alexander. Of all the Ewings, he was the one who made me feel most like a member of the family, and I consider him as I imagine I would a brother if I had one. There is affection and love of a platonic nature, not a romantic one."

Morgan shifted his weight on the bed. "Do I need to know this?"

Jane exhaled slowly. "Yes. And if you decide later that you did not need to know, then you will forgive me because I have a need to tell you." She regarded him now from under raised eyebrows. "Alex loved nothing so much as a scheme, and to his way of thinking, the finest schemes were the ones that involved pulling the wool over his mother's eyes. It is also true that Alex was often in want of money. Even after he began working in the law firm his father founded, Cousin Frances gave him an allowance. No amount would have been enough. He invariably owed more than he had."

"Gambling?"

"Yes. That accounted for most of his debt. Women accounted for the rest. Alex was everyone's favorite."

"Of course," Morgan said dryly.

Jane ignored that. "On one of the occasions that he was feeling desperate for funds, he told Cousin Frances that some female of little means and no social standing was going to bear his child. He went to his mother, declared his transgression, and explained that, naturally, he would do the honorable thing by the young woman. He would marry her."

"It is hard not to be impressed by your cousin's cleverness."

"Yes, well, Alex certainly was impressed with himself. He correctly anticipated his mother's reaction. She counseled him against marriage — forbade it, in fact — and told him she would have no more bastards in the family. A reference to my existence, I suppose. If she said it as Alex reported it to me, then it was one of the few times she acknowledged that I *was* family." Examining her hands, Jane sighed. "I am sorry. That is just a footnote. As I'm sure you realize now, Cousin Frances settled money on Alex to take care of his indiscretion. Alex accepted the money and used it to pay his debt. There was no young woman, or at least not one who was carrying his child. In any event, Cousin Frances never meant for Alex to use the money to pay for the woman's silence. She intended for him to make arrangements with an abortionist."

Morgan nodded. He had an idea now where Jane's story was going, but the ending eluded him. His eyes fell to her mouth. She was biting down hard on her lower lip and when she released it, he saw the only trace of color in her face was a droplet of blood. He rose, went around the bed, and handed her a handkerchief from his pocket. "Your lip," he said. "It's bleeding."

Jane grimaced slightly as she pressed her lips together. She accepted Morgan's handkerchief and touched one corner of it to her mouth. "Thank you."

Morgan sat down again, this time on the side of the bed closest to Jane. "When you're ready."

She swept her lower lip with the tip of her tongue before crumpling the handkerchief in her fist. She tested it a second time before she spoke. "Alex was so encouraged by his success with this particular scheme that he did it two more times before he approached me. His motives were not entirely self-serving. He knew that I was in correspondence with you, and I had already told him I wanted to have my own money before I set out." She held up two fingers when Morgan would have interrupted. "Yes, you wrote that you would send money for my ticket and expenses, but when Alex first approached me it had not yet arrived. I was never concerned that it would not, but it further impressed upon me the need to be independent of whatever you could give. And there was always the thought at the back of my mind that you would change your mind once I was here, or that I would change mine. I told you that when we talked about why I had money."

"We didn't talk about *how* you had money."

"No. I hoped I never would have to tell you." She offered up a self-deprecating smile. "A lie of omission, perhaps, but one I wish was still walking away."

The truth sprints about as far as the barn and the lie walks on forever. For both of the reasons Jane had mentioned, Morgan regretted saying those words aloud. Even thinking them was unfair and hypocritical. "I shouldn't have said that to you."

"No," she said. "You shouldn't have, but it's done now, and the lie stops walking here. I agreed to be part of Alex's scheme to take money from his mother. He believed, rightly as it turned out, that if she thought I was going to be the mother of his child, she would not only pay for the abortion, she would want to buy my silence." Almost as an afterthought, she said, "You understand there was no child."

"I understand." ❖

She released the short breath she was holding. "What Alex did not anticipate was that his mother would handle some of the details herself. She gave the money to David, Alex's older brother, and told him to make the arrangements. When Alex realized what was happening, he tried to intervene. David would not give him the money. He did allow Alex to accompany me to the abortionist, a woman of David's choosing. Alex had no such person to call upon anyway, since every part of his scheming was a fabrication. I did not want to go through the charade, and a charade is all I thought it would be. Alex, though, is quite convincing in his neediness, and I console myself with the knowledge that I am not the only woman who has ignored her better judgment in the face of Alex's pleading.

"David took Alex and me to a brownstone in Brooklyn where none of us were known. They waited in a front room, drinking absinthe and smoking cigars, while I was escorted upstairs. I had prepared a speech to explain the circumstances of my being there, but I never had a chance to say it aloud. I became aware of another person in the room when he pressed a rag soaked with chloroform against my mouth and nose. I clawed at him. I heard him grunt, and I had to be satisfied with that. There is nothing else to remember about my visit. I woke up in the carriage. Alex had his arm around me, and he was shouting at David. I do not recall what Alex said to his brother, but David's reply still resonates. He said I got precisely what I deserved, and the next time Alex thought about marrying one of his whores, he should elope instead of announcing his intentions to their mother first."

Jane's knuckles were bloodless around the handkerchief in her fist. "I don't think either one of them knew that I was awake or whether it would have mattered if they did. Alex attacked David. They exchanged blows, fended more off, and finally stopped when the carriage slowed. They thought they had arrived home, but it was only the driver trying to negotiate bridge traffic. Neither of them looked as bad as Jem did after he was attacked, but David had the worst of it. He did not get out of the carriage when his driver came abreast of the house. Alex helped me up the front stairs on his own. I was not steady, but I could walk. By the time we reached the door, I knew I was bleeding." •

Jane rocked her chair forward and extended her hand to Morgan. She dropped the handkerchief into his open palm. She found it peculiar that her eyes were dry. There were so many moments since leaving Dr. Kent's that she thought she might cry, and yet she hadn't, and she didn't now. She was very cold, though, and what she wanted to do most of all was to go to sleep.

"I was ill with a fever for a few days. Cousin Frances would not permit Alex to send for a doctor. I do not believe she prayed for my death, but it would not have been unwelcome." Bitter laughter bubbled under Jane's breath. "I had my revenge. I survived. It is quite possible that she would have given me any amount of money to never mention what had transpired, but I did not ask her for any. Alex found the money to pay his debt from some other source, his sister perhaps, or maybe from the law firm. I did not want to know if it was stolen, so I did not ask when he gave me one hundred dollars. It was less than he had promised when he first approached me, but I took it and held out no hope that there would be more. I left soon afterward. I am not sure that even Alex was sorry to see the last of me."

Jane unfolded in the rocker and set her feet on the floor. "Until I visited Dr. Kent today, I did not know what had been done to me, and I will never know if Cousin Frances sent me to that awful woman because she truly believed I was carrying her bastard grandchild or because she finally uncovered Alex's scheming and meant to punish me for my part in it. I will also never know if the abortionist was so unskilled at her work that she could not tell that I had no child in me, or if she was instructed to make certain I never bore one.

"Dr. Kent knows virtually none of the

particulars. I did not want to unburden myself to him. He knows what he saw when I asked him to examine me. He says that I should not hold out hope that I will be able to give you a child."

Morgan did not look away from her ashen features. He ached for her. He did not know what he felt for himself beyond relief that she was not dying. That was the fear that had set up in his belly since she met him at the Pennyroyal, the one that he could not name or consider until now.

He held out his hand, palm up.

Jane looked at it, looked at him, and shook her head. "I can't," she said. "I think I might break if I touch you now."

Nodding, he withdrew it. "You made certain we had a conversation about children before we married. Do you remember that?"

"Yes."

"I married you, Jane. You gave me something to think about, and I still married you."

"But you said you wanted children."

"I know what I said, and before that, right out of the gate, I told you I didn't *expect* them exactly. I thought it would happen natural. And that means sometimes things don't happen." His hands curled into fists.

"I reckon there is not a Ewing in New York City I don't want to take a swing at about now, starting with the one you think of as a brother. He'd be a sight less appealing to the ladies with his nose shifted thirty degrees sideways. Your cousin Frances deserves the same, but since her nose is already so far out of joint that it creaks when she sniffs, I'd have to pop her in the mouth. Just a quick jab so she whistles when she speaks."

Now it was Jane who stared at Morgan. Her eyes had widened fractionally. Her bottom lip was trembling.

Morgan said, "I could tear a strip off just about anyone who looked at me crossways right now, but it's not because I'm angry with you. That's what you need to know, Jane. I don't know what I'm supposed to do with what's inside me except hold on to you, and since you won't —"

Jane threw off the blanket and stood. "No, I'm good now. I want you to hold me. I *do.*"

Morgan was on his feet before she finished speaking. He opened his arms and Jane walked into his embrace. She laid her cheek against his shoulder, and he laid his cheek against her hair. His hands rested at the small of her back; hers were clutching his shirt.

In the beginning, she wept silently. Morgan only knew it because he felt her tears making a damp imprint on his shirt. She did not see the wetness in his eyes. He blinked it away when he felt her first shudder. It was followed quickly by great, wracking sobs that she could not muffle even when she pressed a fist against her mouth.

He held her tightly, and she held on. She didn't break. She grieved. Morgan grieved with her, for her, and finally, for himself. He knew that because there came a time when he was aware that her sobs had quieted and that he was standing in the circle of her arms. Neither of them stirred for a long time. There was comfort in their mutual embrace, warmth, and a sense of rightness.

Over the crown of her head, Morgan saw snowflakes drifting and dancing past the windowpane. He lifted his chin and cupped her elbows in his palms. "Look," he said, and turned her until her view was the same as his. "There will be an inch in an hour and six inches by morning if it doesn't blow too hard. Everything will look different."

Jane drew Morgan's hands forward and placed them against her midriff, just under her breasts. She placed her hands on top of his and held them there. "People say that spring is renewal. I suppose that's true, but

I have always liked winter's white blanket."

Morgan smiled. "It *is* beautiful."

"I know I might be longing for spring come February, but for now . . ."

"For now. For now it is exactly right."

Nodding, Jane breathed in deeply.

A moment later, Morgan did the same. The air that filled his lungs seemed clearer. "What do you want to do, Jane?"

She did not answer immediately. "I want to sleep," she said at last. "And I do not want to be alone. Will you lie with me?"

And so he did.

Gideon Welling took off his gloves, dropped them on the ground, and warmed his hands at the fire. After a moment, he hunkered in front of it to let the warmth bathe his face. Ice crystals attached to strands of his thick brown mustache began to melt. He licked his lips.

Marcellus Cooley sat similarly hunkered on the opposite side of the fire. He had his hands out, but unlike Gideon, he was still wearing his gloves. Smoke wafted in his direction. He squinted, turned his head a little to the side. The scar that cut jaggedly through his salt-and-pepper beard from cheek to chin was starkly visible in the firelight. No one took notice of it.

Avery Butterfield reached for the coffeepot, poured himself a cup, and then held it up for other takers. When there were none, he returned it to the grate. He lifted the tin cup to his mouth but didn't drink. He sniffed instead. The heady aroma filled his lungs and expanded the breadth of his barrel chest.

Dixon Evers rolled a matchstick from one side of his mouth to the other as he contemplated whether it was worth the effort to pick up the coffeepot now that Avery had put it back. Probably not, was his determination, so he sucked on the matchstick and scratched the underside of his narrow, beardless chin from time to time.

The fire crackled. An ember popped. No one spoke. They were bone tired from the chase and cold to their marrow. Their horses snuffled nearby, nosing around in the snow for patches of grass. In its own way, the silence was wearing. Only one of them had a plan, and he was keeping it to himself for the time being. Asking for it was, well, *asking* for it, and a fight was probably going to get someone killed. It had happened before. They used to number five, but Cotton Branch was gone now, dropped where he stood because he asked one too many questions. And therein lay the conundrum.

There was no way to identify the question that would be one too many. It was better to ask none at all.

Gideon picked up his wet gloves and placed them closer to the fire. "Did I ever tell you about the time Morgan yanked Jackson's ass out of the pond when he fell through the ice? Mine, too." When they all shook their heads, he went on. "I guess Jack was about twelve. I was fourteen. Morgan must have been nine. Skinny as a rail. Morgan, not Jack. Jack was a chubby one back then. All belly and chins. He dared Morgan to cross the pond out back of our place. Jack figured he wouldn't know where the thin parts were in the ice. Jack was like that. Always thinking about an advantage. It was late March, so there were only a couple of paths across the pond where the ice was thick enough to step."

Gideon held out his hand to Avery and flexed his fingers. Without a word, Avery passed over his coffee cup. "Obliged," Gideon said. The coffee was now the proper temperature to drink, and he did. "Morgan didn't want to do it. Jack and I could see that. I thought that would be the end of it, but Jack kept needling him, calling him names until he found one that stuck in Morgan's craw. Probably something to do with his hair. Carrot stick. Ginger pie. Match head. That sort of thing. Morgan was as touchy as a girl about it back then.

"So Morgan marches his skinny self across that pond and steps wherever he damn well pleases, and when he's safely on the other side, he drops his pants, opens the back door on his union suit, and waggles his bony white ass at Jack. There was no holding Jack back then. I grabbed the collar of his coat, but he wriggled out, and all I had was his coat as he started off.

"He picked his way real careful-like, especially when he got to the middle, but I could tell he wasn't going to make it. I started slitherin' out after him before the ice collapsed and he went under. Crawled on my belly like a snake to the hole, threw out his coat, which I was happy to have now, and tried to pull him out. 'Course, the ice kept cracking and I kept slithering, and I more or less dragged him through the cracks until we reached the other side. I thought Morgan would have run scared by then, but it was the damnedest thing, he was waiting there dangling his pants for me to take. I grabbed ahold of them, Jack had ahold of me, and Morgan pulled. I never would have guessed he was so strong or that I would be so cold."

Gideon's eyes moved from man to man, examining each face. "I reckon I ain't been that cold again until one of you told me it was safe to cross my horse at the Hickory Creek narrows and the other two agreed. I'm still trying to figure out how you came to that conclusion when none of you ever done the same."

He was met with silence.

"Well, here's what I'm thinking. Marcie, you give me your coat. Avery, your boots look to be about the same size as mine. I'll take those and your socks. Dix, I'd be grateful for your gloves and trousers. You fellas can wear my things or not, but my opinion is that it's better if you just set them out near the fire. Have a care nothing scorches, else you won't be getting your things back."

As one, Marcie, Avery, and Dix stood and began to strip. Gideon only got to his feet when he had an armful of clothes. He changed out his trousers, socks, and boots and handed his wet things over. He huddled in Marcie's coat before he put on dry boots and gloves.

He sat down and resumed drinking his coffee while his men dealt with his damp garments. He was smiling genially beneath his mustache when they rejoined him. "Nothing like a story to take you back and put you in the present at the same time. I don't mind saying that I miss Jack, but missing him doesn't change the fact that he didn't always have the best judgment. He should've known the ice wouldn't hold him, just like he should've known not to deal from the bottom of the deck when there's a professional gambler at the table. Worse, you don't keep your gun strapped in your holster. Takes way too long to draw."

Gideon sighed heavily. "But that was Jackson. Always on thin ice. I blame prison some. There's no way around the fact that it changed him. Changed me, too, I expect. You?"

Although he directed his question to no one in particular, they all nodded.

"I figured," he said. "Reckon it changed Morgan, although there's no telling exactly how. Might've made him softer. Maybe harder. Guess we'll be finding that out."

Dixon pulled the matchstick out of his mouth and rolled it between his thumb and forefinger. "You reckon he knows it's us?"

"I reckon he knows it's *me*," said Gideon. "I wasn't aware you ever met Morgan."

"I ain't."

"Well, then. There's your answer. He probably thinks Jack's with me. I don't expect he ever heard that Jack took a bullet eight days out of prison. No reason that he should have, seeing as how Morgan was out three years earlier. He's got the good sense to know by now we aren't just any rustlers, and after you boys roughed up one of his the other night, I figure he has an idea that we number about five or six. Better he thinks that than realize there's only four."

"How's that?" Marcie asked cautiously, knuckling his scar.

"It'll make him cautious, sure, but when we show up at his house, he'll think we have more men watching. Gives us an advantage."

"So we're going in," said Dix. "Don't mind sayin' it'll be a fine thing to get out of this cold."

Gideon chuckled. "Your balls about the size of raisins, Dix? That's not going to change tonight. Not tomorrow either. I'm of a mind to lie low, stay off Morning Star land for a spell. The snow will make us too easy to track, and it can't hurt for Morgan to wonder what's become of us."

"So we're goin' to hole up in the hills," said Dix.

"For a time," said Gideon, "then we're going to Rawlins. Get rooms. Get women. Get warm. And we'll come back when Morgan thinks we won't. Now that I know where he is, I can see that he's not going anywhere. I don't mind saying that there's sweetness in the anticipation of talking to him again. I know it's not the same for you, but you haven't gone wrong by trusting me so far. You got a look around town the other night, got a feel for the layout. Morgan's got a fine hand with a safe, and I'm thinking there's one in the Cattlemen's Trust that he could crack like an eggshell. He owes me, and he knows it."

Gideon's gaze made the circle again. "You're going to benefit from that, gentlemen. Just see if you don't."

Morgan was met with the straw end of Jane's new broom as soon as he opened up the back door. Snow swirled in eddies around him. He shivered in spite of a turned-up collar and a woolen scarf that covered the lower half of his face.

"Stamp your feet," Jane told him. "Hard. Don't track snow on my clean floor."

"Yes, ma'am." Behind his scarf he was grinning. Only four weeks had passed since the first snowfall, and Jane's view of winter's white blanket had changed somewhat. She still enjoyed it from behind a windowpane, but she had no appreciation for it when it came in on a pair of boots. Morgan dutifully stamped his feet.

Jane looked him over before she raised her broom like a tollgate and let him pass. "I thought you were going to ride out with Max. Did something happen?"

"No." He unwound his scarf but let the tails hang over his shoulders. "Max said he could handle it. Truth is, sometimes he just likes his own company. Jem, Jake, and Jessop are fanning out past Settler's Ridge to make sure the cattle have water." He took the broom from her hands. "Come outside with me."

"Morgan, I am in the middle of baking bread."

He glanced at the green-and-white-striped towel covering a bowl on the table. The towel was still noticeably concave. "Dough hasn't started to rise. Come on. I want to show you something."

Jane did not offer a second objection. Even though there had been no sign of the rustlers in weeks, it was not often that Morgan invited her outside. She had resumed some chores that took her past the lip of the back porch and into the weather, but she rarely went as far as the barn, especially if she was unaccompanied.

Morgan waited in the kitchen while Jane collected her coat, gloves, and scarf. There was a pair of black leather riding boots secreted away in the barn loft that he intended to give her for Christmas. It was tempting to present them to her early when he saw what she was wearing on her feet. The dainty calf boots with the pointed patent toes were good for digging up dandelions, he supposed, but not much else. They looked pretty enough, though, and that was as good a reason to wear them as any.

He took the red woolen scarf from her hand and wound it over her dark hair and loosely around her throat. A few wayward strands of hair required tucking under the scarf, and her mouth required kissing before he covered it. She used the pointed patent caps on her shoes to gently prod him. •

When they stepped outside, Morgan took her gloved hand in his. They walked that way to the barn. He only dropped her hand when they reached Sophie's stall.

"She's saddled," said Jane. "When did you —" She put up the flat of her hand for Sophie to nuzzle and spoke to the mare. "So he gentled you after all, didn't he? Sweet Sophie. How pretty you are. Have you let him on your back?" She looked askance at Morgan. "Where are the apples?"

Morgan got one for her and cut it into quarters that he gave to Jane one at a time.

Jane laughed as Sophie took each slice from her palm with the refined manners of a New York debutante. "She's so polite, Morgan. Is that your doing?"

"She's showing off for you. She snorts and roots like a piglet when I put something in front of her."

"Well, I think she is a lady."

"Good. She's your lady."

"Have you —" Jane turned her head sharply to look at Morgan, and Sophie used that moment's inattention to butt her temple. Jane pushed Sophie's nose back. "My lady? What does that mean?"

"It means Sophie is yours."

Jane stared at him. "Mine? Do you mean it?"

"Yes. She's always been yours. Maybe that's why you knew her name."

Jane put her hands on Morgan's shoulders, stood on tiptoes, and kissed him full on the mouth. "It still amuses you that I knew her name, but I don't mind." She kissed him again before she dropped back on her heels. "When will I be able to ride her?"

"I brought you out here to have a lesson."

"Really? Will she take me as a rider?"

"She will. We've all been on her." He pointed to the barn's back door. "Everyone took her out through there so there was no chance that you would see. I wasn't sure they could keep the secret much longer. Jem was near to bursting with it at breakfast."

"I have never had so fine a present at Christmas."

"She's a wedding gift. I meant what I said, Jane. She's always been yours. I cut her from the herd for you." Morgan saw the sparkle in Jane's emerald eyes fade ever so slightly. He shook his head as if he could stop the direction of her thoughts. "For you," he said again. "For my wife. Forget Rebecca. Sophie would dislike her as much as I do."

Jane only offered a mild challenge. "You do not know that."

"I do. They share the same features, and Sophie wears them better."

Jane blinked. "What?"

Morgan tapped Jane's chin and pointed her to Sophie. "Look at her. Long nose. Flaring nostrils. Muscled cheeks. Strong neck. Broad shoulders. She's a beautiful animal."

"I don't understand. You think Rebecca looks like Sophie?"

"Don't you?"

Jane stared at Sophie. In her mind's eye she overlaid it with Rebecca's bold features.

She saw her cousin's face in a new light, one that did not flatter Rebecca in the least. Jane put her hand to her mouth as her lips parted. "No wonder you thought she could pull a plow."

Morgan chuckled. "I never said that. You're the one who mentioned plowing. I said I wanted a strong wife." He nudged her chin back in his direction. "And I got what I wanted. And she's beautiful, too."

Jane batted his hand away and shook her head. "Don't."

"Why can't I say it? It's true."

"You don't go into town enough. It's easy to forget what a pretty woman looks like."

"I never said you were pretty. Well, maybe I did, but I didn't mean it. I just couldn't say the other." He shrugged a little diffidently. "About you being beautiful and all, I'm saying. Partly I kept my tongue in my head because it hurts a mite to look on you that way, like there's a radiant light coming from you that could blind me if I stare too long. Mostly, though, I didn't say anything because you wouldn't believe me. I thought maybe that had passed some, but I guess not. That family of yours sure did twist the way you see yourself. The reasons I want to take a swing at them just keep piling up."

Jane searched his face. She said quietly, "I

never know what you are going to say, Morgan Longstreet."

"Is that good?"

"I don't know about good, but it keeps me on my toes." She came up on them again and kissed him. It would have been easy for her to allow it to linger, but she kept it short and full of promise. "Now, about that riding lesson."

CHAPTER ELEVEN

A brief respite from falling snow in January gave Jane the opportunity to visit Bitter Springs. She was confident enough of her riding skills by then to suggest that she take Sophie and go alone, at which point Morgan looked at her as if she'd sprouted a third eye. He did not argue about the trip, but he insisted on using the buckboard and accompanying her. She thanked him, acknowledging his superior judgment in these matters, and immediately returned to working on her list. Morgan knew he had been had. Oddly enough, he wasn't so sure that he minded it.

Morgan hung back at the entrance of the Cattlemen's Trust and let Jane go up to the teller's cage on her own. He stood with his hands behind his back, occasionally rocking forward on the balls of his feet as he looked around. He was an infrequent visitor to the bank, conducting most of his business when he and his men drove cattle to town to be taken up by the railroad.

Nothing had changed at the bank since his last visit. There were two teller cages, but as usual, only one of them was occupied. Morgan did not recall the man's name. Hall? Hollis? He was a quiet sort and kept transactions brief. He did not allow people to linger at his station, which Morgan thought was wise on his part. Familiarity and chitchat were proven ways to lower a man's guard. Morgan knew precisely how that worked.

The door to the manager's office was open wide enough for Morgan to see Mr. Webb hunched over his desk. To his right, the safe's door was also ajar. Morgan had been in the bank often enough to know it was a practice, not an oversight. Sometime during his long tenure as the manager of the Cattlemen's Trust Bank, Mr. Webb had become complacent.

The safe was a black 1884 Barkley and Benjamin pin and tumbler model with a four-inch steel door and two-inch steel lining. It was impressively large, standing four feet tall and thirty-two inches deep and wide. Empty, it weighed 536 pounds. It was sold with the Barkley and Benjamin name painted in gold leaf on the door. Most banks

added their name. That was true of Cattlemen's Trust, although Mr. Webb had turned
away from the elaborate flourishes used by
Barkley and Benjamin and had chosen plain
block letters instead. He did, however, elect
to use gold leaf.

Morgan's gaze moved on as Mr. Webb
straightened and sat back in his chair. There
was no eye contact, which was the way Morgan wanted it.

The lobby was wide and uncluttered. The
hardwood floors were polished. There was a
table close to the large window that was
mostly used by customers as a place to set
their parcels. Sometimes people sat there to
read and sign papers or study their savings
books, but no one was using it today. On
the opposite side of the bank, Evelyn Stillwell, the barber's wife, was engaged in
animated conversation with Heather Collins, grandmother to Rabbit and Finn. Morgan made it a point not to eavesdrop. He
had never known anything good to come of
it.

"Mornin'," Cobb Bridger said, tipping his
hat to the women as he came through the
door. They stopped speaking long enough
to acknowledge him, then immediately
reengaged in their discussion. Instead of
heading for the teller's cage, he stepped

sideways and joined Morgan. "It must be important, whatever they're talking about. I think it's the first time they haven't asked after Tru. Her condition generally provokes a ten-minute interrogation."

"Umeh."

"Yeah, that's so." He lifted his chin in Jane's direction. "Your wife hasn't been to town for a while."

"That's right."

"Tru was asking after her, wondering if she shouldn't invite both of you to Sunday dinner sometime."

"You discouraged her, I hope."

Cobb's smile hinted at his amusement. "You don't really know my wife, do you?" When Morgan said nothing, Cobb did not press. "I understand you never did run those rustlers to ground."

"No. Never did."

"Last time Jessop was in, he told me there hasn't been any trouble for a while."

"You can trust what Jessop says."

"I do. I'm wondering what you think about it. Is it over, or is it a lull?"

"I couldn't rightly say." Morgan's gaze bored holes into the back of Jane's poppy-trimmed velvet hat, willing her to turn around. Thus far, it had not worked.

"So you're sticking to your story that

they're just rustlers."

"It's like this, Marshal. I *know* they're rustlers. Whether they're something else is still a question, and we've been over it before. Let it be."

Cobb exhaled softly. There was a hint of impatience in the sound. "You damn well know you're not making it easy to do that. You've never come by to look at the sketches I made of those three men."

"No, I never did. It's hard for me to imagine that any of those three would be Jack or Gideon. They'd stay behind, send others to do the scouting."

"That occurred to me," Cobb said. "I noticed you and Mrs. Longstreet came alone. You weren't moving any cattle today."

"My wife is only learning to ride. She's not up to herding cows."

"Funny."

Morgan shrugged.

"I mention it because your visits to the bank generally coincide with a cattle drive. I figure you make a deposit and take care of your payroll."

"You have to find something else to do with your time, Bridger."

"Did I tell you I was studying law?"

"Something *else.*"

Cobb's grin appeared, but it was faint and

fleeting. "Tell me why you're here."

"Finally," said Morgan. "Never thought you'd get done beating around that bush. Trade places with me."

"What?"

Morgan crooked his finger at Cobb and then pointed to the space he was occupying. "Trade places." He stepped aside, waited for Cobb to slide sideways, then stepped into Cobb's footprints. "Look around."

Cobb did. "And?"

"Well, from where you're standing now, you should be able to see that Mr. Webb's sitting next to an open Barkley and Benjamin safe. That makes the pin and tumbler lock, the four-inch steel door, the two-inch steel lining, and all five hundred thirty-six pounds pretty much just for show. So what I'm doing here besides waiting for my wife to open her own account with this fine institution is resisting the powerful temptation to stuff Mr. Webb in his Barkley and Benjamin and tell my wife she's better off keeping her money in a trunk."

"Huh. Maybe I should have a talk with Mr. Webb."

"Maybe you should. And while you're at it, keep an eye on Mrs. Stillwell and Mrs. Collins. I think they've seen the open safe.

They didn't have the time of day for you because they're plotting."

"Are you done?"

Morgan pretended to give the question full consideration. "Yeah. Guess I am."

"All right. Here it is: I've got no problem with you yanking my chain as long as that's all it is. If this business with your rustlers turns out to be something more, then I expect you to get real serious, real fast."

"Sure, Marshal."

"I mean it, Longstreet. If you were here, say, because someone was putting you up to it, then I'd want to know."

Morgan turned to look at the marshal. "I suppose I should be grateful that you're acquitting me of planning a robbery on my own."

"That's what I've been trying to tell you."

Morgan glanced in Jane's direction. She was beginning to gather her things at the cage. "Look, Bridger, if it'll ease your mind some and keep you from following me around like a calf after his mama's teat every time I come to town, then I promise that I'll let you know if something's happened that concerns you and Bitter Springs."

Cobb thought about that. "I have your word?"

"You do."

"Good." He put out his hand.

Morgan hesitated, then he also extended his hand, and they shook.

Cobb said, "Just so you know, I didn't care much for the calf and his mama's teat analogy."

Morgan grinned. "Puts a picture in your head, doesn't it?"

Jane came upon them. "Hello, Marshal." Then to Morgan, "Do I want to know about this picture?"

"Probably not."

She smiled and held up her savings book. "All done. Mr. Hollerman was very helpful."

Hollerman. Morgan held up his index finger as he made a mental note of the name. Not Hall. Not Hollis. "I never knew a bank teller who wasn't happy to take your money. It's when you try to get it out of the bank that they're mean as snakes."

Cobb looked sideways at Morgan. "Your husband's right, Mrs. Longstreet." He tipped his hat. "I have some business with Mr. Webb. Good to see you both again."

Jane opened her reticule and put her savings book inside. "Is everything all right?"

Morgan held out an elbow for her to take. "Everything's fine. Why do you ask?"

"I suppose because he's the marshal, and

you told me once that he was not your friend."

Morgan looked back over his shoulder as he held the door open for Jane. Cobb was walking into Webb's office. Morgan did not envy the banker for the earful he was going to get. "He's not so bad."

"He's not so bad," Jane repeated. "High praise indeed."

Morgan shrugged. "I figure it's what he says to his wife about me."

Ida Mae Sterling placed a plate of almond cookies in front of Jane and invited her to eat. "I've had two more than my fill," she said, sitting down at the table. "And if you don't mind my saying so, you could eat the cookies *and* the plate and none of it would show on your waistline. How tight are you pulling your corset?"

Self-conscious, Jane pressed her palms against her midriff. Even though she was alone with Mrs. Sterling in the hotel's dining room, she only whispered her response. "I am not wearing a corset. I haven't for weeks and weeks."

Mrs. Sterling's wiry salt-and-pepper eyebrows lifted toward her widow's peak. "No corset? Well, then, that's cause to think about this differently." She poured another dollop of sweet cream into Jane's tea. "You need to start eating more of what you're feeding those men. Lord, Jane, but you can slip through cracks where a shadow couldn't go. Morgan looks fit, and I've seen the Davis boys and Max Salter around and about. I can't say they're missing any meals. Are you?"

"No. I'm fine. Really, I am."

Mrs. Sterling continued to regard her suspiciously. "I've known some women who lose weight at first . . . you'd tell me if you were going to have a baby, wouldn't you?"

The question startled Jane into silence. She simply stared at Mrs. Sterling.

"Clearly, I've overstepped. I shouldn't carry on as if I've known you all my life. It's a fault of mine." Mrs. Sterling picked up her teacup and raised it to her lips. Before she drank, she said, "It's on account of Morgan that I take liberties with you."

Jane found her voice. "What accounts for it with everyone else?"

Mrs. Sterling managed to swallow her tea but not without effort. Her small, choking sounds prompted Jane to pat her lightly on the back. She held up a hand and nodded to indicate that she was all right. After she set her cup back in the saucer, she dropped her spectacles to the tip of her nose and dabbed at her eyes with one corner of her apron. "Goodness, but that was unexpected, and dare I say, welcome?"

"Welcome?"

"I wouldn't want you to make a habit of taking me to task, but I confess to worrying about how well you'd do out at Morning Star with Morgan and the boys. Now I'm thinking you don't let them ride roughshod over you."

"Some days are more challenging than others."

"I'm sure. What's this trouble you were having a while back?"

"Trouble? What did you hear?"

"Rustlers."

Jane felt a measure of relief that Mrs. Sterling was not asking about something more personal. "Yes, they showed up just after I arrived at Morning Star, but when the snow began to fly, they disappeared. Morgan does not have enough men to be everywhere at once."

"I don't know a rancher who does, and I don't see that changing anytime soon what with the price of beef falling like it's been pushed over a cliff."

"I am learning to ride. Morgan gave me a beautiful mustang. I am hopeful that in time I will be able to help."

"Ride out, you mean?"

"If that's helping, yes."

Ida Mae Sterling bent her head and regarded Jane over the rim of her spectacles. "Have you mentioned this to Morgan?"

"No."

"Well, I hope you'll let me know how that turns out when you do."

"Morgan is teaching me to shoot."

"That so? I expect he has his reasons. Benton wouldn't let me near a gun. Never did set well with me, but I really had no cause to learn to use one here in town."

"I'm glad you mentioned your husband. Morgan's told me that he admired him but precious little beyond that. How did they know each other?"

"Early on, my husband traveled some in the course of his work. I think it was on one of his visits to Lander — that's up in Fremont County — that he and Morgan crossed paths. You would have to ask Morgan for the particulars. I don't recollect what they were. I'm not sure I ever knew them."

"Was Morgan a young man when they met?"

"Younger than he is now."

"Of course," she said. "Tell me, what did your husband say about Morgan? I ask because it seems to me that you hold Morgan in affection. There's no one else to tell me what he was like as a young man."

"I didn't know him myself, you understand. Just what Benton told me about him."

"It must have made an impression."

"True. Benton never talked much about his work. Like his gun, he didn't really like me near it. I suppose that's why Morgan Longstreet stuck in my head. Benton just started rattling on one day about this boy he met. And 'boy' is what he called him. Said he was smart as a whip but hadn't figured it out yet. Needed some mentoring. Benton would say that when someone needed a good kick in the — well, I reckon you know what part he thought needed kicking — and I think my husband figured he could do the kicking. He said Morgan could make something of a chance if he was given one. Benton aimed to give him one."

Jane waited while Mrs. Sterling took another sip of tea, but when the older woman replaced her cup and offered nothing further, Jane was moved to prompt. "That's all?"

"That's what stuck in my head. You didn't know my husband, but that was a lot."

"Oh. I'd hoped —" Disappointed, she sighed. "I'd hoped for more."

"If there is more, that'd be for Morgan to tell you." Mrs. Sterling tilted her head as she studied Jane. "He's not exactly an open book, is he?"

Jane smiled ruefully. "I don't know anything about where he grew up, nothing about his parents, brothers, sisters, cousins."

"I couldn't tell you about that."

Jane went on. "There are no stories. None. It's as if he did not exist before Morning Star."

"Maybe he didn't." Mrs. Sterling waved a hand dismissively. "Just a fancy crossing my mind. You'll have to press him some if there are things you want to know. You're not afraid of him, are you?"

"No. No, not at all."

"Well, then, you have to keep at him." She pushed aside the plate of cookies and laid a hand over Jane's. "But gentle. You said that he gave you a mustang."

"Yes."

"If he meant for you to ride it, he would have been particular about how it was trained."

"He was. I watched him."

"Then you know how it's done." She smiled encouragingly. "I just recollected something else Benton said about the boy: He has a fine hand and the patience to put it to proper use. I'd forgotten that 'til now. Maybe you want to think about that when you talk to him." She patted Jane's hand, sat back, and pointed to the plate. "Now have a cookie. I'm going to enjoy myself watching you eat until Morgan gets back from the hardware store."

When Morgan arrived at the Pennyroyal, he found Mrs. Sterling in the kitchen but not with his wife. "Where is Jane?" he asked without preamble.

"She walked over to Mrs. Garvin's. I'm surprised you didn't see her. She only left a few minutes ago."

"Mrs. Garvin." Morgan frowned slightly, trying to place the name. "The milliner? Jane already has a fine hat."

Ida Mae made a tsking sound with her tongue as she regarded Morgan sorrowfully. "A woman can always use another hat, but she went there with the idea of finding a pattern and material for something she can wear when she's riding. Mrs. Garvin has books and such that she can look through. Goodness, what has your dander up? Your wife intends to do the sewing; although it seems to me you could part with money enough to see that she doesn't have to."

Morgan lifted his hat, plowed his fingers

through his hair, and then slapped his hat against his leg instead of returning it to his head. "She didn't say a word about it, didn't ask me for money, and she's not where she told me she'd be."

"And yet you're glowering at me."

It did not happen immediately, but Morgan eventually got around to taking a calming breath. "Sorry."

"Humph." Mrs. Sterling returned to peeling potatoes. She gestured with her chin to the plate of almond cookies. "Jane managed to choke down two of those. I think you'll have an easier time."

Morgan picked one up and bit it in half. "What do you mean she managed to choke them down?"

Mrs. Sterling shrugged. "She doesn't seem to have much of an appetite."

"Maybe she was too polite to tell you she doesn't like almond cookies."

"That's probably it."

Morgan wasn't fooled. "Out with it. You're the one who's going to choke on what you have stuck in your craw."

Firmly setting down her knife, Mrs. Sterling regarded Morgan with her most penetrating gaze. "Do you ever intend to tell that girl anything about you?"

"Whoa. What's this about?"

"She has questions, Morgan. Any woman would, living with a man who doesn't have two words to string together about himself. She's looking to know you better, and she's come to me for the blank parts. Apparently there are a lot of them."

Morgan pulled up a stool and sat down. He set his hat on the table away from the potato shavings. "What kind of questions?"

"What kind of questions," she repeated flatly. "Hmm. Can you think of *any* that you've answered about your family?"

Morgan said nothing.

"That's what I thought."

"I don't have family."

"You can say that all you want, but it doesn't make it true."

"What did you tell her?"

"Mostly nothing. I told her to ask you."

"Mostly nothing?"

Mrs. Sterling removed her spectacles, cleaned them with her apron, and then carefully replaced them. "I told her some about you and Benton because she asked. Just a few of the kind things he said about you. I might have mentioned Lander. Frankly, I didn't see the harm in it."

Morgan briefly closed his eyes and rubbed the bridge of his nose. "It isn't your place to say anything."

"You don't think so? Benton was *my* husband. I guess I can talk about him if I have a mind to."

"Sorry."

"How's that again?"

"I'm sorry," he said, more loudly this time.

"That's better. Lord, Morgan, I know you have no one left you're proud to claim as family, but I don't see the sense in keeping them a secret. What do you think will happen if Jane hears about Jack and Gideon? And is it the worst thing in the world for her to know about that Jezebel who raised you?"

A muscle jumped in Morgan's jaw. "I don't see myself ever talking to Jane about Zetta Lee. I don't like saying their names in the same breath."

Mrs. Sterling's slim smile was rueful, her eyes full of regret. "I understand."

Morgan's nod was almost imperceptible. He picked up his hat. "I'll be going. I have to find Jane."

Reaching across the table suddenly, Ida Mae Sterling caught the sleeve of Morgan's coat. "What's going on, Morgan?"

"What do you mean?"

"I'm getting the impression you don't like her out of your sight."

"She was here with you the entire time I

was picking up supplies and listening to Ted Rush talk about the time he almost got lost in the blizzard of '86. That means she was out of my sight."

Mrs. Sterling released his coat and sat back. "I said it was an impression, didn't I?" She looked him over as he put on his hat. "You'd tell me if there was something to worry about, wouldn't you?"

Morgan walked around the table, bent, and kissed her on the cheek. "Dear Ida Mae, you would be the very last person I would tell."

"Humph."

Smiling, he gave her shoulder a squeeze. "You're my family, Ida Mae." And then he left.

Jane emerged from Mrs. Garvin's shop carrying a parcel containing material, thread, and a skirt pattern that Mrs. Garvin made especially for her. Her attention was drawn inward as her mind leaped ahead to laying out the material, pinning the pattern, and cutting the fabric. She was not looking where she was going.

She walked right into the stranger.

"Oh! I am so sorry." Jane smiled apologetically as she bent to pick up her parcel.

"No, ma'am. Allow me." He stooped and

slipped two fingers under the string that held the parcel together. He held it up as he straightened but did not precisely hand it over.

"Thank you," said Jane. "You are very kind. I'll take it now."

"Let me carry it for you. Where are you going?"

"I am on my way to meet my husband. I believe he has been delayed at the hardware store." She held out her hand. "I'll have it back, please."

"It's no bother."

"I understand. I would still like to carry it myself."

Smiling, he gave it over. "You're Mrs. Longstreet." When Jane nodded, he lifted his hat, revealing a thick helmet of brown hair that was only a shade lighter than his heavy mustache. "I thought that was you with Morgan earlier. 'Course, who else would it be? You were coming out of the bank, I believe."

"Yes." She frowned slightly, trying to place his face. He was thin, with sharp, angular features, and stood perhaps an inch taller than she. His eyes were brown. He had a narrow way of looking out on the world, a slight squint that had carved permanent lines at the corners of his eyes. "I am afraid

I do not remember your name. Were we introduced at the reception? There were so many people there. It was overwhelming."

"That's how I remember it, ma'am. And let me say again, congratulations. Morgan Longstreet is a good man. A lucky one also."

"Lucky?"

"Morgan and I go back a ways. I wouldn't be so bold as to say this if we didn't. I meant that he was lucky for getting himself a wife as fine as you."

"Well, I don't know about that," she said modestly. She averted her eyes and gazed off in the direction of Ted Rush's hardware store. "I have to go. Thank you again."

He turned when she started off, but he did not follow her. "You don't want to go to the hardware, Mrs. Longstreet."

Jane's steps slowed, then stopped. She looked back over her shoulder. "I don't?"

"No, ma'am. I saw Morgan going up the steps to the Pennyroyal not long before we met head-on. I said 'howdy,' but I don't think he heard me. Seemed as if he was in a bit of a hurry."

"Thank you. I better go, then." She picked up her pace, and when she reached the corner, she glanced back, this time with no prompting other than her own curiosity. The stranger was gone.

■ ■ ■ ■

Morgan gave Jane a blanket to place over her lap after she was seated in the buckboard. He helped her tuck it in before he snapped a tarp over the supplies in the back of the wagon. Snowflakes dotted the tarp like random chalk marks on a slate. He did not try to brush them off. He climbed onto the buckboard and took up the reins. Before he snapped them, he raised his hand in a good-bye salute to Walt Mangold, who was loitering on the Pennyroyal's front porch.

Jane also lifted her hand to Walt. When he smiled back at her, she felt a little warmer and better protected from the chill emanating from Morgan. She waited until the wagon was rolling before she spoke. "I wish you would not have been so obviously out of sorts with me in front of Walt. You made him uncomfortable. He does not know you very well. I think you made him worried for me."

Morgan stared straight ahead. "Are you worried for you?"

"No. I don't think you are going to beat me."

"Well, that's something."

"I do think you might not tell me why you

are upset. You do that, you know. Not tell me things."

"It's disturbing to me that you don't know what's bothering me."

"I'm sorry. But I don't."

"I left you at the Pennyroyal with Ida Mae. We agreed you would stay with her while I went to the hardware. I expected you to be there when I arrived. You weren't. You went off on your own like you did that time when I brought you to church. It wasn't what was supposed to happen, so yes, I'm out of sorts with you. Should I have said all of that in front of Walt?"

Jane's short sigh was lost in the lift of the wind. A snowflake caught in her eyelashes. She brushed it away. "This is where we differ, Morgan. You think there was agreement because I did not quarrel with you about keeping company with Mrs. Sterling while you went about your business. You took my silence for consent, but to be clear, there was no discussion. When I thought your trip to the hardware store was taking overlong, I decided I would go to Mrs. Garvin's shop. Had I not been delayed by one of your friends, you still would have been eating Mrs. Sterling's cookies when I arrived. It was no pleasure seeing you standing on the porch as I crossed the street, not with that severely disapproving look on your face. Please take note, I crossed the street anyway."

Morgan did not have to look at her. He knew her chin was up. So were her hackles. Absurdly, the first thing he said after taking it all in was, "How did you know I was eating cookies?"

Jane slipped one hand out from under the blanket and touched the corner of his mouth with a gloved fingertip. "Crumbs." She flicked them away.

He caught her by the wrist, turned her hand, and pressed her knuckles against his lips. He pressed a kiss against them before he released her. "When I bring you to Bitter Springs, Jane, I need to have you at my side or know where you are."

"Why?"

"Because . . ." He shook his head. "Humor me." After a moment, he added, "Please."

Jane did not return her hand to the warmth of the blanket. She slipped it into the crook of Morgan's arm instead and moved closer. "It was the 'please' that decided me. Remember that."

Morgan did. That evening, in bed, he did. "Please," he said. "You say it this time. Say 'please.' "

Jane's lips parted around the word she was desperate to say, but he cut her off by nuzzling her mouth with his. She was already maddened by his kisses, teased to the point of near mindlessness, and he was saying "please."

He growled it in her ear the first time he had said it. His teeth nibbled on her lobe and the huskiness in his voice tickled her. He whispered it against the curve of her neck just before he sipped on her skin, and then later when he was on the point of taking her nipple into his mouth. He rolled it between his lips, flicked it with the damp edge of his tongue. "Humor me," he said when he placed his mouth against her belly. "Please." That soft puff of air made her abdomen retract.

His voice was silken against the inside of her elbow and the underside of her wrist. He said the word before he began raising her nightgown, and he said it again when his fingers slipped between her naked thighs.

Sometimes she did things without any encouragement from him. Sometimes anticipation was enough to move her. His mouth circled her navel and then dipped below it. Her thighs parted. She raised her knees and he was lifting them over his shoulders so her calves rested against his back. She could not recall if he had said "please" then. She was beyond caring. She pressed her forearm across her eyes the first time he set his mouth against her warmth and wetness of these other lips. She was all sensation and the darkness helped her seize control of it. She listened to her breathing and the sound of blood thrumming in her ears. She felt her heart beat a rapid tattoo against her chest. Every stroke of his tongue was a lick of fire. Her fingers curled into fists. There was a word lodged in her throat, and when the sharp pleasure of his intimate caress was just this side of bearing, she set it free.

"Please!"

He pushed her over the precipice and she was grateful for the long fall and the soft landing. Her body shuddered, every contraction a sweet one. Pleasure lingered. It seemed to Jane it filled her very pores. A sigh hummed through her as Morgan stirred.

Jane uncovered her eyes in time to see him emerge from under the covers, his thick ginger hair endearingly mussed, a cunning and vaguely smug grin on his face. "You are a wicked man, Morgan Longstreet." She noticed that he was not offended. If anything, it became more evident that his smile *was* smug. Except to lay her hands on his shoulders, Jane barely moved as he entered her. She waited until he was seated and then she contracted around him, folding like the petals of a flower around a drop of dew.

He hardly moved as she did the work of tightening around him. Her legs. Her arms. And especially there, in her warm, wet center. Neither of them spoke. What they communicated was done with touch. Her fingers in his hair, ruffling the ends. His hand on her breast, the thumb tracing the areola. They might have been resting except for the savoring. The sole of her foot rubbed the back of his calf. His mouth brushed her shoulder.

She moved, then he did, or it might have been the other way around. It did not matter. His penetration was deep, full, and the sensation of his erection pressing against her walls made her want to grip him more tightly. He groaned, closed his eyes. The pleasure of withdrawing was intense, the return even more so. He made himself go slowly, as much for his pleasure as hers. Watching her face, the darkening of her eyes, the presence of the tip of her tongue against her upper lip, that was a source of pleasure, too.

Jane did not close her eyes now. She

watched him as intently as he watched her, glad for the muted glow from the bedside lamp that put his face in sharp relief. She fancied that she was reflected in his eyes. The black centers were like dark mirrors. She could not penetrate the depths of them, and yet they did not make her afraid.

Once again she found herself skimming the surface of pleasure. Like moonlight glancing off a pool of water, she thought she would never go deeper, that here was a gentle ripple, satisfying in its own right, and she would simply ride it out. It was that gentle vision that she had in her mind when Morgan dragged her under.

Jane sucked in a breath, and it seemed forever before she could take another. There was no shuddering. What he did to her did not make her shudder. She shattered. If he were not holding her, keeping her secure in his embrace, Jane thought she would never find the pieces of herself. She recognized it as a physical experience, but understood it was not only that. It was spiritual, a state of being so light that she felt as if she were floating, drifting, and then falling into herself once again.

Morgan came moments later. He rocked them both so hard the bed frame juddered. His skin flushed. His spine curved as he lifted his shoulders and pushed into her. Tension pulled his shoulders taut. At some point he had grasped her by the wrists, and he held them on either side of her head as his orgasm pumped his seed into her. Outside, the wind howled, but it may as well have been the sound of his release. It soughed through him, taking his breath and then giving it back.

He collapsed on his back and said the only thing that occurred to him. "Please."

Jane chuckled softly because this time when the word crossed his lips, it sounded like surrender. She drew the covers closer with no thought to searching for her nightgown. She needed to get up and go outside to relieve herself, or use the pot in the washroom's commode, but moving was not what she wanted to do yet. She waited for Morgan to go first.

What he did was fall asleep, and deeply. Smiling, she nudged him on his side when his breathing became a soft snore. She still did not leave the bed, choosing to lie beside him awhile longer and lightly rub his back. He did not wake. It was a guilty pleasure to touch him in this manner. His skin was warm and smooth under her palm. She felt for tension between his shoulder blades with her fingertips. Exhaustion had erased those taut lines, and she was glad for it. Sometimes she thought that peace did not come easily to him. She breathed deeply, letting the scent of him fill her nostrils and then her lungs. The heady, heavy fragrance of sweat, sex, and man made her womb contract. She pressed her thighs together and immediately felt a stir of lingering pleasure. A lovely little shiver went through her, and when it passed, she leaned forward and pressed a kiss to his shoulder.

Then she climbed out of bed.

Morgan dreamed of Zetta Lee. Her hands. Her mouth. She whispered in his ear, "My boy. My sweet boy. Yes. Like that." She sat astride him, her eyes dark and slumberous, her smile languid. She manipulated his cock while he lay perfectly still, his hands at his sides. He was not allowed to touch her. He could watch. She wanted him to watch. In the beginning, and sometimes afterward, that was all he was allowed to do. She lifted her hips and guided him into her. She took her seat slowly. "Don't come," she told him. "It will be very bad for you if you come. Do you understand?"

Beads of perspiration dotted his upper lip. He did not know if he was allowed to nod his head. He did not know if he was allowed

428

to speak. She expected him to know, and if he got it wrong she would punish him. He could not predict the form that her punishment would take. It might be days or weeks before she invited him to her bed again, and he did not think he could bear that. Or she might set him up for a series of humiliations that would bring him to the attention of his brothers. She never struck him. That was what she did to Gideon and Jack when they were out of her graces, and they, in turn, did the same to him.

Morgan nodded and knew he had responded correctly this time when her lazy smile deepened and she began to roll her hips.

"My ginger pie." Her voice was a husky contralto. The pitch set his nerve endings tingling. "My sweet ginger pie is a man now, aren't you?"

Was he?

He was twelve.

Zetta Lee Welling had been his lover for a year.

Morgan said nothing. Even in his dream, he knew when to remain silent.

"Morgan?" Jane placed her hand on his shoulder and gently shook him. "Morgan. Wake up."

He turned on her so suddenly that she

had no time to cry out. It was no less than an attack, and Jane struggled as Morgan lay heavily on top of her and his cock pressed hard against her flat belly. She sucked in a breath in the moment before his hands circled her throat and his thumbs began crushing her windpipe.

Curling her fingers like talons, Jane clawed at his hands. She couldn't speak, couldn't tell him to stop. She abandoned trying to remove his hands and struck at his head with her fists. It took one solid blow to his temple to knock daylight *into* him.

Morgan blinked. The bedroom was dark, but he knew it was Jane under him, not Zetta Lee. He knew it was Jane's slim neck he held in his hands, her throat that he was closing off with his thumbs. Morgan reared back. He had no idea that he left her almost as violently as he had turned on her. He threw off the covers as he rolled away. He could not leave the bed fast enough. Jane was coughing, trying to clear her throat. The sound of her labored breathing made him sick to his stomach.

He disappeared into the washroom and braced his arms on either side of the basin. He tasted bile at the back of his throat. His stomach roiled. Waves of nausea came and went. His hands curled into fists.

He was peripherally aware of light coming from the bedroom and realized Jane must have lit a lamp. He could hear her moving around. He imagined she was looking for her nightgown. He pushed away from the washstand long enough to find a towel and hitch it around his waist. She was holding the lamp in one hand when she came to the doorway, and he was leaning over the basin again.

"Are you all right?" she asked.

He laughed, albeit without humor. "That's the question I should be asking you."

"Then let me answer it. I am fine. You frightened me, but I am fine. Look." She parted the neckline of her gown to reveal all of her throat. "See? I looked in my hand mirror. There is not a single mark."

He did not turn his head. "Show me tomorrow."

Jane closed her gown. "It does not matter if my throat is purple tomorrow. You were dreaming. You did not know what you were doing."

"I did know," he said. "But I wasn't doing it to you."

"Morgan," she said, her tone gently admonishing. "I never thought you were. It happened very quickly. You were talking in your sleep. It woke me, and then I tried to wake you. Perhaps I should not have done. I think I precipitated what followed."

"It's not your fault." He closed his eyes tightly, trying to make sense of what he had been dreaming. It was already vague in his mind, disjointed in the way his dreams often were. He did not know that he talked in his sleep. "What was I saying?"

" 'No,' " she said. "You were saying 'no.' I don't know how many times you said it before the sound of your voice woke me. I could tell you were troubled. I think you might have been frightened. You said it louder. I thought you would wake yourself. When you didn't, I tried."

Morgan nodded slowly. It was coming back to him. Scenes from his life appeared randomly, the years folding back on themselves. "She's still alive," he said, straightening. There was enough light from Jane's lamp for Morgan to see his reflection in the mirror above the basin. He looked weary, he thought, and older than his twenty-nine years. His shoulders were hunched from the weight of the secrets he kept. His own and Zetta Lee's. He bore them like a punishment, the consequence of being made Zetta Lee's ginger pie man at eleven.

"The last I knew," he said, looking at Jane

and no longer at himself, "she was still alive."

"She?"

"The woman I was choking. She liked that sometimes. She would tell me to put my hands around her neck and squeeze while I was fucking her. She'd say 'harder,' but she wasn't talking about the fucking. She was talking about my hands, and I would have to tighten my fingers, press harder with my thumbs, and she would buck and arch like a feral mare that I was trying to ride for the first time. I could barely keep my seat, but I never —" He stopped, put up a hand as the lamp Jane was holding started to waver. "You told me you were strong, Jane. You have to show me now. Do you have the stomach for this or not, because I'm not sure I do. You say you want me to tell you things, and this is it. This is what I want to tell you, and most of what's inside of me is rotten ugly."

Jane stared at him. She held the lamp as steady as she held her gaze. "Go on," she said.

Her calm was no salve for his open wound, but oddly, it gave him the confidence that she would not allow him to bleed to death. The urge to say it all at once had passed, and he spoke quietly, gravely. "I never let go until she told me I could. That was her hold on me. Everything was the opposite of how it looked. No one knew. I never once tried to kill her. She gave me so many opportunities, almost dared me, I think now, and I never took her up on it. Tonight, though, dreaming about her the way I was, I was doing what I couldn't when I was lying with her. Tonight, I was going to kill her. She had me so twisted up inside, I was finally going to kill her."

He saw Jane swallow. He gave her full marks for not putting a hand to her throat. She had to be thinking that he could have strangled her, so he said it aloud. "I could have killed you tonight, Jane."

Jane shook her head. "Who is she?"

"Zetta Lee Welling," he said after a long moment. "The woman who called herself my mother."

"Of course," Jane said. Her voice was no more than a whisper. "That's why you sounded so young."

Morgan watched her set the lamp on the seat of the chair. He knew what she would do. "Stay there, Jane. Stay where you are." She came to him anyway. She *was* fearless. He had been right about her, had always been right about her, and he had been right to be afraid.

He did not know what to do when she put her arms around him. His hands remained at his sides. She pressed her face into the curve of his neck and held on. She was the only person who ever held him in just that way, giving comfort but also finding it. He could hardly bear it that she was touching him, and he thought he would die if she stopped.

He did not know he was crying until she laid her fingertips against his cheek and wiped his tears away. He put his arms around her then and rested his damp cheek against her hair. They did not move until she took his hand and led him to bed.

Jane returned the lamp to the table. "Dark?" she asked.

"No. Let it burn."

She left the wick as it was and slipped into bed but did not draw the covers up until he was beside her.

"Did you think I was going to run?" he asked.

"I think you still might."

Morgan lay back and made a cradle for her head with the crook of his shoulder. She did not hesitate to pin him in place. "Better?" he asked when she was done burrowing.

"Yes. For you?"

"Yes."

"I thought you might insist on sleeping in the other room."

"It occurred to me."

"But you decided against it."

"Because I figured you wouldn't let me sleep there alone, and if you were going to be wherever I was, what would have been the point? Was I right?"

"Yes. I am not worried that you'll try to hurt me again."

"I was never trying to hurt you."

"I know." She laid her hand on his chest. "Where is she, Morgan? Lander?"

Morgan sighed. "You got that from Mrs. Sterling. She told me that you were asking questions this afternoon."

"She said you met her husband in Lander. Is that where you're from?"

"I'm from New York City, same as you, Jane." He chuckled when her head came up as quick and alert as a prairie gopher's. He placed his hand on her crown and applied gentle pressure until she lowered it again. "Unexpected?"

"Yes."

"I was born there. Do you know Five Points?"

"I do. I was not allowed to go there. It's not safe, even now."

"Well, that's where I'm told I was born. My mother, whoever she was, and it's reasonable to assume she was a whore, had the decency to hand me over to the nuns at St. Francis. I was raised in their orphan asylum. At six, about fifteen years after the social reformers sunk their teeth into the problem of homeless, impoverished, and unwanted children, I was put on an orphan train and sent west. I was so certain I was being punished, and perhaps I was. I had friends at the asylum. None of them made the journey with me. Do you know about the orphan trains, Jane?"

"Yes. When Cousin Frances once threatened to put me on one, I made it a point to learn about them. I did not think it was the worst idea she ever had. Perhaps it was that thought lingering in the back of my mind that prompted me to answer your personal notice. Isn't it what I did, Morgan? Put myself on an orphan train? I think, though, that my experience has been quite different from yours. Is that how you met Zetta Lee Welling? Was she the one who plucked you from the train?"

CHAPTER TWELVE

Zetta Lee Welling was the second wife of Hamilton Welling. Hamilton, or Ham as others knew him in the territory days, had used up his first wife putting eight babies in her. The first three were stillborn, and he grieved hard for the son but hardly gave the two daughters that followed an afterthought except to make certain Essie Clare knew she was not to present him with any more girls, dead or alive.

She did not. She gave him two boys, Gideon and Jackson, with another stillborn son in between. Essie Clare begged him not to touch her again, but Ham had it in his head that he required at least four sons to manage what he intended to make of the land, and he got Essie Clare with child two more times. She presented him with two more sons, both alive at birth and both dead within days. Her last baby outlived her by fourteen hours.

Still of a mind to add two sons, and needing a mother for the two little ones he had,
Ham took his sons, ten head of cattle, and
rode to the outpost at South Pass on the
Oregon Trail to wait for a wagon train to
pass through.

He found Zetta Lee right off, and because
the wagon master was happy to send her
packing, she only cost Ham six of the ten
head he was prepared to settle on her family. Zetta Lee always maintained that the
cows were her farewell gift to the wagon
party, not a bride's price. She had no family
to formally accept what Ham Welling was
offering, and besides that, she was as delighted to be gone from the wagon train as
her fellow settlers were happy to see her go.
Even before her husband died because he
was too slow or too stupid to get out of the
way of a runaway wagon, Zetta Lee was at
the center of unrest in the group. The
women were suspicious; the men were smit-
ten. Zetta Lee was in her glory.

She was a widow at nineteen and beholden
to no one, so when Ham Welling proposed
to make her his wife, the mother of his two
sons, and the mistress of Welling & Sons in
the Eden Valley, she accepted. Hamilton was
her senior by sixteen years and range work
had kept him lean and hard. He did not

have a kind face, but he had the kind of face that gave her a little thrill when she caught him looking at her. She was as much taken by the way his eyes ate her up as she was by the fact that he already had two sons. She did not want children of her own. The thought of being pregnant terrified her. There was no surer means of a woman becoming old before her time than producing a litter of brats.

Zetta Lee would later say that one of the things that attracted Ham to her was knowing that she was already broke in. She would also say that he never suspected how true that was. If he thought he was ever the master in their marriage, it was because she let him think it. He put his dead wife's ring on her finger, but he may as well have put it through his own nose because Zetta Lee led him around by it in and out of bed.

Zetta Lee was a hard worker. She made sure Ham had no complaints with her there, and she did right by Gideon and Jack, raising them to benefit from what she had learned through the eighth grade. She never turned Ham away, but neither did she give him the children he wanted. She kept her figure trim, her breasts firm, and her ebon hair glossy, and when he was range riding for days, sometimes weeks, on end, she entertained his friends from nearby Lander who stopped by to see if she needed anything. Or anyone. She always did.

Ham Welling did not know about his wife's interests outside of their marriage bed, and because she let it be known that Ham would kill her if he ever found out, none of her lovers betrayed her — or themselves. The one concession that Zetta Lee made came five years into their marriage. Ham got it in his head again that he wanted another child. He would accept a daughter, if that's how it turned out, but he had an unnatural fear that one of his sons would be Cain to the other's Abel. He did not understand how it was possible to plant eight babies in Essie Clare and not one in Zetta Lee. What he knew was that it was not for lack of trying.

Zetta Lee fell into a melancholy state. She was listless, quiet, and undemanding in bed. She rarely spoke except to apologize for her inadequacies as a wife. She cried a great deal when Ham was around. She ate very little. This went on for three weeks, and just when she thought she might become as mad as Lady Macbeth, Ham took it all back.

That was when she suggested an orphan. They would take on just one boy at first and see how it went. If it was a good fit for their family, they'd choose another later. Zetta Lee was not certain how Ham would take to the idea, but when he said yes, she figured she had bought herself another five years. Raising someone else's child was less onerous to her than bearing one.

Ham had to travel a piece to meet the orphan train. The Union Pacific's rails did not reach as far west back then, and most orphans ended their journey in Indiana. Ham set out from Eden Valley with three of his ranch hands and two hundred head of cattle destined for the eastern markets. He returned a month later with his men, a decent profit from the drive, and a skinny redheaded boy who sat better in a saddle when he was tied to the horn.

Ham liked him because he didn't whine about it.

Morgan Longstreet was a good fit. He didn't look like a Welling, but he took the name because no one ever said he shouldn't. Sometimes he forgot that he didn't look like the rest of them. Mostly it was Zetta Lee who reminded him. She liked to point out that she was different, too. Where Ham and his two sons had coffee-colored hair, Zetta Lee's was as black as a pirate's heart. Gideon and his father shared sharp, angular features that Jackson would also see once his face thinned out. Zetta Lee's face was heart-shaped, her lips fuller, her eyes rounder. Morgan avoided the mirror so he would not have to gaze into the freckled face she told him was angelic.

She called him Ginger Pie. Until Zetta Lee, he had always been "that redheaded boy." He had never heard the word "ginger" used in reference to his hair. He didn't mind so much. She had silly names for Gideon and Jackson as well, but it seemed to Morgan that she used them less frequently and not always kindly. He did not know if the endearment made him special or was meant to set him apart, but it was years before he objected to it, and still years after that before he objected out loud.

Morgan figured he got along with Gideon and Jack about as well as any brothers ever got along. Early on he recognized that Gideon and Jack shared a bond that he would never have with either of them, together or separately, but they did not make it their life's work to exclude him. The three of them made a triangle, and that usually meant that one of them was sitting on the outside. Sometimes that was a good place to be, like when Gideon and Jack were tearing into each other, but other times he was there because he was their target and they were fixing to bury him in a heap of trouble.

They all worked hard on the ranch. Everyone had chores. From the beginning, Morgan was expected to do his share, and depending on the mood of his brothers, he sometimes did their share as well. Morgan learned to ride and rope, and Ham taught him how to break a horse. There was an old hand named Hatch Crookshank who taught him how to gentle one. Gideon, owing to his age, was the first one allowed to accompany his father on a cattle drive. He came back with stories that made Jack and Morgan long to go. They talked excitedly about what they would do when their turn came, and Gideon listened to them with his chest puffed out, like he was ten years their senior and a score of years more experienced.

Jackson was permitted to ride out next. Ham let his sons flank the herd on the left, keeping them together so they could look out for each other. Morgan stood back on the porch with Zetta Lee and watched them go. She laid her hand on his shoulder and comforted him.

"Come inside now, Ginger Pie. I want to show you something."

That was how it started. Zetta Lee took him to her bed, and in the absence of her husband, she broke him in. The two hands that were left behind to help manage the ranch came sniffing around at different times, but Zetta Lee told each one that he no longer pleased her. From the bedroom window, Morgan watched one, then the other, slink away. He wondered if he would leave her like a whipped puppy when she said the same to him.

There were men from town who stopped by. Morgan recognized them from previous visits. He also remembered that their visits usually lasted longer, and he remembered that when they came he and his brothers were sent away from the house. On one of those occasions, Jack had nearly drowned in the pond.

Now Zetta Lee did not let any of them stay beyond a few minutes. Some of them were angry, others merely resigned. She remained firm. She held a Bible in the crook of her arm and told every one of them the same story. She had been visited by an angel, and she was saved.

Morgan knew this because Zetta Lee invited him to sit at the kitchen table when she saw one of the men coming. She gave him a biscuit with honey. He nibbled at it while she spoke to the man. Even then he understood his presence tempered their exchange. After they were gone, she took him by the hand and led him to the bedroom. He forgot about his half-eaten biscuit when she showed him there were other ways he could taste honey.

He thought it would end when Ham returned from the drive. He felt different, but he wasn't sure *what* he felt. Zetta Lee was beautiful, and what she did to him was exciting, but no matter what she said to justify what they were doing, the fact that she was justifying it at all was his assurance that it was wrong. He wrestled with a confession that he practiced when he was alone, and he was prepared to say every word of it to Ham, but Zetta Lee practically dragged Ham to bed when she saw him again, and Morgan felt such a confusing surge of jealousy and betrayal that he said nothing.

And on the second afternoon of Ham's return, when Zetta Lee sent Morgan to the smokehouse on an errand and then trapped him there, he felt both joy and shame as she opened the fly of his trousers, dropped to her knees, and took him into her sweet, hot mouth.

When it came time for him to ride with the others, the cattle drives were much shorter. The advance of the Union Pacific made it possible to take the cows no farther than the nearest depot, in this case, only as far as Rock Springs, a distance of little more than a hundred miles. Zetta Lee complained prettily that she didn't like the idea of her youngest going off with the others, and because Ham considered the ranch was better served by having Morgan manage it than ride, he agreed with Zetta Lee that Morgan should stay back.

Morgan remembered that Zetta Lee had hardly let him out of her bed, let alone out of her sight. He was old enough, strong enough, understood enough now to tell her no, but that counted for nothing. She had him so twisted up inside that he did not know the word when she was around.

Ham Welling came back from that trip to Rock Springs with the bones of his right foot smashed by the chuck wagon's wheel. The doctor came from town to look at it, but there was nothing he could do. It would heal or it wouldn't and that would be that. The foot became infected, then gangrenous, and the doctor returned to Eden Valley to amputate. Ham died three days later, and his wife and sons buried him in the shade of a cottonwood tree.

Zetta Lee spent the evening mourning her husband and all of the following day trying to get into his safe.

Morgan shifted. It only required that small movement for Jane to lift her head. "My arm is numb," he said, a tad apologetic.

"Oh, yes. Of course." She felt a twinge of sympathy for him as he eased his arm back to his side and flexed his fingers. "You should have said something a long time ago."

"I don't think I really noticed." He rubbed his upper arm until Jane took over the task for him. "It feels better when you do it."

"Mmm." She propped herself on an elbow and concentrated on what she was doing. "How did it end, Morgan?"

He stared at the ceiling for a long time before he looked at Jane. "I told her I was done with her. Just those words: 'I'm done with you.' I don't know why I said it that way. Until then it always seemed as if she had the whip hand, but saying it like that, and hearing myself say it, I took it from her, and I never gave it back."

"Was it hard to tell her? I am imagining that you steeled yourself to say the words."

"It wasn't hard. Not then. Not after so long. Maybe if I'd thought about it, I wouldn't have been able to get the words out, but I didn't think. I just said them, and it was done."

"Zetta Lee didn't argue?"

"Some. But she never cornered me again or invited me to her room. She would not humiliate herself like that. I used to wish that she had argued more or set some traps again. When she didn't, it got me thinking that I could have ended it whenever I wanted. Years earlier even. Maybe ended it before it started. It made me feel more responsible somehow."

Jane pushed herself upright and looked down on Morgan. She searched his face, but he would not look at her. "No. She was a wicked woman. And clever. She is still punishing you. You could not have stopped her one moment earlier than you did. She would have manipulated you; she *did* manipulate you. You think with your man's mind when you look back on it now, but you were a *boy* then."

"Sometimes I know that," he said. "And sometimes it slips away from me."

Jane touched his shoulder and angled her head. This time he looked at her and held her gaze. "I grieve for that boy," she said. "I grieve that he has never known peace." She took his hand, squeezed it. "But I love the man who keeps him close and protects him and has the courage to let me know him."

"The boy or the man?"

"Both. The courage to let me know the boy *and* the man."

"Jane."

She closed her eyes briefly, her smile faint but content, and when she opened them again, Morgan was searching her face. "Yes?"

"You said you loved that man."

"I did say that, didn't I?"

"Did you mean it?"

"Do I often say things I don't mean?"

"Right now I can't think of one."

"Well, there is your answer."

"I wish you'd say it again. Straight. To me."

Jane leaned forward and brushed his lips. She lifted her head to stare into his eyes. "I love you, Morgan Longstreet."

His sigh was barely audible, mostly just a gentle rise and fall of his chest. "It feels even better than I thought it might."

"You thought about it?"

"Some." The way his mouth curved made him look very young suddenly and just a little abashed. "All right. A lot."

"I think that's nice."

"Have you ever said it before?"

"I'm sure I must have said it to my mother and father."

"But what about to someone like me?"

"Like you?" She pressed her lips together, thinking.

"Jane."

"No, Morgan. I've never said it to someone like you. Aside from the fact that there *is* no one like you, I have never loved another man and therefore have felt no urge to say so."

Morgan tapped his chest with his forefinger. "It's the boy. He needed to know."

"I understand. It's all right."

"I've never said it to anyone."

"You still haven't."

"Should I say it now?"

"Only if you want to. Only if it's true."

"Do you mind if I wash off the stink of Zetta Lee first?"

"I think I'd prefer it."

Morgan sat up. Jane released his hand as he moved to the edge of the bed. Tightening the towel at his waist, he stood and padded to the washroom. Jane watched him go. When he shut the door she lay down and pulled the covers up to her shoulders. Smiling to herself, she closed her eyes. She did not remember falling asleep.

Jessop cracked an egg against the side of a bowl and prepared to separate the shell with his thumbs.

"Quiet," Morgan snapped in a stage whisper. "I told you, Jane's still sleeping."

Jessop replied in a similar tone. "Then you tell me how I'm supposed to prepare them with the shell still on."

Scowling, Morgan muttered something under his breath and sat back in his chair.

Jem answered for him, sotto voce. "Hard-boiled."

Equally hushed, Jake said, "Soft-boiled."

Max said, "Anyone want more coffee?" When everyone just stared at him, he shrugged and set the pot down.

Jessop turned back to the hot griddle and dropped the contents of the eggshell onto it. It sizzled and crackled loudly on a thin layer of bacon grease. Behind him, he heard Morgan swear softly and everyone else snicker.

Jake asked, "Is she all right?"

"She didn't say she isn't," said Morgan. He glanced over his shoulder to the doorway. "Do you think I should check on her?"

The men all looked at each other, then at him. No one answered.

"What?" he asked.

Jem shrugged. "Just surprised you asked, is all. Usually you do or you don't. Whatever it is."

Max stretched his legs under the table. "Guess she's got you tied up in knots, boss. That sound about right?"

It sounded about right, but what Morgan said was, "You think she's got me in knots because I asked you if I should go back and see if she's all right?"

Max shrugged. So did everyone else.

Morgan picked up his coffee cup. He had it almost to his lips when he said, "I love her."

No one said anything.

Morgan looked at them over the rim of his cup. "Well?"

Jessop glanced over his shoulder. "Hell, boss, I reckon we all knew that."

"Yeah," said Jem. "What made you say it?"

"It's the knots," said Max. "You've got them yourself, Jem. You should know they provoke a man to say peculiar things."

"Well, sure, but it don't happen much at the kitchen table, not without cards and liquor to ease the way. Jessop, how're those eggs comin'? Boss is hungry and talkin' out of his head."

Morgan's mouth twisted to one side. "You all had your fun? Jake, you have something you want to say?"

"Nope, but if you want to say it again, I guess that'd be all right. Sounds like you could use the practice."

Morgan set his cup down. "Does it?"

This time they all nodded.

He cleared his throat and rolled his neck. "I love her."

Jane stepped into the kitchen, a forefinger pressed against her lips. "Shh," she whispered. "You'll wake her."

Morgan scowled at Jake. "You knew she was standing there."

Affecting innocence, Jake held up his hands.

Jane squeezed behind Max's chair to reach Morgan. She stood behind his chair and placed her hands on his shoulders. Leaning forward, she kissed the top of his head. "Don't blame Jake. I told him not to say anything."

Morgan reached back and laid one of his hands over hers. "You heard?"

"I did."

Morgan circled Jane's wrist with his fingers and drew her around his chair while he pushed back. He ignored the resistance she offered as he pulled her onto his lap.

"Morgan!"

He spoke to his men, not to Jane. "You all observed that she has expressed the proper amount of disapproval?"

They nodded. Jem said, "She's a stickler

for what's proper. I noticed that right off."

Morgan cocked an eyebrow at Jane. "See?"

"Morgan."

"I love you." He pointed to his men. "They think you have me tied in knots. They're right. You do. It's a hell of thing, Jane, but I don't even mind. I thought you should know. I figure they already do."

His very public declaration left her quite without words.

"I love you," he said again, and this time he punctuated the declarative with a proper kiss. "Don't fuss. I should have done that the first time we had witnesses."

Jane angled her head against Morgan's, her smile nearly beatific. She regarded her witnesses. "He neglected to kiss me at our wedding."

"Now, that's a damn shame," said Jem. "Sorry. But it is. I've been givin' that kiss some thought. I'm going to bend Renee back over my arm and —"

Jessop slapped his spatula against the griddle. "More like bend her over your knee if you want to get that gal up the aisle."

Jake nodded. "He's right, Jem."

Jane said, "Don't you dare listen to them. Besides, you will want to save something for the reception. The whole town will turn out for that. They did for ours and we hardly knew a soul. I am still running into folks who were there that I have to meet all over again." She started to rise. "Jessop, let me have a turn at those —" She did not finish because Morgan pulled her right back onto his lap. Surprised, she stared at him. "I was only —"

He put up a hand. "Something . . ." He frowned, his thoughts turning inward as he searched for a recollection. "Yesterday — I think it was when we were leaving town — you said something about running into one of my friends. Am I remembering that right?"

"I suppose I may have said something like that. It's true. It was the reason for my delay in returning to the Pennyroyal."

A narrow crease defined the space between Morgan's eyebrows as he continued to frown. "Someone you met at the reception?"

"Your thoughts do take the odd leap now and again. Is this because of what I said about the town turning out?"

"Probably. I don't know. It's been niggling, I suppose."

Jessop put a platter heaped with fried eggs and bacon on the table. "Eat up."

Jem reached out to pull the platter closer. Shaking his head, Max threatened Jem's hand with a fork. Looking glum, Jem sat back.

"Who's the friend?" asked Jessop, taking a seat. "The boss here maintains he doesn't have any friends, or hasn't he told you that?"

"That is what I hear," said Jane, looking at Morgan. "I do not recall the man's name. I am thinking now that he never told me, but he did mention that you and he went back a ways. I think that is how he described it. He knew who I was, so I supposed he must have been at the reception. I said that to him, I believe, although I am not sure he truly confirmed it." She shook her head and offered a helpless shrug. "Really, our conversation was brief, the encounter was rather odd, and I was frankly in a bit of a hurry to find you."

Morgan was thoughtful. "He said we went back a ways? I'd say that's odd since only Mrs. Sterling and I go back a ways, but why did you think so?"

"I am not certain I can explain it. I dropped my parcel, he picked it up, I thanked him, and he did not immediately return it. I think I said I would like to have it back at least twice, perhaps three times before he gave it to me. I found that odd."

"Not very mannerly," Jem said as he slowly walked his fingers toward the bacon and egg platter. "Ow!" He yanked his hand back and glared at Max, who was examining his fork tines for blood. "What'd you do that for?"

"Leave the food for now," said Max. "Can't you see how this is somethin' worth attendin' to?"

Jem nursed his hand and regarded them all with a wounded expression. "I'm attendin'. I do it better with food than without it. Anyway, I guess I got it figured out that this fella doesn't really know the boss, probably wasn't at the reception, and has no proper manners. Makes me think that him comin' upon Mrs. Longstreet like that wasn't an accident. Like maybe he was followin' her, lookin' to make her acquaintance." He sharpened his gaze when he came around to Morgan. "That sound about right?"

"It does."

Jane looked from Morgan to Jem and back again. "Not a chance meeting? You are drawing a conclusion with very little to support it. He said he saw us earlier, coming out of the bank, which is neither here nor there, but it does speak to the dull nature of our conversation. He *does* know you, Morgan. He told me that he called out to you as you were going into the Pennyroyal."

"I didn't hear anyone."

"That's what he said. You didn't hear him. He did know that you were at the hotel, though, because when I started to go toward the hardware store, he redirected me."

Jake said, "Maybe if you were to describe him, ma'am, it'd help one of us place him."

"I think I may have given you a poor impression of him. True, he did not return my parcel immediately, but that was because he offered to carry it for me. I told him I was meeting you, Morgan."

"I'd still like to know who he is," said Morgan. "Humor me. Please." He used those words quite deliberately, and they provoked the pale pink flush coloring Jane's cheeks. Out of sight of his men, she pinched him. He grinned and bore it.

"Very well," she said, looking around the table. "He is older than Morgan, but not yet forty. At least I do not think so. In height and build, he is similar to Max."

"A runt, then," said Jem.

"Deceptively strong," said Max, tapping his muscled bicep.

Jane ignored them both. "His coloring could make him another Davis brother. I'm remembering thick brown hair when he tipped his hat. I think his eyes, though, were brown, not blue, and he had a mustache, very dark, heavy, but neatly trimmed. His face was narrow. I would say he had sharp features."

"A weasel," said Jem.

"No. That is an unkind comparison, and one might infer from it that there is some shifty aspect to his character. He should be judged on his behavior, not on the cast of his features. He is not as pretty as you, Jem, but he is not unhandsome."

Heat blossomed in Jem's cheeks. He ducked his head, but no one at the table thought he wasn't pleased by the compliment.

Jane said, "He was dressed like any of you going into town on ranch business. That is to say he was not dressed like Mr. Webb at the Cattlemen's Trust or Buster Johnson at the mercantile." She turned over her hands and shrugged. "I don't think there is anything else I can tell you."

Jessop said, "I guess that describes just about anyone we know. I had a picture of Charlie Patterson in my mind."

Jake nodded. "I was thinking that it sounded a lot like Ansell Roach over at the Bar G."

Max fiddled with his fork. "Wes Duffy. He's in and out of town regular on errands for the Stapletons."

Jem shook his head. "I got nobody. You, boss?"

"Nothing."

Jane removed herself from her husband's lap and this time he let her go. "Perhaps I will see him the next time I am in Bitter Springs. You can be certain that I will point him out or get his name if you are not there."

"Oh, I'll be there," said Morgan. "You're bread. I'm butter."

"Uh-huh." She reached for the platter of bacon and eggs. "Pass your plates, men. Let's have breakfast."

Gideon Welling folded his cards and tossed them toward the middle of the table. "I'm out." He looked toward the saloon's front window and set his jaw as the snow continued to fly. "Goddamn weather."

Marcie absently scratched his scar with a knuckle. His attention was for his hand and the bid, not the snow. "Guess this means we wait."

Gideon mocked him, repeating the words but not the tone. "Guess this means we wait." His chair scraped the floor as he pushed it back. It made enough noise to attract the attention of the men drinking at the next table. "I guess it damn well does."

Gideon shot a feral glance at the onlookers. "Nothing interesting this way, fellas. I suggest you give us no never mind."

Dixon Evers chuckled under his breath as the other men turned away. "Two cards." He tossed off two and collected a pair from Avery. "Shame about the snow kickin' up again, but I don't mind sayin' that I'm glad we didn't move too fast. Better to still be in Rawlins than back on the range, sittin' around a fire with a saddle for a pillow."

"I don't reckon you're wrong, Dix," said Gideon. "And it pains me enormously to admit it."

Grinning crookedly, Dixon threw in a couple of chips. "Did you consider takin' her right off the street when you had the chance?"

Gideon shook his head. "The fact of it is, I didn't really have a chance. I had her alone, like I said, but she didn't give in easy, wouldn't let me walk with her a spell. I had no opportunity to get her out of sight of the street. I took her for a woman who'd make a fuss before I got her quiet. Besides, we talked about it. It wasn't the plan. Maybe nothing will come of it, but I like to think I'm bedevilin' Morgan."

Avery Butterfield took a card for himself. His rawboned features remained impassive.

"We're not long for this snow, Gideon. No reason you can't get back to Bitter Springs soon. Take a room at that boardinghouse like you planned and get a better look at what really interests you."

Leaning back in his chair, Gideon nodded slowly. "Waiting's never been what you'd call my strong suit. And I've already had a look at what interests me. Morgan's different that way. Real patient. I remember how he worked on my daddy's safe after Zetta Lee gave up. She was crazy mad to get into it. She was fixin' to dynamite the thing when Morgan stepped in. I think he forgot all about the rest of us standing around while he worked. I never saw the like before, and when he opened that door" — Gideon whistled softly, admiringly — "that was something. Sure put a lot of ideas in Zetta Lee's head."

Marcie asked, "What was in the safe?"

"Cash money. Homestead papers from the land office. A couple of pieces of jewelry that belonged to my daddy's mother and a locket that was Ma's. The money was enough to keep us going for a while, and we had a clear title to the land, but Zetta Lee got it in her head that we could do better than cattle ranching, especially in the lean times."

"And you did," said Dixon.

Gideon shrugged. "We did all right. For a time. Problem was, Morgan didn't see the advantages same way the rest of us did, and we needed him for the safes."

"He really has the touch?" asked Avery. "I've heard that some people do, but I've never seen it."

"Could be you'll get the chance. What he can do with a safe is elegant. Always did prefer it to blowin' the damn thing up." He smiled narrowly. " 'Course, that's kinda fun, too."

Jane leaned forward in her saddle and patted Sophie's neck. The mare tossed her head and preened. "Yes," Jane cooed. "You are such a pretty lady."

Morgan chuckled. He was riding Condor, a chestnut gelding who had no interest in Sophie's flirting but liked to nuzzle Jane when Morgan let him get close. He supposed it was because Jane had been baking oatmeal cookies before he suggested they ride out to Blue Valley.

"This must be the most glorious place on earth," she said, twisting right and left to take in as much of the panoramic view as she could. Snow blanketed the landscape. It defined the skeletal limbs of the cottonwood and maple trees, and lay in thick folds along banks of the stream. It frosted the pines until their branches sagged under the weight. The Herefords congregated around green circles where they had pushed away or trampled the snow. Ice in the basin had been chipped away to allow them to enjoy their favorite watering hole.

The sky was halcyon blue. The wind was not stirring, and an icy glaze across hill and valley reflected the sunshine.

Jane was smiling contentedly when she looked in Morgan's direction. "How did you find Morning Star?"

"Ida Mae told me about it."

"Mrs. Sterling? Really?"

"She heard that the eastern syndicate wanted to sell, and she knew I wanted to settle. The first time she wrote to me, it was to tell me that Benton was dead. I wrote back, expressed my sorrow, and I thought that would be the end of it. She wrote again, and I answered, and we fell into an easy correspondence that lasted until I came to Bitter Springs."

"She never mentioned that."

"No," said Morgan. "She wouldn't. She figures things like that are for me to say."

"Does she know about Zetta Lee?"

"Calls her Jezebel, so yes, she knows some

things about her." He shook his head, pointing to himself when Jane arched an eyebrow. "Benton. I don't know precisely what she knows, and I have no intention of asking her. Neither should you."

"I wish you did not believe you had to say that. I suppose I have given you reason to think I might speak to her on any subject concerning you, but I would never about that, Morgan. I would *never.*"

He looked out over the valley. "I'm still getting used to the idea that you know."

"Are there things I don't know?"

"About Zetta Lee?"

"No. I don't care about her. I'm talking about you. Are there things I don't know?"

"Yeah."

"If you had answered differently, I might have called you a liar."

"I figured as much. Is there something in particular you're wanting to know?"

"Actually, yes. I've been thinking about all the talk at breakfast a few mornings back."

Morgan snorted. "There's too damn much talk at every breakfast. You'll have to be a tad more specific."

"About your friend. The one I ran into outside of Mrs. Garvin's shop."

"That was almost a week ago. I hardly remember it."

"Liar."

He grunted softly but did not offer a defense.

"I think you have someone in mind who fits the description I gave you."

"What makes you think that?"

"Something about the way you looked then and your evasion now. Who is he?"

"Not my friend."

"That was my word, not his. He only said that the two of you 'went back a ways.' "

"He could be anyone."

"I realize that. But who do *you* think he is?"

Morgan sighed, rubbed the back of his neck. "I reckon he could be one of my brothers."

Jane's eyes widened. "Whyever wouldn't you say so?"

"Lots of reasons, but mostly because I am trying to figure out what I want to do about it."

"I have no idea what that means."

"I know you don't, and I know it's my fault. Maybe it's wrongheaded, but I still have this notion that there might be things I will never have to tell you."

"If it helps, I will remind you again that I am not going anywhere."

He smiled. "Since you're still here after I

told you about Zetta Lee, it seems like that's something I can hang my hat on."

"Yes," she said. "Hang your hat on that."

For a long moment, Morgan was quiet, then he said, "Did you notice if he limped some?"

Jane thought about it. "No. We did not walk together. He was suddenly there in my path and then he wasn't."

"Jackson limps. He fell halfway out of his saddle during a cattle drive, got his foot caught in the stirrup, and was dragged a piece before Gideon could help him. He put his knee out. It never set right with him after that." Morgan shrugged. "The limp's a good distinguishing feature. Otherwise, it'd be hard to describe them in enough detail to set them apart."

"All right, but everyone at the table except Jem offered a name, and each name belonged to someone who lives in or around Bitter Springs. Your brothers don't, do they?"

"No. The last I knew they were living in Kansas."

"That's quite a way off. Is Zetta Lee there now?"

"Not that I know of. I think she's still in Lander."

"So they might have come back this way

to visit her."

"Possible, I suppose, but there's no love lost between them and Zetta Lee either. And before you ask, the answer is: I don't know. Neither of them ever said a word to me that makes me think Zetta Lee had them in her bed. Same as I never said a word to them. There's enough other reasons they'd as soon choke her as look at her."

"Do you mean that?"

"About choking her? I do."

"So your brother might be here to see you?"

"Probably."

Jane gave Sophie a little kick and urged her forward when Morgan and his gelding began to move across the ridge. "Where are we going?"

He pointed to the next ridge where a stand of pines offered shelter under their broad, white canopy. "We can stretch our legs over there, walk around a bit where the snow's not so deep. I brought some extra shells. I thought you might like to have a chance to shoot."

"Are you certain you want to give me a weapon, Morgan? I might well turn it on you."

Morgan said nothing.

Jane pulled Sophie up.

Morgan looked over his shoulder and cocked an eyebrow at her. "Aren't you coming?"

"When you tell why you think it might have been one of your brothers I met in town. There is something missing because it makes no sense. If it is a brother, why wouldn't he make himself known to you?"

"Either one of them would have their reasons."

"Suppose you tell me one."

"The best I can figure is that he doesn't want witnesses."

"Witnesses to what? Greeting you?"

"Killing me."

Jane stared at him, mouth parted.

"You're gaping," said Morgan.

Nodding, Jane brought Sophie abreast of him. "I am not certain what I want to say to you, Morgan Longstreet, so I am going to sort it out before I say things I shouldn't." She took a deep, calming breath. "Right now, for all kinds of reasons, I am in favor of that shooting lesson."

Chapter Thirteen

Morgan opened the door for Jane and followed her into Cobb Bridger's office. They both stamped snow off their feet at the entrance, although Jane was more delicate about it.

From behind his desk, Cobb dropped his chair onto all four of its legs and stood. He lifted his hat to greet Jane. "An unexpected pleasure, Mrs. Longstreet." His smile faded as he looked at Morgan. "Let's just say it's unexpected."

"I was thinking the same," said Morgan.

Jane looked from one to the other and shook her head. "Now that you two have observed the niceties of social convention . . ."

Chuckling, Cobb came around his desk and showed Jane to a chair in front of it. "Would you like to take off your coat?"

Morgan said, "We're not going to be here that long."

Jane said, "Thank you, Marshal. Yes, I'd like that. After the ride into town, it feels rather cozy in here." She unbuttoned her coat, but when Cobb stepped forward to help her out of it, Morgan warned him off with a glare and did it himself. Jane pretended she didn't know what had happened. Instead of taking the chair Cobb had offered, she walked over to where the notices of wanted men, and one wanted woman, were tacked on the wall.

"Morgan told me about this," she said. "I cannot decide if it is impressive or merely sad." She looked back at Cobb. "But I don't suppose you regard it in either light."

"No, ma'am. It's my job."

Morgan said, "She wanted to see it. Make sure I wasn't up there."

"That's a lie," said Jane. "I wanted to see it. Period."

Cobb said, "Am I getting wind of some kind of domestic dispute here? Because if that's the case, you probably don't want me in the middle of it. Mrs. Sterling, now, she's the one who delights in that sort of thing, and I know she's at the Pennyroyal because I just came from having lunch at the hotel."

Morgan shook his head and said flatly, "Jane knows."

"She knows," Cobb said with as little

inflection. His eyebrows lifted. "She *knows*?"

"Mmm-hmm. She does. I told her."

"When?"

"Not that it matters, but eight or so days ago."

"Six," Jane said as she continued to study the Wanted Wall.

"I guess it does matter," said Cobb.

Morgan shrugged. "Feels like eight."

Looking at Jane's stiff back, Cobb spoke softly to Morgan. "I know that feeling."

One corner of Morgan's mouth lifted. "I bet you do."

Jane turned around and faced both men, but she addressed Cobb. "I wonder what your wife would say if she learned you were someone other than she thought you were."

Humor tugged at Cobb Bridger's lips. "It gives me no pleasure to say so, Mrs. Longstreet, but I can pretty much recite what she said chapter and verse. I had a similar problem. That's why I told Morgan he should let you know straightaway."

"You never told me that," said Morgan.

"Didn't I? Could be because I knew you wouldn't be receptive to hearing it from me. I sure thought about it enough."

Jane said, "You two can sort that out later. It certainly seems you have enough in common to forge a sustainable friendship."

Cobb scratched behind his ear. "Maybe so."

"Jury's still out," Morgan said.

Jane gave her husband a pointed look.

"Maybe so," he said.

Cobb laughed outright and pointed to the chairs again. "Please. Sit down and tell me why you're really here."

Morgan and Jane sat. Both declined Cobb's offer of coffee, and he did not pour any for himself. He returned to his chair and pushed a book and a few papers out of the way.

Jane folded her hands in her lap and began. "The last time I was in town, I met someone who Morgan believes might have been one of his brothers. Morgan did not see him, so we can't be sure." She described the meeting outside Mrs. Garvin's shop and how it meant so little to her that she mentioned it only in passing to her husband. "Morgan and I thought you should know in the event that he returns to Bitter Springs."

Cobb's attention shifted to Morgan. "Is that right?"

"My wife just said so, didn't she?"

Jane interjected, "Morgan said he gave you his word that he would tell you if something happened that concerns you and the town."

"He remembers what I told him," Morgan said. "He's just having trouble believing my word is good."

Cobb sighed heavily. "I'm not questioning anyone's word. I guess I'm a little surprised you're coming forward when all you have is suspicion. When I tried to get you to go along with me before, you weren't having any part of it."

Jane asked, "When was this?"

"He's talking about what happened to Jem," said Morgan. "He had a lot of questions for me when I got here. He thought then that one or two of the men who beat up Jem could have been Gideon or Jack."

"Or part of their gang," Cobb said. "Your husband couldn't confirm it."

"I don't know that they have a gang. In the beginning, there were only the three of us. We were brothers, not much of anything else, not then. That's how I remember it . . ."

"It's not like Ham's safe," Morgan said, joining Gideon and Jack outside on the boardwalk. They stood there for a time, silent and reflective, in front of the Cumberland Bank in Rock Springs until Gideon thought they should move on.

"No point in attracting attention," he said. He pointed to the saloon across the way.

"Let's go to Angel's. Think this through."

They chose a table out of the way even though it was the middle of the afternoon and the saloon offered a lot of empty tables. Gideon and Jack had a pint of whiskey to share. Morgan had a beer.

"Tell us about it," said Gideon. "Zetta Lee said it was like Daddy's."

"Last time she was here, it might have been. Or it could be they just look alike to her." Morgan gave his brothers a frank look. "Or, and here's what I'm really thinking is the truth, she just said that to get us here."

"So what are you saying? We should go back with nothing to show for it?"

"I didn't say it, but yes, that's what we should do."

"I don't like it," said Jack. "And Zetta Lee *sure* isn't going to like it."

Morgan lifted his beer and drank. He wiped his mouth with the back of his hand.

"Jesus," said Gideon, rolling his dark eyes. "You look like you're about twelve when you do that. If you'd grow some hair on your lip and chin it would take care of that foam for you. I should have bought you a sarsaparilla."

"Would have rather had a sarsaparilla. This beer's sour."

Jack said, "Forget about that. Can you do

it, Ginger Pie?" He held up his hands, palms out, when Morgan scowled at him. "Sorry, but Gideon's right. You look about twelve. So, can you?"

"I don't know. It's a Newell and Chester. I don't have a feel for what it might be like. It could take longer than usual."

"What's that?" asked Gideon. "It takes forty minutes instead of fifteen? We go in at night, like we always do. Bankers don't expect that. It ain't been done until we done it, and no one knows it's us. There is no one looking out for the place come nightfall. We saw that plain enough for ourselves last night."

"That doesn't mean there's no risk," said Morgan. "There are still people around. Most of them in and out of this saloon." He jerked his thumb over his shoulder in the direction of the Cumberland Bank. "You haven't forgotten the proximity, have you?"

Jack snorted softly. "We ain't virgins staring at a twelve-inch pecker. We've done this before. Three times."

"Not with a Newell and Chester. I'm not going in there."

Gideon and Jack did not miss a beat. They spoke as one. "The hell you're not."

That night they left Rock Springs with a little more than fourteen hundred dollars from the Cumberland Bank in their saddle-bags. No one saw or heard them. Mr. Horatio Cumberland discovered the theft the following morning when he opened the safe to put cash in the tellers' drawers. He remarked that it was unnaturally thoughtful of the thief to shut the safe after relieving it of its cash contents. No documents were stolen, no jewelry. The office was left tidy, too. He mused aloud that if he had to be robbed, it was better done by a man with a light touch than one with four sticks of dynamite. Mr. Cumberland hired someone that afternoon to stay in the bank at night until the new safe was delivered.

It had taken Morgan twenty-seven minutes to open the safe once he was kneeling in front of it. He might have done it in less time, but the gun Gideon held to his head while Jack stood guard made his feel for the tumblers a slippery thing.

The Cumberland Bank robbery was the last time they worked alone. Gideon and Jack decided that they needed help in the event that Morgan could not be counted on to do his part. Gideon did not relish the idea of turning his gun on Morgan again; for that matter, neither did Jack. They agreed it was best done by a third party who had never heard Morgan answer to "Ginger Pie."

Morgan opened two more safes for them, one in Leadville, Colorado, the other in Logan, Utah, and still it wasn't enough. Their number grew to six, and Gideon and Jack had to hold the reins tight on their little group as dissension grew. Zetta Lee, too, thought they could take more risks and make Morgan's role less important. They set a bonfire in the middle of the night on the Union Pacific tracks west of Rock Springs and allowed Morgan ten minutes to open the safe in the mail car. At eight minutes Gideon started setting the charges. At nine, Jack lit the fuses. Morgan felt his bones rattle when the safe blew. He was standing forty feet away by then, in the flickering light of the distant bonfire, apologizing to the mail clerks for destroying their car. His brothers dragged him off as soon as the payroll money was packed away.

The postal clerks would tell the Uinta County sheriff and the detectives who rode with the Union Pacific that they felt a little sorry for the redheaded fellow who did his best to crack the safe. Hard to work, they said, under the kind of pressure he faced, what with the six-and-one-half-inch barrel of a Remington pointed at the base of his brain. The clerks said they never feared for their lives; no one ever asked them to open the safe. It seemed the only person that might meet his maker that night was the young'un.

Morgan's red hair and youthful features were the two clues that circulated throughout the territories and Colorado. Posses were formed. The Union Pacific sent a special investigator to assist in gathering information. They were still compiling a list of robberies where safes had been cracked when word reached them that the Jones Prescott Bank in Cheyenne had been broken into two nights earlier. It was the freshest trail; they decided to follow.

The raid on the bank had been made while it was still dark, but dawn was breaking as the robbers were leaving town. There were witnesses, not to the robbery, but to the departure. Two whores sharing a cigarillo on the second floor balcony of the Flower Garden saw six men riding out. Five of them wore a hat. The one who didn't, the redheaded boy, looked up as they were passing, and smiled at them. They told Benton Sterling, the marshal from Bitter Springs who was part of the posse by then, that looking on that boy's smile was the purest pleasure they had known, excepting the time they entertained Duke Forte when he came through town with his trinkets and toys.

It seemed to them, they added, that the boy wanted to be noticed. Why else would he be holding his hat instead of wearing it? Why else would he look up and give them a smile so full of glory it made them blink?

It was an observation worth considering, Benton Sterling thought.

There were two more robberies before the law narrowed the search in and around Lander. As best the detective for the Union Pacific could tell, the first robbery for this gang had likely been the Walker Trust. No one had reported a safecracking, not one that was done without explosives, before that. Once they arrived in Lander, it was inevitable that they would finally find Morgan Longstreet.

The eight-man posse had to admit in court that Mr. Longstreet was more or less hiding in plain sight. They came across him herding cows toward a watering hole on the Welling homestead, and he didn't raise an eyebrow as they approached. Benton Sterling would testify that Morgan Longstreet not only surrendered his rifle and his sidearm, he looked as if he were relieved to see them.

That wasn't true of Gideon and Jackson Welling or the other three men they found working the ranch. Shots were fired before the Union Pacific's investigator could state why they were there. It seemed the adage was true: a guilty conscience needed no accuser.

A man named Paul Viola was killed when the deputies returned fire. No one else was hurt. Zetta Lee Welling came out on the porch wearing an ice blue taffeta dress and three ropes of pearls around her neck. She had a shotgun in her hand and a feral look in her eye that stopped every man except Morgan Longstreet in his tracks. Morgan's long stride carried him up to the porch while no one else was moving or even paying attention to him. He wrested the shotgun from Zetta Lee's hands, emptied it, and tossed it into the yard at Benton Sterling's feet.

Gideon and Jackson Welling gave up their guns. It was Zetta Lee who encouraged it. Morgan had gone crazy, she told them. Her boys did not need to die because of it. Once their guns were on the ground, the other two men dropped their weapons as well.

They were taken into custody. The posse searched the house, but they never came across money that would point to the robberies. Zetta Lee told her sons to go with the law and she would arrange for lawyers and their defense. She knew they were innocent. Everyone else would know it, too

Morgan straight-armed himself out of his chair and went over to the stove to take Cobb up on his offer of coffee. He held up the pot, but he had no takers. Jane's lips were pressed together. It was how she had collected herself the first time he'd told her the story. He had not wanted her here, but she would have it no other way. It was important to her that Cobb Bridger heard the story in its entirety, not the broad strokes that Morgan had given him when he first came to Bitter Springs. She didn't trust him to say it all, and Morgan knew she was right. The case she made was dead-on, but it did not follow that he was comfortable owning it.

She'd had her back up that night, pointing out all the ways in which circumstances mitigated his participation in the robberies. And then she'd set her hands on her hips and told him that he kept his secrets because he would rather have people think the worst of him, or think nothing at all. She even cursed some. She cried a little, too. It broke his heart to see that.

She never talked once about leaving him, though. She went after him like she was a hammer and he was a nail. It felt good that she cared so much, and when he told her that, she flew at him again, this time calling him a horse's ass because *of course* she cared so much. She *loved* him. Horse's ass and all.

Recalling that, Morgan had a faint smile on his face as he returned to his chair. "You pretty much know how it turned out from there, Bridger. Zetta Lee came forward but not in the defense of anyone but herself. She claimed we had stolen from her right after Ham died and that opening his safe was surely what put us on the road to ruin." Morgan chuckled under his breath, although the sound had an edge to it. "Road to ruin. She really talked like that. Gideon and Jack pointed fingers back at her, but no one took them seriously, especially when I did not support them. I reckon that if they're around, it's because they want their pound of flesh."

"I thought it might also be for the money," said Cobb.

"From the robberies, you mean?"

Cobb nodded.

"There's no money, but that doesn't mean they won't want me to get them some. They had the impression that Zetta Lee gave most of her share to me and that I had it squirreled away where none of them could touch it. I have to believe she put that in their heads because there was some advantage in it for her. That's how she thought. I saw no point in trying to convince them differently."

Jane said, "Morgan had neither conscientious nor competent representation at trial, Marshal Bridger, and my husband said nothing in his own defense. It is a character flaw of unimaginable proportions."

"I'm getting that impression." Cobb leaned back in his chair and said to Morgan, "This is how Benton Sterling figures into what happened. *He* spoke up for you."

"Yes. He wasn't alone, but he carried on the loudest. Seems like the jury heard him because I spent six years in the territory prison, and the rest of them went to Leavenworth. It was the express mail train robbery that got them the ten-year sentence in a federal prison. You know about their early release."

"I do," said Cobb. "But we're only talking about your brothers. The other two that went in with them died there."

"Bobber Metcalf and Wayne Corley."

"Right. Metcalf and Corley."

Jane reached over and laid her hand on Morgan's forearm. "What can you do, Marshal, to protect my husband?"

Morgan looked down at Jane's hand and then at Cobb Bridger. He smiled a trifle crookedly.

"Yeah," said Cobb. "I know *that* feeling, too." His blue eyes swiveled to Jane. "I think Morgan is more interested in what I am prepared to do to protect you, assuming, that is, that anyone is in need of protection. The first thing we have to do is establish the identity of the person you met. I'm fair with a sketch. I used to have to do it a lot in my previous work. Should we go over your description again?"

"Yes," Jane said firmly. "We should."

Morgan sat quietly, drinking his coffee and listening to Jane describe the man again. This time, though, she had Cobb Bridger to ask her questions, and Morgan had to admit that the marshal understood how to gently tug on her memory to get a more complete picture. Bridger also had the skill to literally *draw* on her memory. His pencil flew over the paper as he sketched and shaded and erased and sketched again. Jane went to stand at his side to watch the portrait take place, offering a suggestion that broadened the man's nose and another that shortened the distance between his eyes.

Morgan did not look at the picture as it was being composed. He watched Cobb's steady hand and the way Jane nibbled on her lower lip as she carefully considered her words. Sometimes she closed her eyes. He admired the effort she made to be precise. She spoke as if their lives depended on what she said.

It was very likely that they did.

Morgan finished his coffee at the same time Cobb set down his pencil. Jane had pronounced herself satisfied with an emphatic, "That's him." Cobb had then lifted the sketch and blown away shavings left by the gum eraser. The paper lay balanced in the palm of his hand until Morgan finally nodded.

Cobb pinched the sketch between his thumb and forefinger and held it up for Morgan to see. He said nothing, letting the work speak for itself, and waited.

Jane also waited. She held her breath, searching Morgan's face for some indication of the outcome.

"I haven't seen my brothers in almost ten years," Morgan said. "They were shackled together and being escorted out of the courtroom the last time I saw them. I remember thinking Jackson would have killed me right there if he could have reached me. The look in his eyes when he turned back and saw me standing beside Benton Sterling . . ." Morgan's voice trailed off. He shook his head. "I'm realizing that fifty years could go by without seeing him and I would still know him at a glance. That's not Jackson Welling."

Morgan leaned forward and placed his empty coffee mug on the corner of Cobb's desk. He extended his hand for the sketch and when Cobb gave it over, Morgan held it up for Cobb and Jane to get the perspective he had. With his free hand, he pointed to the narrow, sharp-edged face. "This is my oldest brother," he said without inflection. "This is Gideon."

Walt was standing in the Pennyroyal's foyer when Jane and Morgan walked in. He greeted them warmly, took their coats and Morgan's hat, and started to show them to the dining room. Morgan put up a hand, halting him, and inquired about a room.

Jane stopped as well and regarded her husband with considerable surprise. The request was unexpected. "I thought we were going to eat and then return to Morning Star."

"Do you object to hot running water and a bathtub so big that —"

Jane raised her hand and placed it over his mouth. She would swear she could feel the imprint of his wicked smile against her palm. "Excuse my husband, Walt. He forgets himself."

"Oh, it's all right, ma'am. I've heard the like before and more besides." He put a finger to his own lips. "It's not in me to talk about things I shouldn't, and I reckon Mr. Longstreet knows that."

Jane dropped her hand when Morgan nodded. "I will depend upon your discretion, Walt. Please, tell us that you have a room."

"Sure do. Just the one. Number six at the end of the hall. You want to sign in now? Mrs. Sterling will be real happy to hear you're spending the night."

"Show me the book," Morgan said, "and then show us to a table."

It was almost two hours later that Jane and Morgan followed Walt up the stairs and were escorted to their room. Jane unpinned her hat and held it against her midriff while she collapsed backward on the bed. She lay like that for a time, eyes closed, legs dangling over the side, and enjoyed the splendid comfort of doing nothing, thinking nothing.

Morgan tossed his hat on the seat of a chair and laid their coats over the back of it. He lit a lamp on the dresser and another on the bedside table before he knelt at Jane's limp feet and began to unfasten the laces on her boots. She made funny little whimpering sounds of contentment as he worked the boots off.

"Are these too tight?" he asked her, dropping the first one to the floor. "Maybe you need a new pair. We can do that tomorrow morning before we leave."

"There is nothing wrong with them. Barefoot is simply better."

"Oh. Well, in that case . . ." He reached under her skirt all the way to the garter above her knee and began to unroll her stockings.

Jane's sigh defined bliss. "I believe you would make a most excellent lady's maid."

"Did you have one?" He lifted one of her feet and pressed his thumbs into the ball and sole. She actually shivered with pleasure. That was encouraging.

"Of my own? No. But if there was an important event that required my being turned out like a new penny, Rebecca's maid had to make time for me. She minded a great deal less than Rebecca."

"I've noticed you never write to her. To

anyone." When he paused his massage of her foot while he waited for a response, she curled her toes and let him know he should go on. "I thought you would write to Alexander."

"The express mail train crosses the country both ways. You have not seen any letters from him, have you?"

"No."

"There is your answer. I rarely think of him, of any of them, actually." Jane whimpered again when he found a sweet spot in the tender arch of her foot. "I know the circumstances of being separated from our families are very different, but did you think much about them during your incarceration?"

"I guess I did. In the beginning anyway. Trying to forget something — or someone — is the wrong way to go about making peace with it. At least that's what I'm learning. Putting that memory front and center makes it a wall you can't see over or get around. And if you put the damn thing so far behind you that it's hardly a recollection anymore, the next thing you know it's biting you in the ass."

"Like Gideon and Jack."

He nodded. "Exactly like Gideon and Jack. So I guess the only way to go on without slamming into walls or getting bit is to keep it all beside you and acknowledge it from time to time." He gave her foot a little tug. "Of course, it helps if there's someone around to keep you steady while you're doing that."

Jane dabbed at an errant tear that slid from the corner of her eye. "You say extraordinary things, Morgan Longstreet."

"Huh."

Levering herself up on her elbows, Jane regarded him with a watery smile and a slightly arched eyebrow. "Sometimes more than others."

He grinned back at her. "How about I draw milady a bath?"

Jane groaned feelingly and fell on her back a second time. "Yes, please. Milady will be ever so grateful."

"Oh, I'm counting on that."

Jane was barely awake when he came to fetch her. He considered turning her more comfortably on the bed, covering her with a blanket, and letting her lie there, but then she extended an arm toward him in an elegant, graceful gesture and that made up his mind. Pulling her to her feet, he guided her into the bathing room, where he relieved her of everything right down to the tortoiseshell combs in her hair. He held her hand when she stepped into the tub and kept holding it until water lapped at her breasts. When he was certain she wouldn't sink and drown, he laid towels on a stool and then carried her clothes into the bedroom. He stripped there, adding his clothes to those he had arranged on the chair. When he looked over at the bed and saw Jane's hat was still on it, he moved it. She would not thank him for crushing it in a frenzy of lovemaking.

He was still grinning when he lowered himself into the tub.

Jane roused herself enough to look at him from under one partially raised eyelid. "I am not going to ask *what* you are doing. That seems obvious. It is the *why* that eludes me."

"Back scrub?"

Jane was aware of the water rising as Morgan settled himself comfortably in front of her. "That is more easily accomplished if you are sitting on the stool *outside* the tub."

"I was thinking of my back."

She opened her other eye but not by much. "In that case, you're facing the wrong way." She made a circling motion with her forefinger. "Be careful. I should not like it if you slipped in a puddle on your way to bed. You might be carrying me."

"And I thought your hat was all I had to worry about."

"What?"

"Nothing." He rose up, turned, and put himself in the space Jane made for him between her thighs. She was holding soap and a sponge in her hand, so Morgan drew up his knees and leaned forward. At the first pass she made, he bent his head forward and closed his eyes.

Jane pressed her knuckles against her mouth to cover an abrupt yawn. "I do not know why I am so tired."

"I can think of a couple or three reasons. Strain. Lack of sleep. And polishing off everything Mrs. Sterling put in front of you at dinner. It was a heavy meal, plus you ate more of my apple pie than I did."

"That is an exaggeration. I ate perhaps a third of your pie."

"And all of your own."

"Mmm. Mrs. Sterling was happy, though. Did you notice? She thinks I don't eat nearly enough."

"I'm not unhappy about it. I don't think you eat enough either. Not lately anyway, tonight being a notable exception."

"There is altogether too much interest in my appetite. I am so full now, I believe I have a belly."

Morgan reached behind him. "You do."

"That is not my belly." She lowered his hand.

"Oh. You do."

Laughing under her breath, she slapped his hand away and returned to applying the soapy sponge to his back. For a time she did nothing but make slow, lazy circles. "Are you satisfied with how things turned out today?"

"I will let you know in about an hour."

Jane squeezed the sponge over his head. Spitting and sputtering, he grabbed it out of her hand and leaned back so she was pressed against the sloped end of the tub. Her arms went around him and her legs followed. It was difficult for either of them to know who was captured and who was cradled. What was important was that it did not make any difference.

They remained like that until the water began to cool. Morgan nudged the stopper with his toe and drained about half the tub before he added hot water. They immediately returned to positions of sloth.

Jane soaped Morgan's damp, ginger hair and amused herself making furrows and peaks and curls while he washed. When he was done, she helped him rinse his hair. She would have washed herself, but he kept the sponge and soap and took what Jane told him was an unnatural interest in her hygiene.

Water did accumulate in puddles on the floor but that happened as they were getting out. Jane stole both towels that were on the stool, one for her wet hair and the other to wrap around her shivering torso. Morgan had to find another, and that delay meant Jane was already turning back the covers when he arrived at the bedside.

He whipped off the towel she had tucked around her head, but he let her keep the one she was clutching to her breast. "I don't understand why, Jane, but I find your modesty very, *very* fetching."

She tumbled into bed, taking the towel he had hitched around his hips with her. "We are different that way," she said, regarding the state of his erection with unabashed interest. She lifted the covers and patted the place beside her. "Come here, Mr. Longstreet. I believe I can help you with that."

"I'd be obliged if you would." He extinguished one of the lamps and crawled into bed.

Under the cover of the blankets, Jane surrendered her towel.

They made love with no urgency, but taking their time was satisfying in its own right.

Slow exploration made the places they had been before seem new. There was wonder in the rediscovery of how sensitive Jane was to his lips at the hollow of her throat, and how responsive Morgan was to her fingertips at the nape of his neck.

Their kisses lingered, wet and slow and deep. They tasted at their leisure. Sometimes they teased, but not often. It was more than either one of them wanted to do just then.

When Morgan took her breast into the hot suck of his mouth, Jane lightly held his head in the cup of her palms. The contractions were sweet. She closed her eyes and concentrated on them.

When Jane's hand made a languorous sweep of his thigh, Morgan held himself very still in anticipation of her palm slipping over that curve and making a nest for him. When it happened, he held his breath. She squeezed.

It meant something that intimacy could also be play. Jane laughed in short, staccato bursts when he learned she was ticklish at the base of her ribs. He kept coming back to the spot because the sound of her laughter was transcendent. Morgan's laughter was deeper, vibrating in his chest, lodging in his throat, and it overtook him every time she whispered something outrageous in his ear. Her breath was warm, damp, and he did not think she knew half of what she said, but it tickled him that she said it.

"What about here?" he asked, sliding his fingers between her dewy lips.

"Mmm."

He removed his hand. "Good to know."

She parted her legs a fraction, but his fingers did not return. She accused him of having no mercy. That merely made him grin.

Later, she asked, "Here?" Her fingers were making a trail from his neck to the base of his spine. The twin dimples just above his taut buttocks were her targets. She felt for the impressions, found them, and pressed.

"Mmm."

They agreed that indolent lovemaking did not lend itself to eloquence. It seemed they were too lazy for words.

She straddled him. It seemed fitting since she had learned to ride. Jane liked seeing him from this angle, his eyes filled with her. She drew his hands to her breasts and guided their caress. She lifted her hips and then slowly lowered herself onto his cock until she found her seat.

Neither of them moved. This was also part of the play, and they might have stayed in their still, carnal pose if the absurdity of it had not struck them at the same time. Their simultaneous shouts of laughter changed the tempo of everything.

Jane rocked her pelvis, rising, falling Morgan stroked her. His fingers pressed the flesh of her bottom. He added his thrust to hers. The rhythm was shared. They heard the same pulse, the same percussive beating, and their bodies responded to the familiar cadence effortlessly.

Jane's dark, damp hair fell over her shoulders as she arched backward at the moment of orgasm. Morgan's eyes followed the extension of her slender neck, the thrust of her pink-tipped breasts, the lift of her abdomen, as her breathing grew shallower. He heard her gasp, catch her breath, and then her shudder rolled into him like water spilling over a dam. He clutched her hips as though he needed to hold on. His muscles had reached a state of tension that could not be sustained, and when they released that coiled energy in one long spasm, Morgan thought he might come out of his unbearably tight skin.

For the third time since entering room number six, Jane collapsed on her back on the bed. Naked, although hardly conscious of it, she did not try to cover herself.

"You are exhausting," she whispered.

"I am too tired to return the compliment."

Jane was able to raise a small smile. She laid a forearm across her eyes and nudged Morgan's shoulder with her free hand.

"What?"

"More coals in the stove, please."

"You could pull up a blanket."

"I do not think that is a good idea. Not when you find my modesty fetching. I don't think I could be fetched right now."

Morgan gave her a sideways look, but since she couldn't see him, his suspicious peek was lost on her. Grunting softly, he rolled out of bed and padded to the cast-iron stove. He added coals to the belly of the stove and then went to the bathing room to wash up. When he returned, Jane was lying on her side, her head propped up on an elbow. She had a sheet draped over one shoulder and across her torso. One of her long legs was exposed from thigh to toe. Modestly covered, she looked like a goddess.

Careful not to disturb the arrangement of Jane's sheet, Morgan climbed into bed and drew the blankets on his side up to his chest. He had just settled comfortably into the mattress when Jane touched him on the corner of his mouth with her fingertip. Since it was the corner with the crescent moon scar, he knew what she was finally going to ask.

"Fishing," he said.

"Fishing? I'm not —" She smiled and lightly tapped the scar with her fingernail. "I see. You were answering the question I hadn't asked. How very prescient."

"Prescient. There's one I haven't heard before."

"It means —"

"I got it now."

"Tell me about fishing."

"There's not much to tell. Gideon and Jack were fooling around by the lake, snapping their rods and casting long and wide. One of them, and I swear I don't remember who, snagged me with his line. Hook caught me in the mouth because I was yelling at them to watch what they were doing. Zetta Lee stitched it up, and Ham whupped them both with his belt. I was crying, carrying on, begging him not to do it. I think he figured out what I was really trying to tell him because after Zetta Lee finished her stitch work, he whupped me, too."

"And that put you back in your brothers' good graces?"

"Sure did. For a time."

Jane chuckled quietly. "Fishing." She leaned over and kissed the corner of his mouth. "Most of the time it gives your smile a wry twist."

"And the times that it doesn't?"

"It gives your smile youth."

That made him grin. He drew her hand to his lips and pressed a kiss to her knuckles.

Jane repeated the question she had asked him earlier. "Are you satisfied with how things turned out today?"

Morgan did not make the question less important than it was with a flippant answer. "Yes," he said. "I'm satisfied. Going to see Cobb was the right thing to do."

"I feel better knowing that he will be watching for Gideon's return, and when we get back to Morning Star you'll tell the others what they can expect."

"They know most of it. And Jem's already had a knock-down-drag-out with three of the men running with Gideon."

"But now you have remarkable likenesses of all of them except for Jack, and you will know him immediately. I think it was good of Marshal Bridger to make sketches for us to take back."

"It was."

Jane slipped her hand under the covers and rested it on Morgan's chest, just above his heart. "How did you come by the money to buy Morning Star?"

"Did you put your hand there because it's comforting or because you think my heartbeat might tell you if I'm lying?"

"Because it's comforting, although the other sounds as if it might have some merit. Are you going to lie to me, Morgan? And by lie, I mean evade the truth, omit the truth, turn the truth on its head, or otherwise prevaricate."

"I rustled cattle and saddle horses. That is about as straight as I can say it."

Jane's lips puffed as she blew out a breath. "I tried to imagine what you might say and how I would feel about it before I asked."

"How are you doing with that?"

"My conscience is pinching me."

"Like your boots were."

"Yes, about like that."

"Maybe this will help some. I stole the cattle and horses from Zetta Lee."

"You did?"

"Uh-huh. It was a spell after I got out before I could go up to Lander. I wasn't even sure that she would still have the place, and I wasn't going there to see her anyway. I wanted to pay my respects to Ham, see his grave again, and more or less apologize for what became of that legacy he was so keen to have.

"I had been thinking on the problem of

what I was going to do when I got out. Mrs. Sterling had written to me about the old Burdick place, and I had some ideas about what I could do with a spread like that. No money, though. I had to work for a rancher in Uinta County until I had enough to buy one of his old saddle horses. I left for Lander that same day.

"When I got there, I did what I set out to do. Ham's gravesite needed a bit of tending, so I did that, too, then I looked around at what had become of Welling & Sons, and the only thing I decided that would keep me from putting my hands on Zetta Lee was to steal her cattle."

"Welling & Sons," Jane repeated quietly.

"Ham's brand was a complicated thing. He had it forged when Essie was carrying their first child. He told me once that he started using it right after that baby was put in the ground because he was so sure there'd be another."

"Poor Essie."

"That's what I thought, but Ham figured he was just being optimistic."

"What was the brand?"

"A *W* with an interlacing *S*."

Jane used her index finger to trace the letters above Morgan's heart.

"Ham was always fussing about it come

branding time. If you didn't place the brand just right, especially if you got it upside down, it looked like —"

Jane smacked him on the chest, not hard, but hard enough to get his attention. "Morning Star," she said. "It would look *exactly* like your brand at Morning Star." She traced it again, this time with an *M* and the *S* twining through it like ivy. "It *is* your brand."

"I'll be darned." He caught her hand before she slapped him on the chest again. "You have violent tendencies, ma'am."

Jane was not contrite. "If that is true, you should stop nurturing them. I thought you named your ranch Morning Star because it speaks to what is on the horizon. It is hopeful and grand and —"

"Romantic?"

She sighed softly, nodding. "Yes, romantic. Now I learn that it was merely practical."

"I don't know. It's a little romantic. I could have named my place Morgan's Sanctuary or Mostly Stolen. Those are practical."

Jane laughed in spite of herself. "If those were the other choices, then you did well." She sobered some, inching closer. "How was it that you were never caught? You are the one who told me the law deals harshly with cattle thieves. More harshly, it seems, than they do with bank robbers."

"Caught? I don't think Zetta Lee knew that any of her cattle were missing until spring. By then I was long gone. She did not have enough hands at the ranch to ride the property, and fences had not been repaired in a long time. The only man I recognized still working for her was old Hatch Crookshank."

"The one who taught you to gentle horses."

Trust Jane to remember, he thought. "Yes. The same. He was Ham's friend as much as his best hired hand. Zetta Lee would have done well to trust him, but she never warmed to anything he had to say. The state of the ranch spoke to that, and it made what I was doing about as easy as buttering toast.

"Beef prices were good then. I drove small herds southwest across the open range to the station at Kemmerer, not far from the territory line. No one knew me there. Ham had never registered his brand because the station inspectors at Rock Springs knew him when he started out. I registered his brand as mine but made sure the inspectors understood the proper orientation for the iron. I sold the cattle to start, got enough for a stake in a rolling poker game on the

Union Pacific, and tripled what I had. I went back for more cattle and did it all over again. When I returned the third time, I already had an agreement with the syndicate to purchase the ranch and money down on the contract. I took fewer cows that time because I had no intention of selling at market. That's also when I stole some of the horses."

"And you escorted your spoils to Morning Star."

"Escorted? I suppose that's accurate. They were real cooperative; it didn't feel like much of a drive. There was some good stock left from when the Burdicks owned the ranch. The eastern speculators hadn't done right by the land or the cattle, but there wasn't anything that could not be repaired over time. I didn't need Zetta Lee's cattle or her horses. I took them mostly for —"

"Revenge?" asked Jane.

"I was going to say I took them mostly for sentimental reasons, but I won't argue with revenge."

Jane's soft laughter tickled her lips. "All right." She traced her initials on his chest.

"Branding me?"

"I am, yes." She tapped him again. "What happened to the money from the robberies?"

"Split and spent. Zetta Lee got most of it. She considered that fair since she did the planning. There wasn't one of us who trusted banks, but no one thought that Ham's safe was a good place to put money either."

"Not with you around, certainly."

"I believe that factored in their opinion."

"So?"

"So everyone had a hidey-hole. Mine was an old stump I hollowed out about a hundred yards due north of where Ham was buried. Yes, I spent some time looking for it when I was up there. Found the stump, but there was nothing inside. Before I looked, I told myself I wouldn't take the money, or if I did, I'd return it to someone, maybe Mr. Cumberland at the Rock Springs bank. Since there wasn't any money, I can tell myself that I would have resisted the temptation to keep it, but I think I know better."

"What happened to it?"

He shrugged. "My best guess is that Zetta Lee found it after the trial. She probably knew where it was all along. Same for Gideon's and Jack's."

"Don't you think your brothers might have gone back to Lander to get what they left behind?"

"They might have. Or they might not have

seen the sense in it, knowing Zetta Lee the way they did."

"Where did she keep her money?"

"I don't know. Probably close. If something was important to her, she didn't like to let it out of her sight."

It was the same if some*one* was important, Jane thought. She did not say it. Morgan was probably thinking it as well. "Her bedroom, then. In her mattress. Perhaps under the floorboards under the bed."

"Maybe there was a false bottom in the trunk where she stored extra linens."

"Hah! You could not resist reminding me, could you?"

"Apparently not."

Jane injected some starch into her tone. "You must be very pleased to know you can get your hands on my money anytime you like. *I* have to present my savings book. *You* merely have to present yourself."

He chuckled. "I have money there as well. And Cattleman's Trust holds my mortgage. I have more to lose if Mr. Webb opens his safe than if he keeps it closed. And you heard me tell Bridger, given enough time, that 1884 Barkley and Benjamin he keeps in his office is probably not that difficult to get into."

She feigned a disapproving sigh. "It is

distressing that you know the kind of safe he has."

"Again. My money is there."

"Still, you know the *year* that safe was made, and you were in jail when it was manufactured."

Morgan said modestly, "I did some reading."

"You did some reading," Jane repeated, shaking her head. "It is no wonder that Cobb Bridger walked in your footprints every time you came to town." She poked him in the chest. "And don't pretend you did not enjoy that just a little."

CHAPTER FOURTEEN

The thaw Gideon Welling had been waiting for finally arrived in the middle of February. He did not move his men out immediately, not when the trails and roads were muddy enough to trap a horse. Instead, he bet on a freeze to follow, and when it arrived bearing biting winds and no snow, when ground was hard and easy to cover quickly, he judged it was time to leave Rawlins.

No one objected. Marcie was pretty sure he had contracted the pox from one of the whores. Dix didn't have much to show for all the nights he spent playing poker. Avery Butterfield was tired of drunks trying to pick a fight with him just because he was the biggest man in the saloon and they figured — hell, he didn't know what they figured. He was the biggest man in the saloon, for God's sake.

They got their ten-dollar horses and forty-dollar saddles from the livery, mounted up, and set out for the Morning Star ranch.

"Hey, Marshal Bridger."

Cobb was about to step inside his office when he heard the greeting. He backed up and turned to face the street. "Hey, Rabbit." He put up a hand to greet Finn as well. The boys were riding in the buckboard they used to take visitors to the Pennyroyal, but this afternoon they were alone in the wagon. "Where are you off to?"

Finn, who held the reins, brought the wagon to a halt when it was abreast of Cobb. He pulled down his red woolen scarf so he could be understood. "We're going out to Morning Star."

Cobb's eyebrows puckered as he frowned.

Rabbit said, "He's talkin' about Mr. Longstreet's ranch. Sounds a heap better than callin' it the old Burdick place."

Realizing the boys had misinterpreted the reason for his look, Cobb nodded. "It does sound better," he agreed. "So why you are going out there, and do your granny and pap know?"

Finn said, "You sure got a powerful interest in what folks are doin'."

"Part of the job," said Cobb. He stuffed his hands in the pockets of his long coat to keep them warm. "And you haven't answered the question."

Rabbit jerked his thumb over his shoulder to point to the bed of the buckboard. "That crate is for Mr. Longstreet. Delivery all the way from Chicago. Probably something from one of those catalogs, but Finn and I are on our honor not to do any investigating."

"Yeah," said Finn. "We got the same powerful interest in folks that you do, Marshal, only we ain't got the credentials to make it anything but nosy."

"Is that right," Cobb said wryly.

Finn either missed the edge of sarcasm or, more likely, chose to ignore it. He said, "Sure. That's why Rabbit called out to you. We were goin' to stop here anyway."

Cobb turned his attention to Rabbit. "Oh?"

"We got to thinking that maybe there's something you want us to do for you since we're headed out there. You got a message for anyone? Maybe you want to send a pie or some cookies along. You know, just to be neighborly."

"Uh-huh. Just to be neighborly." He glanced back at the crate. "When did that come in?"

"I reckon about a week ago," said Rabbit.

"Pap held it thinkin' someone from the ranch would be in and could take delivery, but no one's shown up for a spell. That's why it's our job now."

"Yeah," said Finn. "And it's not so far to the ranch house that we can't get there and back before dark. Not that the dark bothers us. You know we do our best work at night."

"I do know that." Cobb was not warm to the idea of the boys going out to the ranch again, but he had no compelling reason to stop them. He had seen Morgan one time since he and Jane visited his office together, and Max Salter had been in town shortly after that. They had nothing to report. The ranch was quiet and there were no signs of anyone riding the outskirts of the property.

Then there was the crate. Cobb estimated it was three feet high, four feet wide, and another three feet deep. All kinds of things could fit into a box like that. It was tempting to look inside, but not even his credentials made that right or legal. He let it go.

"All right," he said. "I guess I could send you out there with something from Jenny's bakery."

"Is there a message?" Finn asked hopefully.

"Yes. Give my best to Mrs. Longstreet."

"That's it? You ain't goin' to make us

deputies? Rabbit and me figure we could be transportin' somethin' of great significance."

Rabbit added, "Could be there's gold. Guns maybe. Bottles of good whiskey packed in excelsior. It's heavy enough. We've been speculating."

"I bet you have. All right. Both of you, raise your right hand. Your *right* hand, Finn. Good. From this point forward, you are my special deputies, charged with the safe transport of this box to Morning Star ranch. Your commission ends when you report back in. I'll be waiting for you."

"Mrs. Longstreet's real nice," said Finn. "She could invite us to sit for a meal like she did the last time."

"Fine. Eat. But when you get back here, find me. Go on. You know where the bakery is. I'll meet you there."

A sharp, bitter wind buffeted Jane as she removed sheets from the clothesline. She collected wooden pins in her mouth as she moved along. It was difficult to know if the sheets were dry or merely frozen. They were certainly stiff.

"Here," Max Salter said. "Let me help you. I don't even think you should be doing this."

Jane blinked. Like an actor stepping out

to address his audience, Max had parted two sheets to make his entrance. Jane plucked the pins from her mouth and dropped them into the pocket at the front of her apron. "Here, take these." She thrust the crackling sheets into his hands and quickly went down the line, removing shirts, shifts, and a union suit.

"Why shouldn't I be doing this?" she asked.

Max shifted his slight weight from side to side and shrugged.

"Careful, Max. Stay steady or you'll be three sheets to the wind."

He laughed. "That's a good one, ma'am."

Above her armload of clothes, Jane smiled humbly and tilted her head toward the house. "Inside. Now." The wind whipped her dress so hard that the ruffled edge of her petticoats turned up. She hurried off without looking to see if Max was following her.

He was. He got inside, wrestled the door shut, and dropped his load on top of the one Jane had put on the table. She was facing the stove, warming her hands over it. He held up his gloved ones, wriggled his fingers.

"Yes, I know," she said. "It was foolish to go outside without gloves. I can't find them.

I can't find anything these days, Max. Wherever I am, my mind is somewhere else."

"I don't think that's unusual, considering your circumstances."

"My circumstances? My circumstances are no different than anyone else's. We are in this together, aren't we?"

"Oh, certainly," Max said quickly. "We are, of course we are. I was just thinking that . . ."

Jane arched an eyebrow, waiting. "Yes? Thinking that . . . ?"

"Well, that it's probably harder on you. You're left behind, aren't you? Today you're with me. Yesterday it was Jem. Before that it —"

"I understand what you're saying, Max, but I don't agree with you. It's harder on my husband. He can't stay here all the time, and it tears a strip off his skin when he has to go."

"I hadn't thought of that." He took off his gloves and stuffed them in his pockets. "It must be a hell of a thing to have your brothers turning on you the way his are. Jessop and Jake were talking about it the other day, and they couldn't imagine it until Jem started waxin' poetical about Renee. Still, they didn't really turn on him."

"No, they wouldn't do that." Jane turned her back on the stove and began emptying her apron pocket. She tossed the pins into a basket on the table. The ones that missed, Max picked up and threw in. "Did I hear Morgan right this morning? They were riding out past Blue Valley?"

"Yep. Piney Hill. Settler's Ridge. Leastways, the boss and Jake were going that way. Jem and Jessop were riding up to Hickory Lake."

"So it will be dark before they get back."

"For the boss and Jake, sure. Jem and Jessop should come riding in before then. You thinkin' about supper?"

"Yes," she said, although she was thinking nothing of the kind. "I was wondering how many would be here for supper."

"I've got my chores done. I could help."

"It would be lovely to have company." When Max started to unbutton his coat, Jane stopped him. "No, not yet. I need eggs. Six if you can encourage the hens to give them up. And you will probably want to put your gloves back on. Not one of them was kind to me this morning."

"Good idea. And the next time you go outside, wear your coat."

Jane accepted the tit for tat and waved him off. While he was gone, she folded the sheets and clothes and carried them to the bedroom. Max was not back when she returned. Supposing the hens were not being kind to him either, Jane put the basket of clothespins in the pantry and selected the items she needed to make Eggs Susette.

She dropped six fist-sized potatoes in the sink and placed everything else on the table. Watching for Max out the kitchen window, she scrubbed the potatoes with a brush and then pierced each one a few times with a fork before placing them in the oven. Afterward, she sat at the table with her cookbook to review the recipe. Realizing she was going to need two more eggs, she stepped onto the back porch to call for Max.

She had no opportunity to say his name. A gloved hand arrested her speech as soon as she opened her mouth. At the same time, an arm circled her waist and pulled her back hard enough to make her lose her balance. Her assailant supported her. She stared at the bell she was supposed to ring. It hung in its proper place, and it was well outside her reach.

"He'll be coming along directly, Mrs. Longstreet. Don't concern yourself that he won't."

The words were directed into her ear. The tone was calm; the breath was warm. It surprised her that she recognized the voice because their only exchange had been so brief, but she was confident that it was Gideon Welling who was holding her.

Jane made no attempt to struggle. She held herself still but not relaxed. He was holding her close enough to feel her tension.

"You know there's no point in screaming," he said. "You're not hurt and no one except for that fellow in your henhouse is going to hear you. He'd probably want to come after you, and that would surely get him pain for his trouble. That sound right to you?"

Jane drew in her lips so they would not rub against the palm of his leather glove. Her nod was almost infinitesimal.

"Good," he said pleasantly. "I'm going to take my hand away, step to the side, and you're going to go back in the house. I'm going to be right behind you. We're clear on that?"

When she nodded again, he did exactly as he said. So did she. Immediately upon entering the kitchen, her eyes darted to the gun rack. She did not realize that some small movement of her head had given away the direction of her glance until Gideon spoke.

"That's a fine Remington you've got

there. Good for long range. Go on, you have a seat at the table while I remove temptation. That's right. Over there. All the way at the other end." Gideon removed the Remington rifle from the rack, examined it, and then did the same with the Winchester. "Another fine piece here. There's an empty space. That must be what Morgan's carrying. I don't see him riding out without one."

He did not seem to expect a response, so Jane said nothing.

"You stay where you are, ma'am, while I attend to these."

His confidence that she would do as he wanted made Jane set her jaw, and yet she knew it was not misplaced. What were her choices when Max's situation was unknown to her, and she had no means of escape? She watched him disappear with the rifles and listened to his footsteps for some indication of where he was taking them. It was a good strategy on his part, she thought. She would never find them quickly enough to use them.

On the other hand, he had left her alone in the kitchen where there was an astonishing array of weapons. Jane chose her sharpest paring knife and put it in her apron pocket. Even if he found it, it was easily something she might have been carrying in her apron before he accosted her. Jane made certain she was sitting exactly as he left her when he returned to the kitchen. Even the cookbook was still open in front of her.

Gideon sniffed the air. "What's in the oven?"

"Potatoes." Jane felt absurdly delighted that he appeared to be disappointed.

"Huh. Well, that's something at least. Are you going to have enough for guests?"

"I would have to know how many guests."

"How many potatoes you got in there?"

"Six."

Gideon nodded, satisfied. "I reckon that'll do us fine." He wandered over to the window and looked out. "You being so accommodating and all, I figure you remember bumpin' into me in Bitter Springs."

"I do."

"You know who I am?"

"Gideon Welling."

He looked over at her, a narrow smile creasing his face between his mustache and his new growth of beard. "So you figured it out. I'll be damned."

"Most likely."

Gideon's eyes sharpened momentarily, then he chuckled. "Yeah. Most likely." He pointed to the cookbook. "What are you making with those potatoes?"

"Eggs Susette."

He whistled softly. "Eggs Susette. I don't believe I've ever tasted the like before."

"I've never made them before."

"So this is in the nature of an experiment. No harm in that. I always think it's good to try something new. Like comin' here. This is new." He looked out the window again.

Jane merely stared at his profile.

"Where is Morgan?"

"Around and about."

"See? Now, that's an unacceptable answer. I'd hoped for better since we are getting along so well." He stood back from the sink and began to unbutton his coat. He casually parted it to reveal his gun belt and the weapon riding low on his hip.

"Is that a Remington .44-caliber?"

"It is."

"The Model 1858 or the 1875?"

"Jesus. Do you have ice water in your veins? Either one will shoot you dead."

"Mr. Welling, my blood has been running cold since you waylaid me on my own back porch. You made a point of showing me your gun so I thought you meant for me to remark on it."

"Lord, help me. It's the Model 1875."

"Do you carry an extra cylinder or find that you can reload as fast without exchanging it?" Even from her current angle, Jane could see that Gideon's dark eyebrows were rising toward his hairline. He did not answer her question, though. Instead he pointed toward the window.

"Here they come," he said. "And none too soon to my way of thinking." He went to the door and opened it. "Stay where you are, Mrs. Longstreet. There's no cause for you to be jumpin' up like someone lit a fire under you."

Jane sat, but she did so slowly and with what she regarded as a certain air of dignity.

"About time," Gideon said.

Jane pressed down hard on her lips to keep from crying out when she saw Max. He was standing, but only just. The men on either side of him were more responsible for holding him upright than he was. The tender flesh all around his left eye was badly swollen. If he had any vision there, he would not have it much longer. Blood still oozed from a split lip. His jaw sagged oddly to the left, and Jane wondered if it was broken. She knew the moment he saw her because he made an effort to stand taller. She shook her head, and her eyes pleaded with him not to do anything that would make his situation even worse.

Max's hands were bound. Jane could see

that his knuckles were bloody and swollen. She admired his pride for still holding them in tight fists. It must have pained him. She also noticed that his gun had been taken away.

Jane dragged her eyes away from Max's bruised face to look at the men on either side of him. They had not emerged unscathed, but Max had not been able to return the damage proportionately. The larger of the pair, a man with a barrel chest and broad, sullen features, also had a cut lip, although his blood was already drying. The other was chewing on a matchstick and working his jaw from side to side. He did not have the narrow range of motion that Max did, but Jane could tell he was nursing a substantial blow.

"Please let him sit over here," Jane said. "So I can tend to him."

The two newcomers regarded her with a mixture of surprise and suspicion; however, they both looked to Gideon for their orders.

"You better do what she says," Gideon told them. "My brother's got himself a wife full of sass and brass. Put him over there beside her." He pointed out the men as they helped Max to the table. "Big fella's Avery. The other one's Dix. Dixon, but mostly he goes by Dix. This is Mrs. Longstreet."

"Ma'am," said Avery.

"Ma'am," said Dixon.

Jane wished they had scowled at her. Their mannerly greetings and polite smiles were more disturbing. She wondered if anyone expected her to introduce Max.

"That's Max," Avery said to Gideon. He set one of his large hands on Max's shoulder and pushed him into the chair that Dix held out for him. Once Max was down, they both pushed the chair close to the table.

Gideon said, "Did you get anything out of him besides his name?"

"No. He's not much of a talker."

"Well, we'll see if that changes." He looked at Jane. "What do you need to look after him?"

Jane told him, and Gideon sent Avery to collect it. "A basin of fresh water also. Please."

Gideon jerked his head toward the sink, and Dix went to fetch it. "Did you take care of the horses?" he asked.

"Out of sight, just like you wanted," said Dix. "Marcie's finishing up. He should be along directly."

"And the others?"

"The others? Oh, yeah. Everyone's exactly where you want them."

"Good. We're settling in."

Dix put a bowl of water in front of Jane. Avery returned from the washroom and placed the items she had asked for beside the bowl. He handed her a washcloth.

"You two can go into the parlor for a spell. Warm yourselves at the fireplace while I get acquainted with my sister-in-law. I'll send Marcie in when he gets here. Don't get too comfortable. Everyone's got to take a turn outside on lookout." When they were gone, Gideon removed his coat and hung it on a peg beside the empty gun rack. He stuffed his gloves in a sleeve and placed his hat on another peg.

Jane watched him run his fingers through his hair in a gesture that was reminiscent of Morgan. It was unexpected, and Jane confronted her first moment of real despair since Gideon Welling had appeared. Searching for composure, she began to minister to Max's wounds.

Gideon pulled out a chair at the end of the table opposite Jane, spun it around, and sat. "He's lucky."

"I doubt that he thinks the same."

"Maybe not, but it doesn't change the fact that he's not dead. That makes him lucky."

If those were Max's choices, Jane was inclined to agree. She did not say so, choosing instead to concentrate on bathing his face. She gently touched his jaw and encouraged him to try to move it. He did, but with great care. "I'm so sorry, Max."

"Why are you sorry?" asked Gideon. "If Morgan were to apologize to him, I could understand. But you? Seems a mite excessive."

"I sent him out for eggs."

"Well, then, you're right to be sorry."

"Which I still require."

"What? Oh, you mean the eggs. Marcie can get them before he comes inside."

Jane dabbed alcohol on a cotton ball and pressed it against Max's lip. His head reared back and his eyes watered, but he did not make a sound. "Hold that there while I see to your hands." He brought up his bound hands to his mouth, and Jane carefully washed his battered knuckles.

Gideon watched her ministrations. "You're good to give your man so much kind attention, but it's likely only a temporary balm, you understand."

"What do you mean?"

Max spoke between clenched teeth. "He means they're going to plant more fists in my face."

Jane's head swiveled to Gideon. "Is he right? You're going to hurt him again?"

"Maybe. Where is your husband?"

"I told you. Around and about."

"Then, yeah, he's right."

Jane wrung out the washcloth hard. "For God's sake, how can I possibly know where Morgan is? It is a ridiculous question. Morning Star is twenty-six square miles. That's more than sixteen thousand acres. He could be standing in the middle of any one of them right now."

"Where did he set off to?"

"Blue Valley."

"That doesn't mean much. What direction and how far?"

She looked at Max. He shook his head. Jane told Gideon anyway.

"And the others?" asked Gideon.

Jane hesitated, and then relented. It seemed little enough to tell him. He wasn't going to ride out to meet them when he could wait at the house to announce his presence.

Gideon lightly tapped the top rail of his chair. "What has Morgan told you about me?"

Jane was keenly aware that Gideon's question served him alone. He did not ask, "What has Morgan told you about *us*?" It came to her suddenly that Jackson Welling might not be one of the "others." She could not say what the consequences might be, but in spite of not knowing, she asked, "Where is your brother Jack?"

Gideon did not answer immediately. His head tilted to one side as he studied Jane. He knuckled his beard. "He's outside."

Jane shook her head. "He's not. You are lying." She was not certain it was true until she said it, and then she was very certain that it was. "Yes," she said with confidence. "You are lying."

Gideon pointed to his right eyelid. "Was it twitching? Sometimes I don't notice it, and I can't really stop it, so . . ." He held up his hands in a helpless gesture. "I would not want to play poker with you."

"Where is Jackson?"

"Nebraska. A little place called Falls City."

"He did not want to join you?"

"He did, except that he couldn't, seein' how he got himself murdered for cheatin'. At cards, you understand. Not with a woman."

Jane offered no condolences. Her face remained a mask, and she went back to attending to Max.

"You haven't asked why I am here. You probably figured out this isn't a regular family reunion."

"Yes. Your actions have spoken to that. It

seems clear you have business with my husband."

" 'Business.' That's as good a word for it as any other. Yes, I have business with my little brother." Gideon suddenly leaned back and called into the front room, "Avery! Go outside and see what's keepin' Marcellus. He should have been here by now. And while you're out, get —" He cocked an eyebrow at Jane. She held up eight fingers. "Get eight eggs."

Avery appeared in the doorway, shrugging into his coat. "Eight eggs." He sniffed the air just as Gideon had done earlier. "Am I smelling potatoes bakin'?"

Gideon nodded shortly and pointed to the door. When Avery lumbered off, Gideon said, "Shouldn't you be seein' to those potatoes about now?"

"It has not been long enough."

He shrugged. "Guess you would know. Just don't get any ideas about ruining our dinner for spite. That'd be real inhospitable, and frankly, it would piss me off."

Jane ignored him. She sat back and critically eyed Max's injuries. She wrung out the washcloth and applied one corner of it to a runnel of dried blood on his jaw just below his ear. When he winced, so did she. "I'm sorry." He waved off her apology as she withdrew the cloth. Jane sighed inaudibly and turned to Gideon. "Except for seeing to his pain, I am done here. I have some headache powders in my dresser that could help him if you will allow me to get them."

Gideon jerked his chin at Max. "You have a headache?"

Max glared at him and said nothing.

"That's a no, then." He offered Jane an apologetic smile. "It's the nature of some people to shoot themselves in the foot."

Jane had no comment. She put the salves, alcohol, bandages, and cotton balls together, and then folded her hands in her lap under the table. She stared steadily at Gideon. His lips twitched, but not his eye. His amusement rankled but Jane gave no hint of it. She was very aware of Max's presence and knew he would insert himself if there were the slightest indication he should do so. It was for that reason that Jane looked away first.

"You got any whiskey?" asked Gideon.

"I could make you coffee."

"That'd be fine, but I'm still waitin' for an answer about the whiskey."

"In a cabinet in the front room."

Gideon did not move. "Hey, Dix! You find the whiskey?"

The answer came back immediately. "Sure did."

"Then bring it in here."

Dix appeared in moments with a bottle and a glass. He set both down in front of Gideon. He rolled the matchstick to the corner of his mouth as he spoke. "Your brother ain't much for spirits. This is all there is."

"You looked in the cabinet?"

Dix nodded.

"You and Avery had some, though."

"Yeah, we did. Warm us up, you know."

Gideon looked as if he were going to come out of his chair, but a disturbance coming from the back porch actually kept him in it. "See what that's about."

Dixon's hand hovered near his gun as he went to the door. At the last moment, he stepped sideways and peeked out the kitchen window. "What the —"

Jane was disappointed that surprise did not cause him to swallow and choke on the matchstick. A gust of wind swept into the kitchen when he pushed the door open. From her vantage point, Jane could not see who was on the porch. Max could, though, and she looked to him for understanding. When she saw his lip begin to bleed again as a frown stretched his skin, her heart

533

began to hammer.

"Hey, Mrs. Longstreet," Finn said as he crossed the threshold. His eyes widened when he saw Max. "Well, hey there, Max. What happened to you?"

Jane spoke quickly so Max did not have to. "He was in a bit of a scrape. Fooling around that got out of hand."

Rabbit came up behind Finn and nudged his brother farther into the room. He got a good look at Max, shook his head, and then said to Jane, "Didn't know about you having company, Mrs. Longstreet, but the extra hands turned out to be a good thing. Got a delivery for you. Well, for Mr. Longstreet, but I reckon it's all the same, the address being Morning Star ranch. Anyways, that's why we're here."

Gideon was on his feet now, watching Avery back through the doorway carrying one end of a crate that was putting some strain on his shoulders. Marcie had the other end of the thing and was puffing a little as they maneuvered it into the kitchen.

Gideon swore softly. "Couldn't you leave it on the porch?"

"They were not having any of that," Marcie said as he and Avery lowered the crate to the floor.

"They?" He forked two fingers at Rabbit

and Finn. "You mean these two? You're taking orders from these two?"

Avery's broad features reddened in a way that could not be explained by his encounter with the outdoors. "It's kind of hard to explain, but yeah, I guess we did."

Gideon jabbed his fingers at the boys again. "Who are you exactly?"

"Exactly?" asked Rabbit, whipping off his hat to reveal an unruly head of dark blond hair, some of it sticking straight up. "I'm exactly Cabot Theodore Collins, and I go by Rabbit on account of no kid wants to be called Cabot Theodore." His chest puffed. "And I happen to be about as quick as one."

"I bet you are," Gideon said under his breath. His eyes swiveled to Finn. "What about you?"

Finn also removed his hat. "Carpenter Addison Collins, and folks know me by Finn. I named myself, and it stuck on account I only answer to Carpenter when it's my gran who's saying it."

Gideon looked at Jane as he pointed to the crate. "Do you know what that is?"

"No."

He swore under his breath and rubbed his forehead. "Marcie. Avery. Put it in the front room. Dix. Take Max and make him comfortable somewhere. He should probably lie down." He stepped to block the boys' view of Max's bound hands as Dix led him out of the kitchen. "You fellows want to sit down?"

Rabbit and Finn exchanged glances. It was Rabbit who spoke. "That's real kind of you, sir, and the potatoes sure got my mouth to waterin', but our pap expects us back before dark, and mostly we do what he says."

"Even if you leave now, it's going to be nightfall before you get back." Gideon nodded toward the window to draw their attention to the lowering sun. "Go on. Sit down." He did not frame it as a request this time.

The boys sat, Finn taking Max's chair and Rabbit taking the one opposite his brother. They flanked Jane.

"They should go back to town," Jane said.

"They will. Maybe with an escort, seein' that it'll be dark soon. I reckon you boys came out here with a wagon."

"Yes, sir," said Finn. "Our pap's buckboard."

"Where is it now?"

"That one fellow with the scar — Marcie, I think you called him — he took it to the barn and said he would look after our mare. He helped us get the crate off first, and we stood by it just in case there were villains around on account of there could be just about anything inside it. We're speculating that we took shipment of gold bars."

"Huh. Gold bars. So you boys must like adventures."

"Sure. We had us a few."

"Well, let's just say you're having one now."

Finn nodded, and Rabbit joined him. Neither of them looked at Jane.

She started to rise.

"Where are you goin'?" asked Gideon.

"The potatoes. They're done. And I *still* need eight eggs."

"I'll get 'em," said Rabbit.

Gideon put out a hand. "No. Stay where you are. Marcie will get them." He hollered for his man, told him what he wanted, and Marcie shuffled out, shoulders hunched to brace for the cold.

At Gideon's nod, Jane finished straightening and walked over to the stove. She wrapped a towel around her hand and removed the potatoes from the oven. She heard Gideon clear his throat in a warning manner when she picked up a knife. "I need to slice open one end of each potato." When he did not say anything, she began to make the cuts, acutely aware of how closely he was watching her.

Marcie returned with the eggs. The hens had not pecked his eyes out as Jane had hoped, but she observed that he had fresh scratches on the backs of his hands. She resisted the urge to tell him that he should have worn gloves.

While she prepared the Eggs Susette, checking the recipe from time to time, Gideon engaged Finn and Rabbit in conversation. It was truly his only recourse because shutting them up was not so easily accomplished.

Occasionally she caught him looking out the window, judging, she supposed, the onset of nightfall. It was impossible not to think about Morgan's return. He would see the boys' horse and buckboard in the barn when he came back. He was familiar with both, and he might be surprised that Finn and Rabbit were still here so late, but he would not be suspicious. He would walk in the door prepared to greet them and come face-to-face with Gideon Welling.

Jane poached six eggs in a gently rolling boil while she lined the scooped-out baked potato shells with a mixture of mashed potatoes, finely chopped ham, dried parsley, the whites of two eggs, butter, and cream. She removed the poached eggs with a slotted spoon and carefully slipped one into each shell. While she was wondering if she could toss the hot water at Gideon without scalding Rabbit, he suddenly appeared at her side and removed the pot. He gave her a crooked, knowing grin as he emptied the water into the sink.

"Thought I could help," he said.

Jane held her breath as something caught Gideon's attention; he leaned forward and stared hard out the window.

"Avery! Here. Now. Dix! You and Marcie keep an eye on the front door."

Jane said, "Please let the boys go."

"No."

It was said with such finality that Jane did not argue. She placed a hand on Rabbit's shoulder and smiled at Finn. She meant to reassure, but there was a tremor in her fingers and her chin wobbled. She averted her head and quickly blinked back tears. Beneath her feet, the floor shook as Avery's heavy footfalls pounded through the house.

Gideon held up his hand as he continued to look out the window. "Two of them. They just went into the barn. I can't be sure who they were. They'll see to their horses first. Maybe . . ." He crooked a finger at Rabbit. "Why don't you come with me, son?"

Jane shook her head vehemently. "No. I'll go. The boys stay here."

Gideon's chuckle was without humor. "I know you heard a question there, but it really wasn't. The boy comes with me. Dix! Get in here. Sit with Mrs. Longstreet and Finn while Avery and I mosey out to the barn."

Jane took a step forward, but Rabbit jumped up and blocked her progress.

"It's all right, Mrs. Longstreet. I don't mind goin' with these gentlemen, and you got supper there to think about. I'm kind of curious about those potato cups you're makin'. Sure would like to try one."

Jane nodded because she couldn't speak. She ruffled the hair at Rabbit's nape before he jammed his hat back on his head. When Gideon held out an arm, Rabbit marched right up and allowed himself to be nudged out the door.

Finn had a lopsided grin for Jane. "Don't worry about Rabbit. He does all right fendin' for himself now that he's thirteen. Now, if he had asked me go, well, that'd be a worry for everyone, even me."

Jane thought he was extraordinarily philosophical about it.

Finn set his folded hands on the table with great aplomb and regarded the man who was charged with keeping them in the kitchen. "So," he said gravely, "what sort of name is Dicks anyway? No villain should have a name that sounds like his man parts."

The Eggs Susette was ready to come out of the oven when Gideon, Avery, and Rabbit walked back inside. Gideon had Rabbit firmly by his coat collar. He marched him up to the table, kicked out a chair, sat him down hard, and then he pushed the chair in until Rabbit's chest bumped the table.

"Was that necessary?" asked Jane. "He's a boy."

"He's man enough to tell your hands to shoot me when I was holding a gun to his head."

"Oh, yes. Of course you would do that. It is a very tired tactic, Mr. Welling, and one that shows a singular lack of imagination. To use it on a child to elicit the cooperation of the ranch hands is unconscionable."

"Lord, ma'am, but you have a mouth on you."

Finn leaned forward and whispered to his brother across the table. "She does kinda, but it's real pretty how she says things."

Gideon shot daggers at Avery and Dix when they snickered. They backed out of the way. "You see?" he said to Jane. "They got something to say about everything, just like you. What you should be saying is,

'Thank you, Mr. Welling, for not killing the men who help my husband run the ranch.' Ain't nobody died, so you can get right down off your high horse. It'd be a mistake, though, to think I won't pull the trigger on any one of you. Have a care. Your men —" He gave Rabbit's chair a shake. "What're their names again?"

"Jem and Jessop Davis."

"Yeah. Your men, Jem and Jessop, are trussed up proper in the bunkhouse, and Avery's goin' to watch over them once you give him his supper." He went to the china cupboard, took out a plate, and handed it to her.

Jane chose the largest of the potato shells to give to the big man. She placed it on the plate and asked him if he wanted coffee. He thanked her politely and added some whiskey to his cup when she gave it to him.

When he was gone, she asked, "Are the rest of you going to sit down to eat? One of your men is still at the front door."

"I know where my men are. Marcie! You want something to eat, come here." Gideon sat and grunted softly when she handed him his supper.

Marcie and Dix ate standing up although there was room for them at the table. Jane put a plate of food in front of each of the boys. They recognized immediately there was nothing left for her.

"Finn and me can share one of these," Rabbit said. "You take the other."

Jane shook her head. "No. Thank you, but I don't really have an appetite."

Finn looked her over. "I heard that's true sometimes when you have a delicate condition." He shrugged when Jane simply stared at him. "Just somethin' I heard."

"What's he talking about?" Gideon asked Jane.

"I am sure I do not know. Finn, what are you talking about?"

He shrugged again. "Well, I don't really know either. Seems like no one wants to tell me, but I heard Mrs. Sterling sayin' somethin' about it to my granny."

Jane pointed to herself. "Saying something about me?"

"I thought it was about you." He dug into his potato shell with a fork. "I could be wrong."

Gideon pouched a mouthful of egg and potato and ham in one cheek and spoke around it. "You're pregnant?"

"If I were, I would hardly tell you, but as it happens, I am not. Finn is correct in that he is wrong. Whatever he heard, he's mistaken the meaning."

Gideon swallowed, nodded. "Damn shame. That'd get Morgan's attention. His wife *and* his child. I don't know that I'd even have to hold a gun on him." He took another bite. "Damn shame."

Jane sat down. She supposed she did it without any awkwardness, but in her mind, she had a vision of reeling toward the chair and collapsing in it as her knees folded.

She was pregnant. The enormity of the miracle made her want to shout and weep and, oddly enough, fling herself at Finn Collins. She had not known, not even suspected. The possibility that she would bear Morgan's child had become so remote to her that it had all but ceased to exist, and now she was confronting it for the first time in the presence of a man who wanted her husband dead.

Jane considered the clues to her condition that she had assigned some other cause: fatigue, little appetite, distraction, moods that made her weep, an improved appetite recently, and a belly that had a slight, but definite, convex curve. There had been a lapse in her courses, but that had happened before and pregnancy was never at the root of it. And there had been some spotting. The truth was, with so many things to occupy her mind of late, she had not given it much thought.

She wondered if Morgan had. It seemed he noticed everything about her. Had he noticed this?

Gideon picked up a whiskey bottle at his elbow and reached behind him for a cup. He passed both to Finn. "Here, give this to her. Seems like things are catching up. She's as white as bitterroot."

Finn dutifully slid the bottle and cup to Jane.

She stared at it for a long moment before she pulled the cork from the bottle and poured a generous finger. She placed the cup against her lips before she permitted herself a small, secretive smile. Then she sipped.

It was Marcie who spotted Morgan and Jake riding along the fence line. They were darker silhouettes than the blue-black sky. He poked his head in the kitchen door, made his announcement, and ducked outside again. At Gideon's direction he went to the smokehouse.

"You stand over there," Gideon told Dix. "Behind her. Not too close, but keep your hand ready and steady."

"You want me to shoot her?"

"Not now, for God's sake. But maybe,

yeah. We talked about this."

"I know, but she made supper for us."

"She didn't make it for *us*. She made it for *them*. Morgan and the help. We stole it."

"Well, yeah, but . . ." Dix found himself on the receiving end of Gideon's dark glare and took his place behind Jane. But not too close.

Gideon waited partially out of sight at one end of the china cupboard.

And waited.

Jane knew how long she could expect Morgan to take from the time he reached the barn until he walked up to the house. She didn't know if Jake would come with him right off. Sometimes the hands came in a little later, giving Morgan and her time to be alone before they showed for supper. If Jake went to the bunkhouse first, he'd be confronting Avery on his own. Jane suspected Avery would employ the same tactics as Gideon. Jake would be just about helpless if one of his brothers was put in harm's way.

Jane's lips barely moved as she ticked off the minutes in her mind. Finn and Rabbit sat preternaturally still. She thought of the knife in her pocket and the child in her belly and wondered if she would be able to act, and if she should.

Her head lifted as the door opened and Morgan came through alone. He had a beautiful, welcoming smile for her, and she held on to it in her mind's eye as it faded away. He was taking in everything at a glance and understood the consequences of acting even before the slight shake of her head warned him to do nothing.

His hands went up, not down. "Gideon. Is that you sheltering on the lee side of the china cupboard? I'm shutting the door now." He backed up to the door and pulled it closed. The wind died immediately and the house was quiet. "You're really too big to hide there. Do you remember when you could fit in one of these cupboards?"

Gideon stepped out. His gun was drawn.

Morgan's eyes stayed on his brother, not his brother's gun. "If you're going to shoot me, I'd be obliged if we could go outside. It's not a thing for women and children to see."

"Take off your gun belt."

Morgan slowly moved his hands to his buckle. "It's been a lot of years, Gideon. It seems we should say hello at least."

"Slide it over this way. Low, like you were playin' tenpin with it." Morgan pitched it across the floor, and Gideon kicked it out of the kitchen beyond everyone's reach. He pointed to the empty rack near Morgan's head.

"I saw it," said Morgan. He spared a brief look for the trio at the table. "Jane. Boys. Are you all right?"

Jane pressed her lips together, nodded. Finn and Rabbit each raised a hand just above the table.

"Good. They have nothing to do with what's between you and me, Gideon."

"That's why they're not dead." He ended the sentence abruptly. Although he did not say it, the word "yet" hung in the air.

"Where are my men?"

"Around and about." Gideon chuckled lightly. "That's what your wife said to me when I asked where you were. She came around, though. You got more to worry about than your men, Morgan. I come to make things square between us. You owe me. I need you to think about that. You got a nice place for yourself. A wife who's real fine to look at when she's not talkin'. So many head of cattle that I bet you didn't know the half of what we took. Sure, you had three years out before Jack and I saw the light of day, but I think you've done better than can be explained by dumb luck. Zetta Lee says you got what was comin' to you for all those years you were her own special ginger pie."

He raised a couple of fingers. "Now, don't go all twitchy on me, Morgan. You don't want to ruin this before we get under way. Besides, Zetta Lee's gone. Same as Jack's gone. She can't spread her legs or her stories. And Jack? He's all done with cheating."

"You killed them?"

"Not Jack. Not my brother. But Zetta Lee was nothing to me except the whore who sent us away. I went to see her in Lander before I found you. She wasn't livin' on the ranch. Sold it off for a place in town and swore to me that she didn't get much for it. A lot of her stock was gone. Cattle thieves. The house was not worth anything, but she did have the land. You know what she did with that money? She bought herself a brothel. Ain't that a kick in the teeth?"

Gideon smoothed his mustache with his thumb and forefinger. "Do you really have a problem with me shooting her dead in sight of our daddy's grave?"

CHAPTER FIFTEEN

Jane pressed a fist against her mouth. It was not enough to suppress her whimper. She saw Morgan set his jaw and knew he had heard her. Gideon was either oblivious to her distress or uncaring of it because he began to describe the final minutes of Zetta Lee's life, those minutes when she realized his intention was to kill her.

For the first time since entering the kitchen, Finn and Rabbit actually looked afraid. Jane wanted to take them by the hand. It might have reassured them, but it would not have made them happy.

"Enough." It was Morgan, not Jane, who spoke up. He surprised Gideon into silence. "That's enough," he said quietly. "If you need to tell someone, tell me, but not in front —" Morgan spun around as the back door opened. A second gun was pointed at him.

Gideon holstered his Remington. "Give

him some space before he takes it out of your hands."

Marcie pulled the door shut and then kept his back to it. He looked around, nodded to Dix, and then came back to Gideon. "Everything all right?"

"As it should be," said Gideon. "Did you check on Avery like I told you?"

Marcie nodded. "He's fine. Those three boys sure are fit to be tied." The long scar running through his salt-and-pepper beard meandered a little as he chuckled. "And I mean it exactly like I said it. Mmm-mmm-mmm. Especially that one we acquainted ourselves with over at the Pennyroyal. He's spittin' mad. You'd think no one ever got the drop on him before."

"All right," Gideon said. "You've had fun."

Morgan turned his back on the gun and faced his brother. "Where's Max? He said three boys. What did you do with Max?"

"He's resting. There was an altercation, I guess you'd call it. Your wife fixed him up."

Jane said, "He was a little worse off than Jem. They put him in one of the bedrooms. I haven't heard a sound from him since."

Gideon smiled pleasantly. "See? He's resting, just like I said."

"There're four of you?" asked Morgan. "I'm counting four. Three here and one in

551

the bunkhouse."

"Let's just say you don't know the half of it."

"Eight men? I don't think so, Gideon."

"Four," Jane said quickly. "He wanted me to think there are others, maybe two more, but there aren't."

Gideon screwed his mouth to one side as he shook his head. "I don't like her much." He pointed to Dix. "If she opens her mouth again, shoot the little fella there." His fingerpost moved to Finn. "Yeah, you. And stop squirmin'. You got ants in your pants?"

"I gotta pee, mister." His eyes darted to Jane. "Sorry, Mrs. Longstreet, but I gotta go real bad."

Gideon said, "Good thing you got here when you did, Morgan. I learned a little about the advantages of patience while I was in prison, but those lessons are fading some in my mind. You understand?"

"Let Finn step out on the porch."

"Jesus. Marcie, take the boy outside." He drew his gun and held it on Morgan while Finn practically danced his way to the door. He jerked his chin at Rabbit. "You gotta go, too?"

Rabbit shook his head. "No sir, leastways not yet."

Morgan asked, "What are you boys doing

out here anyway?"

Before Rabbit could respond, Gideon raised his gun a fraction and drew Morgan's attention back to him. "They brought you something. A crate. It's pretty heavy. They're speculating it's gold."

Morgan had an apologetic smile for Rabbit. "Sorry. No gold."

"We didn't *really* think there was gold in it. We had cookies and pie, too, like the last time, but they're still out in the wagon."

"Sure wished I had looked," said Morgan. "I suspect we could use some pie and cookies about now."

Gideon snorted. "And here I was thinking it was a real shame they were wrong about the gold. That would have squared us, and we wouldn't have to concern ourselves with the Cattlemen's Trust."

"So that's your game here. The Cattlemen's Trust."

Before Gideon could confirm it, the door opened and Finn stumbled into the room. Morgan had to grab him to keep him from falling.

Marcie shut the door so hard it vibrated. "He *pissed* on me." He pointed to his right trouser leg. There was indeed a wet stain below the knee.

Morgan quickly pushed Finn toward his

chair to get him out of Marcie's way. Marcie looked as if he wanted to club Finn, and that was probably only to make shooting him easier. Gideon's reaction surprised Morgan, though. His brother was laughing.

"Damn, Marcellus. The boy said he had to go, didn't he? Couldn't you get out of his way?"

Marcie grunted and drew his gun. He pointed it at Finn. "Dix, don't you concern yourself with shootin' a kid. If Mrs. Long-street says somethin', *I'll* shoot him." With that, he turned the gun on Morgan.

Gideon holstered his weapon again and knuckled away a tear at the corner of his eye. "I don't know what you think, Morgan, but I'm kinda wishin' Jack was here to see this. He never did cotton to taking things too seriously. I liked that about him. It skewed his judgment some, but that was Jack."

Morgan did not respond.

"Right," said Gideon. "Have a seat. Time for plain talk."

Morgan sat at the head of the table. He had a reassuring smile for Jane that encom-passed the boys, and a dark, narrow look for Dix standing at Jane's back.

Gideon stepped to the side until he had Morgan's face in view. He leaned a shoulder against the wall and folded his arms across his chest. "Here's what I'm proposing, Morgan. There is a Barkley and Benjamin in the manager's office at the Cattlemen's Trust. I've seen it. I even had a chat with the manager after the marshal left, just to get the feel of things. Made a little deposit, too."

Morgan recalled that Gideon had said something to Jane about seeing them coming out of the bank. Bridger might have still been inside when Gideon went in. Morgan recognized the opportunity that he and the marshal had not been able to see at the time. Under the table, his hands curled into fists.

"You know about Barkley and Benjamin safes," said Gideon. "I remember that you're particularly good with them."

"I hope you brought dynamite. It has been a long time since I've touched one."

"Oh, I don't think that will matter. As for dynamite, I figure I've got three sticks sittin' right here at the table, another in a bedroom, and three more hog-tied in the bunkhouse. That should be enough to blow up Morning Star and pretty much make a ruin of your life. You understand what I'm sayin'?"

Morgan nodded.

"Good. We'll stick to what we know and

to what we know works. My men have done some scouting. They had a look around Bitter Springs before they checked in with the marshal. Most folks will be in bed soon. The ones who aren't will be at the Pennyroyal or Whistler's Saloon. That'll make the alley behind the bank a quiet place. We go in through the back, get you settled at the safe, you perform your magic, and we leave."

"We? I'm leaving the bank with you?"

"Of course. Wouldn't be right to leave you behind. Anyway, if I kill you there it won't exactly look like you did it on your own, and I think preserving the illusion for a little while makes sense."

"All right, but why do you think anyone will suspect me? People around here don't know about me, what I've done."

"Maybe. Maybe not. But they'll come to it because I'll be leaving somethin' of yours behind. That'll bring the marshal and his men out this way first, and we'll be long gone."

"Well, I can tell you've thought a lot about it. Do you know what you're going to leave behind? It should probably be my hat."

Gideon looked it over. "I suppose that might work. There's nothing special about it, though."

Morgan removed his hat and placed it on

the table. "What's special is this." He pointed to his hair. "There are probably one or two threads of it in the crown. Besides, if anyone does see me slinking through town, they're likely to catch sight of my hair first. I'm known by that."

"It *is* like a struck match. Sure, we'll leave your hat."

Morgan nodded. "So how do we do this? I figure everyone's not going into Bitter Springs."

"Marcie and Avery stay. Dix comes with you and me."

"Then we are all coming back here?"

Gideon shook his head. "No, Morgan. You do your best work under pressure. Like I said, we will stick to what we know. You will want to pay attention to the time. Once we leave, Avery and Marcie will also take notice of the time. You will do the same. I'm figuring about eight, maybe nine miles as the crow flies to town. We can be at the Cattlemen's Trust in forty minutes. Of course, how long it takes you to open the safe will determine the outcome for these folks at the table and the ones you can't see. I figure you'll have an hour left once we get to the bank. The less time you use fiddlin' with the safe, the more time you have to get back here. If Marcie and Avery don't see you one hundred minutes after we leave, there will be nothing for you to come back to. That's clear, isn't it?"

"I have not opened a safe in nine years, Gideon. I've never touched an 1884 Barkley and Benjamin."

"See? You know it's a Model 1884. That's what I'm talking about here." He pointed to himself. "I didn't know that. Marcie? Dix? Either of you know that?" When they both shook their heads, he went on. "I guess you did something to keep up. You always set store by book learnin'." He dropped his hands to his sides and pushed away from the wall. "Now, who do you want to take with us? Never hurts to have extra insurance."

"No," Morgan said. "They stay here. I will come back for them. *All* of them. They stay here."

"I'm thinking along different lines. It seemed polite to give you a choice, but I can see how that could be a hardship for you. I don't mind making the pick, although I do wish I had better pickings."

"No," Morgan said again.

"Stay in your chair. It'd please me to have your wife along if she didn't think I cared about her opinions, and Rabbit over there is a little too bold for my tastes. Now, Finn here, depending on how you look at it, either pissed on Marcie or pissed him off. Maybe he did both. That makes him the best one to come along, seeing as how Marcellus is staying here."

Jane opened her mouth to protest and clamped it shut when Gideon cocked an eyebrow at her.

"That's right," he said. "I don't care for your opinions, and if Dix shoots the boy because you have it in your mind you can talk now, I'll just take the other one." He jerked his chin at Morgan. "How the hell did you meet this one?"

Morgan did not look at his brother. He only had eyes for Jane. The slender smile that lifted the corners of his mouth touched his gaze. "She answered my personal advertisement."

"Mail-order bride? You don't have another one in that crate in the front room, do you?"

Morgan waited until Gideon was done laughing at his joke. "No. That's a sewing machine." Still watching Jane, he said, "She told me once that she had one when she lived in New York." He saw tears well in Jane's eyes and watched her bite her lower lip to keep it from trembling. She, too, was remembering their first morning in this house, in this kitchen, when he was critical of her apple green dress with the white polka dots and ruffled neckline because it was too pretty. *I shall miss the sewing machine I had in New York,* she had said, *but I do well enough with a needle and thread.* She told him she would make aprons, and she did, and every time he saw her wearing one, he thought of the sewing machine. "Unlike you, Gideon, I care a great deal about the things she says."

"Huh." He scratched behind his ear. "You always were a ladies' man. Now I know why. You poke them *and* listen to them. I just poke 'em."

"Shut up, Gideon."

A soundless chuckle made Gideon's shoulders rise and fall. "Let's go. Take your hat." He walked behind Morgan to get his hat and coat. "Finn, you got anything you want to say to your brother before you go?"

Finn nodded and stared at Rabbit with solemn regard. "I reckon we should've ate more of those cookies. Maybe had some of the pie."

Rabbit nodded. "I had that in my mind, too."

"Touching." Gideon finished buttoning his coat. "C'mon, Finn. This way. Morgan, you follow. Dix, you're the caboose. Marcie, I'll fire one shot to let you know when to start that hundred minutes. You have your pocket watch?"

"I do."

"Then we are out of here."

Jane thought she was prepared for the report from Gideon's gun, but when it came, she shuddered from head to toe. Rabbit was lifted out of his seat. She slid a hand toward him. With his brother gone, there was no reason not to accept her offer. Apparently he thought so, too. He slipped his hand under her palm and allowed her to give it a squeeze, and then he turned his hand over and took hers in his. Jane had no words. It was as lovely a gesture as there ever was.

Marcie put his gun away and sat at the table for the first time. He set his pocket watch in front of him. "You think he can do it, Mrs. Longstreet?"

"Of course he can."

"Good to know. I have to say, I've had my doubts about this plan all along, but Gideon had it in his head that it had to be done this way. Just desserts, he called it." He glanced at the stove. "Is the coffee still hot?"

She nodded and started to rise.

"Sit. I don't mind doin' for myself, not when there's no gang to serve." He got a

561

cup and went to the stove. "Now, on the trail, it's a different matter. Someone gets up to get himself a cup and suddenly you got someone else yellin', 'Man-at-the-pot.' That means you're obliged to carry the pot and give a fill-up to anyone who wants one." He returned to his chair and sipped his coffee for temperature before he took a swallow. "This is real good. You have any fancy fluff-duffs?"

Jane frowned.

Rabbit said, "He's talkin' about fancy cakes, doughnuts, food like that. Must be the just desserts that got him going one way on that track."

"Nothing like that," Jane said evenly. "But I understand there is a pie and cookies in the wagon in the barn."

"I heard that, too. Guess I'll be leavin' them there." He drank more coffee. "You haven't asked. That surprises me a little." When Jane did not respond, he said, "You haven't asked me how I come to throw in with Gideon."

"I do not want to know."

Marcie spoke as if she had not. "Prison." He slowly traced his scar with a fingernail. "I wouldn't want to say what I did to get there in front of the boy, but I could take you in the bedroom and show you."

Jane showed no reaction that she could control. It was not possible to keep blood from draining out of her face.

Marcie glanced at the pocket watch. "One hundred minutes is a long time for some things. Not enough for others. What do you say, Mrs. Longstreet? Would you like to buy some time for your husband?"

Morgan and Finn rode abreast. Gideon led the way. Dix was still the caboose. Morgan rode Condor, the same saddle horse he'd had under him all day. He would have preferred a fresher mount, but Gideon insisted on the gelding. Finn, though, got Sophie when she proved too recalcitrant for Gideon to mount. She was used to someone lighter in her saddle these days, so Morgan suggested Finn, but he already had it in his mind that he would be the one riding her back to Jane. She would fly for him, and she had the heart to do it.

"We can cover the ground faster," he told Gideon. "Finn can keep up."

Gideon looked over his shoulder. "Worried that there won't be enough time?"

There was no point in responding to his brother's mockery, so Morgan didn't. He glanced over at Finn. The boy was staying in the saddle, and that was the best that could be said for his seat. The only animal the Collinses owned was the mare that pulled the station buckboard. Finn and Rabbit spent considerably more time behind her than on her. Sophie was taking her lead from Condor, not Finn.

"There's the graveyard," Finn said, pointing up ahead. "I guess I know the shape of that cottonwood. It's about as gnarly as my granny's hand." He cupped a hand around his mouth so his loud whisper would be sure to carry ahead to Gideon. "Hey, mister, you know the quickest way to get to the bank, or do you want me to show you?"

Gideon slowed so Finn caught up to him. "I got a way figured out."

"And I probably got a better one. I've been all over this town one time or another on adventures with my brother. You tell me how you want to get there, and I'll tell you if it's good."

Gideon looked over at Morgan. "What do you think?"

"I'm for listening to him. He's got a stake in this. His brother's back there."

"All right," said Gideon. "Out with it."

Finn laid out a route that would have them skirting the edge of town and then turning sharp and heading straight through the alley that would bring them to the bank.

"It's roundabout," said Gideon.

"It'll be quick on horseback," said Finn. "The other way, the best way if you don't want to be noticed at all, is on foot, but I got it in my head that bank robbers want to have their horses close by the bank, not tied up at the graveyard."

By the time they reached the edge of the cemetery, Gideon had made his decision. "You take the lead, Finn. I'll be right behind you."

"I need to be with him," Morgan said. "He can't control Sophie."

"Go ahead. As long as I control you, I don't figure we have a problem."

Morgan caught up to Finn and grabbed Sophie's reins. When he leaned over, he spoke as loudly as he dared. "When the time comes, Finn, you listen to me."

Finn's widening eyes were the only indication that he heard.

Jane watched Marcie tear two of her tea towels into long strips. She knew what he would do with them, and she warned Rabbit not to fight. He sat there like a stoic, accepting the restraints as Jane was ordered to bind his feet to the chair legs and then bind his hands to the spindle rail at his back.

Marcie stuffed part of his handkerchief in

Rabbit's mouth when Jane's hands began to shake. He finished off binding the gag with the last strip from the towels and checked Jane's work.

"There's no reason we should be disturbed by the boy carrying on, and it'll make that other fella crazy. Shall we go, Mrs. Longstreet? There's five minutes waiting for you on the other side of paradise."

Bile rose in Jane's throat. "You said ten. You agreed to ten minutes."

"What I agreed to is that ten minutes with me gets you five. You want ten, then you have to give me twenty. You think you can bring me up twice? There's a whore in Rawlins who could do that, but I think she gave me the pox."

Rabbit started to wrestle with his bonds. The chair jerked and bounced on the floor. The table jumped.

Jane shook her head. "Rabbit! Stop. Ten minutes. I can get us ten minutes. It could mean everything." She bent and waited for him to meet her eyes. "You will not cry." She kissed his forehead and brushed back his hair at the temples. "Whatever you hear, you will not cry." She forced a smile. "You will get a stuffy nose and not be able to breathe. I am buying ten minutes so we can *all breathe.* Do you understand?"

566

He nodded. He closed his eyes when Jane used one corner of her apron to dry his wet lashes.

"That's it, Rabbit. Keep your eyes closed."

He did, and when he could stand it no longer, he opened them. Jane and Marcie were gone.

Finn's route got them to the back of the bank without incident. It had also been his idea to ride in pairs as they approached because folks who might see them would have little concern about two riders. Four at once would have made people pay attention. Finn and Gideon were standing at the back door before Morgan and Dix dismounted.

Gideon rattled the door. "It's locked but seems like it doesn't have a bar, or someone forgot to bar it. That was careless." He stepped aside and took a lock pick out of his vest pocket and handed it to Morgan. "You'll need this. How many minutes left, Dix?"

Dix had to hold out his pocket watch at several different angles before he caught enough light to make out the position of the hands. He announced there were fifty-eight minutes remaining at the same time Morgan was opening the door.

Gideon gestured for Morgan to precede them. He got a good grip on Finn's collar and pushed him forward. "We'll go in together," he told the boy. "Dix, you separate the horses like we talked about and keep an eye out here." He closed the door.

"Matches?" asked Morgan. "I can't see a damn thing."

"I put them in Finn's pocket. Go ahead, boy. You light one."

Finn felt around in his coat pockets, found them, and struck one against a wall. "How about that, Mr. Longstreet. I didn't even feel him put 'em there."

Morgan did not waste a moment or his breath admonishing Finn about being too impressed by Gideon's sleight of hand. He was already moving to the interior door that led into the lobby. Behind him he heard a heavy thud followed by a string of colorful curses from Gideon.

"We're all right," Finn called to Morgan. "It was just the iron bar that should've been across the door. Your brother found it." He hunched his shoulders as Gideon squeezed harder around the back of his neck. "Ow, mister. It ain't my fault it fell on your foot. I didn't knock it over."

"I could've shot you. Shut up and keep going."

Finn averted his head as he lit another match. He and Gideon hurried after Morgan.

"Blow it out," Morgan said when they came up behind him in the lobby. "No more until we get to the manager's office. There are no windows in there. Come on. We only have to get past the tellers' cages. You can make them out well enough."

Morgan swore under his breath as he came up on Mr. Webb's office.

"What is it?" Gideon asked.

"It's locked. I need the pick again." He held out his palm. He was conscious of every second that ticked away until Gideon put the pick in his hand. Putting his shoulder against the door, Morgan inserted the pick and carefully twisted it. He felt the lock give. The knob turned in his hand.

"Give me the pick," said Gideon. He pocketed it. When his hand came up, he was holding his gun. "Go on. What are you waiting for?"

Morgan realized he was holding his breath. He closed his eyes and exhaled slowly. Then he opened the door.

Jane paused outside the open doorway to the room where Max was being held. She felt Marcie's hand at the small of her back, urging her forward, but she resisted. Max was lying on the bed, staked out as though for human sacrifice. They had taken his boots. His hands and stocking feet were tied with strips from one of the sheets that Max had helped her take down from the clothesline. It did not seem possible that it had only been a few hours ago. Until Gideon made his announcement that they were guaranteed no more than one hundred minutes of life, time had passed very slowly indeed.

"I want to look in on him," she told Marcie. "He was bound very tightly. Look at his hands. His fingers are swollen."

"What do you think you're going to do about it, Florence Nightingale?" He poked her with two fingers to keep moving.

Jane was satisfied that she had already done something about it. At the sound of her voice, Max had lifted his head and was staring at her through his one good eye. Jane immediately turned in the doorway and planted a hand on the frame on either side. This barred Marcie from entering, but more importantly kept her face from his view. When Max started straining against his bindings, she shook her head. It wasn't enough to keep him from doubling his efforts when Marcie's face appeared at her shoulder.

"Max! Stop! Please, stop. Whatever happens, Max, you need to tell Morgan this is what I wanted. I want you to promise that you will do that for me. I could not ask Rabbit. It would not be fair to him."

She had no idea whether Max committed to doing what she asked. Marcie grabbed one of her wrists and pulled it behind her back. He might have hurt her if she had struggled. She did not. She reminded herself that he was taking her where she wanted to go.

Gideon kicked the door shut once they were inside Mr. Webb's inner sanctum. No one moved until Finn struck a match and located a lamp. He burned the tips of his fingers lighting it because he did not want to use another matchstick. When Gideon cuffed him, he merely shrugged and sucked on his fingertips.

"Put the lamp on top of the safe," said Gideon. "Then sit your ass in that chair."

"Mr. Webb's chair?" asked Finn. "Behind his desk?"

"Don't get too excited. No one's asking you to run the place."

"Do what he says, Finn." Morgan knelt in front of the safe. "And stay put." Morgan set his ear to the safe's door and spun the lock.

"He should watch, though," said Gideon. "And learn. It might figure into his future."

"Shut up, Gideon. I need to hear this, not you. Is there a glass anywhere around?"

"No."

"Finn, look in Mr. Webb's desk drawers."

"Already found it." Finn held it out to Gideon. "Right next to the bottle of sassparilly he takes for his rheumatism."

"Clever boy." Gideon passed the glass to Morgan, who put the open end flush to the safe door. Gideon pushed aside some papers on the desk and hitched his hip on the edge. He rested his Model 1875 Remington against his thigh.

Morgan pressed his ear against the bottom of the glass and spun the lock again. He began to work in earnest. He estimated he could safely take five full minutes to crack the combination. He decided he would use every one of them.

"How much time?"

Gideon checked his watch, a gold-plated timepiece that had once belonged to his father. It was the only thing he took from Zetta Lee when they parted ways. He used a thumbnail to flick it open. "Fifty-four, no, fifty-three minutes."

■ ■ ■ ■

Jane did not permit Marcie to push her into the bedroom. She walked in under her own steam, chin up, shoulders braced.

"You ain't goin' to the gallows," Marcie said. "Or the — what's that French thing with the blade that cuts —"

"A guillotine."

"Yeah. You're not goin' there either. Like you told your man in the room, this is what you want. It's real good of you to say that. Eases my mind some that it won't come to rape. You'll understand that I've had my fill of that accusation."

Jane picked up the folded linens at the foot of the bed and carried them to the rocker. She set them down and turned to face him. Her eyes dropped to his gun belt. "You can put your gun on the dresser, or if you like, you can put it on top of the wardrobe."

"What I like is to keep it at my side."

"Your whores do not complain?"

His crooked grin changed the line of his scar. "Seems funny hearing you say somethin' like that." His eyes grazed her from head to toe. "I'll give up the gun if you loosen your hair."

573

Jane hesitated. The idea of this man touching her hair was repugnant. She had only ever unwound her hair for Morgan. He acted as if she were giving him a gift. Sometimes she thought it belonged more to him than it did to her, and now this man, this awful man, wanted to touch it.

"Yes," said Jane. "Of course." She put her hands to her head and began to remove the pins.

Marcie unstrapped his gun belt and put it on top of the wardrobe. "Guess you better come over here." He crooked his finger at her. "I don't think much of calling you Mrs. Longstreet. What's your name?"

"I *am* Mrs. Longstreet, and I prefer that you remember it, but if it troubles you, you may call me Frances. I would not mind that terribly."

"Frances. That's where you get your starch. I like Franny better. I have a notion that it's a bit softer."

"Do you think so?" Jane dropped her pins and combs on top of the linens and walked toward him. She stopped at the other side of the bed. "Shall I turn back the covers?"

He smiled. "You're goin' to stay all proper about it. I like that. No, you can leave the bed as it is and just lie down. I'll cover you."

Jane smoothed her apron with damp

palms and nervously licked her lips. The brief darting of her tongue brought his attention to her mouth. She worked to keep her breathing steady. "I do not want you to kiss me."

He cocked a wiry eyebrow at her. "What you want is five minutes, remember? Let me see what you have, Franny. Come here."

Jane went. She did not have to feign reluctance. And when he pulled her close, dug his fingers deep into her hair, and ground his mouth against hers, she did not have to feign despair.

The pins clicked. The tumblers fell. Morgan put the glass on top of the safe.

"You got it?" Gideon asked.

"We'll see. Stay where you are. Let me see if this works first." Morgan placed a hand around the long brass handle and gave it a pull. The door opened, revealing neat stacks of bills, valuables, certificates . . . and one more thing.

He had only seconds to act; Gideon was already on his feet and trying to get a view of the interior, but the position of the door blocked his efforts. When he moved to get around it, Morgan shoved it hard at him. The heavy steel door struck him solidly in the side before he could get out of the way.

"Cover your eyes, Finn," Morgan said.

Finn did. He made himself as small as he could in Mr. Webb's big chair and pressed the heels of his hands hard against his eyes. Something in the deadly calm of Mr. Longstreet's voice warned him to do that.

Morgan already had possession of the gun that had been placed in the safe for him when he gave Finn the directive. Jumping to his feet, he took quick aim with the Colt as Gideon was lifting his own weapon and fired.

Jane squeezed her eyes shut as she set one hand on Marcie's hip and the other in her apron pocket at the level of his groin. Her fingers folded around the hilt of the paring knife. Her knuckles brushed his button fly as she twisted the blade and aimed. Her touch had stirred his blood. Jane hoped all of it had settled between his legs.

She struck hard and sure and the knife sliced through layers of fabric as easily as if she were back in the kitchen slicing potatoes. She kept that in mind as she struck again.

And again.

Gideon got off one shot as he staggered back. The bullet ricocheted off the door. It was Finn, not Gideon, who cried out. Morgan pushed the door out of the way and grabbed the boy out of the chair with one arm while he kept the Colt aimed at his brother. That Finn could stand at all he took as a good sign. He pushed the boy behind him.

"Drop the gun, Gideon. You set the rules. You know I don't have time. Drop it!"

Gideon looked at the open safe and then back at Morgan. "You knew I would come for the money. The gun was waiting for you. I bet you knew the com—"

Morgan fired again, this time taking aim at Gideon's wrist. The bullet only grazed him, but it was enough to make him drop the gun. "Don't move! Finn? No, stay where you are. Hold on to me. Were you hit or were you frightened?"

"My right leg's burnin' somethin' fierce, Mr. Longstreet, but I reckon I was scared pretty good, too."

"All right. I'm going to get you to Doc Kent's."

"There ain't time," said Finn. "You said yourself, you don't have time."

Gideon chuckled. Blood was seeping from the wound in his shoulder. He slipped his injured hand under his coat and pressed his palm against it. "Hard choices."

"You let me hold the gun on him," said Finn. "I know all about ridin' the longhorns of a pretty big dilemma, and you shouldn't have to wrestle that steer now. You gotta go. Dix will be here. He's got to have heard the shots."

"You heard the boy. It's a pretty big dilemma. I'm guessing you'd want to know that I left your missus with a man who served time for raping his sergeant's wife."

Morgan loosed Finn's grasp on him and stepped forward to kick Gideon's weapon out of the way. With Gideon's attention at his feet, Morgan flipped the Colt in his hand, held it by the barrel and clubbed Gideon in the side of the head with the ivory grip.

Gideon slid down the wall to the floor, where he slowly toppled sideways.

Morgan picked up the Remington, took out the cylinder pin, removed the cylinder, and thrust the gun into Finn's hands. He further surprised the boy by hefting him over his shoulder. "We're leaving by the front door."

They made it halfway across the lobby when Dix called from behind them to stop. Morgan turned, fired twice, and dropped Dix where he stood. He was done picking locks, so when he reached the bank's entrance, he kicked the door until it gave way and then he carried Finn outside to where the wind was biting and brisk and where people were congregating in spite of it.

"You cut off my goddamn cock!" Marcie screamed. "Jesus, lady, you cut off my —"

Jane shoved him away and stepped back at the same time. His fingers were so deeply embedded in her hair that he took some of it with him. For a moment, tears blurred her vision. She was still able to see the spread of blood staining his trousers before he bent over and cupped his groin. Only seconds passed before blood began to seep through his fingers.

Jane thought she would be sick, but when she held up the bloody knife she was filled with an eerie calm. She made quick, jabbing motions with the knife so that he was forced to bob and weave and protect himself at the same time. Tears flooded his eyes. One of them followed the path of his scar. Jane did not care.

When she had backed him into the washroom, she slammed the door shut and leaned against it just long enough to catch her breath. On the other side of the door, Marcie stopped howling and began to whimper. She imagined that he was checking the condition of his parts. Jane doubted that she had cut off his penis but wondered if perhaps what she had done was not worse. There was so much blood, so much bright red blood, that she thought she might have cut into his femoral artery.

"There are towels in there. Use them to press hard on your injuries."

"Go to hell, lady. I'm gonna bleed all over your goddamn floor."

It occurred to Jane that he was angry enough that he might live after all. She dropped the paring knife in her apron pocket and walked to the other side of the wardrobe. She put her shoulder against it and heaved. Her feet slid on the floor and the wardrobe did not budge. She dug in again and pushed harder. This time it slid inches. Again, and it moved far enough to block half the washroom door. She stopped using her shoulder and put her back into it instead. The wardrobe moved the rest of the way.

Jane stood on tiptoes to reach Marcie's gun and holster. She caught the edge of the belt with her fingertips and pulled it toward the edge. She carefully took it down and removed the gun from the holster. After tossing the belt aside, she opened the cylinder, saw that all chambers were loaded, and closed it again.

Satisfied, she went to the adjoining bedroom and freed Max. She gave him Marcie's gun. She picked up Morgan's Colt on her way to the kitchen. It was lying on the floor just where Gideon had kicked it. She set it on the table while she untied Rabbit.

"Are you hurt, Mrs. Longstreet?" It was Rabbit's first question when she removed his gag. It was the same one Max had asked.

Jane looked down at herself. Her apron front was stained with blood. Marcie's blood. "I'm fine."

Rabbit's cheeks ballooned as he blew out a long breath, and then he dared to ask the question that Max had not. "Did you really cut off his piss whistle?"

Ted Rush was the first person Morgan recognized when he waded into the crowd. He put Finn in Ted's arms and told him to take him to Dr. Kent. "Finn will tell you everything. Send Bridger after me." He grabbed Ted by the collar when the man stared dumbly at him. "Send the marshal after me!"

Morgan let him go, spun on his heels, and ran off toward the alley. Someone in the crowd must have thought it would be a good idea to shoot him first and sort it out later because he heard Finn scream with bloodcurdling ferocity to drop the gun. So much for the ordinance against carrying.

He ducked into the alley and ran to the back of the bank. He untied Condor, but it was Sophie that he mounted. If the gelding could keep up, he was welcome to come.

Morgan took the straight route out of town that none of them had discussed going in. He wanted to be noticed now. He and Sophie emerged from the alley as if they had been catapulted from a slingshot. The crowd scattered, and no one tried to shoot him this time. Their trail down the middle of the street was as true as a compass needle and as quick as a bead of mercury.

Avery surrendered without drawing his weapon except to toss it on the bunkhouse floor. It pained him some that he was outmaneuvered by a man who could only see out of one eye and a woman who had to hold her gun in two hands to keep it steady. They had him crosswise before he knew what was happening. His chest made for a very large target.

The boy entered when they called for him and cut through the ropes that secured all three Davis brothers to the bunkhouse's center post and to each other. They stood, shook out their cramped limbs, massaged their wrists, and then took turns raining blows on Avery's head, his stomach, and occasionally his groin. Jem, in particular, seemed to enjoy every punch he landed.

They stopped when Mrs. Longstreet called a halt, but by then, Avery was already on his knees.

The brothers made the same short work of tying him up as they had of beating him up.

Once Morgan set Sophie on her course, he never looked back. He carried no timepiece except the one in his head. He counted out the seconds, the minutes, and he, the godless man, prayed that he would arrive in time.

Rabbit brought the buckboard to the front of the house. He was flanked by Jem and Jake on one side and Jessop and Max on the other. They were mounted, ready to ride. There had been no debate, no disagreement when Jane had said they must go. They were waiting for her now because she had gone back into the house at the last moment. There was something she had to do, she told them, before she went out to meet Morgan.

They let her go. Not one of them would stand in the way of her unwavering faith that Morgan was coming back.

When she left them, she was wearing her black velvet hat with the spray of scarlet poppies. When she returned, the hat was gone, replaced by a red woolen scarf. It covered her hair and wrapped around her throat. The long fringed tails were knotted once.

Rabbit held out his hand to help her up. She thanked him, thanked all of them, and then the wagon began to roll.

Morgan saw them as silhouettes. Four men on horseback, two people in a wagon. He thought Sophie must have seen them, too, because she dug deep and *flew*. The last hundred yards were a blur, but Sophie's speed did not wholly account for it.

Jane jumped out of the wagon before Rabbit brought it to a full stop. She spread her arms high and wide as Morgan pulled Sophie up hard and threw himself out of the saddle. His momentum carried him into Jane's embrace. He lifted her off her feet. She held on as he spun them round and round. She thought his shout of joy, of relief, rode the wind all the way back to Bitter Springs.

He set her down and cupped her face. He kissed hard. He kissed long. He unwound her scarf to thread his fingers in her hair . . . and stopped.

"Jane?" He felt for pins, for combs. There were none. He gently ran his hand over the crown of her dark hair until he reached the blunt, cropped ends at the level of her jaw. The ragged cut went all the way around. Sifting through it with his fingertips, Morgan bent his head and placed his mouth against her ear. "You are my life, Jane. Whatever's been done, *this* will grow back."

It was then that his strong, fearless warrior wife burst into tears.

EPILOGUE

May 1892
Morning Star Ranch

Jane and Morgan stood on the front porch of their home to see the last of their guests off. Jane waved. Morgan alternated between nodding and tapping his hat brim with a fingertip. They both smiled, though, and that was the lasting impression they made on every person who rode away that night.

People had begun arriving at Morning Star in the early afternoon. They brought hot, covered dishes, and cold ones packed in dry ice. Walt Mangold and Mrs. Sterling arrived with cases of liquor and a keg from the Pennyroyal. Morgan and his men roasted a cow and two pigs. Cobb Bridger brought his wife and new baby and a crate of fireworks he had ordered special from St. Louis for the occasion. The mayor came with his fiddle and two banjos and had no trouble finding folks to pick and strum.

Jem Davis proposed to his sweetheart, *again,* but he was feeling the drink by then and no one was certain if he would remember that this time she said yes. Ted Rush stayed close to the liquor and told stories to folks who did not mind hearing them, *again.* Finn stationed himself behind the smokehouse and showed off his badge of courage to anyone who paid Rabbit a penny to see it. When his granny caught him with his pants down wiggling his hip at Priscilla Taylor, she took a broom to both boys, *again.*

It was the best kind of day, perfect, peaceful, and in a good way, predictable.

The picnic was Jane's idea, and Morgan fell in with her plans because opposing them would have put him in the bunkhouse. There still had been snow on the ground when she conceived of the idea, and on one of her trips to Bitter Springs, she put it to Ida Mae Sterling. At that juncture, only a calamity of biblical proportions could have stopped it from happening.

There had been no calamities in Bitter Springs since the night of the robbery at the Cattlemen's Trust Bank. Ted Rush was still trying to name the event because he thought it deserved that kind of notoriety in the town's collective memory, and because he played such a critical role in saving Finn's life. After all, Morgan Longstreet singled *him* out to take young Finn to the doctor, and Ted had sacrificed his good wool coat to the boy's bloody wound. Most everyone learned that very night that while the ricochet from Gideon Welling's gun had cut a furrow in Finn's thigh, the injury never veered toward fatal. They let Ted go on because he was a force of nature on the order of a howling wind and sometimes you just had to hunker down and let him blow.

Folks knew now that when the first shots were fired, Marshal Cobb Bridger was at the station house talking to Jeff and Heather Collins regarding the whereabouts of their rascal grandsons. As Cobb would recollect later, the gun reports were so distorted by distance and obstructions that he did not recognize them for what they were. Jefferson Collins had heard them as well, but he had checked his watch thinking it was an approaching train and that he had mistaken the time. Heather had tilted her head to one side and cupped the ear she generally kept close to the ground, but in the end, had only shrugged.

Cobb was curious, but he wanted to finish his conversation about the boys. By any measure that he applied, Finn and Rabbit were late returning to town, and he was of a mind to go after them. First, though, he needed to know if Mr. or Mrs. Collins had an explanation for the boys' tardiness that he was not privy to.

The station agent and his wife were discussing that between themselves when the next incongruous report echoed their way. Frowning, Cobb put up a finger to halt their conversation and walked to the station entrance and opened the door. He stepped out, waited, and . . .

Drop the gun! It came to him clearly, a youthful, earnest voice as familiar to him as his own. He ran to the edge of the platform then and peered down the street. He could see that people were congregating in front of the bank, and moments later, he recognized Morgan Longstreet, hat in hand, red hair as bright as a signal flare, charging out of the alley and riding hell for leather toward Morning Star.

Cobb had wasted no time mounting his horse and riding straight for the crowd. Finn was waving a gun, screaming and squirming to get out of Ted Rush's arms, but when he saw Cobb, he flung the gun to the ground and began to sob. The bystanders provided some help interpreting Finn's disjointed story, although Cobb had a sense of the whole of it long before they did. He quickly deputized Jim Phillips and George and Buster Johnson to handle the growing crowd, the bank, and the bodies, and then he set off out of town.

He had come upon Jane and Morgan sheltering in each other's arms about a mile short of the ranch. He slowed his horse when he saw them and gave them a wide berth, joining the group he saw up ahead instead.

Their version of events at the ranch was about as disjointed as Finn's had been, but Cobb understood enough to recognize he had at least one arrest to make, and maybe two, if Marcie was still alive. If he wasn't, then there was a body to remove and a washroom to scrub before he was allowing Jane to go near her home.

He deputized Max and the Davis brothers, just so they knew they were answering to him for the time being, not Morgan Longstreet. He turned them around, and they headed back to the house. He was not even sure that Morgan and Jane knew they were leaving.

Marcie was not dead, or even castrated, but he had bled like a stuck pig — which they all agreed was an apt description — so there was plenty of work for them to do in the washroom to make it right. Rabbit was sent to sit on the front porch to direct Jane to stay outside when she and Morgan returned. No one wanted to tend to Marcie's wounds once they got a good look at them, so Cobb gave him a wadded towel to stuff down his trousers, and Jessop and Jake carried him out to the bunkhouse to keep Avery company.

Cobb made a final inspection of the house before pronouncing it fit for Jane's return. Jake cleared the table, washed and dried the dishes, and dealt with the firebox and ash pan in the dragon. Max removed the remnants of the torn sheets that had been used to tie him to the bed and straightened the covers. Jessop put away the folded linens that were sitting on the rocking chair in Jane's room, and placed her hairpins and combs in a shallow dish on the dresser with others like them. Jem and Cobb walked the wardrobe side to side until they put it back where the markings on the floor indicated it belonged. Jem admitted he was confounded that a slip of woman like Mrs. Longstreet could move it on her own, but Cobb had some experience with women who could move heaven and earth if they had a mind to. For any one of them, a full wardrobe was hardly challenging.

Cobb gave Marcie's gun belt to Jem along

with an armload of bloody towels for burning. As Jem left by the back door, Cobb opened the front one and invited Morgan and Jane into their own home. He thought he had accounted for everything until Morgan helped Jane off with her coat, and he saw the bloody condition of her apron. She had followed the direction of his glance and quickly tore it off, but not so quickly that Morgan had not gotten an eyeful. While he and Morgan were still staring at each other, Jane ducked between them and went straight to the front room's hearth where Cobb had built a welcoming fire. She took something from the apron's pocket that Morgan and Cobb only recognized as a paring knife when she held it up to the light. She regarded it for a long moment and then tossed it and the apron into the fire.

Cobb stayed long enough to hear what happened from all sides and not a moment longer. He told them later it was like conducting an orchestra where none of the musicians could read sheet music.

He had his own part to tell, the most important being that armed with several well-reasoned arguments — and his gun — he had convinced Mr. Webb at the Cattlemen's Trust that the only way to save his bank was to let Morgan Longstreet rob it.

That was the plan they had come to the afternoon Morgan and Jane sat in his office and discussed protection. Morgan believed his brother would ask him to crack the Barkley and Benjamin, and Cobb was inclined to agree. They talked about whether he could really do it, but in the end decided it could not be left to chance. Morgan alone was given the combination to the safe, Cobb put a gun inside it, the iron bar was deliberately not placed across the bank's rear entrance, and Mr. Webb lived in such a state of anxiety from one day to the next that even his medicinal sarsaparilla in blends that exceeded twelve percent alcohol failed to calm his nerves or ease his rheumatism.

Dixon Evers was the only casualty of the robbery, although it looked for a while as though Marcellus Cooley might succumb to infection. Doc Kent eventually pronounced him fit enough to hang. It was not the part he played in the thwarted robbery, or even the attempted rape, that drew the death sentence from Judge Darlington. It was the cattle rustling. Cobb Bridger tracked down a branding inspector at the Rawlins station who remembered Marcie bringing in some cattle with an unregistered brand. The closest markings the inspector could find belonged to the Morning Star ranch, but the bars at the top and bottom meant the iron was not a match. He did not have time to investigate his suspicions, but he did not allow Marcie to sell the cattle at his station. The inspector proved to be a good witness at trial.

Marcie would not turn on Avery or Gideon, so there was nothing to connect them to the cattle thieving except common sense. Judge Darlington liked the idea of hanging Avery Butterfield for the company he kept, but ruled with the law instead. Avery was fined five hundred dollars for being offensive in the eyes of the court and thrown in jail until he figured out a way to pay it.

Gideon had another charge that separated him from his men. He had confessed to killing Zetta Lee Welling, and he had made this admission in front of Morgan and Jane Longstreet as well as the two young deputies who had been sworn in earlier that day. The sheriff in Fremont County cleared the way for Gideon to be tried in Bitter Springs. No one thought that jurisdiction should stand in the way of jurisprudence.

Judge Darlington gave considerable weight to the statements made by Marshal Cobb Bridger's deputies. He heard testimony from the Longstreets first and certainly found them credible, but he made no secret of the fact that he, like everyone else crowded into the room that day, was looking forward to what the young lawmen had to say.

Rabbit presented the facts gravely and gave a good accounting of the events and Gideon Welling's declaration of guilt. When Finn took the witness chair, he eased into it slowly and carefully, reminding the court that he had been shot, although his wound was considerably healed by then. He related Gideon's confession and how it had come about, and no one, not even his grandmother, doubted his veracity. He also managed to insert the story of how he had pissed on Marcie's leg and told him it was raining.

Gideon Welling hanged the following day.

Jane slipped her hand into Morgan's and pulled him toward the porch swing. "Come. They're gone. I cannot hear them any longer." She turned her head a little and listened. "No, not even Rabbit or Finn."

Morgan sat and gave Jane's hand a tug. She followed him onto the swing and drew her legs up. "Are you pleased with yourself?" he asked.

"Can't you tell?"

"You look pleased, but then you glow all

the time now."

Chuckling, she drew his hand to her belly. It had a curve that he could palm with his hand. "I am very pleased with myself." She gave him a little poke in his side. "And with you. You were a good host, and I think you might have actually enjoyed yourself."

"I am not admitting to that."

"Mrs. Sterling noticed it."

"She's not always right."

"True. She was right about my pregnancy, though, and she will always be able to claim it. When I looked around at our guests today, I don't think there was anyone here who did not know before I did, including you, and they still take some perverse delight in telling me that. The women, that is. The men don't dare."

"No, they wouldn't. You have a reputation."

"I know," she said, leaning her shoulder into him. "Sometimes it is difficult to know whether to laugh or to be dismayed."

"As long as you know you did right."

She nodded. Sometimes she wondered if she could have done anything differently, but she never thought she had done wrong. "I was very careful not to be seen with a knife in my hand today. That's why I asked Jenny Phillips to cut the pies and Mrs.

Sterling to slice all the cakes."

"I noticed, but I doubt anyone else did."

She patted his thigh. "You are still a terrible liar. You do much better omitting facts than offering ones that you know to be false."

"I thought you didn't like that."

"Well, I don't, but I suppose it is better than an outright lie."

"All right."

"All right? Just like that?"

"Yes." He started to gently move the swing. "Just like that."

Jane lifted Morgan's arm and ducked under it so that it covered her shoulders like a shawl.

"Are you cold? Should we go in?"

"What I am is replete," she said. "I do not want to move."

Morgan had no objection to that. In time, he felt her head grow heavier and knew she had fallen asleep. He bent, pressed his lips to her hair, and then laid his cheek against it. She did not stir, and he thought that was as it should be. She had earned this rest, as had he.

The quiet in her settled in his heart. In these moments, the peace that had eluded him all of his life became what she was, his companion. He walked with his past at his side now. He walked with her.

With Jane, all things were possible.